For the women who felt a lightning-bolt connection with a man they knew would ruin them—and walked away from the fire before it turned them to ash.

ALSO BY CAMILLA ANDREW

The Sanguine Sorceress (The Essence of the Equinox 0.5)
When The Stars Alight (The Essence of the Equinox
Book 1)
We Will Devour the Night (The Essence of the Equinox Book 2)

AND THE AGE OF SUMMER WILL RISE

Book Three Of

THE ESSENCE OF THE EQUINOX

CAMILLA ANDREW

CONTENT WARNING

This book contains sensitive material including but not limited to: explicit sexual content, on-page sexual assault, emotional and physical abuse in a romantic relationship, body horror and gore.

For more information regarding this series, please visit:

www.aninkwellofnectar.com/The-Essence-of-the-Equinox/

PRAISE FOR CAMILLA ANDREW

"The Essence of the Equinox trilogy opens with a celebration of love and ends with the daybreak of new devotion. The magical clashes with the political as different factions race to staunch the rot of chaos once and for all. This is a dazzling conclusion to a series where the darkness yields to light. For readers of fantasy who love women in all their complexity, this is not one to miss."

Ladz, author of *The Cradle of Eternal Night*

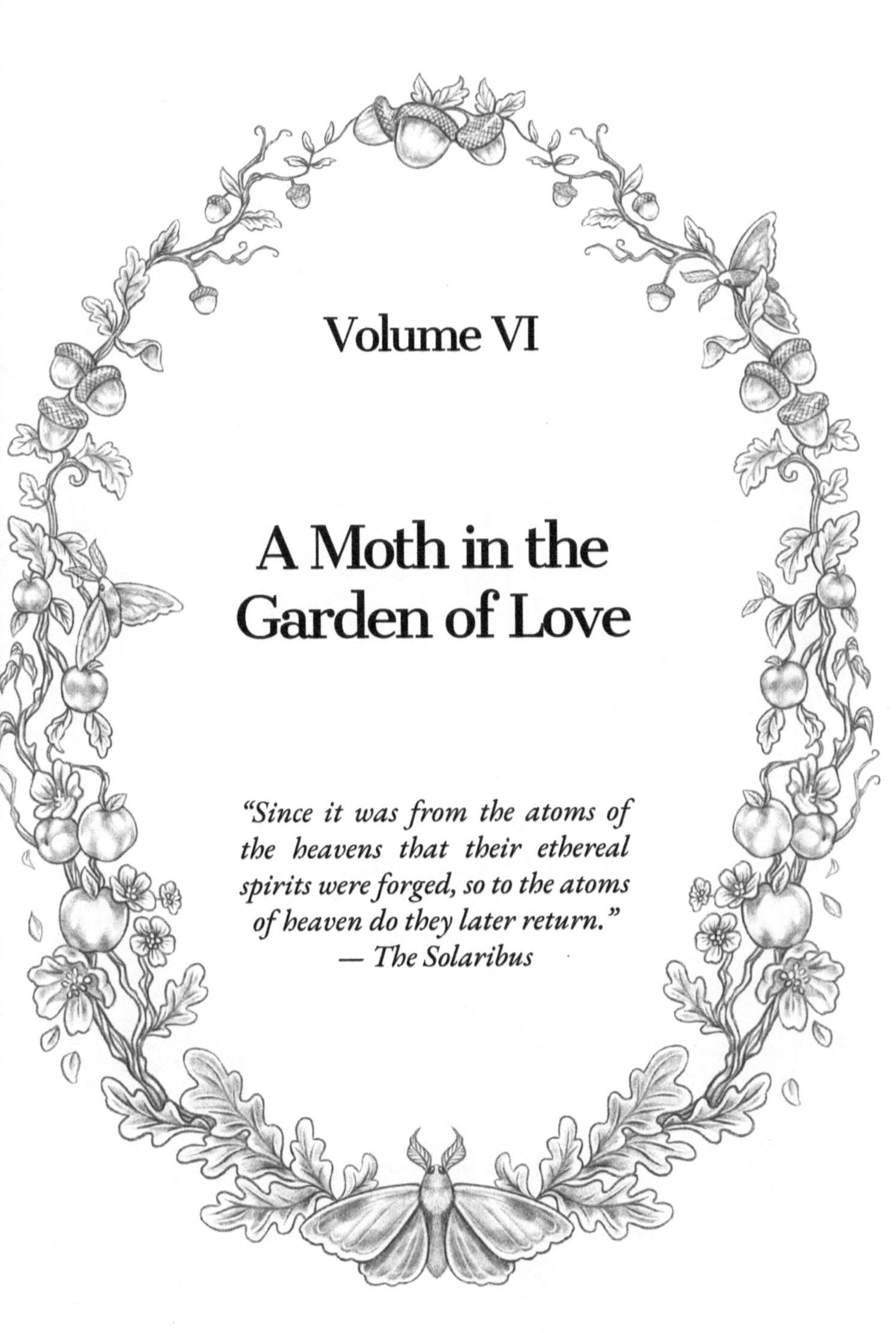

Volume VI

A Moth in the
Garden of Love

"Since it was from the atoms of
the heavens that their ethereal
spirits were forged, so to the atoms
of heaven do they later return."
— The Solaribus

I

UBJECTS FLOODED THE ICE-GLAZED STREETS OF
MORTOS. The upcoming celebration had been the talk of
the town for months: the marriage of the rex to the star
princess from across the sea.

While many were wary of their unprecedented union, the rex soon tempered the bruised egos of his nobles with strategic grants of land, lowered taxes, and arranged marriages to eligible brides. The more religious-minded saw their worries soothed when no grand catastrophe struck the lands of Mortos for such an unholy match: No leviathan beached itself from the depths of the ocean to doom the isle to a watery grave; the crops did not wilt in revolt and sprout ergot; infants did not petrify in their mothers' wombs and slide out cold as stone.

Since the wedding had been announced, the star princess had

immersed herself in the kingdom and its subjects. She shipped purple calla lilies to the tea rooms of noble occasselle and black roses to the village of the blood sorceresses.

The qarna smiled in thanks as she handed them tinctures brewed from the rex's laboratories—remedies that could kill pain and eradicate a fever, as even the power to destroy could serve its purpose. Their children waved to her on their way to the wooden schoolhouses, whose renovation had been overseen by her exacting gaze.

She filled the great hall of the Citadel with the starving and senile, serving them bowls of rich chestnut soup splashed with apple brandy—a fall recipe from her Soleterean roots, something warm and hearty to keep one's strength over the winters.

The people migrated from the hinterlands to the city in order to see her, to catch a glimpse of the smile that could banish a chill from even the bitterest frost. She would be found perpetually at the rex's side, ebullient and animated where he was guarded.

This conflict in nature was what intrigued the subjects most. Where the princess would flit from table to table chattering to all, the rex would remain elevated high on his regal platform. The only time he transformed from his austere stance would be when the princess sat herself on his lap and encircled his neck while he secured her lower back with his hand. Her presence caused everything glacial in Darius Rex's features to soften, making something far less monstrous of their immortal regent. He seemed to be as commonplace as any other fool in love.

The princess now resided in the bridal lodge where all prospective reginas awaited their nuptials. In true Mortesian custom, Laila was to be stashed away like a prize for her rex to come and collect, where he'd pay the necessary toll to her gatekeepers before they eased the passage. The toll could come in many forms but was often paid in gifts—an act that was overseen with rather heavy appraisal.

Laila pivoted from one side to the other to examine the scarlet velvet of her wedding gown flowing into a billowing skirt. Floral cream lace lavished the neckline, the sleeves slit to reveal an elaborate underlayer of matching beading. Her meticulous eye had overseen its design in great detail to cater to traditional forms of Mortesian bridalwear while still having her own personal flourish.

Once she had completed her critical inspection, she turned to find her maid of honour approaching.

"You look magical," Elvira declared with awe.

"Thank you." She smoothed her hands down her gown, a blush tinting her cheeks. She hadn't realised before the words were uttered how they would make her long for her starlet entourage across the sea.

She turned back to the mirror and forced a smile to will away the faint pang of despair. No one would be in attendance from her homeland to wish her well on the path towards wedded bliss. Even her bridesmaids were occasselle strategically chosen by Darius.

"Are you certain about this?" Elvira asked as she crowned Laila with a wreath of black roses, a silk veil edged with scarlet lace fastened over the top. "Marrying him?"

"I'm certain that I love him."

Elvira paused before nodding. "My mother always told me that was a fool's wish. To hope to marry for love."

"Then what were you to hope for?"

"She said the key to every successful marriage was to have a hefty dose of fear."

Laila frowned in dismay. "Fear of your husband?"

"Fear of each other. For you were to enter one of life's most sacred covenants, in which only one can prevail."

"Well, that's certainly... morbid." Laila grimaced, appalled that such a sentiment could be seen as profound.

"A fortune you are to be spared such advice!" Elvira smiled, choosing her words carefully. "The rex will make an exceptional husband. There are many who would slay to be seated where you are now."

And didn't Laila know it. The resentful stares she'd garnered since the betrothal was announced had left her feeling pockmarked.

"I'm just happy not to count you among them."

"Well, I can't say I'm not envious that you'll be regina, but far be it from me to stand in the way of a love as grand as yours." Elvira smiled wider until the corners of her eyes crinkled. "I can only aspire for Caius to adore me as much as the rex adores you."

The sound of whips thrashing outside caused Elvira to rush towards the window to gaze at the sky.

"He's here!"

The white carriage lowered to a stop beside a stepping path paved with opalescent stone. Darius stepped out when the driver opened the door for him, and he gave a loving stroke to one of the six albino hippogriffs fluffing out its wings.

Tucked away in the cradle of the crooked forest, the emerald green izba had a storybook quality to it, with all the sinister underpinnings of a fable to be taught.

Darius risked a glance up at the window to seek the silhouette of his bride behind the gossamer drapes. His heart rose to lodge within his throat. He swallowed it down again and reached back into the carriage to retrieve three parcels to appease her gatekeeper. One bridesmaid was an insignificant fort to contain something far more precious than all the hidden treasuries of the Citadel. In a just universe she would've been surrounded by her kin, fawned over and coddled. But then she would not be preparing to accept the hand of a demon for a spouse.

Darius shook away the faint thrum of inadequacy that gave him, having no use for it. Years could pass and he would never know what possessed Laila to turn away from crown and country in order to become his bride, but he would vest everything in his power to ensure she never again wanted for anything in this life. Even if it took him an eternity to prove.

He straightened his white cloak as he made his way up the path, the back hand-painted gold with beads and stones embroidered with patterns of his insignia. His white overcoat glistened with lace and gilt detailing, cinched at the waist by an elaborate gold belt. Ornate buckles adorned his silk shirtfront, also in gold, and his draping half-sleeves twinkled with sequins. Small prisms of colour flowered along the stones, refracted from his golden boots as he clopped towards the door.

Before he could reach for the handle, Elvira arrived at the porch to obstruct him. "Stop right there!"

"Come on, Elvira." Darius tilted his head to one side, a mischievous crook appearing in the corner of his mouth. "Just allow me a little peek."

Elvira folded her arms together in defiance.

"You are a hard lady."

"What's in the box?" Elvira jutted out her chin towards the parcels. "It had better be up to snuff."

"I'll let you be the judge of that." Darius set down the boxes and opened the first one to reveal an ornamental eagle egg, the holy representation of Callus. The egg was enamelled in translucent pale green and decorated with gold roses, emerald green leaves, and a latticework of rose-cut diamonds. Inside was an ivory miniature of the pavilion found at Château de Rosâtre cushioned on satin lining.

Elvira's lips parted in delight as she reached out to touch one of the roses. "It's beautiful."

"My first gift represents the place where Laila agreed to be my wife and serves as my first pledge as a husband—to provide a marriage as eternal and evergreen in love and happiness as the garden before you.

One as full of new beginnings and prosperous growth as the egg from which the son of Calante emerged."

Darius put away the first gift and then retrieved the second parcel. This one held a solid gold pocket watch engraved with a depiction of arctic volcanoes against a backdrop of star-filled skies.

"This represents my promise to realise our vision of unification between our respective nations. A vision that will certainly take time but shall be fulfilled."

Elvira took the watch and lifted the case to examine the silver face carved with vine-like motifs, while rose-gold hands, and finely painted numerals.

The last offering was a round satin box of dark chocolate truffles lavishly coating a soft caramel centre with crystals of fine sea salt. The truffles were shaped like hearts and lightly dusted with a gold-leaf shimmer.

"As to my final pledge—I offer my heart, the sharp and bitter tang of it that has softened to sweetness at the centre. I ensure that she will always be nourished and fed by my affections for her and that our marriage will never be starved for kindness."

With his offerings presented, he now kept his head bent to await the verdict. "Does my tribute please you?"

Elvira hummed in thought, perusing each gift at length for full effect. When she was content she'd worked up enough of an anticipatory sweat in the bridegroom, she nodded. "I say yes!"

Darius's face splintered into a grin as Elvira threw open the door for him. Though rather than step with brazen pride through the threshold, he instead remained rooted to the spot as a figure descended the steps towards him.

To say the sight of Laila in her wedding gown took his breath away would be too trite a commentary to make. More accurately, it would seem that she had thieved him of voice, pulse, thought, even motion, the very second he had seen her appear. He had been rendered inanimate as an ice sculpture, until the proximity of her warmth thawed him to life.

Faced with little more than stunned silence, Laila glanced down in uncertainty and did a little pivot for display. "I may have gotten a little carried away adding Soleterean flair." She folded her hands together primly. "I hope it's not too unfitting."

"You're perfect," Darius said instantly.

Laila started, then smiled.

"Shall we?" He held out a hand to hers, gloved in sheer white.

She slid her hand into his, and, like this, they took their first steps past the threshold.

The ceremony took place within Gravissia Cathedral, the country's largest place of worship. Despite the lack of Soleterean attendance, its eburnean interior had been dressed to suit it. Thick garlands of red roses snaked around the pillars and pews, their sweet effusions effortlessly intermingled with the scent of age and incense. Flaming candles banished the shadows left by a gloomy winter morning and looked, from a distance, to be flickering stars.

A wailing choir heralded the arrival of the regal couple, backed by the sonorous drone of an organ. Guests stood to immediate attention as the carved oak doors croaked open to receive them up the aisle.

Laila recognised several by face alone. Their expressions were an unpredictable assortment that ranged from envy to acquiescence. She was grateful to not see Delanus's face among them, at least, for he'd been stashed away in the dungeons until further notice. She clung tighter to

Darius's elbow as they reached the altar, a raised platform awash with the crimson light of the sky pouring through tall leaded glass windows.

They took their seats on chairs of tufted red velvet directed by the priest where the tabernacle depicting the holy trio of Calante, Anara, and Callus passed judgement upon their union.

The priest stretched a length of scarlet ribbon and bound one of each of their hands together. On their free hands, he cut a line across their palms with a ceremonial dagger and squeezed them together so that drops of their ichor flowed into a goblet of red and white wine—his black and her gold blurring into one stream. "This cup and its content shall represent the intertwining of two beating hearts into one immortal rhythm. Drink in the knowledge that you are choosing to unite yourselves in passion and in power, in body and in blood."

Locking their arms at the elbow, Darius tipped the wine carefully between Laila's lips before the gesture was returned. "With this sip, I bind my heart to yours until its very last pulse."

Next, the priest poured the volcanic ashes of Mount Occassus into a ceremonial bowl and summoned chaotic blue-green flames to rise up from it. "These flames represent the everlasting power and might of our god, Calante. They shall be used to imbue the seal of this marriage with the same unbreakable cord—one that can only be severed should death part you."

Laila flinched in remembrance of Elvira's earlier words on how marriage was a sacred covenant only one could survive.

"Place your right hand into the right hand of your groom."

She swallowed, having heard whispers of this part, and looked cautiously towards the enchanted branding iron now infused with the blue-green glow of chaotic flame.

"This will only sting a moment," Darius assured her, twisting her hand to face her inner wrist upwards. His hand shook as he aligned the iron with her wrist, knowing what must come next.

Laila stifled a cry of shock as he pressed the iron down onto her skin, sizzling the Calantis crest with his initials onto it. Her eyes misted with tears as she watched the steam clear from her newly applied marking. It hurt. Far more than she had ever anticipated it to. But it was a brief sear followed by a swiftly ebbing throb.

To offer a reward of sweetness, they were given a slice of red apple to share between them. Darius slid the slice gently into Laila's mouth, offering her the larger bite, before splitting it down with his own teeth while his thumb stroked soothingly over her brand.

"Seems we know from which side the roost will be ruled," the priest commented in jest at the unequal halving of the apple.

With this gesture their union was officially sealed, and the audience rippled in applause that progressed to standing ovation.

The priest led the couple to the centre of the Cathedral, where they stood on a regalia-emblazoned rug to perform the Crowning. Here was an amendment to the ceremony reserved for those of royal standing, as after several prayers the priest placed crowns over the heads of the bride and groom.

The first crown was Darius's—a domed silhouette split into two hemispheres like a cracked skull, a red velvet cap in the centre. It was encrusted with innumerable black diamonds and white diamonds, while arching across the great wound were six diamond-encrusted eagles.

The second was Laila's—nine ruby and diamond stars set into a scroll-like diadem.

Thus marked the closing of a chapter and the beginning of one anew. For no longer would one speak of Laila Rose as the dutiful daughter of aether, Princess of Soleterea and Espriterre. From this point forth she was the bride of chaos, the Stella Regina of Mortos.

II

INE SNOW PELTED THE NEWLYWEDS AS THEY DEPARTED the cathedral and fielded through the uproarious mob of guests tossing rose petals in their path. Once safely concealed inside their carriage, Darius sat across from her and took her left hand in his own. "So how does it feel to be the regina of Mortos?"

"It'll take some getting used to," Laila admitted, glancing down at the brand on her wrist. A new mark to pair the one on her spine that bound her to a different dynasty. "I've been a princess for so long. I never imagined this to be the next step."

"Well, I'll be certain to assuage any doubts you may have." Darius stroked his thumb over her marriage brand, causing a faint flare of pain from the burn.

"There are no doubts." Laila's smile radiated unwavering

affirmation. "If there's one thing I've known in my bones since I left that garden, it's this: I want to be with you. Always. I don't ever want us to be apart. So just hold me close."

"Oh, I'm not ever letting you go." His gaze had sharpened with conviction. "Not even something as meagre as death will keep me from your side."

Laila lifted his hand and let it rest upon her cheek in comfort. "It had better not." She leaned in to capture their first wedded kiss in a gentle, lingering peck before drawing back slowly to nuzzle her nose against his.

"And now that I have you alone, I have one final gift to present." He gave her a carefully wrapped parcel bound in a red velvet ribbon.

Laila slowly unravelled it and peeled back the paper to reveal a copy of his most beloved leatherbound tome, *The Question of Evil*, in near pristine condition.

"My favourite book, complete with my annotations." He lifted the cover to show the bookplate inscribed with his signature and flipped through the pages scrawled with his elegant penmanship.

"You're giving this to me?" Laila's voice was soft with disbelief.

"You said you'd like to know me better." He shrugged one shoulder. "What could be more intimate than reading the most influential text I'd ever read?"

Laila closed the book with the gentlest thud, caressing her hand over the aged leather. "Thank you. This... means more than I can say." A mite of guilt nibbled at her. "I know it runs counter to custom, but you've left me feeling quite spoiled. I'll have to find something to return the favour."

"You've given me yourself," Darius said frankly. "There's nothing I could want more. No greater offering than that."

The wedding carriage took the newlyweds through a tour of the city. At each major landmark they drew to a halt and exited to receive exaltation from their subjects. The later festivities returned them to the Citadel, where the grand hall had been decked for reception.

Floral arrangements of red roses, chrysanthemums, and lilies accented with black feathers and lacquered branches were arranged in lace-wrapped vases. Froths of cream chiffon with a decorative layer of black lace clothed the tables. Candles in red and gold burned inside the gilt figures of eagles exhaling smoke from strings that coiled around the waxed antler centrepieces.

The wedding cake sat on a dedicated table—six tiers of glittering black fondant decorated with calligraphic patterns and the royal seal in gold leaf. An extra layer of red icing cloaked the top, giving it the guise of being slowly engulfed by rippling silk.

When they arrived, hot black soup was being served by the pail. Blood was squeezed from the hearts of a mated pair of swans, and the hearts were then marinated in strawberry brandy and mixed with plum syrup, dried cherries, apple vinegar, and honey.

A servant offered them each the exsanguinated organ that remained, stuffed with herbs and spices, and encouraged them to take a bite.

"If we finish them off it is meant to be an omen for eternal fidelity," Darius explained, locking his elbow with hers to present the heart from his hand.

"Then let's hope we both brought bottomless stomachs," Laila quipped, taking a bite of the soft, elastic meat. She felt the acuteness of her mother's absence with every juice-filled chew, thinking for the first time how she might have liked to have her here.

For good or ill, they were briefly interrupted from the completion of their course by the arrival of another round of servants carrying skull-shaped decanters adorned with garlands of roses. Tall glasses of polugar peppered with strips of gold leaf were poured to toast them. The guests took a drink in salute and then commanded the couple to kiss away the bitterness. Laila giggled as Darius covered her mouth with a chaste peck to the chime of glass and chants of encouragement.

Other small plates of the evening had been hunted by the groom the night prior to prove his worth: pinkish sun-dried roe from a mermaid, the sweetbreads of an elusive white hart, and the grilled hatchlings of a wyrm, all chosen to improve fertility.

Throughout the meal guests lined up to offer them gifts and well wishes.

"I must admit to this generosity being far more than I expected," Laila observed as she held up the monogrammed porcelain dishes and the bottle of wine vintaged on their wedding day.

"Nothing quite brings Mortesians together like a wedding or a funeral," Darius said. "Lifelong blood feuds have been put aside to honour these."

"Useful to know."

With every rule, of course, comes an exception. As the razor-sharp footsteps of their upcoming guest would soon prove.

Darius sensed the rich herbal perfume of his mother on the horizon before she approached, his fangs itching for prominence. She arrived with her own fangs gleefully on display, her cloth-of-gold letnik sparkling with emeralds and rubies. The traditional dress seemed to serve as a pointed insult to Laila's less than conventional gown. A marker of her eternal unbelonging.

"So you actually went through with it?" Serafina asked in mock surprise. "I'd hoped you would come to your senses long before now."

Laila bristled in response, but she wasn't going to rise to the bait. "I assume you've come to bestow your well wishes at long last, Domina Blackwood?"

"You are an optimist, Your Majesty." Serafina cackled in delight. "I've always admired that. I suppose one would have to be in your case."

"Though you may not believe it, I happen to love your son. And he loves me. We are going to make each other very happy."

"Oh, you foolish, foolish girl." Serafina tutted. "You've no idea what you've just committed yourself to. But you will in time. I only hope by then it's not too late."

"You and I are family now, Domina Blackwood. So for the sake of Darius, I think it best we start afresh and move forward with good intentions. Enjoy the food and drink." Laila leaned forward with a menacing quality to her lowered voice. "And get out of the way."

Serafina stepped aside with relish.

"I do not understand why you insist on having her here," Laila commented sharply once Serafina melted away and helped herself to dessert. Rosewater meringues filled with mousseline cream and honey stewed figs served as the perfect finisher for the meal.

"Because for now she is useful to me," Darius said, stroking his hand up and down her arm in comfort. "Though rest assured, the moment that ceases you won't see hide nor hair of her."

"One can only hope," Laila muttered, though petulantly she couldn't stifle the resentment that at least his mother cared enough to spew her venom.

"And I'm sorry Amira isn't here for you." Darius leaned in to nuzzle Laila's temple, rightly sensing the true root of her anger. "But you know I always am. And I always will be."

"I know." Laila sighed so heavily she sagged with it. "I thought... perhaps at least she would've cared enough to disapprove. If not to see me married." It had been the silence in response to the invitation that had cut her worst of all. As if she'd been excised from Amira's life as well as her heirship.

"Well I, for one, am immensely glad," Darius scoffed. "You've suffered her unreasonable critiques for long enough, Laila. It's time you stopped seeking them out, searching for reasons to doubt and self-flagellate yourself. You made a choice to pursue your own happiness, and there's nothing wrong in that. Even if she might not approve." He took her hand in his and lifted it to his lips to give it an affectionate graze.

Just then an announcement sounded that it was time for their wedding waltz, and Darius led her onto the dance floor with an urgent tug. They wrapped an arm around each other's waist to the sound of an opening flute, circling each other like eagles giving chase before the transition into strings had them lacing their fingers together.

Warmth flooded Laila's cheeks as he led her in a waltz. Though they'd done nothing obscene, the fluidity and grace he used to guide their bodies made her feel as though they were engaged in something far too intimate for onlooking eyes.

They were so enthralled by the dance and with each other, Laila almost missed the stealthy arrival of an unexpected guest. The last guest she would've expected to see.

The appearance of Lyra de Lis in the distance almost caused Laila to stumble over her steps, but she held her poise with finesse until the final instrument had ceased to play. Darius spun her under his arm and to his side as they both took a curtsey to applause. Then she broke his hold to approach her friend and ascertain her realness.

"Lyra?" Laila's legs quivered the nearer she drew to the sprite. Lyra's cream suit seemed scandalously close to the groom's own attire, adorned with the golden sun symbols of Caelestis. "Is that really you?"

"Flesh and blood," her former sprite guard declared with a wry grin.

Laila breathed out a laugh as she took Lyra into her arms. "I thought I'd never see you again." Tears starred her eyes as she drew back to look at her friend, framing her face within her hands.

"Ah, it'll take more than that to be rid of me." Lyra grinned before leaning in to press their foreheads together. In the distance, she sensed the inquisitive gaze of Darius burrowing through her skull and resisted the urge to return it with a scowl. "Can we talk somewhere?"

Laila glanced over her shoulder to see Darius's expression and threw him a comforting look. "Of course," she said, turning back to Lyra. "Let's go to the courtyard."

"Lead the way."

They walked onto grounds freshly powdered with the earlier snow, the stagnant waters in the fountains now frozen a viscous black.

Laila hugged her arms together once they'd vacated the humidity of merriment and heat from the feast and exhaled a soft cloud. "When did you get here?"

"Today, actually." Lyra slid her hand into her pocket and strolled towards the fountain. The leer of chimeras figurines followed her motion. "We're sorry we couldn't make the ceremony, but I suppose it was just as well. I'm already too late to stop you."

"Lyra." Laila pressed her lips together as her thumb stroked over her marriage brand. Then her brow furrowed. "We?"

"I'll explain later." Lyra picked up a stray stick and used it to poke ice off the edges of the fountain rim. Then, sensing the futility of her task, she threw it away. "There's a part of me that still wants to beg you to come home with me. Isn't that insane?"

Laila did nothing in response except to breathe in deeply.

"I thought if I saw you with him. Saw you happy. Then I could get past it, but..."

"Oh, Lyra." Laila shook her head and reached to take her hands. "You say you wanted to see me happy. Well, I am. And the best gift you could give me is to be here and accept it."

"Then it seems that's where I fail you, yet again." Lyra looked down at their hands and slowly parted them. "Because I still can't."

"I see," Laila said, running her wrist through her hand. "So why come?"

"Because I couldn't live with myself if I went without seeing you," Lyra said, swallowing. She reached to brush one of Laila's curls from her cheek. "I understand now this might have been a sharper stab. Perhaps it's time I let her take over from here."

"What do you mean?"

A carriage door swung open nearby, creaking with the unloading of its passenger.

"Maman." It had been so long since she'd said the word that Laila nearly choked on the exhalation of it. Her hands twitched with the urge to reflexively primp and preen in her mother's presence. "You're here." The sight of her was dizzying, causing her lips to rise in elation. She felt torn by a desire to embrace, but she withheld. "I didn't think that you would come."

"I very nearly didn't." Amira hobbled forward with the use of a gold lion-headed cane, the black strains of her chaos-polluted veins still prominent. "I knew it would pain me too much to see you on this day. Like this. Ready to throw away everything we've worked towards without even an ounce of guilt. I can see now that I was right."

Laila fiddled with her hands, eyes downcast. Her fleeting hopes for reconciliation were flattened by the force of reality. "I'm sorry, Maman." Even now she felt foolish for expecting her mother to see the error of her ways, that her grand exit would catalyse a period of self-reflection. "I didn't mean to disappoint you."

"Well, you have. Deeply. What you did left a wound upon my heart that has never sealed. I keep asking myself where I went so wrong that you would turn your back on me when I was desperately ill, grasping for survival, to walk into the arms of a monster. Did you ever think about me while you were frittering time away over floral bouquets and fabric swatches? Did a thought to my wellbeing ever even cross your mind?"

Laila swallowed thickly, nausea roiling in her stomach. Her throat burned with the acidity of her stifled words. "I often agonised over what I would say to you in this moment. How it might make you feel if I admitted the truth. Because the truth is... I didn't. I didn't think about you at all. The last six months have been the lightest I have ever felt in my life, and I realised it was because the weight of you was lifted from it."

"I beg your pardon—"

"No, no. You don't speak. I need you to listen to me for once, because it needs saying. Because if I don't do it now I don't think I ever will. My whole life you've made me feel as though I were a burden to love, and I didn't realise how long I'd believed that to be the truth until I met someone who loved me when I wasn't even trying to be worthy of it. Until I met Darius. And there are moments when I can still scarcely accept even that. I let your claws sink into me so deep that there are mornings when I wake up in dread and expect for him to change. But when I look in his eyes I know that his love for me is impenetrable. And for that reason alone I do not regret walking away from you."

The speech was uttered with such conviction that Laila became red-cheeked in passion. It depleted every ounce of strength from her, leaving her trembling and infirm. She put her hand on her stomach as if to steady herself, bracing for the onslaught of her mother's verbal riposte.

Amira was too stunned by the act of being silenced to immediately respond. Then the laughter came, low and mocking, as she shook her head in dismissal. "Well, I hope that declaration was cathartic for you, Laila. Did you expect me to feel cowed and remorseful for expecting the best of you? For pushing you to reach new heights? You spoiled, selfish girl. How truly pathetic you are, chastising me because I didn't pet and kiss you enough. I gave you everything! I made you who you are today. And now look at you, the greatest achievement you can speak to is having a monster's love? Ha! What a pittance in the face of the greatness you almost held."

"You can keep your pity, Maman. And you can keep your scorn. I have no need for either. You might have made me what I am today, but that accounts for the good just as well as the bad. Perhaps I wouldn't have accepted a monster's love if I hadn't been raised by one."

All traces of mirth drained from Amira's features in an instant, leaving behind only a stony indifference. Her eyes glimmered like amethysts as she lifted her cane to point it accusingly in Laila's direction. "If that is truly how you think of me, then from this point forth you can consider yourself on your own, Laila. When this farce of a marriage inevitably crumbles, don't even think of weeping to me in the aftermath. Let's see what face your occasso beau reveals now you're fully in his clutches." Her cane tapped with a steady staccato as she turned on her heel to her carriage. "Come, Lyra."

Lyra's eyes flitted between the two solarites, dithering in uncertainty.

"Lyra!"

The guard jolted and rushed to follow her.

Laila clutched tighter to her abdomen as she watched them leave, her stomach tangling into inextricable knots. Her legs were shaking and her throat had constricted so tight that there was no getting any thread of breath through that needle. She crouched down until she was on her knees, rocking back and forth as she willed herself to breathe.

Darius found her like this not long after. Though rather than try to pick her up, he crouched down with her and reached to gather her gently into his arms. "It's all right. You're all right."

With the safety of his arms around her, she allowed herself to crumble.

A carriage arrived after midnight to send them off on their honeymoon. And like this, they waved goodbye to their guests, who tied cloth dolls to the back of the coach to guard against evil and sent them off.

Laila watched as the industrial landscape of Gravissia dispersed into forests of blue-grey trees. Unidentified howls and screeches welcomed them into the untamed wilderness.

"It's tradition to spend the two weeks of marriage going back to our roots," Darius explained as they reached the clearing for a lodge not unlike her bridal one. This one was composed of dark wood with similarly ornate wooden lace surrounding the door frame, windows, and eaves of the roof. "We are to live simply, like hunters, removed from all material distractions to keep our focus on mating."

"I see," Laila said, who in a better mood might have had a wittier retort for such an amorous suggestion. "No servants, then?"

"We'll be completely alone," Darius confirmed. Then he smiled. "Not to worry, I will serve you. Keep you fed and warm. You won't want for anything while we're here."

She managed a smile at that as he lifted her out of the carriage, carrying her up the steps to the porch and past the threshold. Once there, he spun her around before setting her down, and he brought her close to cup her cheeks.

Laila squealed in delight before settling into a laugh, leaning her forehead against his.

"Feels good to hear that laugh again," Darius said, stroking his thumb along her cheek. "Are you all right?"

Laila nodded, sliding her hands from his neck down to his chest. "Tell me you love me."

"From the bottomless pit of my heart."

Her smile grew stronger as she brought him into a kiss.

He broke it briefly to rest his nose against hers, breathing her in. "Do you have any idea how happy you've made me?"

She kissed him again, arching her body into his. Her arms slung around his neck to pull him even nearer. Yet they were still too far apart for her liking. And too well-clothed. She wanted to feel his skin against hers, and their bodies entwined as he proved his adoration with more than just words.

Darius parted them for breath. "We should probably take this upstairs."

"If you insist." Laila pouted in disappointment.

"Upper floor, first door on the left." He kissed the tip of her nose. "I'll go fetch our luggage."

"Don't keep me waiting."

She watched him leave for the carriage with a spring in his step, suppressing a laugh as she turned to explore the house. The interiors were rustic and intimate, with a large fireplace in the sitting room and a velvet divan she could imagine sprawling across during cold nights. The kitchen had been newly stocked, and a well-kept cast iron potbelly stove sat waiting in the corner, eager for use.

She crept upstairs to enter the bedroom and surveyed the massive alcove bed enclosed within a frame engraved with grape leaves and vines and frolicking nude couples. The bed was draped in piles of fur and scattered rose petals with a trail leading from the doorway.

Rather than take the bait, Laila went into the adjoining bathroom, where she found a round hot spring tub carved from oak and a porcelain basin atop a matching pedestal. It was here she chose to settle as she removed the veil from her hair and followed it with the garland of roses, which she let carelessly fall into the basin. With her hair now uncovered she took a moment to glance at herself in the mirror, willing away the faint gnaw in her stomach that still remained from her mother.

A knock on the door distracted her, and she opened it to find Darius had left her luggage waiting. Straining her ears, she heard him heading back downstairs and took the suitcase in with her to change.

She unclipped it to rummage through her numerous nightclothes and decide upon an appropriately enticing set. She brought out a two piece negligee of peach-coloured silk edged with yellow lace and pulled the capelet top over her head, tying the wraparound waist into a large bow at the front. After that, she let down her hair from the jewelled pins that ensnared it and shook free her buoyant curls.

Content with her look, she re-entered the bedroom to find Darius already there. He had stripped down to his wedding drawers of sheer white cotton, the bell-shaped legs flaring into a deep ruffled flounce of hemmed lace inset with birds, a white satin ribbon bow on each leg. The cotton was just translucent enough that the sight of him made her mouth dry.

He was pouring them glasses of deep red wine, his body glistening with the light oil he'd applied each time he moved in the candlelight.

Laila approached him silently, not wanting to disturb such a pleasant scene, but she knew better than to expect she could sneak up on him.

The moment he sensed her he looked up with a smile and handed her a glass. "Thought you could use a drink."

Perceptive as always. Though only one thing was certain to quench her thirst.

Laila took a sip from the wine, finding it rich and decadent. The potency gently soothed her mind. "Do they really expect us to spend two weeks simply mating?"

"That's the general gist of it, to get a bride with child." He quirked a brow ironically, downing his drink before setting the glass aside. "Rather unfortunate for us, I'm sure. That isn't to say we can't still give it a solid effort."

She smothered a laugh as he brought her in by the waist.

"But as much as I'd love to keep you in bed, there's still plenty else I'd like for us to try. I could take you ice-skating. Show you all my favourite little fishing spots. Spend some time exploring the ocean."

"That sounds nice." She took another long drink. "I'd like that."

"All in due time, princess." His hand found its way to her bow as he smirked, lightly tugging it free.

"Not a princess anymore," she reminded him, feigning affront. A difficult façade to maintain when the sight of his smile alone had her throbbing between the legs.

"Of course," he acknowledged, biting his lip as the bottom half of her negligee descended to her ankles. "How does 'my queen' sound?"

"Much better." She finished her glass and then let it drop to the carpeted floor.

He brought her into a kiss, a chuckle vibrating into her mouth before she shoved him back and left him glancing at her in faint bewilderment.

"I didn't say you could kiss me."

Darius responded to this with the most self-satisfied smirk imaginable. "So it's like that, is it?"

Laila hummed in affirmation. She flattened one palm on his chest to guide him to the bed and pushed him until he was up against the headboard. Then she stripped off his drawers, tossing them away. His body tensed with anticipation as she mounted him, making a throne of his lap.

"Hold onto the bed frame," she ordered. She gave a small whimper as the air slithered up her exposed skin and sent the top half of her negligee along with it. "You're going to need to."

He ached to disobey her decree and seize those bountiful hips, the dainty sliver of a waist that so tempted him. But he made like a good little monster and clutched the engraved wood.

"Don't move," she told him sternly. "If you move, I will stop."

"They warned me of this," he couldn't help but quip as she nestled close until their chests compressed. He could feel the heat from her arousal against him. "Marriage has made you quite the demanding tyrant."

She started by sliding her hand down her stomach, between her legs, finding her clit and stroking it between her fingers. She closed her eyes with a deep, throaty sound of contentment.

Darius had to keep from rocking forward. "Laila—"

"Don't move." She continued to slide her fingers with expert precision, bringing herself to the brink in little time.

Darius suppressed a whine at this exquisite torment. Watching her pleasure herself right in front of him, that beautiful neck inclined as she made those high, breathy exhalations—and he couldn't touch her at all.

Laila allowed her orgasm to pass through her with an electrifying quiver. Then she reached to take him in hand.

Darius let out a choked sound as her fingers enclosed his shaft and stroked him gently from base to tip. His neck tilted back in recline as she slowly built up a coaxing pace, and he had to hold still to keep from thrusting into her palm. While he ached for release, her touch alone was soothing. He didn't want her to cease just yet.

Laila bit her lip mischievously as she edged just close enough to take in the tip of his arousal. She kept her hold on him firm as she continued to caress him and allow only the tip of him inside.

Darius's moan rumbled deep in his chest. The tantalising closeness of her was almost too much to bear. He knew with one brisk motion of his hips he could end her taunting and be fully embedded in her but he remembered himself in time to recall her demand from before.

Thankfully, she decided to be merciful, and he wasn't left waiting long before she clutched his shoulders for grip and let herself sink onto him, her chest plummeting as though she were in freefall.

Laila closed her eyes in relief; his girth always soothed the ache in her just right. No words in her vocabulary could encompass it—in either her language or his. It went against all reason that their bodies should fit so exquisitely together, but she was never one to question that which gave her pleasure. A warmth like having too much of a full-bodied wine filled her belly. "Stay there. Stay right there." She joined their mouths together in a tender kiss, the tips of their noses touching. Then she clenched her muscles tight around him, making use of her impeccable muscle control to pulsate around his shaft.

"God, Laila." His voice grew strained and desperate. His fingers dug into the wooden frame until it splintered.

Their bodies melded together as if they were made for exactly this—a fusion of flesh transmuting into love. Yet no union could have been more abominable than this. More ill-fated.

"You're doing well so far," Laila said, moving his length inside her. She paid particular attention to the way he twitched and tensed, ceasing all movement when it seemed he might be veering too close to the edge.

Darius couldn't take it for long before his fingers were chipping away at the bed. He detached them to land on her hips, seeking the softness of her flesh.

"Darius—" Her breath caught in her throat as he grabbed palmfuls of her buttocks to move her on his lap at a fervent pace, his pubic bone flattened against the hood of her clit.

Laila shuddered from the headiness of it, her eyes rolling back. She could feel her legs going weak from the potency of overstimulation in multiple areas. He wasn't so much moving as he was guiding her movements, scaling them both towards their climax.

"I need you to come for me, Laila," he murmured in her ear, deep and husky in a way that made her whimper. She was close. And if he kept using that lascivious tone she'd be even closer. He claimed her lips in a kiss, prying her mouth open to his and tracing the edge of her tongue. "Come for me."

She could feel herself weakening from the intensity of his stare. The soulful earnestness of him being so ravenous for connection. Until at last her body obeyed.

They cried out in unison through the waves of pleasure that followed. The sensation was overwhelming, all encompassing. He was submerged in her, swept up in the throes of her orgasm until he shipwrecked against the shore of her thighs.

"Oh gods, *Darius*," she cried as he circled his hips in a way that sent her orgasm rippling all the way through her clenching stomach, her chest, her throat, until her body slackened.

He held her through the comedown, kissing a trail down her throat to her breasts, stroking his hand through her dampened hair.

"You get minus points for cheating," she murmured.

"You seemed to be enjoying it well enough."

III

ONG AGO, BEFORE THE WORLD WAS BORN, THERE *was nothing in existence but chaos. A writhing black Abyss. Vast as an ocean! That was before Asemani came, descending from on high to split a wedge through the Abyss to craft the world. She summoned the four elements and imbued aether at the world's core, and from this she created the forests, the mountains, the seas, and the desert.*

Once Asemani had finished her task she decided she wanted to bring life here. So she filled the seas with fish, the forests with beasts, the mountains with birds, and the desert... Ah. The desert she gave the most precious gift of all. There she set those made in her image to cultivate the elements, and companions to support them.

When Asemani saw that her humans were a success, she drained pure aether from the sun and mixed it with the elements, sending it down in the shape of a flaming bird with rainbow-coloured feathers. A phoenix. This phoenix would immolate itself in the desert and spread aether through its core for humans to access. This would bestow on them the ability to tame chaos, to manipulate the forces of the elements to create Perfection in the image of Asemani herself. But chaos was not quite so easily thwarted...

Elina strained to keep her eyes from fluttering closed as the *Solaribus* continued to narrate its first chapter. She had gotten worryingly thin. Her muscles held the same firmness as damp paper, and the slightest bump was enough to leave her skin a patchwork of bruises.

Fortunately, she didn't need to lift the book to delve within the rice-paper pages, for, when read, each word would ignite with a fiery glow and conjure an enchanted orb of light to animate the scripture in sound and image.

Since her attack by a mutated Naveen (an unfortunate casualty in Sadik's dabblings with chaos magic) had robbed Elina of both her magic and mobility, she turned to her final refuge in the form of accruing knowledge of her condition through books. Having not been reared in the temples of Caelestis, her knowledge of solarites was patchier than those under the umbrella of Caelestic worship, but after she'd consented to the experimental treatment offered by Dr Isuka to be injected with a serum made from ichor of the solarites, her interest in their origins had grown tenfold.

In Thalistan, they knelt in prayer before the snake goddess Naya who ruled the earth and all that could be seen, touched, experienced. The skies and the underworld were therefore unreachable voids of pure emptiness to them, bereft of life and frightening as a result. A fear that soon proved worthy of heeding when from one came ethereal maidens and the other malevolent fiends. Both arrivals altered the course of humanity irreparably, but what this did not achieve was causing the

Thalit people to lose faith in their goddess. Elina, too, had kept up the practice.

Elina absorbed the animation as it continued to unfold, familiarising herself with it. First was the descent from the sky of the asteroid that shattered into star fragments. These fragments embedded into the white clay and would later form the solarites' bodies. Here was where many beliefs splintered, for the Ahian religion the Thalit practised believed that Naya was the one who bestowed bodies to the solarites, whereas Caelestians vehemently argued it was all Aṣemani's design.

Thankfully, little debate was held over what happened next. The part that Elina in particular had been searching for. The Phoenix of rainbow feathers set their bodies alight with a breath of heavenly fire and imbued in them a spark of immaculacy.

"Sorry to interrupt, Mata Panja."

Elina flinched when she saw Dr Isuka standing at her bedside, as if she'd been caught doing something tawdry. She hadn't heard her come in, but that was to be expected. Even if Elina hadn't been so entranced by the *Solaribus*'s theatrics, the scholar's tread always sounded as if she walked on beds of feathers.

"No need to worry," Dr Isuka said, offering what appeared to be a friendly smile, though it lacked anything but straining muscles. "You can help yourself to any books you like to occupy your time. I was hoping we might discuss how you're feeling."

"I'm still showing signs of anaemia." It had been one of the first symptoms discovered in humans afflicted with chaos magic. Bruised skin. Paleness. Weakness. Fatigue. Cold hands and feet. "How are my red blood cell counts?"

"Still cause for concern, I'm afraid."

Elina smothered a sigh. "From what I understand, there are different layers to how chaos can manifest when it gets in a body."

"Ah, indeed. Severity can depend on the power and proficiency of the inflictor. There can be smaller, localised wounds that are easier to immediately treat. Lower hexes or bites and scratches from unintelligent beasts will differ from curses administered by occassi, for example. And from more generalised afflictions that require stronger treatments. Yours is the latter, like the solarites attacked in Aurea Park. In your case, you also had some of your aether depleted, which weakens your body further."

"Should I be taking more of the tinctures?"

"It'll help for now. But we'll still need to tackle the root cause." Dr Isuka wrinkled her nose. "Occassi blood is... putrid. It has lower oxygen levels than a regular mortal's. A chaotic effect, I'd imagine. Their bodies have evolved to allow them to survive this, but obviously to a person..."

"What about a stronger dosage?"

"I'd be careful with that. Due to your mortality, there is every chance your body won't be able to fully sustain the purity of the elixir."

"Then the true mystery is how we get it out of me. And keep it out."

They'd tried several remedies over the course of her stay, both of scientific origin and Elina's own homemade brews. Each case was the same. It would eradicate traces of chaos for a time, but it would always bounce back as vicious as ever.

"I'm wondering something."

"What?" Dr Isuka asked.

"You ever seen what happens to a solarite under the effects of chaos magic?" Elina had noticed the absence of solarites among Dr Isuka's ghastly menagerie.

"I can't say that I have," Dr Isuka replied, lips sagging with this sudden gap in knowledge. "Why? What are you thinking?"

Elina could feel herself on the brink of some form of breakthrough, and the process had a way of making her tired. "There is something about solarites. Whether it be their bodies or perhaps their capacity to produce their own aether. It gives a layer of protection to chaos that we mortals do not have. I was thinking... well... maybe it's the Phoenix."

"Yes..." Dr Isuka put a gloved hand to her lips in thought. "Yes, that would make sense, but what are we to do with such knowledge? The Phoenix only descends once every seven hundred and fifty years."

"That's true, but a tiny spark remains inside every solarite. Right? And I was thinking of the case studies of those affected and injured. Most of them perished instantly. Others lasted but were impacted heavily still. Only one dynasty appears to have fully shaken it off... Can you guess who?"

"The Roses."

"The line directly descending from Esterre Rose." Elina nodded. "The First."

"You believe the Roses are the key to unlocking this whole mystery?" Dr Isuka squinted. The coincidence of a Rose having wedded herself to a Calantis struck her as too grave. To her, it could be nothing other than a divine-delivered message from above. Her face lit with rare glee. "A smashing observation, mata!"

Dr Isuka walked her fingers along a vial rack of blood samples, counting them one by one. From her collection, she selected the first sample from Elina Panja and smeared it on a glass slide, moved it within the range of a microscope, and narrowed the scope until her blood cells were visible.

What she observed was a sparse number of red cells among darker, shrivelled cells. She hoped the serum from the Rejuvenation Pit she used to resurrect Dominus would work towards giving better results next time. The second sample was from a chaos-afflicted solarite after the tragedy in Aurea Park. The cells were golden and charged, vibrating with power, but some were blackening at the edges still—the sign of a celestial fighting off invasion. The last was a sample she'd recently extracted from an occassella undergoing treatment from the Rejuvenation Pit. Much like Dominus, her chaos was only "in remission," lurking for the opportunity to re-introduce itself.

Isuka's conclusion matched Elina's: There was something about solarites that allowed them to resist chaos magic in ways that other aether-sensitive individuals could not. And that same something might be what was needed to eradicate chaos from occassi.

Solarites first had their bodies set by holy fire breathed from the Phoenix, and that spark was passed down from mother to child upon the completion of their moulding. Phoenix fire, among other abilities, was known for its purifying properties. Asemani had, in the scriptures, first used phoenix fire to create life from the great abyss of nothingness.

Therefore, it stood to reason that phoenix fire was the missing ingredient they'd been searching for. But how could they harness it? When a solarite died, the flame went out of her at once. And the Phoenix only visited the land once every seven hundred and fifty years, the next visit not due for another seven hundred.

Dr Isuka rubbed her chin before picking up a nearby compact mirror to summon Dr Mielette.

"Good evening, doctor." Dr Mielette greeted her with a serene smile. "You have new information for me?"

"I may have something." Dr Isuka drummed her fingers on the table. "How was the Rejuvenation Pit created?"

"It's been a family secret for generations," Dr Mielette graciously informed her. Her tone betrayed nothing of what she felt on this, but then nothing she said ever had. "It's the regenerative properties, you see.

It's similar to our blood but on a more advanced scale. Our foremother sacrificed herself to create it."

"I *see*." The pieces were slowly coming together for Dr Isuka. A great act of aether magic on the part of a solarite, powerful enough to exhaust herself. "It's not strong enough..."

"I do beg your pardon?"

"I have been thinking about your connection to the Holy Phoenix. How it distinguishes you solarites from any other creature of this land. I do think... This may be the missing component we need. But—"

"You think we need a Rose to do it?"

"Esterre was the first," Dr Isuka said. "We cannot discount that connection having an effect on her bloodline in comparison to yours."

"Amira Rose tried to lay hands on a phoenix feather two hundred years ago but was thankfully thwarted. Stars know what would've happened had she succeeded." Dr Mielette's voice flattened. "However, I am sufficiently intrigued by your theory and shall have to look into it further. Thank you, Dr Isuka."

IV

VOLCANIC BELCHES FROM THE LAVA PITS BENEATH Delanus seeped through his prison rags and caused an itch to prickle beneath the shoddy fabric. He shook it off without care. A little heat would do him no harm in comparison to the glacial rage of the rex when he'd ripped Delanus's appendages away one by one.

For that reason alone he'd been grateful to be granted leave from the wedding, and for the subsequent absence of the newlyweds on their honeymoon. The last thing Delanus could stomach was seeing Darius soft-eyed and fawning over his bride.

Poor Delanus. He was foolish enough to consider that after the loss of his fangs and claws he couldn't suffer anymore indignities at the hands of his sovereign. He forgot Darius's bottomless capacity for sadism could never be sated.

This was why he couldn't stop his shoulders from clenching in anticipation when someone opened the door to the dungeons. A streak of panic went through him at the screech of heavy metal and the hollow clunk of footsteps as his eyes swept the room for the person who could've entered.

Fortunately for him it was only his daughter, having made herself comfortable enough to indulge in some of his finest whisky.

"Oh, it's you." Delanus exhaled his relief.

Sabina smiled in greeting whilst swirling the amber liquid in her bottle. "Thought you could use a belated toast to the rex's happiness."

Delanus blew his lips. "By all means, don't let me stop you. I'd have a glass of my own, if you don't mind." He massaged his temples and sank back onto his lumpy mattress with a loud sigh. "Still cannot fathom what Darius was thinking, choosing her. What is the use of a foreign bride if she cannot deliver on foreign relations?"

"You truly have it out for the regina." Sabina chuckled dryly as she poured her father a glass of whisky. "Why does she irk you so?"

"Because she *took* what's... ours." Delanus sniffed as he reached through the bars to retrieve the glass. "You should be at the rex's side, not her."

"And by me... you mean you." Sabina gave him a pointed look. "That's what this is all about for you in the end. Worming your way as close to the rex as you possibly can. One would think if only you had the womb—"

Delanus sneered into his glass before he downed the shot. "Don't be disgusting."

"I'm not wrong though, am I?" Sabina tilted her head, lips broadening. "You of all people have given him so much. You devoted yourself heart, body, and mind, and what has he ever done to thank you in return but to demand... more." Her smirk diminished into a sorrowful frown. "I should be glad to have escaped that fate, I think." She stared into the translucent liquor and found her reflection in it.

Delanus yawned, overcome with a sudden heaviness. "Why do... I... feel..."

"As he has more to demand from you, still."

The whisky glass fell from his fingers, spilling the last remaining dregs. Then Delanus collapsed alongside it, groaning softly.

Sabina moistened her lips and put the bottle to one side.

"You did well." Serafina emerged from the shadows to look over his unconscious form. "Didn't suspect a thing."

"Is he—" Sabina paused for a breath. "Do you intend to kill him?"

"Hopefully not!" Serafina pursed her lips. "That would be rather difficult to explain away, wouldn't it? No, he'll be fine. I have practice with this sort of thing. He shouldn't remember anything that takes place from now to the near future." She unlocked the door to his cell and started to arrange his limbs neatly, crossing his arms and pushing his legs together. "I'm going to need your help."

Sabina hadn't taken her eyes off of her father.

"Are you all right?" Serafina looked her over. "If you have doubts, I can tell Darius—"

"No." This was a test, Sabina was sure. For him to gauge who held the depth of her loyalty. She wouldn't fail it. "Let's take him down to the laboratory."

They stuffed his body inside a trunk and carried it down to Serafina's quarters. The rooms that had once been Darius's before his ascension.

When they arrived past the secret tunnel into the laboratory, Serafina changed into a starch white lab coat.

Sabina couldn't stand the sight of the place as soon as she laid eyes on it. It was too immaculate. Too sanitary. The gleam from the glass and the metal nearly blinded her.

"I should hope this will do for a specimen." Serafina stepped forward to unclip the clasps of the trunk. "However, I would've rethought the target in this instance. Your father has suffered enough at his hands, wouldn't you agree?"

"Darius is going to appoint me as prime prefect in his absence," Sabina said, as if that explained it all. She was following his path when he became rex, trampling on the bodies of her relations in the quest for power. "For the time being, my father will be said to be banished from the Council in disgrace."

"My, that's quite the advancement!" Serafina's face lit up with invigoration. "You've the Vidua instinct in you. I say again you would've fit in well there."

Sabina glanced away from her. She couldn't tell whether that was a compliment or an insult.

"I can see you still think the worst of that." Serafina tutted at her as she hauled Delanus's body out of the trunk to toss him onto a gurney. She peeled back his eyelids to ascertain his lack of consciousness. "And what if things go awry?"

Sabina breathed in deep. "I am to say he went mad in prison and that he... took his own life." Her gaze flitted over to him. "It shouldn't be difficult to manage considering his disadvantages."

"Of course. Though a gruesome tale to speak of, to be certain." Serafina rolled up her sleeves, casting a glance to Sabina. "Now, I'll warn you... You're not going to want to be around for what's next."

Sabina was already halfway up the stairs by the time the words were uttered.

Serafina clicked her tongue. She thought it exceptionally cruel for Darius to ask Sabina to be the one to do this. But she understood the logic behind it. To have a reliable underling, one must ask them to muddy their hands with the most unthinkable acts as a display of loyalty and material for blackmail.

She leafed through the contents of her heartless research, flipping page after page before closing the book. "Well, we're going to want to plug your mouth with something." Serafina scrunched her nose as she looked over his unconscious face. "This will certainly wake you up."

She wrapped a clean rag around his face and tightened it. Firmly. Then Serafina ripped open his shirt to expose his chest. After that, she dipped her hands into volcanic ash to dust them and extended a claw. She carved a rune above his heart that welled with blood, spidering along his exposed skin. "Let's see... First, I'm going to test removal and then re-insertion. It should give me some clue as to whether there's a certain period of heartlessness that can be sustained without permanent damage."

Serafina blew out from her mouth and closed her eyes to chant. She gesticulated wildly above the rune on Delanus's chest until it ignited with a glow. As her chanting intensified, a pulsating lump pushed forward from Delanus's chest, which stretched further and further out.

The sheer force of it was enough to make Delanus's eyes fly open as his first scream of the night came muffled through the rag.

He twisted and turned, frantically trying to focus his multiplying vision on anything before him. He held no recollection of what had come to pass before he'd ended up where he lay. There was only a resounding sense of numbness, countered by the pain of being gripped by sharp claws.

That was when he grew aware of Serafina's hand in his now-open chest, squelching muscle and viscera around his beating heart.

He mewled meekly at first before the cry gained strength. He attempted to strike her, but his limbs were bound. Never had he missed the use of his claws and fangs more than when Serafina coaxed his heart out with a gush of blood.

Serafina raised the organ to inspect it. His heart pulsated vibrantly with fear, still tethered to his body.

Delanus screamed in anguish, but his wails were too deafened for anyone to hear.

Serafina blew softly on the plumes of steam rolling up from her herbal brew before holding it up to her face. She closed her eyes, parting her lips to inhale through her mouth. The vapours purified her sinuses. She felt the indomitable burn of it up her throat and through her nostrils. The discomfort only lasted for a moment before being replaced by weightlessness.

"What are you doing?" Sabina eyed the brew with wary interest, staring down into the bubbling blackness in an attempt to decipher its contents. The scents emerging from it were earthy and resinous, organic.

"Renewing my energy." Serafina's voice was smooth as caramel. "A sorceress must take care not to overexert herself on blood magic usage. Particularly after challenging feats."

"I see."

As was her duty, Sabina kept her lips sealed and her head turned, yet part of her was still troubled by the prospect of Darius becoming heartless. She was too young to remember Lanius's downfall, but her father relayed the unfortunate tale to her when he became prime prefect, telling her of how it paved the way for Darius's own ascension. It frightened her to think the same misfortune might befall him, as it was through Darius's progressive rule alone that she'd been pedestaled from the leering hands of lower lords desperate for a mistress.

She'd seen the fates of barren girls who'd not been deemed suitable enough for the convent or midwifery. A lifetime of preening and pleasing and pleading. *Please like me, I'll do anything.* Darius demanded a great many things from her, but at the very least none of them involved her on her back or knees.

"Can I ask why you did it?" Sabina leaned her shoulder against the wall and crossed her ankles. "For Lanius, that is. Why make him heartless?"

Serafina's head tilted in faint amusement as she reached to neaten a few coal-silk strands of her hair. "It's been a while since someone asked me that. Not even Darius did."

"I'm just curious. It seems like something one would do out of some... misguided act of fondness. But you refused Lanius when he desired to make you his regina, did you not?"

"Do you know what the leading cause of death is for occasselle, Sabina? It's not childbirth or war or attacks from other creatures. It's our husbands. Especially when we become nuisances. Especially when we become bores or disappointments. Eternity is such a long time to be shackled to a nag without hope of trading in for a better model. Occassi pride can't take the shame of an amicable separation. That implies inadequacy on the part of themselves or the marriage. And *she* cannot be allowed to find someone better than him, after all. She must simply cease to exist."

Sabina couldn't suppress the rueful smirk that came to her lips, finding nothing Serafina said untrue.

"The Vidua Nocte were founded upon these principles. Only we are widowing ourselves from occassi as a whole." Serafina took one last whiff and placed down her bowl. "But yes, I loved Lanius. Once. And when I was at his court we had a formidable partnership. I even persuaded him to stop that barbaric practice of female mutilation. However, in the end, I knew I couldn't be his regina and be a sorceress. I had to choose."

"And Darius Rex? How did he come into it?"

"Darius was... an accident. Yet not one unwanted by me, by any means. Had he been, he would never have escaped my womb. But you see, the Vidua Nocte have our ways, and that means no ties to occassi. Not even sons. I raised it with the leadership, thinking that if I could explain how politically expedient having a rex's bastard around could be, I could sway them... but how could I be exempt when we had asked so many occasselle before and after me to make such a difficult choice? And so eventually we put it to a vote—you can guess who won—and I took my sweet little blue-eyed boy and I laid him out on the slab."

"You really would've killed him?" Sabina looked temporarily startled.

"I still ask myself that sometimes." Serafina raised a shoulder. "Lanius removed the decision away from me, however—perhaps the only thing he ever did that I praised him for."

Now, she wondered whether such praise would be misplaced, having seen what their mixing had led to—a lethal alloy of his mother's silvered shrewdness and his father's callous steel.

She often caught glimpses of Lanius's tyrannical silhouette trailing behind him, and she felt a fear sedated by love. Yes, love. For in spite of it all she could never excise that pang of longing to hold her son to her breast and plead for forgiveness.

A naïve fantasy. The moment she made her vows to the Widowlands, she'd signed a tacit agreement that, if need be, she would raise a blade to slay even her own flesh and blood for the good of the cause. She only wondered if she could.

V

ARIUS LED HIS BRIDE THROUGH FROST-LACED branches of fir trees towards a lake frozen into a lustrous black mirror. Its darkness was so dense that their reflections seemed to return distorted as some sinister half of their souls.

"Try not to be too nervous," Darius told Laila as they approached the edge. "It'll be a little slippery at first, but just remember that I've got you."

Laila eyed the lake sceptically, clutching Darius's arm. "You're sure it's strong enough to hold us?"

"Mortesian ice is impermeable," Darius assured her. "And with those skates made of waxed qarnun bone you ought to be able to glide over the lake with ease."

Laila glanced down at the skates he had given her, unconvinced.

He stepped onto the ice first before starting to tug her with him. "Come on."

"Darius, no!" Laila's heart thundered as she dug the blades of her skates into the marsh to root herself.

"Come on." He chuckled but ceased pulling her forward. He held her hands gently and looked into her eyes. "What are you scared of?"

Laila wanted to say otherwise but couldn't keep her trembling legs from betraying her. She knew she looked needy and foolish to him and prepared for the moment he berated her reticence. But why ever would he? She supposed it conjured a long-buried memory of a pageant her mother had forced her to enter, demanding she do tightrope ballet on a translucent cord of spider silk to give the illusion she was dancing on air. When she'd fallen and broken both her legs, her mother had shown no sympathy, only giving her days to regenerate before pushing her back out to perform.

You healed, didn't you? So what is there to fear?

"Promise you won't let me go?" Laila grazed her lip with her teeth in uncertainty.

"Never." Darius caressed her hands and threaded their fingers together. "Not until you're ready."

The affirmation made her relax. She let him lead her onto the ice, stumbling as she went, but his hold on her was iron-firm. At first she clutched his hands and let him lead her; her skates glided across the ice with little resistance.

"You can use me to balance yourself," Darius instructed, pressing them palm to palm. "Push me along, I won't fall."

She did as he said, using him as a pillar to lean against as she strengthened her control over her quavery legs. It took her a few moments to gain her bearings, but once she did she found she was able to lessen her reliance on him by small increments. Then she let him go entirely.

"Oh!" Laila spread her arms like a flapping bird for balance.

Darius reached for her immediately in concern.

Rather than meet a chilly humiliation on the lake, she skimmed across it until a lightness rose in her chest. She released a cheerful vapour of a laugh that warmed the frosty air, kicking up speed until she was soaring.

"Oh, it's like flying!" Laila sighed dreamily, arms still spread and eyes closed to enhance the sensation of being airborne.

Darius couldn't help but be entranced by her delight. The contented way her lashes swept low and left crescents on her cheeks. Under the moonlight, her glistening skin had become a spectrum of iridescent colour.

Unwilling to be outdone, he started to cross her path in smooth figure eights, leaping over a large expanse of the lake in a series of twirls with a graceful landing.

Laila scoffed as she watched him. Though there was an undeniable allure to seeing him move with such fluidity. "Show-off."

He threw a smirk over his shoulder as he skated backwards past her. "You know, it's been centuries since I've properly done this. When I was a boy this used to be one of my favourite activities to do in the world. I found it calming."

"Why did you stop?" she asked, struggling to keep up with him. Her legs twitched to try one of his twirls, but she lacked the confidence to commit.

"My father thought it silly for me to waste time on such a frivolous pursuit when I could be training instead. Plus he didn't care for how much I liked to take after occasselle in my dance movements..."

Laila looked at him the way she often did when he faltered during talks of his childhood—with a gentle, coaxing encouragement. "You suffered under him for so long."

Darius swallowed, slowing to a stop. "We all did, I suppose."

Laila skated over to take his hands in hers. "That's why it's important you're here now. As rex. You can make it so that no little boy will ever know shame for wanting to dance on the ice."

"Well, it's half the reason I invested so much into chimera creation. Gradually, I hope to replace a large bulk of our troops with it. Encourage us to pursue other things than martial warfare. Keep our numbers stronger in the event of conflict. We have enough combatants in this country. What we need now are scientists, philosophers, poets. If only they could see that."

She lifted his hands to her lips to warm them with kisses. "I'll help them see it."

"What would I do without someone like you by my side?" Darius's voice softened with tenderness.

She leaned in to peck him lightly on the lips. "I'm going to try a twirl now."

"Are you sure?" A note of consternation entered his speech as she slipped away from him. "It's a lot trickier than it looks."

"Oh, come on, how hard can it be?" Laila scoffed as she took a few skates forwards for momentum. "You just build up to a jump and—"

Unfortunately for Laila, her hubris had taken her far closer to the sun than her feet did. And instead of the balletic leap she'd envisioned, she halted midway in a jagged wobble before collapsing to the ground.

Having sensed this blunder before it came, Darius rushed to break her fall. He ended up flattened between his wife's weight and the freezing moisture of the lake for his trouble.

Laila landed on him with a muffled sound of pain before bursting into laughter.

"Well, I'm glad you find this so amusing," Darius said flatly, resistant to joining her mirth. The lake's sharp nips were already eating through his furs.

Laila strained to stifle her giggles as she straddled him, stroking a loose lock of hair from his eyes. "This wouldn't have happened if you'd just let me fall."

"Force of habit." Darius rolled his eyes. "Seems even now I can't bear to see you harmed."

"What a fool for me you are." She smiled, touching her forehead to his.

The ice crunched beneath them in warning, forcing them to scramble to their feet.

"So much for Mortesian ice being impermeable." Laila cast him a withering look as the splinter lengthened beneath their feet.

"With the force of our bodies combined I suppose it got a little more than it bargained for." Darius seized her hand, pulling her along. "Come on, we just have to make it to the edge before—"

His speech was cut off when Laila's skate scuffed an uneven ridge of ice, pulling her hand from his. She fell to her knees, swiftly encircled by a snaggle-toothed ring of fissures that threatened breakage.

Laila couldn't move, couldn't think, couldn't do anything but call out "Darius!" before whatever thin barrier remained between her and the abyss disintegrated and sent her plunging into blackness.

Darius still stood with his hand outstretched, clasping the air for her before he registered her absence. Upon seeing her swallowed by Mortos's desolate depths, horror gripped his chest. He thrust his hand without hesitation into the bone-chilling water to tear her free.

Laila resurfaced with a fragmented gasp, thrashing pathetically. She was chill as a corpse and riddled with shivers, unable to clamp her shuddering jaw as she huddled against him for warmth. Solarite bodies were not built to suffer cold, and the Mortesian lake had felt like fornicating death.

"It's all right, I've got you. I've got you now." Darius picked her up, wishing his powers could do something of use. "Can you warm yourself?"

Laila's chin wobbled with an attempt at denial.

"Hang on tightly, then. We'll get you back to the lodge."

He kicked off the skates and sped down the snow-slickened path they'd used at an ungodly pace until they were at the porch, where he slammed the door open with his back to carry her inside.

He set her down on the divan, stripping her wet clothes away before discarding them into a pile. Then he turned to the stove and fed it wood to burn.

Laila's teeth chattered as she slid her forearms beneath her breasts in a frantic search for warmth. If she could heat herself even somewhat, her power could do the rest. But the ice in her felt marrow deep.

Darius kept bouncing from wall to wall, snatching furs from every corner of the lodge and bundling them into a cocoon to encase her. He lifted her from the divan to the floor, placing her closer to the fire.

"The furs will do their best, but you'll need body heat," he thought aloud, scrambling to remove his own garments before he crawled within the swaddle he created. Her skin was so cold it seared him, but he ignored his discomfort to hold her near.

Laila wound herself around him like a coiling vine, slipping limb through limb until they were fully entangled. She buried her face into his chest to warm her cheek with a whimper.

"I'm sorry," he murmured into the crown of her head. "It's my fault. I let you go."

"'S not... your fault..." Laila quivered as she nuzzled into him, pressing a cool kiss to his collarbone. That he should blame himself when the fault lay entirely with her made her heart swell with love for him.

Darius cradled her to him, rocking her back and forth until the ice within her receded.

The night terror snuck in like the subtlest of thieves.

Darius tossed and turned in the midst of a sweat, covers thrown off, lips rapidly moving with incomprehensible murmurs.

"Darius?" Laila put her backhand to his moistened brow. "You're burning..."

She hadn't noticed it start, having fallen asleep with his whispered assurances that all was well. Of course she'd believed him. How could she not? Darius had always faced any infirmity with a certain amount of grace and aplomb. He was the sort who, upon having received an appointment with Death, would meet him early at the threshold and politely request he come at a more convenient hour.

Imagine her surprise, then, when she awoke to discover the impossible. Her occasso was in the throes of ephialtes. She observed his violent tremors and flushed cheeks with helplessness. "I'll go get you a damp towel."

"No." His hand snapped around her wrist. "Please... don't... don't leave."

She'd never heard such desperation in him. It melted her heart. "I'm here." She took his head and brought it to rest in her lap. Her hand caressed through his damp hair. "I'm here."

He reclined onto her warmth with a soft whimper.

"Hmph. Pathetic."

Darius squeezed his eyes shut as the apparition of his father leered at him from the foot of the bed. Lanius's fury was so vivid and real that Darius almost cried out.

"I see even after having helped yourself to my crown, you're still the snivelling whelp you've always been."

"No." He shook his head violently. "Stop."

"Darius?" Laila gazed down at him in worry.

"Look at you—whining like an infant at her breast. I underestimated how desperate you always were to crawl between the legs of any wench who'd spread them for you and hope she'd keep you there. Rather than cast you out... like your mother."

"Be quiet!"

Lanius unhinged his jaw until his face was nothing but torn skin and stringy ligaments. *"Yes... that's what frightens you, isn't it?"* A torrent of cruel laughter poured out from his black throat. *"Never keeping the soft touch of a maid's love. Knowing that there is a rot deep in the core of you that, once exposed, will cause her to scamper away..."*

Dr Emica Hariken slithered up from the darkness to gurgle at him accusingly, a waterfall of chaotic essence spilling from her lips.

"I'm so sorry..." he snuffled, chest hitching with a sob.

Laila shushed him. "Don't apologise. You have nothing to be sorry for."

Her voice was an anchor to the present, and he clung to it for dear life. "No... you shouldn't have to see me like this. I'm..." His throat rolled with a swallow. "I'm so worthless."

"Oh, Darius." Laila's eyes watered. "Let me find something to help you."

"No. I don't need anything. Only you." He closed his eyes and breathed slowly in an attempt to steady his pulse. "I hadn't suffered this in so long that I... I thought I was past this. I thought I'd stopped being so weak."

Laila's chest flared from the revelation along with the tone of self-loathing he'd taken. "Tell me how to help you." She cradled him close and put her lips to the crown of his head. "Please."

"I—" He couldn't say it. Yet he must if he was to surpass this trial. Letting her know how much the threat of losing her nearly drove him to despair. "I... I need you to stay with me, Laila. Say you'll never leave me. I can handle anything else with you at my side. Anything but that."

"I won't." Laila brushed his hair aside and kissed his clammy forehead. "I'm not going anywhere, Darius. All right? I'll be here with you for as long as you need."

He exhaled something between a laugh and a weep, already feeling his pulse wane. "I have done so many terrible things. Awful things."

"I know."

"You don't."

"I do know. And I've loved you through it whether you deserve it or not." Her hand sought his, and she laced their fingers together, her thumb stroking over his knuckles. "I always will."

She kept him encased in her arms as he whimpered and murmured through the rest of the nightmare, sweating profusely. Each time, she shushed him and wiped his brow, doing her best to keep her breathing even. Once he'd settled into a twitching state of rest, she too succumbed to her fatigue.

VI

O FURTHER IMMERSE HIS REGINA WITHIN HER NEW kingdom, Darius planned a tour to the furthest untamed hinterlands of Mortos. They intended to visit every town and city, both familiar and new, graciously accepting the hospitality of the occassi landmasters that took them in.

Their first stop was Skarlvile—the domain of Domitia Orlovia. Both had decided it best to get her out of the way. The illustrious matriarch would surely take offence if she were not positioned as the opening act of their honeymoon tour and the first to cast favour on their union.

The domina had her qarna lay a path with swan feathers towards the threshold of her gate. Laila was all smiles as their carriage descended, accepting their salutations and the fresh hollyhocks the qarna placed into her bejewelled hair.

"Thank you, thank you." Laila and Darius waved them off and

parted through with careful nudging towards the Orlovis estate, where Domitia awaited.

"Well, if it isn't our stella regina." Domitia laughed heartily as she cupped Laila's face, peering down her nose like she was inspecting a cut of meat for quality. "Mm, it gives me great pleasure to be the first to look upon your newly crowned bride, Darius Rex. She wears her post-wedding glow well."

"We wouldn't dream of giving anyone else the privilege," Darius said.

Domitia pressed an approving kiss to Laila's forehead. "Welcome to Skarlvile. Please come inside."

Laila tried not to cower at the ferity etched into Domitia's smile and followed her indoors. The heat roaring from log-fire furnaces made a tight-clenched fist around her body. Already she could feel a sweat forming, but it wasn't from the cloying temperature alone.

Domitia led them into a hexagonal dining room and presented her carved oak table and chairs. Wolves flanked her family crest above each seat, while grotesque pig heads frozen in open-mouthed squeals decorated the arms. The sight seemed ominous, so Laila almost dithered but retained enough grace to take her place on the blood-red velvet chair Darius pulled out for her.

"So, how long can we be expecting your stay?" Domitia snapped her fingers and beckoned one forward to serve them mulled wine.

"We shan't be stopping long." Darius crossed his legs and tented his fingers. "We have plans to tour the kingdom and return to the Citadel in a full moon's period. You'll enjoy our company for only a night, I'm afraid."

"Well, I hope this splendid meal I've prepared will make your swift passing memorable."

The servants arrived to lay the table with Domitia's bounty. Salmon pie with a crackling golden crust embossed with the Orlovia family crest. Grilled octopus tentacles, thinly sliced, sprinkled with chives and garlic and swimming in green mustard. Poached salmon wrapped in pickled cucumber ribbons. There were even roasted bat wings caramelised in pungent truffle honey—a rare delicacy.

The qarna worked at a slow and sluggish pace, half-deadened, it would seem, from the tedium of their task. Only a closer look would reveal the true cause behind their lethargy.

Laila spied a faint splotching of welts and two puncture marks at the wrist as the qarnina neared to offer her a plate of nettle bread rolls. She took one with a tender smile as her chest started to throb.

"I do suppose you'll pass by my son Caius along your journey," Domitia continued with a loud slurp from her glass. "He has taken a bride of the Snegnia clan all the way in Skorbjeva."

"Ah, yes, indeed. Your last one to be wed, if I'm keeping count." Darius chuckled, miming the number with his fingers. "The reach of your descendants has certainly spanned far and wide, Domina Orlovia."

"That it has." And she took every opportunity she could to flaunt it before each seated monarch. "My lord husband often jests it's a shame we did not bear a daughter for you. We ought to have conquered the kingdom by now."

Darius made a mirthless sound and took a sip of wine.

"But of course then you wouldn't have found love in your solarite bride. How are you enjoying the bread, Laila Regina?"

Laila jolted upon the address, tearing her eyes from the qarnina.

"You've not taken a single bite out of it?" Domitia arched a brow. "Is it not to your liking?"

Laila glanced at the bread held in her tightly clenched fingers, powdering crumbs into her lap. "Apologies, I—" She dropped the bread onto her plate. Her mind had drifted the moment the bite marks had seized her focus and refused to let go. "I—I have to ask—"

"Yes?" Domitia straightened in her seat.

"How long have you been biting this qarnina?"

Domitia's lip curled. "I beg your—"

"What is your name?" Laila turned towards the server.

"Y—" The qarnina glanced towards her mistress before deferring to the order of her monarch. "Yula, Your Majesty."

"Tell me, Yula." Laila leaned forward to touch her wrist. "How long have you been being bitten?"

Yula swallowed and shrank her hands into her sleeves.

"It's all right, don't tell me now," Laila soothed. Her eyes hardened to stone when they reached Domitia. "This will stop. Immediately."

"Your Majesty," Domitia scoffed in amusement. "This will hardly resolve matters. Qarna are very weak-willed creatures, feeble. If we stop giving her venom now she will die of wanting it."

"Then a solution: You give venom in a much more diluted form as a medicinal brew to curb the cravings. But I better not hear of you biting her or any other qarna. Otherwise there shall be consequences."

Domitia's lips had scrunched at the suggestion, further diminishing into a puckered circle the more she spoke. "Your Majesty, surely you cannot—"

"I believe your regina issued an order," Darius said.

Laila kept her smile muted, affirmed by his support. "Is there a problem?"

Domitia's hand squeezed her goblet until it bent. "Yes, there is." She set down her glass before it shattered. "I had hoped for a pleasant meal with you both, and now it has been tarnished. I see no reason why you feel the need to concern yourself with how I run my household, favouring the welfare of common filth over the loyal subjects who make it the greatness it is."

"Perhaps the reginas of old might have turned a blind eye, but I see it as my duty to serve all who reside in Mortos, no matter how wealthy or poor, how powerful or meek—"

"A darling sentiment where you're from, I'm sure." Domitia's lips curled into a saccharine sneer. "I suppose I cannot fault your newness, but I believe your husband's duty should be to inform you of how things function in this country."

Darius took a slow sip of his wine before setting down the goblet. "Tell me, Domitia, which of your sons would it hurt you the least to lose?"

The question came so unexpectedly that it left Domitia's mouth agape.

"Take your time." Darius made an encouraging gesture. "I can imagine it is a difficult question to answer."

"Your Majesty..."

"Name one."

Laila's smile faltered as she turned to look at Darius, finding no anger in his demeanour. Instead there was a relaxed, affable ease to him that struck her as almost playful.

Domitia's face had darkened considerably, now posed with a choice no mother in their right mind could ever respond to.

Eventually, Darius sighed. "If you don't choose then I may have to choose one for you—"

"Marcus."

Darius chuckled. "Middle child. Wed to the weakest family. What a positively mercenary pick. Very well, Marcus will be the first one I shall use as fodder in the chimera pits should you speak out of turn again. Believe me, there are plenty of vultures who'd be happy to swoop into his seat in the aftermath." His voice didn't raise a decibel above a stern, lecturing tone delivered with the utmost politeness. "Gone are the days where you wielded your sons as a bludgeon against past rexes. Your numbers may be bold and your influence encompassing, I shall grant you that. But I rely on a new army now." He cocked his head like an adult before an errant child, waiting patiently for an answer. "Do you understand?"

Domitia had gone ashen, her pupils heavy and round, before she unleashed a loud and uncomfortably long cackle that made Laila flinch. "Well, when you put it in such terms, Your Majesty, how can I answer but in the affirmative?"

"Then let us resume dinner."

"One other thing." Laila stood up and approached a still trembling Yula, taking her forearms to lightly squeeze. "As a gesture of goodwill, I would like to take this qarnina into my service." She pivoted towards Domitia. "Consider it a coronation gift to me."

Domitia gave a small chuckle, realising her intent, and dismissed it with a bored flick of her wrist. "She's all yours, Stella Regina."

"Go wait in my quarters," Laila whispered, guiding the qarnina to what she hoped to be out of harm's way for the foreseeable future.

Laila requested a tincture be brought up from the kitchens with diluted occassi venom mixed with healing herbs. When it arrived she stirred the ceramic spoon in the bowl herself and puffed to cool it. Then she pricked her finger with the edge of a hairpin and added a few drops of her ichor.

"It'll help to heal your injuries," she explained when Yula shied away from the offering, expecting more tricks.

Her eyes darted over the medicine in doubt, assessing risk, before she snatched it from Laila's hands and consumed it in one gulp. "Thank you," she gasped, wiping her mouth with the back of her hand.

"I require no thanks." Laila dipped her hands into her lotion of rose petals and strawberry seeds and moisturised her hands. "I am merely performing my duty."

"There—" Yula traced the rim of the bowl. "There are others like me. In the household. She bites them all, you know. It's how she keeps us complacent now they can't kill us anymore."

"I know." Laila sighed as she sat down on the edge of her bed.

"Somehow it's worse than when they made us corpses, because at least we didn't have to feel it," Yula said. "But what can we do? Even if we manage to take them back, the process of weaning them from venom is often fatal in itself."

This was my doing, Laila realised. She had pushed for the abolishment of the Culling with Darius, and the occassi had gone on to evolve a crueller torment to take its place. It seemed the more she dug her feet into the abyss to drag this country out, the deeper she ended up sinking.

"I'm taking you with me to the Citadel, where I can guarantee there will be no biting. Back where I hail from, treatments were developed to ease the detrimental effects caused by dependency on moongrass. I am uncertain how they will measure in the face of the full potency of occassi venom, but I can assure you they will ease the effects."

Yula's shoulders drooped, eyes watering until a tear slid with a plink into her bowl. It didn't take much for Laila to gather there would be loved ones here she'd be leaving behind.

"I am sorry, Yula," Laila said, then a thought crossed her mind. One that gnawed in her stomach. "I understand if you wish for me to retract my command—"

"No." Yula shook her head and sniffled. She rubbed her eye.

"Domina Orlovia is a ruthless beast. If I stay I'll die. I know that much. I—I want to live. My family would want me to live."

Laila nodded. "Stay in my room tonight. Do not leave it. If anyone asks, you are my personal attendant and I have strict orders that you are to remain here at my beck and call. Understand?"

"I understand." Yula's back straightened. "What would you require of me, Your Majesty?"

"I order you to come over here and get into this bed. Because you seem exhausted. I shall retire with the rex tonight."

Yula spared no moment before cuddling underneath the silken sheets, smoothing her hands over the softness with a sense of awe. She was out in seconds.

Laila tucked the covers up to Yula's chin and smoothed her fleecy hair from her forehead before walking into the adjoining room where Darius was resting.

He was seated upright, ankles crossed, thumbing through a tome before he looked up at her. "Has our impromptu guest been settled for the evening?"

Laila nodded as she gathered up her curls in her hands. "I apologise for the disruption I caused tonight."

"Don't be." Darius set his book aside. "I won't deny Domitia can cause quite the diplomatic headache, but she's needed her ego checked for centuries."

Laila fiddled with a ribbon she picked up to tie her hair.

"You're so far away." Darius slipped off the bed and took her in his arms, pressing a kiss to her shoulder.

"Did you mean what you threatened?" Laila looked up at him. "When you said you'd cast down her sons?"

"What Domitia said to you today was unacceptable. I needed her to know it wouldn't be tolerated. If that requires some extreme action on my part, then yes. For the sake of defending my regina... yes."

His words set her heart aflutter as she found herself at war with herself between appreciation and dread. Thrill and fear. She couldn't decipher which of them had conquered by the time his lips came down to eclipse hers.

"Now come to bed."

Laila gave him a mischievous look. "Is that an order, Your Majesty?"

"Yes."

Laila smoothed her palm along his chest, saying nothing. But the glint in her eyes communicated more than words. "And if I refuse?"

Darius chuckled and walked her back against the wall so she was pinned beneath his weight, unable to escape his unrelenting gaze. "I think I'll find a way to make you yield."

Laila squealed in laughter as he hooked his arms behind her knees, struggling to keep quiet as he carried her off to the bed. She landed with a bounce when he dumped her onto it and crawled in beside her.

"So, what did you think of *The Question of Evil*?" He propped his elbow up on the pillow and rested his cheek on his fist, eager for her response. He'd seen her flipping voraciously through the weathered tome of his favourite novel during the length of the tour.

"Well, the work was thought-provoking, but in the end I found it rather solipsistic."

"Solipsistic?"

"It was too narrow in scope."

"And what is *that* supposed to mean?"

"What could be more self-involved than an author reducing other races to nameless hordes and congratulating himself on his hardened detachment as he pontificates the ethics of brutalising them?" Laila threw her hands up. "It's all so... bloodless despite the nature of his work. Stodgy, tedious prose mired in apathy."

"How scathing! You truly didn't like it at all, then?"

"Well, I wouldn't say that. I am not sorry I read it. And I found the subject matter interesting. I suppose I wished for more depth. More... personhood. Volgis reduces his opponents to numerals and forgets that there are *lives* within them."

"Sometimes that's necessary. During a moment of crisis you can't always stop to factor everyone as an individual of inherent worth. If your people are starving and suffering and, in a split-second decision, you can slaughter a village to get their food, then that simplification in one's mind can make all the difference."

"Perhaps... but that is not satisfactory to me."

"Well, if you were in danger I know I wouldn't hesitate. Your worth outpaces thousands in my eyes. Would it not be the same for you?"

"I'd... have to think about that."

Darius sucked in sharply. "Cold-blooded." He shook his head at her. "And what precisely would you recommend to counter my stodgy philosophical tomes?"

"*Dandelion Whispers*." Her response was immediate. "One of my favourite novels, told in prose poetry. It's steeped in symbolism and metaphor and romantic atmosphere, with much scathing social critique on the nature of court politics. Which I think you might appreciate."

"I'll give it a gander."

"Her works aren't for everyone but what I love about her is she always manages to give everyone a sympathetic face. It makes watching the machinations unfold much more satisfying to me."

With their conversation concluded they curled up together and slowly drifted off to sleep. That night, Laila dreamed she discovered Darius's heart cast out into the snow. The organ was black and shrivelled like a raisin, half-deflated on its side. She frowned as she drew nearer to rescue it, scooping it up in her hand and shaking off the glaze. Frost gnawed deep into the tissue and left it striated with white. It weighed heavy in her hand like a stone, like it had never once beat.

Softly, she took it in both hands and started to massage it, hoping against all odds that the warmth of her touch alone would inflate it back to life. She handled the task with diligence and care, as if she had never done anything more important in her life. Only when she felt a faint throb in her hand did she finally stop and carry it inside with her.

By the warmth of the fireplace she took trimmings of fragrant herbs and stuffed the heart like a pastry, folding over the flaps of muscle, and left it for three days. When she returned, the heart had sprouted blossoms, and she discovered a rosefinch had made a bed within its folds.

The last thing she remembered before she awoke was Darius coughing up tufts of pink feathers. Each time he tried to speak his larynx trembled with the shrill, musical whistle of a bird.

VII

WHENEVER A SOLARITE PERISHED, THERE WAS NEVER a body left behind. Instead, whatever tie she held to her physical body extinguished and she dispersed into atoms. For this reason, instead of a traditional burial, they observed solarite passings by placing a small porcelain figurine into the dynasty shrine as a representative for them and laying the table with objects they once favoured.

Amira's face turned grim as she saw all the figurines being brought into the cemetery. Some were cradled close, moistened with tears and lavished with kisses. Others were adorned with garments and flowers as if they were dolls. Some were spoken to as if they were animate. Others were observed in silent reverence as their kin knelt in prayer.

It had been a solemn reckoning to observe how much their numbers had truly dwindled. Solarites were never plentiful to begin with, but Dominus's assault had pushed them towards endangered levels. The cane she used to aid her aching limbs was a sore reminder of what was lost that day.

She could only manage a few rounds to bestow her condolences before the chaos still present in her body inflamed her joints. Then her skin started to ooze a pungent, sulphuric substance that stung worse than venom the moment the air touched it.

She gritted her teeth, pressing her thighs together to keep them warmed by her body heat as one of her ladies came over to check on her.

"Madame," said one of the sprites. "You really should make use of this." They presented her with an aerochair that would levitate her across the grounds.

"I can make my way," Amira said flatly. It was a last roar of pride from the wounded lioness. She refused to become reliant on these aids. If she couldn't make the journey up a pitiful cemetery there was no reason for her to rise up from bed again the next morning.

She brought one foot forward, but the immediate rush of air onto her weeping skin brought an acute sting to the back of her knees. She couldn't even stand. Much less walk.

"Madame?" Her guard looked on at her in concern.

Pity, she thought miserably. *Once they feared me and now they pity me.*

"Just put me in the chair and get it over with," she said, muted so as not to portray her weakness. She couldn't think of anything more embarrassing than to show how much she was still impacted by the attack. "And fetch my blanket."

She didn't understand why she kept reaching for that accursed thing.

Somehow it had become her only comfort after a long, dreary

session of light treatment, having her body expunged of the lingering dregs of chaos. Afterwards, she would find herself within her chambers, glass of summer wine in hand, and with a sharp snap of fingers would direct one of her sprite maids to bring said blanket to her. Then she'd be on her favourite chair with the shawl spread across her lap.

Once the sprite had brought it to her she commanded for it to be laid across her lap. She smoothed her hand over the fine weaving and every pristine little silk bow tied at its edges. A small smile came to her lips in spite of herself at the immaculacy of its condition. She still remembered when she'd demanded it made, how she'd scoured the wares of every travelling merchant with the utmost critique in search of the perfect fabric. In the end she'd decided on cloud fleece, for it was gentlest on a starlet's skin. Only the best would be had for Amira Rose's future daughter.

And hadn't she given her the best? Had she not clothed Laila's delicate skin in the most exquisite of silks? Had she not fed her by hand the most delicious puréed meals? Had she not enshrouded her in every luxury that could be known to a crown princess of their kind, and then some? And what did she receive in return but to be shunned as a monster?

The thought was enough to turn her nostalgic reverie to rage as her curled fingers embedded in the fabric. Had she less remarkable control over her impulses, a mere tug from her supernal strength would be enough to tear the blanket in two. Instead, she lifted the blanket to her nose and inhaled the faint remnants of Laila's sweet baby scent to snuff her temper.

It wasn't long before her private time was encroached upon by none other than Lucrèce Mielette.

"Your Luminosity." Lucrèce gave a light curtsey.

"No need for courtesies, Lucrèce," she said with a dismissive wave, folding the blanket and draping it over the arm of her chair in a decorative fashion. "This is a solemn day for us all. You are no stranger by now."

"But of course." Lucrèce accepted the invitation and made herself quite at home sitting beside Amira in her dynasty crypt.

"To what do I owe the pleasure?"

"I understand this might not be an appropriate time to broach the issue but, in my grief, I must. I have come to ask what more you intend to do with regards to occassi migrants. They still appear to be travelling throughout the continent at quite steady numbers, and after... recent events, I believe it unwise to permit them such ease of way."

"I made my thoughts on the matter clear when we voted on a Mortesian embargo during Parlement." Amira stroked her blanket. "What happened in Aurea Park was the lone action of a lunatic. Darius Rex has been very forthcoming that he intends to reimburse Soleterea for the damages wrought with reparations paid in yearly instalments. He has also issued a formal apology on his brother's behalf. We've not had any comparable incidents before or since. I have no desire to stir the pot unnecessarily, Lucrèce. Treating occassi as though they're criminals the moment they set foot on shore sends a message. An adversarial one that's sure to have repercussions overseas."

"And you wouldn't want to give reason for them to exact their frustrations upon your daughter while she remains firmly within the Mortesian rex's clutches?" Lucrèce astutely guessed.

Amira tightened her lips into a firm line.

"It's understandable to miss her." Lucrèce glanced towards the baby blanket. "And to worry for her. You are a mother as much as you are a monarch, and that's an impossible balance to strike."

"After everything I did for that girl..." Amira's breath hitched with the formation of a rant. "All for her to desert me for a monster while insisting *I* am the brute. Was my conduct truly so poor? I treated her no worse than my mother treated me.”

“Starlets don’t often have the foresight to understand their mothers until they become one themselves.” Lucrèce smiled in sympathy. “All you can hope for is that she’ll come to see your perspective.”

Amira made a sardonic noise.

“Give it time,” Lucrèce insisted.

“But in answer to your request: I do not intend to restrict occassi movement. At least not explicitly. I do, however, believe we need to allocate more funds to an anti-chaos department in the Iron Clan.” Amira put down her glass. “I shall discuss it with the commandante.”

“As I’m sure would be best.”

Lyra grunted as she stood beneath the piping hot stream of her water spout, its heat painting vengeful pink wings on her shoulder blades. Steam swirled around her in profuse clouds as if she herself were burning hot enough to turn everything to vapour as it touched her. Sometimes it felt like it. That this rage in her was enough to blacken her to the core. Only alcohol was enough to quiet it—as the table full of empty bottles in the other room could only attest to.

After the wedding, she’d turned in her Lightshield uniform and shield, and her sole comfort since had been the endless tap of gin from the local public house. In spite of her spotless reputation, the people lacked judgement so long as she paid, and she’d soon taken to it as a second home. Far superior to the taunting vacancy of Le Creissant, now haunted by the absence of far too many solarites. In the end she could no longer bear it. The wordless accusations. The crippling sense of failure. Each time she closed her eyes her mind repeated the scene of

Aurea Park engulfed in screaming and smog. The emaciated remains of starlets when the first tendrils had retracted, their bodies black-veined and polluted with chaos.

Losing Laila had been the final push she'd needed. For she could no longer keep up the pretence that she'd upheld her duties. She'd lost her very charge to the claws of a monster. What greater shame could there be?

She rubbed her sleepy eye with her palm. After yet another night of gin-soaked misery she needed a shower to shake her awake. Once she was rinsed through she palmed for the lever and ceased the water, walking nude into her bedroom.

A soft noise escaped her lips as she acknowledged the invitation on her desk. It was the newest atop of a pile of correspondence with the same split wax seal of a honeybee. This one demanded her presence for dinner and indicated that a vehicle would collect her. Whether she willed it or not.

Lyra set aside her resentment and pulled out her most presentable garb from her moss-covered wardrobe, a cream suit made of lily petals. Once she'd dragged it onto herself she went to meet the driver outside, climbing into the car with little more than a wave in his direction.

The aeromobile took her to the Astrial, a famed bistro on the outskirts of the capital. The establishment was acclaimed for its palatial interior including its stained glass roof, brass pilasters, and floral ceramic friezes.

"Welcome." The sprite valet took her coat. "Please follow me."

Lyra entered into the foyer and glanced over the patrons chattering with stems of rose-shaped wine flutes in hand. She sought the hostess among them, but the solarite discovered her first.

"Ser de Lis?"

Lyra jolted instantly at the sound of her name. "Where the bloody oblivion did you come from?!"

Lucrèce retained her perfectly composed tone, arms folded behind her back. There was something unnervingly varnished about her—not a single crease to be found in her filmy silk gown or a scuff on her leather shoes. She almost seemed more stone than skin. "I am most pleased you were able to join us."

"Well, well, well." Lyra straightened to acknowledge her. "Ought to have expected your dynasty was to have a heavy hand in all this."

Lucrèce's chuckle was a light ringing sound, causing the butterflies in her cloud of hair to flit their wings. "If you'd join me, I have a special place picked out for us. We can talk better that way." She turned and glanced over her shoulder to beckon Lyra to follow.

Tough crowd, Lyra thought as she stood to follow her. She wondered if this wind-up doll ever unwound. The name Lucrèce had been bandied about during times when Lyra had tried and failed not to overhear Laila trading gossip among her peers. Her icy demeanour was infamous. Courtiers often referred to her as the Glass Figurine.

Lyra hurried to keep up with her but found that wasn't difficult with Lucrèce's delicate, precise steps. A ballet dancer, if Lyra were to guess from her svelte build alone.

Lucrèce had booked their table in a cosy alcove next to one of the hand-painted mosaic tile walls depicting Asemani. Something about seeing the sun goddess in her flowing silk robes surrounded by her starry descendants always instilled Lyra with an immeasurable sense of calm.

Lyra approached the empty seat, though before she could touch the chair, it glowed gold with aether and withdrew for her, then pushed her in once she'd sat.

Lucrèce gestured to the carafe. "Help yourself to some nectar wine if you'd like."

"I'm fine," Lyra said, swallowing away her thirst. "I was hoping we could launch straight into the matter of things."

"Of course." Lucrèce nodded in approval. "We were hoping to meet with you sooner, but with the current state of affairs there's been some delays."

Lyra warded off the memory of anguished cries she'd buried deep in the back of her mind. She'd started to regret not taking up the offer of a drink. "Understandable."

"Plus, you've been rather difficult to contact." This was said with the merest hint of reproach.

"I needed... time to myself." Lyra flexed her fingers and laced them together. She was more than happy when the cold berry soup seasoned with pansies came, and she picked up a spoon to occupy her hands. "But I'm here now."

"As you should be." Lucrèce's lips tilted upwards in an approximation of a smile. Although her eyes creased, the pastel blossoms on her lids and the tiny butterfly on her lash line remained impeccably placed. "Because we have a proposition for you."

"What kind of proposition?" Lyra took a sip of soup. It had a sharp flavour with the slightest sweet aftertaste.

"There may be an ingredient missing from our elixir," Lucrèce said. "An elusive ingredient which, if located, may be vitally important to our research."

Lyra paused and scooped up more soup. "Sure you trust me with such a monumental task?"

"We all make errors. See this as a chance to re-ingratiate yourself to our esteem. Should you be willing."

Lyra put down her spoon and drummed her fingers. "What kind of ingredient?"

"We require a feather from the Holy Phoenix."

"Wait, wait—" Lyra held up her hand. "Please tell me you are not requesting that I *desecrate* the sacred Holy Phoenix? The spirit that replenishes our connection between our world and the Astral World? This could have worldwide ramifications on our connection to aether—"

Lucrèce gave her an appraising look. Her enigmatic air both intrigued and irritated Lyra, who wanted to huff hot air at her until she defrosted.

"Right. Too much preaching."

"You sprites never fail to amuse." Lucrèce shook her head. "No desecration will be necessary, Ser de Lis."

"But the Phoenix only appears once every seven hundred and fifty years, and in case you hadn't noticed, it's been only fifty since its last sighting."

"I'm aware," Lucrèce said. "However there is… an alternative method to evoke the Phoenix. And it requires contact with Esterre Rose."

"She hasn't been seen for at least…" Lyra blew air from her mouth. "Three hundred years."

"She resides fully in the Astral Realm along with our Elders. If we want to contact her it must be done on hallowed ground in Setâre Island. And we shall require someone from the Rose bloodline."

Lyra flushed, having immediately thought of Laila. "The impératrice?"

"The impératrice is unaware of our mission, and I'd prefer it remains that way."

The thought of it sat uneasily on Lyra's shoulders, as did everything about this secretive little sect she'd encountered thus far. "Then who?"

"I have someone in mind," Lucrèce said, "and I want you to approach her. It can't be me, as I cannot risk her asking me too many questions."

Lyra nodded. "All in the aim of ridding the world of chaos." She took another few spoons of soup before noticing Lucrèce's bowl and glass were untouched.

"Are you not going to have anything to eat?" Lyra asked. "You've not touched the soup."

"I do not need to play-act at these things." Lucrèce tilted her head to one side. "So why pretend?"

VIII

SADIK DRANK HIS FILL OF SPICED RUM AND GINGER beer. He set down the drink with a relieved sigh and folded his hands behind his head, allowing the Malakian sun to bake his oil-slicked muscles recently loosened from a massage. Yasmin's delighted squeals travelled up on the breeze as she paddled in the sea at the shore, Elina close behind to watch and guide her.

He couldn't prevent the smile of pure contentment that came to his lips. These were the perfect moments worth living and having lived for. Whatever hardships he'd suffered through this past year alone were irrelevant compared to the knowledge that he had his innermost heart's desire in his grasp here and now.

His relief was miserably short-lived.

The sky, once glistening bright, became overwrought with a black whirlpool of clouds spitting out blue shards of lightning into the ocean. The waters rippled with a crackling current that awakened several unmentionables lurking below.

Sadik started upwards at the sound of a roar as a webbed hand appeared from the water, followed by an arm suffused with slimy scales. The sea monster surfaced with razor-sharp fins and needle teeth, its piercing shriek summoning an army of mutant black crabs the size of small dogs that scuttled onto the shore.

Oh, gods. Sadik's legs went numb from fear as more and more sprouted up from the seabed, approaching his beloved and child with menacing hatred in their blank white eyes. More than simple hunger. This was pure *malice*.

"No!" He scrambled up from his towel with futility and tripped over his legs into the sand. Yet still he crawled, helpless and impotent as the crabs claimed Yasmin first.

"Stop! Please!"

Yasmin squealed as the crabs tore off her limbs in a prolonged and playful torment. "Amma! Appa, help me!"

"Yasmin—"

"Elina, don't!" Sadik sobbed as Elina raced into the mass of the crabs to save their daughter, only to be taken next and scattered into pieces of bloodied viscera.

He didn't fight back when they surrounded him, covered him, slowly peeling the skin from his back and face and fingers until—

Sadik lurched from the dream with a gasp, his sheets and body both saturated in sweat. Each night as he struggled to sleep, he saw himself and those he loved attacked by monsters with gnarled, serrated claws. They flayed open his ribcage and pecked his innards to tiny gibbets. They plucked out his eyes. They squawked in his ears until the drums were bleeding.

"Bad nightmare?"

Sadik flinched to discover a new doctor sitting on a chair beside his bed. He pulled up his covers to preserve his modesty. "How did—how did—?"

"I get in?" The doctor cocked her head to one side. "Dr Mielette was kind enough to allow me a visit." She gave the room a onceover. "My, how far you've fallen. I recall the club and car you had were a far sight more ostentatious. Reeked of new money insecurity."

Sadik rubbed at his eyes twice, hoping he was dreaming. "Who *are* you?"

"My name is Dr Akira Isuka. I am a longtime scholar of the chaotic arts, and haven't you made quite the awful mess with it?" She tutted and wagged her finger at him. "Fortunately, there are ways for you to remedy that."

"What in oblivion are you talking about?" Sadik snapped, too tired and disoriented to make sense of this unexpected nighttime guest.

"You seem overwhelmed." Dr Isuka's voice had taken on a cloyingly sweet tone of patronisation. "Why don't you let me do the talking, hm? Your beloved was forced to turn to me after your reckless actions endangered her. Your beloved, whose life currently hangs in the balance. And will continue to do so if you do not act exactly as I say—"

"Elina?" Sadik scrambled to get out of bed. "Where is she? I want to see her."

Dr Isuka spoke an enchantment that stripped the soundwaves from Sadik's voice. "That's better. As I was saying, we require your aid in a certain task. Dr Mielette tells me you've been having nightmares, yes? Ones that involve being torn apart by monsters? Have any of them ever included a figure such as this?" She presented the image of a large creature crossed between a wolf, eagle, and man.

Sadik squinted closer at the image before recognition jolted his heart.

"I see." Dr Isuka rolled the parchment. "That is Calante."

The god of chaos?

"Yes. It seems he has begun to visit you now, as I suspected."

Discomfort prickled along Sadik's spine. *Why me?*

"Because you invoked him," Dr Isuka said, "the moment you used that book." She gestured at his eye. "The deal you made with the occasso wouldn't have been enough. That was a deal you made with one of Calante's underlings. The grimoire is how you contact him personally, and now you've been marked."

Sadik had sunk further and further into the covers, shaking his head in disbelief.

"He'll be coming to get you."

No! Even without a voice, his scream was palpable.

"I cannot stop it." Dr Isuka sighed. "It's a power that's beyond me. But we may be able to. If you come with us."

Where?

"To the Mountain." Dr Isuka straightened her clothes. "It's our research facility in Odaka where we'll be able to run tests and monitor you closely. Even Elina is there, waiting for you. Isn't that nice?"

He trusted little the geniality of her tone but knew he had few options. He was a cursed man walking, and soon Calante would be coming to claim his soul. Sadik swallowed. This undertaking seemed near suicidal and yet he knew very well he had no means to refuse. So he nodded.

"Good boy." Dr Isuka smiled, rising up from his bed. "I'll let Elina know you were asking for her."

Wait, he cried out soundlessly and stuck out his hand. *Wait. Tell me how she is. Tell me—*

Dr Isuka closed the door behind her.

IX

HE HONEYMOON ENDED QUICKER THAN THE newlyweds would have liked, and throughout it Darius attempted to explore all the sights he had promised.

He took his bride underwater to the glass-orbed metropolis that was carried on the back of a leviathan. They toured for a day before moving on to cursed pirate ships sunk to the bottom of the sea, overflowing with gems that glittered more than Laila's skin. Darius pacified the restless souls with a sea shanty to fish out an egg-shaped opal ring for him and parures for her studded with canary diamonds and pink sapphires.

Next, they visited an ancient library full of tomes with words long dead and forgotten. Darius read her verses from a language that had not been uttered for millennia, and though Laila could not understand, the mere significance of the words on her ears was enough to make her weep.

On the final day, Darius cracked open the tomb of a perished artist and rattled his bones to awaken so they could sit for a portrait. Laila watched the elegant precision of his finger bones as the skeleton put paintbrush to canvas. She thought of what fortune she had to find someone willing to raise the dead for her so she might have a chance to enjoy this lost talent.

When the portrait was finished, she hugged it close to her chest as the carriage brought them hurtling back to the Citadel courtyard. By then it was nightfall, and Darius carried a slumbering Laila into his kingly chambers. Both were too exhausted to do anything but undress and climb into bed together, knowing that by morning their strenuous careers as monarchs would commence.

Laila woke first, having slept soundly atop her husband's chest, and began kissing a trail down it in the hopes of rousing him.

Darius was in no eager hurry to face the world, and he couldn't keep himself from responding to the feel of her lips. His own parted with a deep sigh. "If you carry on this way you're going to awaken a very different part of me."

"Then we'll definitely be late for the Council," she scolded, playful as she kissed a trail back up his chest. His prefects already thought her a conniving seductress enough; being held up in bed during their first meeting as rex and regina would only strengthen the impression.

"A tragedy," he said. Then he sat up and seized her by the waist to bring her onto his lap.

"Darius—" Laila's breath hitched at the force he used to hold her there. He was looking at her with that dark glint in his eyes. The one that made her chest tighten. "We shouldn't—"

He kissed her, ceasing her protestation. Laila couldn't remember why she was even arguing with him. Her stomach fluttered as he shifted them round so they were embracing side by side. He parted her thighs, draping one leg over his waist and massaging the crook of her knee.

Their kiss was a languid indulgence, embarked on for the pleasure of its own sake. There was no desire for more even as their moans and writhing grew more intense. One couldn't say how long they would have happily remained in this position had a knock on the door not disturbed them.

Laila whined when Darius lifted his mouth from hers.

"That'll be our breakfast." Darius detached himself from Laila to vacate the warmth of the sheets. Then he turned towards the door to invite in the servant.

Laila gave a feline stretch as she rolled onto her stomach. Her lips puckered upwards in a contented sleepy smile.

"Thank you, Kirill." Darius received the tray. "You may take your leave. The regina and I are not to be disturbed."

"Yes, Your Majesty."

Closing the door behind him, Darius took the tray back to bed. He lifted the monogrammed lid to reveal its content. Beneath were devilled eggs blanketed with smoked salmon and red caviar, a side dish of anchovies, and a stack of buckwheat blini smothered with lingonberry jam. Two flutes of mimosa sparkled alongside it.

Laila leaned towards the miniature feast in interest, the sheets receding from her to teasingly unveil the supple arc of her spine. The star-studded pattern of her dynasty marque glistened. Darius caught himself fondly tracing the rose with his gaze.

He couldn't fathom a better scene than this. The finest painter he could sponsor would not supplant the glow in his chest at the mere sight of Laila comfortably wrapped in his sheets with no signs of departure. No rushed scrambling for lost clothes. No hurried farewell as she slinked back to her quarters.

"What is it?" Laila asked, glancing up to meet his stare. She picked up a devilled egg and plucked off small bits of it to sample.

"Nothing. It's just... one of the first signs I knew I loved you was when I realised the nights were no longer enough. I'd often envision us having countless mornings just like these where I'd wake up to your smile and kiss you good morning and we'd laze about having breakfast in bed." His fingers glided along the dip in her back. "I never thought it would happen."

A smile blossomed on her lips as she moved in to kiss him. She bumped her nose against his. "Well get used to it. We can have as many of these mornings as you want."

⌘

Their arrival to the Eyrie was thankfully punctual.

Darius had Laila seated to the right of him—as opposed to his prime prefect, who had now been relegated to the left. Only instead of Delanus, it was now Sabina who had taken his place.

Laila's eyes lit up when she saw her and her lips broadened into one of her brightest smiles.

Sabina took in the smile with a pang of discomfort and glanced away from her. "Might I ask why the regina is present for this meeting, Your Majesty?"

Laila tried not to take it to heart, but her expression visibly withered. She couldn't help but feel guilty for the part she'd played in Delanus's punishment and the subsequent spectacle Darius made out of him to show an example.

She wondered if perhaps Sabina blamed her, too.

"Yes, I've been meaning to announce that." Darius stood from his chair. "As of her coronation, Laila Regina will henceforth be present for all Council meetings. You are to treat her as an authority and seek her guidance and approval for all matters of the state. In the event I am absent or indisposed, she will take on duties as regent, and official documents may be stamped by her seal. You might all start getting used to the sight of her."

A ripple travelled through the prefects in response.

Laila had come to anticipate this. The resentful, furtive glances. The thinly veiled animosity. She made herself immune to it, holding her head high as she rose from her seat.

"I thank you, Darius Rex, for bestowing on me such a hefty burden of responsibility." She brightened her face with a smile. "I hope I do right by you, and by Mortos as a nation."

"Does anyone have any concerns regarding my decree?" Darius swept his gaze across the room, head tilted in daring.

A quick darting of eyes in the direction of Sabina in Delanus's place was enough to stifle their tongues.

"Good." Darius took his seat. "Let us commence the meeting proper." He gestured for Laila to receive the proverbial baton. "Whenever you are ready, Laila Regina."

Laila cleared her throat. She suppressed her urge to fiddle with her fingers. This was to be her defining moment. However she performed here would set the tone for how Darius's prefects would regard her for perhaps the rest of their reign.

"During our honeymoon, Darius Rex and I were in talks on how we intend to progress the interests of Mortos going forward. We have since drawn up a series of objectives we wish to enforce both now and in the future." She caught a glimpse of Darius from the corner of her eye, the slight upturn of a smirk in the corner of his lips. He was remembering their sauna this last night, of course, when they'd solidified the final details of their proposal.

She snuffed the memory.

"Rather than bore you with talk, however, I have decided it is better to show you."

She extended her hand towards the ironwood table and, with a graceful dance of her fingers, conjured an illusory miniature of the Mortesian landscape, which rose from the wood like a spectre.

"This is Mortos as we currently know it. The impenetrable forests, the black sand beaches, the icy mountains. Long dominated by the precarious whims of nature. Darius Rex and I have put together ideas on how we might minimise that in the future. Which will start first with agriculture." She gestured to the farmlands, irrigation systems, and erected glass houses with yellow roofs designed to control temperature and sunlight. "Vysteria has long benefited from the use of ætherglass panels. These will absorb aether from the atmosphere and transform it into constant sunlight and warmth without relying on the elements, allowing for year-round growth in spite of the season. This should greatly increase the efficiency of harvesting crops and maintaining livestock, thus making you less prone to constant famine. This shall coincide with Darius Rex's research into pest control and soil health."

She waved her fingers along her map and formed the appearance of a rail track in mid-air, barely scraping the treetops of the forests and the sides of the city buildings. "After that is accessibility. Much of Mortos's development is inhibited by restricted access and dangerous travel. We will improve this by decluttering and enhancing the infrastructure of the streets and roads and eradicating feral wildlife to ensure safe passage. A locomotive will be implemented for speedier journeys between the cities and the hinterlands. Much like ours back home, it will utilise aether power to levitate for both overground and underground travel." A modelled train wove its way along the imagined track.

Here was where she saw the first splint of wonderment in her audience. She repressed a smile.

"Now you might be wondering how we intend to deal with aforementioned wildlife. Well, that is where Darius Rex comes in. He has graciously proposed we begin a new regiment where instead of being trained as warriors, young occassi will be reared as hunters, further serving the country by clearing it of feral beasts. In turn, Darius Rex will expand upon chimera creation to replenish the troops we lose to this unit, keeping our armies strong."

She turned to beam brightly at him, recalling their conversation on the ice. "Any questions?"

"How soon are you expecting all of this to be implemented?" asked Brutus, who in spite of his unfortunate name happened to be a scholar.

"We expect to see most of this enforced within ten years," Laila said. "Twenty at most."

"And how do you expect to lay hands on the ætherglass?" Augustus asked. "Last I heard, you and your impératrice mother were on poor terms, were you not?"

Laila received his question with a thick swallow. Yet she refused to waver. She wouldn't let him know how much the prompt of her mother was exactly what was needed to unsettle her. "Mortesian salt." She thought back to how Dominus had saved her with it two decades ago. "The deposits in the mines here are more potent than ours and help to deep-purge curses from the body. Many solarites are still unfortunately suffering after... the attack. If we offer them your salt, they'd likely be amenable to trade for it."

"You'd barter *medicine* to your own mother?" Augustus chortled. "You are colder than I thought."

A prickle formed on the nape of her neck. She could tell her façade was waning the more satisfied with himself Augustus grew. "Well, I—"

"The focus for today's meeting is to be relegated to affairs *directly* impacting Mortos, Prefect Augustus." Darius inserted smoothly on her behalf. "I would therefore ask that you withhold your concerns regarding matters overseas for another time." He rose from his seat to encircle his arms around Laila's waist. She leaned her weight against him minutely for comfort, too subtle to be of notice. "We will be seeking you out further on an individual basis to discuss your role in this proposal. For now, this meeting is concluded."

Laila waited until the room was completely cleared of everyone but Darius before she let herself unravel. Her illusion disintegrated into golden embers as she bowed over the table. "Almost made a total fool of myself towards the end."

"You did not." Darius reached forward to tuck her curls behind her ear. "You conducted yourself with grace and aplomb."

"Perhaps he's right." Laila struggled to diminish her aggravation. "Perhaps this plan is too cold. Too cruel—"

"Laila, look at me." He took her by the waist and turned her to face him. "You do yourself a great disservice by magnifying your shortcomings. Your plan is a good one, and you needn't feel reservations about bartering with your mother for something you need. Calante knows she wouldn't. Now, you had a slight hiccup and you pushed through it. I am proud of you."

Her chest lightened in relief. She rested her head in the crook beneath his chin. "Thank you."

He kissed the top of her head. "I have something that I think might cheer you up."

"What's that?"

"Come with me."

Darius led her towards the painted glass doors of the newly installed solarium and opened them up. He then stepped aside to allow Laila to fully view his gift to her.

"I had construction begin just before the wedding so that it would be completed in time for our return from the honeymoon."

Laila entered under a glass dome coloured yellow in mimicry of the sun. Light filtered into the solarium as a warm glow that moistened her skin with its dewy heat, causing her skin's natural shimmer to glisten even more.

Darius watched the seeds of her delight blossom across her features, as all around her were roses bushes of every type. Lush blooms of velvety texture lined up in a beautiful assembly of colour, so much like the garden that nestled within the grounds of her ancestral château. Though this engineered artifice would never quite match up, he wanted to restore to her a slice of comfort in this dour fortress.

Laila reached forward to touch a rose, tracing its smooth surface before turning back to him. "I can't believe you did all this," she said, her smile brimming once more with dazzling glee.

He slid his hands into his pockets, finding himself temporarily sheepish in front of her gratitude. "I know it's a far cry from being able to eclipse the beauty of your home, but—" He withdrew his hands to take hers. "I would hope that it would make you somewhat happier here if you felt like you had a piece of it with you."

Her expression softened. "Thank you. I—I really appreciate it."

He raised her hands to his lips to kiss them. "Perhaps we could have another picnic here like that time we did during the midsummer."

"Oh, I'd love that!" she declared. Then she began to plan in exhaustive detail her vision for how this might be accomplished. "Perhaps on one of the benches here—oh!"

A golden bunny leapt out from between the bushes and gave Laila a start. She rose up onto her hind legs to sniff at her with a tiny pink nose.

"Ah, I see you've met Fleur," Darius said, plucking free one of the rose petals to tempt her for a nibble. "I thought you could do with a companion here. One less... Mortesian in character than our local wildlife."

Laila had noticed that the bunny was lacking a conjoined head. Or sabre teeth. Or extra eyes. "She's lovely." She crouched down to pet the bunny, noticing a pink ribbon fastened around her neck. "So she'll live here?"

"I thought it was convenient." Darius shrugged. "Fewer stray occassi to think of her as a quick meal."

Laila's smile dropped at the implication.

"She'll be quite safe here, I promise you." Darius gestured around the walls. "This place is rigged to alert me to intruders."

Laila's happier expression returned by increments as she picked up the bunny to cradle it. "Well now, Fleur. How about you and I get to know each other?" She took a seat on a white-painted bench to feed her rose petals as Darius looked on.

X

PACKAGED IN LIKE SARDINES WITH THE OTHER occupants with no hope of reprieve, Lyra gave a sigh of relief once she stepped on land. She'd never much cared for sea travel, finding it arduous and stifling. She was grateful to once more feel her boots on solid ground.

The sea air was a cool massage on the nape of her neck, providing temporary relief from the baking sun. She hadn't been this far south since she and Laila had taken a period of recess at the Malakian mainland. She was beginning to remember why. The arid heat was far too overpowering for her sprite constitution and she was cursing herself for forgetting to put on a veil.

How fortunate that Lucrèce had transport waiting for her past the docks. Lyra breathed a sigh of relief when she saw the palanquin, the iridescent sheen of its jewel-toned coating reminding her of a beetle.

"Step in," Lucrèce called from the open door and gestured inside. Her cloud of tight coils were flowering bright pink peonies. Neroli-scented air from a humidifier was seeping out in a cold gust, providing an irresistible allure. "If you would, ser. We really ought to hurry along."

Lyra didn't hesitate to climb inside and nestle in the corner out of the sun.

Lucrèce flicked open her butterfly wing fan and handed it to her. "You may want this. They call this the Land of Undying Sun for a reason. Welcome to Setâre Island."

Lyra had heard of this island in her history lessons, said to be the oldest in the world and so preserved in its original state that only travel on foot or by animal was permitted. She'd always longed to see the landmarks that had been built from crystallised pure light. One of the continent's greatest wonders.

The journey took them past sightseers and pilgrims making their way to visit the Setâre Tree. Most of them were clothed in simple white cotton garbs that covered them head to toe and made them look like drifting spirits.

Lyra slumped on her seat with her knees spread. "Where are we off to?"

"To my temple," Lucrèce said, tapping on the digits of her compact mirror with agile fingers. Each solarite dynasty had one allocated specifically for ancestor worship. "There we will stay and make our preparations to commune with the spirit of Esterre Rose."

"Do you know whom we intend to use as our host?"

"Yes, Aurélie. Amira's mother. She resides here in Setâre at present to impart holy blessings to travelling pilgrims. I want you to approach her and request to have her bless you."

"You want me to *lie* my way through?"

"I want you to do whatever it takes to get what we need."

Espionage. A skillset that was not her forte. Lyra's forehead creased as she clutched her drumming temple. The heat paired with the weight of the task bearing down upon her was too much to take on at once.

"The solarite temples are a well-known holy retreat for sprites," Lucrèce explained. "I suggest you infiltrate as a regular pilgrim. Say you've lost touch with your faith and require some spiritual healing. Shouldn't be difficult with your wayward recent past. Leaving the Lightshields."

Lyra stiffened her jaw but could say nothing in dissent.

The palanquin slowed to a stop outside of the Mielette temple. Lyra took a moment to admire the gilt stucco coruscating under sunlight—it glistened like a comb of honey, so befitting of the bee emblem of the dynasty. She wandered past the ogee-arched doors into the grand hall, her steps echoing on patterned marble tiles.

Lucrèce entered after on a foot that was far too silent. She made a whimsical gesture with her fingers, and an acolyte soon appeared to bow before her. "Please see to our luggage," she directed the young dark-eyed girl. "We've had a long journey and it is almost sundown. Join us to break our fast."

"Yes, Your Beatitude."

After that, the rest of the temple came alive, and soon the aroma of sizzling meat and spices wafted through the draughty halls.

Lyra's stomach burbled with want as a dining area was set with gilt plates and firedrakes grilled meat to perfection with well-timed puffs of fiery breath. The acolytes sliced through the meat easily with laser-tipped fingers and stuffed it into pita bread between wedges of fruit.

Lyra feasted on lamb soaked in pomegranate juice and goat meat stuffed into figs, her roiling stomach from her turbulent sea-treading journey long forgotten. She was so hungry she forgot to feel self-conscious of Lucrèce's abstinence, but when questioned by the acolytes the solarite proclaimed herself to still be fasting.

"I feel better connected to my aether when I withhold from indulging in earthly pleasures," Lucrèce explained. "Each time we eat earthly food, drink earthly water, lie with earthly bodies, we are further tethering ourselves to this plane. That, as it so happens, weakens our strength. All these material things... They act as tethers holding me down to the floor. When I allow aether to nourish me I am light as a bird."

By the end of the feast, Lyra's belly was full and aching and she couldn't fathom taking another bite, but then the acolytes popped open a cork of blessed summer wine and sprinkled their cups with gold dust to toast to the sun goddess.

The melody of wine tinkling into glass was an irresistible siren call to her, and soon Lyra found herself deep in her cups of it until she could do nothing more than stagger to the nearest bedroom and fall fast asleep.

At dawn, the huma bird sounded its aubade and called the acolytes to engage in their first prayer. The lyrical cadence of hymnals serenaded Lyra through the lattice windows as she awoke to take her bath.

Steam swirled up from the oscillating bodies of candlefish as they kept the water heated. She sank deep in the tub of rosewater until she could taste its perfumed fragrance tickling the back of her throat.

In Setâre, the water was blessed and steeped in gold roses to purify both body and soul. Lyra felt anything but pure. The abyssal tar of occassi blood clung to the surface of her skin no matter how the golden candlefish in the water tried in vain to nibble her clean.

It wasn't guilt for the bloodshed that stained her, but rather the sheer absence of it. At a certain point she'd forgotten even how to take pleasure in monster-slaying. Instead the task was empty, thankless, and repetitive, and she regarded it with the same unpleasant apathy of having to shovel shit.

So she let the fish eat her raw. For she knew when she prepared to complete this next mission her mind needed to be balanced, weightless. She would need to be able to withstand not only the heat but the intense pressure of crafting a convincing series of lies.

To survive, it would be best if she shrugged off all her emotions—including the rage she kept strapped as a sword across her back, ready to unsheathe at will.

Part of her wondered why Lucrèce even thought to choose her. Surely there were ample sprites clawing for the opportunity to do her bidding who were vastly more suited. Ones who did not stare a little too longingly at the decanters of blessed summer wine before having to tug themselves away.

Even now the thought of wine was enough to make Lyra's throat ache. She didn't think herself a habitual enough drinker to confess an addiction, and to be certain it had not progressed to such a point of no return for her. It was mostly a numbing agent to keep herself softened around the edges, to soothe the raggedness of her temper. But now she would have to face the prospect of no longer having such an aid.

Just how long would she last?

Lyra sighed and covered her face with her fingers, leaving red streaks of heat down her cheeks as she dragged them down. In spite of the already pounding heat of Setâre, she had taken her water boiling and allowed her skin to dye pink as a prawn's. She remained in the bath until the tendrils of steam settled and she knew it was time to reluctantly vacate.

She dressed sullenly in the bedroom in her soft cotton garb, but against her sensitive skin the material prickled. Ignoring it, she made her way to the dining area where Lucrèce was sitting before a plate of doughnuts flavoured with saffron and rosewater. Lucrèce did not eat them but seemed instead to be basking in their aroma as she took a long, indulgent sniff.

"Good morning, Ser de Lis." Lucrèce raised a doughnut towards her in salute. "You really ought to help yourself to one of these while they're still warm."

The fried pastry did look appetising, the sort of sticky sugary treat that Laila would've gorged herself on. She could already envision her at the table humming with pleasure, chipmunk cheeks frosted with confectioner's sugar—

Lyra put that thought immediately out of her mind. The last thing she desired was to be reminded of *her*. "Why not?" She grabbed the baked good and sank her teeth into it, savouring its chewy texture.

Nearby, acolytes were brewing coffee in a pot over coals blanketed by sand. Lyra had never cared much for coffee—a pot of chamomile would do her fine and would've been most welcome—but she accepted the cup they offered her and took a few sips out of politeness.

"Not quite wine, but I believe you'll make do, yes?" Lucrèce gave her a wink.

Lyra couldn't tell whether the joke was at her expense or not.

"Are you ready to embark on your mission?"

Lyra put down her cup. "I suppose."

Lucrèce slanted her head to one side. "Something is troubling you." She laced her fingers together. "I can read it all over your aura. Tell me."

Lyra resisted the cringe that came over her features. She never liked the way Lucrèce's eyes—with those blue-violet irises patterned with galaxies of stars and space matter—seemed to spear directly into her soul. She'd met her gaze only once since meeting her, and the vast emptiness she found there inspired enough dread never for her to attempt it again.

"I don't think I can do this mission," she said.

"Why not?"

Lyra bit the inside of her cheek. "You need to find someone else. Someone more suited. Someone who isn't... so angry. Such a liability—"

Lucrèce held up a hand. "Your anger is not a burden to me, Ser de Lis. It is a gift. I *need* you vengeful—it's the only way we shall win this. The reason the occassi are thriving now is because the others have allowed themselves to soften into forgetfulness. But you remember everything, don't you? You remember your uncle. You remember Aurea Park."

Her chest panged at the mention of each injustice. "Yes."

"Carry that with you. Let their deaths not have been in vain. Or what will you do now? You've abandoned the Lightshields. You've lost your princess. Do you intend to spend your existence languishing in obscure misery? Or perhaps you'd care to join your loved ones in the Astral Realm where you will see them again."

See them again. Lyra's eyes started to water as she wondered if, perhaps, that was what awaited her at the end of all this. Léandre's calm smile. One she hadn't seen in so long she almost couldn't quite conjure his face. He had ascended to the realm of music, softness, and light where suffering did not exist and there were no more screaming urges from a relentlessly demanding body so eager for food and rest.

Was that why Léandre had been so eager to toss his life away all those years ago? She more than understood now. But, like him, she couldn't abandon hers without doing at least one thing worth showing for it.

"All right," Lyra said. "I'll do it."

She started her journey before the sun got too high.

Lyra was grateful for her foresight as the red sun peered over the horizon. It allowed her reprieve from the merciless heat to bask in the softer clarifying air with its green tinge of eucalyptus. She gulped as she shielded her eyes to find the Rose Temple in the far distance. She'd never been this close to seeing a solarite Elder, but tales of them were infamous by now. At five centuries old, solarites started to take their leave from the public, secluding themselves from the prying eyes of mortals for their own safety.

Pious sprites in need of spiritual guidance would visit in the hopes of receiving access to dormant powers in their aether sensitivity. Esteemed knights of legend were granted abilities to teleport, make holographic doubles, to run along walls as if gravity failed to bind them.

That was, of course, if you were worthy.

Lyra had wanted it for herself one day. Of course she had. Yet how could she when her sword and shield were stained far more with the ichor of those she'd failed than the blood of those she'd slain?

She stifled her envy as she crossed the threshold of the temple and caught a whiff of rose-scented incense. Inside the room were meditating sprites, looking purer than ever in their white robes, levitating cross-legged in golden orbs of aether.

Her task was to remain trained on the prize—she needed Aurélie, not the gifts she'd bestow on her. And there the solarite was, seated right at the other end of the hall on her gilded throne.

A veil kept her face mercifully obscured, but even at a distance Lyra could see the light teeming from within her. Her celestial soul had expanded beyond her body to exude a radiance so strong that she'd blind anyone who looked directly upon her.

The idea settled uncomfortably in Lyra's stomach, but she was curious, too. Thus, she walked forward with reckless abandon until someone moved to impede her.

"What's your business here, young sprite?" A robed acolyte approached her and gave an appraising look.

"I've come to pay my respects to an Elder," Lyra said, keeping her head bowed. "I am in need of spiritual guidance."

"Allow her through."

The order came directly from Aurélie herself. She had an otherworldly voice, like sunlight trickling through the gaps between leaves.

The acolyte bowed and stood aside. Then Lyra stepped forward to bend the knee herself. "It is an honour, Your Beatitude."

"Tell me, child, what brings you here?" Through her veil, Aurélie's eyes were white as milk, opalescent as pearls. As was her hair. Her pigment had been lost to time, eaten away by the light.

"I have lost my way, Your Beatitude," Lyra said. "I've come to you in order to rediscover my path."

It was not an untruth on her end, but a sweat prickled on the nape of her neck when Aurélie cocked her head.

"Come take my hand." She extended her palm, which was covered in a pearl-speckled lace glove.

"I—" Lyra swallowed.

"It will tell me more of what guidance you seek."

The moment of truth. She'd been coaching herself for this for so long, but still she could feel her courage faltering.

Not too late to turn back, she thought. Her feet urged her to do just that. She squashed the desire and took her first tentative step forward, then the next.

Was there any way she could approach this near goddess and keep her heart sheltered from her gaze? No. She could only exert some minor influence over what it was she showed her.

"As you wish."

I can do this. She set her mouth firm and walked forward with more confidence and deliberation than before. Then she placed her hand in Aurélie's and closed her eyes.

❧

When she opened her eyes, her palms were buried in mounds of hot sand.

Lyra withdrew them with a sharp yelp of pain and flapped them frantically for a breeze that did not come to soothe them. Twisting this way and that, she searched for anything to let her know where she was and saw nothing but vast sands lengthening on and on with no hope of anything in sight.

"Hello?" *she called in vain. Nothing answered.*

She stood up to move even as the sun kept searing holes through her cotton robes. She sought the temple she left behind, wandering and wandering, as behind her a brisk, sweltering breeze came over her footsteps to disappear them from sight.

"No..." *Lyra fell to her knees as she tried in vain to press her palms in the place where she knew she'd stepped last.*

It was to no avail, as the further she wandered the more lost she grew. By the time she thought to give up, she'd been baking to the point of begging for someone to stick a fork in her and call her done. That was when Laila came to her.

"Well, isn't this the predicament you've found yourself in." *Laila tutted at her as Lyra keeled over at her feet. The sound of Laila's laughter was the sweetest song after nothing but the crunch of her own footsteps.* "All this effort... just to ruin my own chance at happiness."

"I never—" *Lyra coughed raggedly.* "Never did this to make you unhappy. I just wanted to make you see—"

"See what? That I'm better off with you?" *Laila slanted her head in derision.* "Better with someone who'd continually take the side of my mother over me? Who would never put me first over your self-righteous pride?"

Lyra struggled to swallow, but her tongue felt like worn leather in her mouth. "Darius... will... hurt you..."

"I think you need yourself to believe that," *Laila said.* "It makes you feel better for trying to ruin us. Then you don't have to confront the fact that I chose him over you because he could offer me something more and better than you ever could."

She couldn't deny that it stung, hearing the words from Laila's lips, though she knew Laila would never have been cruel enough to say them. That at the end of it all Lyra's unwavering allegiance to duty, to a higher calling, had been what had broken them apart. And what did she have to show for it now? What had it all meant?

"Laila... please..."

"Please?" *Laila mimicked in a crude imitation.* "I never knew you to be so pathetic. Why don't you just roll over and die here? After all, who else is left to miss you?"

Miss you... *The words glided over the smooth sand and rang endlessly in her ears.* Miss you...

Lyra's eyes burned, but she was too empty for tears. And there wouldn't be any use for them anyway. So she pushed to her feet and kept going even as Laila's laughs cruelly mocked her on the way. Until she could move no longer.

She collapsed again in the sand, her aching muscles screaming for release. As she looked up at the white disc of the sun blaring down upon her she thought about how far she'd come. How close she came. How for all purposes this would be a good place to rest.

"That's it, you sleep now," *said a soothing male voice as gentle hands brought her head to lie on his lap.* "You've travelled a long way."

"U-uncle..." *Lyra rasped through chapped lips.*

"It's all right to rest. To take a breath." *He stroked her hair softly.* "Just so long as you remember to wake up at the right time after."

"I don't want to wake up anymore." *Lyra heaved a dry, tearless sob.* "I've kept going without you for so long and I can't... I can't..."

"You can," *Léandre told her firmly.* "And you will. Because that's how I raised you. You take a few hard knocks but you keep on swinging. My little lyre..."

He hugged her close in a way she hadn't been since she was a spriteling. Lyra let herself be held.

"Oh, I've missed you so much." *Léandre kissed her forehead.* "But it's all right now. You're where you belong. You're with me."

Lyra placed her hands on her uncle's arms and felt his warmth, his rugged strength, wound so tight around her she doubted she could escape if she tried. "I'm with you," *she said.* "I'm with you."

His hands were on her, picking her up and carrying her away. A figure wearing the bejewelled mask of a phoenix examined her face for signs of breathing before looking to her companion with a nod. "We've seen what unrest dwells inside her heart now."

"Then let's take her."

Lyra smiled, a weak, frail impression on her lips as she allowed the vision of her uncle to take her home.

XI

IRRITATION BUZZED BEHIND DARIUS'S LIDS LIKE AN ANGRY hive. For hours, he and Laila had been going through petitions after announcing their aetherglass initiative and were now debating which solarite dynasty would be the best to attempt to ally with to distribute aetherglass in Mortos.

"The Guillories are the best bet for trading luxury goods." Laila placed a silver chess piece over their dragon sigil. "But, of course, the Vitales control the ætherald mines. I think if we have a Guillory act as a proxy buyer they are far less likely to reject. We can refine it here once we've received it."

Darius pinched the corners of his eyes. "Do you have someone you can contact who would be amenable to this?"

"Oriel Guillory was one of my ladies. We haven't spoken since…"

Laila tapered off to silence. "However, I nurtured her as a mistress into her current position as a bank owner. I'm sure if I contact her she will at least hear me out."

"Yes, you should make the arrangements." He sighed heavily. "And I shall see to making sure no landmaster or blood sorceress tries to impede our plans."

Monarchs had always prided themselves on keeping subjects in line through savagery, and in the past he might have indulged this out of dulled apathy—if not for Laila by his side, trying to mediate her way through a more diplomatic avenue.

They accomplished a flourishing symbiosis between them. He with his firm hand and animal cunning, his intimate knowledge of the brutishness that pulsed within the blood of his kin. And she with her patience, her empathy burrowing through into the minds of her opponent, trying to lure them to her side with breadcrumbs of a reward.

Together they were a balanced scale. Him in his dark purple kaftan embellished with gnarled dragonbone painted iridescent. Her in her frail overlayer of Soleterean lace upon green silk, delicately trimmed with flowers.

Such harmony did not come without external pressures to rattle it. None more trying than the mother of the rex, whose upcoming petition would prove to be the most stress-inducing yet.

"Well now, I hear you two have been causing quite the spectacle of late." The low croon of Serafina's voice appeared before the occassella herself.

"Thank you for coming, Mother," Darius said with an air of dismissal as though he meant to imply the opposite.

"The pleasure is all mine." Serafina made a mocking curtsey. "I feel this meeting has been a long time coming."

"You know why you're here, then?" Laila asked, straightening slightly in her seat. She didn't want Serafina to catch her with her spine bent.

"Indeed. It seems you fancy yourself Mortos's new saviour, here to thwart the bloodthirsty dragon of the Vidua Nocte and our mighty food hoard." Serafina's teeth bared in delight. "I must assert myself to be quite resistant to such a course of action, and should it be given the go-ahead, my girls and I will not accept it without a fuss."

Darius rubbed his temples with a groan. "Do be reasonable, Mother. You've always known that the Citadel's relations with your ilk have only ever been a balm to a gaping wound. We have no desire to see the Vidua Nocte disbanded. But your days of running amok unaccounted for have gone on long enough. From this point forward, all blood sorceresses will require official registration by the Citadel to practise. In return, you will be made a protected class under Mortesian law. A tax of fifty pounds will be claimed by the Citadel for any sacrificial trees planted, which you must pay in crops. You must also provide a roster of said tributes prior to any ritual for our review. Failure to do so may lead to a penalty up to and including lifelong imprisonment."

"Oh, you're a frisky one, aren't you?" Serafina tilted back her head and chuckled. "And yet so very close to pushing my limits."

"Make no mistake, Mother." Darius's gaze was smooth and impenetrable steel. "You answer to me and not the reverse. Whatever intimidation tactics you think you may have will be no match for how I choose to retaliate."

The two sized each other up for a charged pause, fangs barely restrained.

Backed into a corner, Serafina knew she ought to detonate the most explosive weapon in her arsenal. That of truth and revelation. Still she withheld in the fear of expending it too soon. Such a thing would be better left timed to perfection and maximum impact.

As she was planning to stand down she noticed the most remarkable thing—Laila placing her hand over Darius's in a pacifying touch.

"Perhaps we can come to a less adversarial arrangement." Her suggestion was a light pattering of rainfall over woodfire smoke. "Let's spend the day together, Domina Blackwood. I'm sure we can come to something that suits both our needs."

"Are you certain?" Darius locked their fingers together, in no way eager to relinquish Laila into the company of his uncouth mother.

"We'll be fine," Laila assured him with a windchime laugh and pecked his cheek before standing. "Is that all right with you, Domina Blackwood?"

"Please." Serafina's dimples grew pronounced as she smiled sweet enough to sicken. "It'd be my pleasure."

Laila descended the steps to join Serafina. "You must excuse Darius. He's quite tense these days. But I thought it was high time you and I had a proper tête-à-tête."

"Hm, I'm sure," Serafina said, straightening the fur cuff of her shuba. "Your presence seems to work wonders for him, though."

Laila dipped her chin in modesty, cheeks rosening with a blush. "To your quarters, then, so we can have a proper discussion."

"Oh, I have plenty to tell you, Your Majesty. Believe you me." Serafina's lips were a hybrid of a smirk and a sneer. The honorific took a barbed edge of derision on her tongue.

"Very well, then." Laila nodded in acquiescence.

Since the wedding, the sorceress had become a more permanent fixture at court, and Darius had benevolently donated his previous dwellings for his mother to reside in.

Laila was surprised to find the moment she entered that Serafina had taken up her knitting. Of all things.

Serafina creaked back and forth in her cushioned rocking chair as if she'd never left, looking the picture of a domestic Mortesian baba.

A swift glance around showed Laila that she'd made herself quite at home here. A row of nesting dolls had supplanted Darius's old clock on the mantelpiece. And those same eerily constructed tableaux of taxidermied animals mimicking civilisation were scattered about the room. She tried not to look at their fixed, unblinking eyes.

"Well," Serafina declared as she looped her yarn around her needles. Her claws were sheathed in the gold filigree armour all blood sorceresses wore, but it made her no less nimble. "Why don't you take a seat there, pet? And for our first subject, I'll polish up your mythology."

Laila took a seat next to Serafina by the fire and watched the orange glow stroke along the edges of her savage features.

"This one's an ancient tale, diligently passed down from mother to babe like milk." Serafina took up her knitting again. "There once was an old god named Calante, and he wanted a world of his own. So he decided, what better than this one? He walked for a time as a king among mortals, indulging himself in all pleasures of the flesh: food and sex and wine and raw, chaotic magic. However, the other gods didn't like that much, so to spoil all of his fun they erected a prison for him forged of frost and fire, tossed him into a pit, and threw away the key—"

"I've heard this one before," Laila interrupted.

Serafina smiled with venom. "Not quite like this, I'd imagine." She looped her yarn once more. "As I was saying. That wasn't quite enough to stop our dear Papa Calante—fellow was the stubborn sort. So instead, he imparted a piece of himself into this world to stretch beyond the bounds of his prison. He created life, replications of his own image. Monsters, abominable things, raised up from the deepest, darkest caverns of the underworld. And thus the first occassi came to be. But this was not to be enough for him. Calante didn't want one measly little iceberg scraped out in the corner of the globe. Oh no. He wanted everything. And so he took himself a beautiful bride from among his new children and he marked her, like this." Serafina traced along her temple, referring to the scratch pattern found on all Anara's images.

"And bestowed upon her the gift of bearing his son. Once his child was reared, he would possess him, ushering the world that denied him into a new era of blood and chaos."

"Something tells me the story doesn't quite end in his favour," Laila said.

"Now, now, you stop interrupting. I'm just getting to the best part. See, Anara gave birth to the son of god and named him Callus. From his first scream, a great and terrible blight befell the island we now know as Mortos. Famine and plague and natural catastrophes ravaged the lands as trees moulted their leaves until they were bare and rivers were stained red with blood. As the boy-cub grew to adulthood, Calante reached out to whisper to him, bond with him, nurture him, in the event that he would finally be ready to occupy. But he did not account for the treacherous heart of Anara, who, driven to desperation in her bid to free the lands from this blight, thrust her hand through the chest of her only son and tore his heart out bare."

Serafina's chair released a groan as she stuttered to a pause.

"As Anara stood above the dead husk of her child, his heart in her hand, his blood spilling out onto the fields, she watched as, for a moment, the earth grew beautifully fertile and flowers sprouted in the flow of his innards. When the others came for her she did not fight them. It is as grave a sin as any for a mother to smite the life she created." She added the finishing knots to her swatch.

"And so they took a stake of white birch, skewered her on it like a prized pig on a spit, and they set her alight. As she burned, maggots and lice and vermin spilled forth from her and they had to purge them all, right down to the very last centipede, to ensure she wouldn't escape her fate. Though what poor, dear Anara ultimately failed to account for was that Callus had already conceived a son of his own who would go on to have his own son who would go on to have a son after that. That final little thread connecting its way between our world and the underworld and weaving its way through to the current living heir of House Calantis."

"So what you're saying is that you believe the Calantis line is the living successor to your god?"

"So the books would have it. The magic that surrounds that House has always been something of a stronger strain. It is why no family other than them has ever dared sit upon the throne. Few would even hear of it. Through each pulse of a Calantis beats the heart of Mortos."

"And Darius is the only one left." Laila gathered her arms about her in a chill. "That must be why they're so desperate for him to produce an heir."

"And Darius's refusal has been mightily bothersome." Serafina's smile turned grim. "Oh, some don't nearly believe in it as strongly now, but traditions are traditions. The pair of you are making a show of baulking them... I wouldn't be surprised if that leads to repercussions." Serafina plucked her needle from her finished swatch and launched it to pierce right between Laila's eyes.

Laila caught it instantly in her hand. "Hm." She peered at the needle's sharp point. "Perhaps it's time for a change, then."

Serafina smirked, unperturbed by Laila's agility. "You may fancy yourself a couple of persecuted visionaries, but we both know this is about power. About leaving your mark. How else but to be the first to claim they finally brought the Vidua Nocte to heel? Well, don't be fooled. Dismantling us will do far more to hurt this country than to help it. If nothing else, I should hope you learn that today. Occasselle come to us because we're the only ones who care enough to right a wrong that goes unpunished simply because it serves a husband, a father, a prefect who buys sex. The ladies in the tea rooms know well enough what happens, but they blind themselves. They think if they play along they'll be spared. We know better. And we open our arms when they come to us all the same."

Laila wrapped her hands around the arms of her chair. "I'll tell Darius to ease his demands. But I have some of my own. I can't allow you to continue to sacrifice indiscriminately. Especially not infants. And we will require your full cooperation with the Citadel's aims from here on."

"Should you desire for the Vidua Nocte to play nicely with your aims then my demands are simple. I want ownership of the Widowlands and surrounding areas in my name. Not a male guardian. With this I will claim the sorceresses and anyone who seeks refuge as my tenants and have the right to defend it from trespassers as I see fit."

Laila turned the request over in her mind. From her time scouring the annals of Mortesian history she'd come to learn that the Widowlands had been left in a purposefully ambiguous state. It came under the rex's sovereignty officially, and only through the tacit endorsement of their occupation had the Vidua Nocte been allowed to continue. "Under Mortesian law, a landmaster has the right to defend their property with deadly force," she quoted from recollection. "Something you've so far had little trouble achieving without legal precedence. If we were to do this, how can we guarantee a mass slaughter will not follow of the likely disgruntled husbands and fathers who'd pursue the fleeing occasselle?"

"I care little for order and justice, Stella Regina." Serafina teased the moniker on the edge of her tongue in such a playfully wry manner that it felt intimately familiar. It struck Laila how much Darius had taken after her. "As an owner I will be granted legal protections and be able to contest on behalf of my tenants to remain on my property. This I could either achieve through negotiation or combat. Regardless, my main priority is escorting the occasselle from their homes safely. The rest is your concern."

Laila frowned at this. "If the occassella could attest to her mistreatment—"

"Your intentions may be noble, Your Majesty, but this isn't Soleterea. It'd be arduous enough to prove one has laid their hands upon a body that will heal as swiftly as ours. Have her thrust before a panel of male judges eager to decry her a whore and a liar and the chances of success all but vanish. It would only impede those who wish to flee. And I reiterate, it's the fleeing I'm concerned with."

"And what happens if a husband agrees to release his bride to your custody only to replace her with another?" Laila countered. "It's all well and good to prioritise an escape strategy, but what you're suggesting will only ever be temporary. We need a remedy that tackles this at the root, that spares more than one."

Serafina regarded her with a renewed sense of interest and disbelief. "To think I first believed you were all an act. But you truly are pure as the driven snow, aren't you? That makes me pity you all the more. I now regret you've chosen to dedicate yourself to this land, Your Majesty, because you don't belong to it. And you certainly won't mend it."

"Your son said the same thing to me once, and I made him a king." She allowed herself a small smile of pride. "Now I may be a dove-hearted idealist unversed in the ways of your land, but I'd dare say if those who'd doubt me expelled half as much of your effort supporting me... we might achieve more than you can imagine."

Serafina was too entrenched in her cynicism to be convinced. "What did you have in mind?"

"Any occasselle who wish to flee may do so, and you can retain custody of them. If the husband or father protests, it will be resolved by Citadel. I'll allow you to claim sacrifices from occassi proven guilty of violent crimes towards occasselle... if and only if they prove unrepentant beyond reasonable doubt. They need to be given a chance to turn a new leaf. A fair one. But if they persist..." The leer of Dominus cast a shadow across her mind. "Then you may enact justice."

Serafina's lips broadened. "We may make a true Mortesian of you yet."

Laila's mind was still haunted by their conversation after she returned to the rex's chambers. So much so that she sought the bed immediately and crawled underneath the covers. There, she waited for Darius to arrive while inhaling his scent for comfort.

Darius himself entered not long after to fling his cloak on a nearby chair. Her chest lurched with happiness when she saw him. It couldn't be helped.

"Did you have a productive discussion with my mother?"

"Yes, she... enlightened me on a lot of things."

She thought of a world where she had done the smart, sensible thing and let him leave her in the Château garden. Would it have spared them all this strife to set her heart aside in the aim of something larger? Perhaps. And yet, when the questions stirred all it took was a whiff of his scent surrounding her to abandon them. What did that make her?

Laila decided to pivot back to his mother. "Are you certain it's a good idea to have a roster where blood sorceresses can become easily identifiable, since so many of them are fleeing dangerous circumstances?"

Darius paused briefly from hanging up his shirt. "I can see she's gotten to you already. I understand your hesitation, but yes, the pros outweigh the cons in this case. If you want to protect the sorceresses from mass retaliative violence then it's far better to put a name to the face. And we cannot disregard how dangerous they are."

"Your mother has expressed a desire to own the Widowlands outright. She thinks that legitimacy will provide a stronger shield."

"Even more reason to tax her and require a registry, no? If she wants to become a landmistress then she will need to abide by the regulations, the same as anyone else. There are no special exceptions."

Laila couldn't argue with his logic, but she was still troubled. She sighed and smoothed the sheets over her lap. "Is it cruel of me to... understand the Vidua Nocte? Why they are how they are?"

"Cruel? Perhaps. But an understandable cruelty." Darius walked over and kissed her forehead, reverent and worshipful. He lifted the sheets to climb into the bed next to her. "You are only ever callous in the interest of kindness, my queen. It's why I adore you. But I think it's best we continue this conversation another time."

As he drifted off to chase the hope of a dreamless slumber, another night invader slipped into Darius's mind to cause him strife. This time Delanus was the culprit, holding out his torn out heart as it spurted pulsations of black blood. He regarded his own organ with the glazed-over apathy of someone who had seen the same sight over many months, as if it were mundane as a sunrise.

"You know you cannot succeed in this... this foolish venture..." Delanus turned his pitiless stare to Darius now. "You think the heart you have to worry about is the one beating inside your chest. When the real weakness sleeps soundly alongside you."

Envy, malice, and something akin to insult cast a dark tint over his eyes as they fell over Laila. He looked at her as if she had robbed something from him and was keeping it withheld. Delanus squelched the heart in his hand, tighter and tighter, until it burst into globules of viscera spattering across his features and slithering down to his neck.

"That's what you ought to do with it. That's how you'll attain the true power you were meant for." He reached towards Laila, palm gooey with organ meat, claws curled to carve through her chest. "Let me show you the way."

Darius leapt up from his pillow in a sweat, panting heavily. His chest flared with the dread of a nightmare not long shaken. It wasn't until he cast eyes on Laila, watching the steady assurance of her breathing, that he was able to relax.

He slid a hand down his face before he peeled back the covers to depart, knowing that he wouldn't be able to calm himself into rest again. As he was putting on his shirt he sensed Laila rouse to drape her arms around him, pressing her lips to his nape. "Come back to bed."

Darius shivered from the pleasant tingle down his neck, remaining steadfast. "I'm meeting some people for a hunt."

"In the middle of the night?" Laila's lips pursed in displeasure.

"It's almost dawn." Darius brought her mouth to his and kissed her until she was slack. "Sleep. I'll be back before you know it."

Laila stifled a disgruntled noise and clutched the covers to her in place of him. "It'd better be swift. Else I'll come looking for you."

He reached out to brush her hair from her shoulders, massaging her neck. "I shall hold you to that."

Laila crooned in pleasure as he kneaded his way to the base of her spine, where she was most sensitive, until she returned to sleep.

With that he went on his way, leaving the rex's wing and descending down the steps into the lower bowels of the Citadel where his hidden lab dwelled. He took a moment to compose himself before he entered the tunnels, hearing the sounds of his mother hard at work on her most recent subject.

She still had her hand rooted deep within Delanus's chest cavity when Darius arrived, her patient gurgling before she tore his heart clean out.

"Any news?" Darius asked in interest.

"He's still alive but somewhat numb to pain." Serafina stared at the pulsating organ in her hand. "He screamed far more the first time I took it out."

"Hm." Darius took a step closer to scrutinise the tranquil expression of the patient. Then he backhanded him. Hard. Delanus's head whipped to one side with a crack in his spine but he was motionless otherwise. "Disappointing. We may yet need another. I suggest you keep working on him until he shows no signs of improvement."

"Oh, goody." Serafina's tone was nothing short of sardonic.

"Delanus at least informed us that there is a margin of time you can remove the heart and place it back in the chest while keeping things... mostly intact. However, it's not quite enough. The experiment continues until we reach some form of success."

"Crude but sensible." Serafina clucked her tongue. "You weren't *truly* serious today about enforcing a tax on the Widowlands, were you?"

"I most certainly was."

"Darius." Serafina gave him a look of reproach.

"I will also consider the terms Laila has brought to me on your behalf. But let's be reasonable, Mother. If you want to be a landowner you'll be getting the same responsibilities."

Serafina scowled. "Tell me, how long do you intend to keep lying to your lovely wife?"

"I fail to see what concern that is of yours."

"Well judging by your self-congratulatory strut, you've not long left her bed. If we are to continue these late night engagements, I dare say she might start getting suspicious of where you're slinking off to every night." Serafina gave him a mocking gasp as a thought came to mind. "Maybe you ought to take on a concubine."

Darius scoffed, arms folded as he leaned against the wall. "Laila would be livid if she thought I was with someone else."

"Precisely." Serafina gestured with her free hand. "She'll be so mad with jealousy at the thought you might be going to see your mistress that she'll not want to hear any details. Not to mention it'll keep her focus strictly on the perceived competition rather than where it truly should be."

Darius tilted his head back and creased his brow in derision. "I'm not going to take on a concubine just to throw Laila off the scent."

"You don't have to take her to bed, Darius. You only need to put on a decent enough show of having her think you are." Serafina shrugged one shoulder as she slapped the still bleeding heart in her hand on a tray. "Though by that point I suppose it's all the same to her, isn't it?"

"What you are suggesting is vile and callous. I would never put Laila through such strain. Should she need to be distracted then I'll distract her, but you can keep your vulgar assertions to yourself."

"Let me be certain I've understood," Serafina said, picking up a damp towel to wipe her hand. "You have no issue continually lying to your wife about your illicit pursuit. A pursuit which, considering her rather irksomely virtuous mien, would unquestioningly lead her to desert you, but it's misleading her to believe you might be sticking it elsewhere? That's going too far?" She couldn't help but snort with amusement. "You truly are Lanius's son."

"What is that supposed to mean?"

"It means back when you were conceived and Lanius wanted to

push for marriage, someone else in his court suggested I be taken on as a concubine to legitimise you. Since I wasn't exactly fitting calibre for a wife. I refused, of course. And Lanius promptly had that prefect killed, believing him to have dishonoured me. You wouldn't think it, but back then he was quite sentimental. Like you. And like you, he made things all the harder for it."

"Your counsel has been duly noted." Darius waved her off as he picked up his mother's open grimoire and studied her notes thus far.

"Why do you even want this? The heartlessness?"

"Why did my father want it?" Darius asked.

"He saw himself as being indispensable to Mortos." Serafina rolled her eyes with a scoff. "That he was the rex they would need to keep it eternally strong and flourishing. You saw how that turned out."

"And I am the same. The moment I seated myself upon that throne I knew that Mortos was in great need of reform and I, perhaps only I, would be the one with the necessary insight and skill to see it through. I also understood that there would be those who resist. Who might desire my blood for even thinking of it. And for that reason I need a strong foundation. To be so unconquerable no one would dare challenge me, and hence here we are."

Serafina arched a brow at his words, at her former lover's clear echo in them. "You truly think yourself alone so remarkable?"

"Not alone," Darius conceded, his lips curling into a wry approximation of a smile. "That's where my father failed. He was too arrogant to see that what Mortos needed changed from when he ascended, and being heartless robbed him of self-reflection. And he didn't have Laila. You saw how she was with you today. Mortos needs her just as much as I need her. She balances me. I'm doing this for her too."

Serafina huffed. "Then why can't you tell her?"

"Because everything about her that makes her benevolent, fair, and hopeful would never be able to stomach something like this. So I bear the weight of that transgression. She need not know it ever occurred. She will keep her light."

"This country changes people, Darius. You can't shield her forever."

"Maybe not, but I see it as a mission worth undertaking."

After all, Darius had married for nothing but love. Pure, dizzying and nonsensical love. It was the kind of love that strengthened and guided him along this slaughterous path of axing innocents down by the dozen—all so he could build a castle out of their bones for her.

XII

SADIK GLANCED APPREHENSIVELY THROUGH through the window to the blue mountains ahead as he reached for his flask of rum. The thought of being at the mercy of the stone-faced Dr Isuka as she poked and prodded at his mind was enough to drive him to drink. He took a long sip to let the liquor warm him, but the alcohol didn't help his already existing drowsiness, and so he soon did away with the vice.

What a fool he had been to trifle with chaotic forces. So much wasted time he'd spent salivating for his own magic, and what had it brought him but this? Driven to the ends of the continent while the woman he loved and his child remained helplessly out of reach. He clutched the corners of his eyes and rubbed at them. When he landed, he would need to figure out what to do. How to fix all of this.

His airship landed inside a cave, and from there he knew he had begun to serve as a prisoner for another form of sentence. When he exited the airship, a guard approached to place cuffs on him before leading him towards the lift and down into the tunnel of the laboratory.

Dr Isuka awaited him at the lift's entrance, hands folded behind her back. "Welcome, Sadik Yilan. Please follow me."

Sadik squinted before the blinding lights as he followed along behind her. He strained his neck to make sense of his immaculate surroundings, so white they resembled the porcelain veneer of a tooth. "Where's Elina?"

"Why, straight ahead." Dr Isuka canted her head towards the patient ward.

There she could be found, tucked in bed. Sweat-sheened and pale from sickness. Weight had melted from her bones and left her emaciated. And her hair had thinned—those long luscious locks he'd once lovingly run his fingers through were falling off in patches.

A soft moan came from Sadik's lips at the sight. He staggered towards her and collapsed to his knees to take her clammy, clawed hand in his to raise it to his lips. If he hadn't experimented with those men, Naveen would never have sought his aid when the chaos magic turned him into a monster. He never would've touched her.

Elina roused, sensing she was being watched, her eyes narrowing when they met Sadik. Before he could plead his apologies, she greeted him with a smack across the face. The impact echoed through the laboratory's sterile halls and brought some wandering residents to a standstill.

Sadik hissed in pain as his cheek throbbed with her handprint. "I guess I deserved that one." Of course the first time he'd been graced with the touch of her palm again had been out of wrath.

"What is he doing here?" Elina demanded.

"We'll require the use of him to find out more regarding your condition," Dr Isuka said. "He'll be kept quite out of your way, I assure you."

"He'd better be."

"Elina—" Sadik stepped forward. "Please. At least let me tell you how sorry I am—"

"Don't speak." Elina shoved a finger in his face. "Not another word. You gave up that right the moment you put me in this bed." Her chin wobbled as tears fell from her eyes. "Then you left me... all alone..."

"No!" Sadik shook his head. "Never."

"Stay away from me if you know what's good for you." With that, she swivelled onto her side and showed him her back.

"Elina..." Sadik reached for her but caught himself in time. Stifling his tears, he brought himself up to return to the scholar with his head held low.

Dr Isuka tutted to herself. "Shall we?"

Sadik's cheeks burned from the glint of reproach in her eyes. "Take me where you need me to go."

Dr Isuka showed him into a new room where pulsating membranous pipes fed ætherald energy into a biomechanical machine.

Sadik took in the throbbing contraption and its dizzying kaleidoscopic glow. "What... is that thing?"

"It's an oneirometer. We use it to study the subconscious." Dr Isuka gestured to the numerous display screens of crystalline glass. "Once connected to the machine we ought to be able to see what's going on in one's mind. It will record dreams as they unfold, and then we can examine the footage."

Dread crept up behind his shoulders as he realised, at the centre of its fibrous casing, was a chair large enough to fit a man of his size. "No—" He staggered backwards, right into the arms of a guard. "Wait—" He squeaked his heels against the polished flooring as the guard pushed him forward. "You can't... you can't mean to keep me trapped inside that thing!"

"It'll only be temporary, Mr Yilan." Dr Isuka drew out a chair to sit as Sadik wrestled against the sprite to no avail. "We need to see what's going on inside that head of yours."

"Please, doctor!" Sadik ceased trying to break through the marmoreal grip. "Please. I haven't slept properly in weeks. The things I see in those dreams... I can't go back there. I can't. I beg your mercy. There has to be another way."

Dr Isuka exhaled. "I am sorry. Perhaps..." She glanced to one side, contemplative of her next words. "Perhaps you should've thought of all this before you wrought such mayhem on us all."

Sadik gave her a look filled to the brim with sheer odium. "I thought the occassi were the worst this world had to offer. But you... you plummet to depths I didn't even think were fathomable."

"Put him in the machine." Dr Isuka made a dismissive gesture.

"Upon my damned soul..." Sadik grunted as the machine stretched open to engulf him and then a series of tendrils suctioned to his head with a pop. "I hope Calante comes to drag us all down into oblivion." A dispersal of gas puffed inside his nostrils and caused Sadik to cough as the fog compelled him to sleep.

Once his eyelids succumbed he was gone from the realm in a blink and awoke at the bank of the Nether.

Though he had been here many times before, the horror of it was swift to assault his mind, leaving the fear that lurched in his chest just as raw and potent as the first time he'd encountered it.

A river stretched before him, but there was no water, no lustre or light within it, nothing inside but a bottomless umbra. Even the very act of looking seemed to drain a bit of soul from Sadik's eyes.

Come closer, the chasm seemed to urge. *Fall*.

He tore himself away, struggling against the pernicious impulse to take a step forward, and took in what else was there.

A rickety maze of rope bridges criss-crossed the river, providing the only visible means of travel. There were no boats Sadik could see, and the nature of whatever substance filled it didn't seem amenable to swimming.

Where does it lead? Sadik dared himself to wonder as he squinted ahead to where the bridge disappeared into the insatiable dark. Suppose the bridges didn't even go the whole way across? He wouldn't even be able to tell until his foot met water instead of wood.

Left with no option other than to travel forward, Sadik took a breathless step onto the bridge, exhaling it when it held his weight, and carried on.

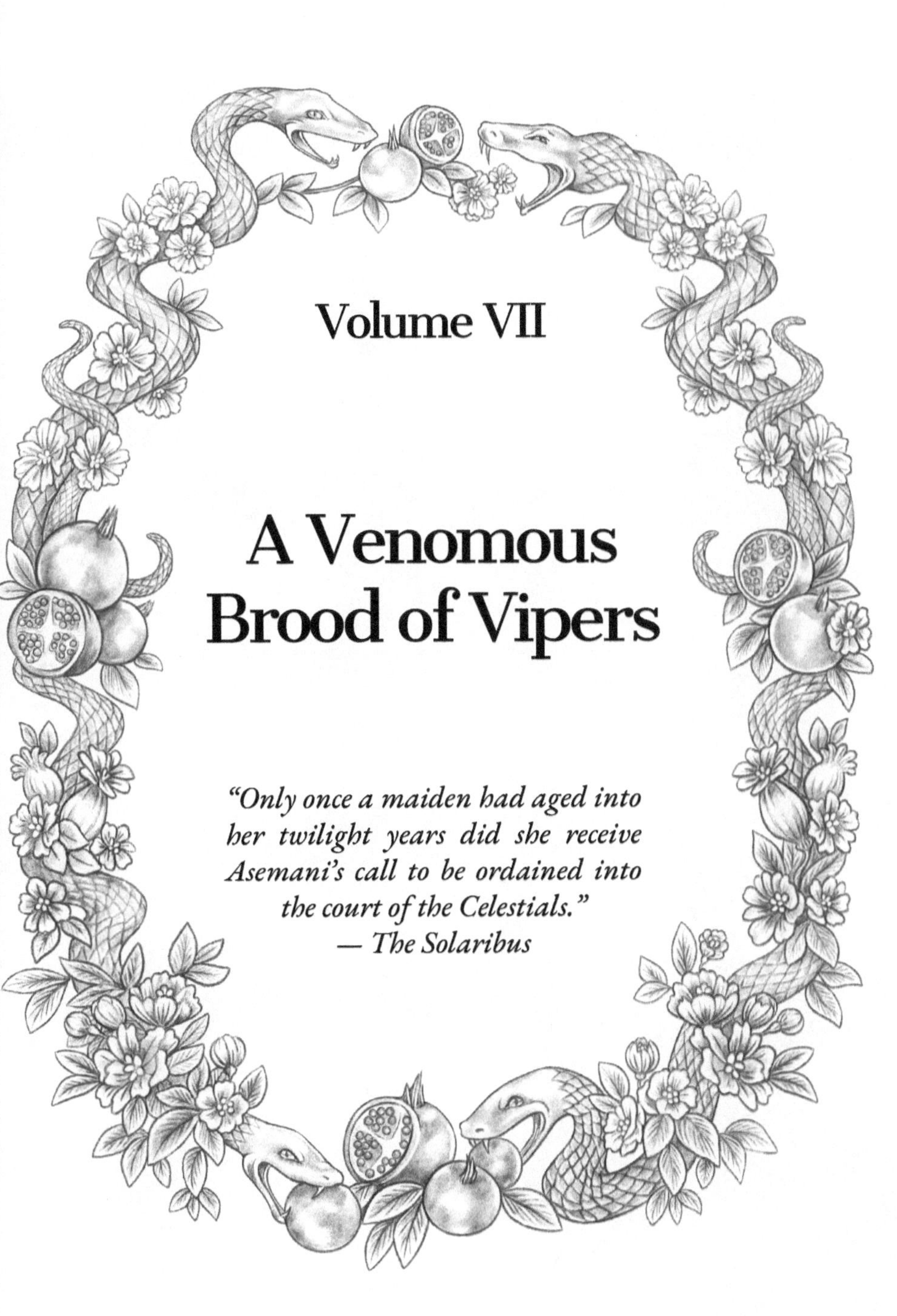
Volume VII

A Venomous
Brood of Vipers

"Only once a maiden had aged into
her twilight years did she receive
Asemani's call to be ordained into
the court of the Celestials."
— The Solaribus

XIII

SHOVEL-MOUTHED CHIMERA SCOOPED COPIOUS mounds of dirt into its gullet to clear a path for Mortos's first train track. Then apelike hybrids, with their multiple arms, came cradling tracks and bolts that they lay diligently, metal clanging through the air as they hammered them down. Afterwards, they erected a tunnel forged of strong vines, thorny brambles, and impenetrable thickets, designed to ward off any dangers to the travelling locomotive.

Serafina loomed above on the branch of an ancient oak and observed them from beneath her hooded cape, her mouth set into a grim line. She couldn't deny she was impressed with the versatility of Darius's inventions. She never would've thought them good for anything but battle fodder before this. Yet seeing these creatures now, tools gripped intelligently and applied with purpose, she understood the folly of her earlier dismissal.

It would be these creatures, along with the carts full of aetherglass they intended to spread throughout the country, that would lead to the extinguishment of her freedom. Not swiftly. Serafina knew well that Darius and his insipid wife would do their best to uphold a reputation of being merciful. So they would legislate them out of existence first, citing their obsolescence when advancement surpassed the breadth of their power. Then, once they were sufficiently stripped of legal protection, Darius would have free rein to subjugate them as he pleased. Finally, he would satiate the centuries-long grudge he'd had brewing in his hateful heart.

If no other virtue could be spoken of Darius, it had to be said he had patience in spades.

"Perhaps I ought to have sacrificed him after all," Serafina murmured to herself. Alas, she had not been bestowed the gift of foresight. Maybe then she would never have even touched Lanius, and all this could've been avoided.

She sighed heavily, knowing it was no use to dwell on past mistakes. She must look to the future now for solutions to put a stop to this and save her sorceresses. So she leapt down from the tree branch she'd been using as a vantage point and scurried home.

The Widowlands was no easy place to reach—a slender oasis cradled deep within the feral heart of the Mortesian wilderness. Serafina cast a protective rune over herself to ensure that no stray hungry monster would be tempted by her.

She smiled in relief as the idyllic sight of painted houses adorned with white wooden lace came into view. The grass made a lush crunch underfoot and rebounded as soon as she stepped off of it. Abruptly, her path was obstructed by a string of running, squawking chickens being chased by an occassella.

The sight startled Serafina, hand clutched to chest, but it soon gave way to a laugh. She swept her gaze over the herds of cattle, sheep, goat, and swine free roaming over pastures to feast on wildflowers and grass to their hearts' delight. Like all Mortesian wildlife, they were two-headed with flowering moss dripping from their horns.

She plodded down the quartz footpath paved for convenience around the village's amenities, passing the apothecary where healers brewed medicine; the stalls of handwoven clothes, baskets, and finished goods; the open kitchen where residents were spooned bowls of chicken and mushroom soup from a bubbling cauldron.

When she got to the kitchen she found her sorceresses in quite the state of unrest. Doors had been left ajar, chores abandoned, and a cluster of bodies had gathered. Only one cause could've been the source for this.

A new stray had come in during her brief absence at the Citadel.

Serafina parted the gossiping occasselle to observe the arrival for herself and found the new occassella in the arms of Katerina, one of her most devoted sorceresses.

A once beautiful countenance was now marred by savagery—her eyelids were puffed and swollen shut over empty sockets, and the rest of her face was so battered it left Serafina searching for recognition among the lumps and bruises. She would heal in time, one of Calante's few mercies, but the alterations to her spirit had yet to be assessed.

It didn't take much to guess what had happened to her and what she'd fled from.

"When she came here her eyes had been smashed in their sockets," Katerina explained, carefully guiding spoonfuls of soup to the runaway's lips. "She travelled here by herself, using sound and smell alone."

The runaway slurped noisily at the sustenance given to her, a task made difficult with the welts on her lips. But her tenacity alone was enough to spark admiration. The same fortitude for survival that had delivered her here.

Rage flared inside Serafina, soon offset by a despondency that further gutted her with each case she encountered. It never got any easier to see her fellow occasselle in such a horrific state. They'd been reared as predators. Apex of the food chain. Unconquerable and incontestable except at the hands of their own patriarchs' fists—whether it be a husband or a father.

"Tell me her name."

"It's Priscilla," Katerina said, stroking down her silver-white hair.

Serafina nodded. "Now tell me the name of the bastard we're about to sacrifice."

This always went a number of ways. There were those who were resistant, who tried to play coy. As if they didn't know exactly what would happen once they crossed the threshold to the Widowlands. As if it weren't clear from the very name what they were about. Not that Serafina could not understand. The obedience of a subject to its master was a hard bond to break.

Then there were those who came vengeful. Who wanted the bloodshed. The sacrifice. And the eventual power that came with it. They'd seen the stakes ahead of time and decided it was them who should live instead of their terroriser.

Which one would you be, Priscilla? Serafina pondered.

Priscilla smacked her lips together once she'd finished what she could of her soup. "I want him to suffer twice as much."

Oh, if that didn't bring a little smile to Serafina's lips.

The sorceresses made good on their promise. Once they lured Priscilla's pig of a husband safely from his flock, they gave him a treatment more than befitting of such a swine.

Wild cackles decanted through the air, flooding out the shrill pitch of his screams as they each went to work on him. They took turns putting a potato peeler to his cock and shaved off portions of his member until he was a raw, bloodied stump. The occasso squealed an awful racket at each swipe of the blade, the strips of his much prized virility hitting the floor with a wet slap.

By the time they were through he was begging for the obelisk, and the ancient obsidian doors had come to life with swirling runic patterns. It opened with a gasp of anticipation, eager to accept its new sacrifice.

As with all the others, they stuffed him inside and let the spikes squelch his body to a pulp and juice his blood into the birthing pit, where Priscilla descended to begin her new life as a sanguine sorceress.

Serafina stood aside from the cheering crowd as Priscilla swam in the font of her husband's essence, observing it all from a distance.

Katerina took note of her reticence and moved close to join her. She didn't say anything, but she didn't have to. She knew Serafina well enough to know her presence was enough.

"It's going to get harder to finance this land if Darius's plans come to fruition," Serafina said. "And harder still to defend it."

"I wouldn't be worried." Katerina pulled a mocking face. "Darius is merely showing off. Trying to impress his little star queen. It's her we need to watch out for, if you ask me. Her and her grand visions for the country."

"Sadly, whatever designs she has he seems more than happy to indulge." Serafina glanced her way. "If I knew it would be so easy to steer him by his cock, I might have asked you to marry him."

Katerina snorted. "That would not have worked. Darius had passion enough for me to be certain, but he loves his Stella Regina with a ferocity that far surpasses that. He's a fool for it, though. They won't last."

"You believe so?"

"How can it if she doesn't even know who he is?"

"Love can blind and so can power. She wouldn't be the first regina to fall victim to it. Even if I did tell her, I can't be certain she would believe me, and that's not even to say what Darius might do to retaliate."

"It's a tricky one." Katerina nodded in agreement. "However, there are other ways to drive a wedge between them. All it needs is just a little nudge in the right direction." She prodded Serafina with an armoured claw. "I'd do it myself, but I doubt he'd touch me now. However, her position as an heirless regina is ever so fragile. Cast enough doubts about her ability to suit the role of consort and let the court do the rest."

Serafina hummed in appreciation. "You are wicked."

"And you love me for it."

The aim was clear, then. If Laila left Darius of her own accord it would spare Serafina the repercussions of having it traced back to her. Thus she must find a way to spew her poison and sow instability in Laila's position as consort.

Since the seal of Darius's matrimony had dried upon the parchment, Katerina had not once stepped foot on the Citadel premises. Now, however, it seemed the whistle of the draughty halls had compelled her presence as she edged her way into the Regina Wing.

It did often cross her mind that this might have been hers in another life, under another set of circumstances, one in which she had not seized blood sorcery as a liberation from having to barter her body. Not that Darius would have wanted it. It was never love that brewed between their bodies but rather something transgressing that. Something that ran deep.

Katerina *loved* that she inspired the wolfish appetite in him to chase her, devoting himself to her with such a persistence, a constancy, that she knew he would always be there waiting should such a time come for her to want him again. That she could make him whine with desperation after she'd spent a night in his bed, begging her to claim him. She didn't have his heart and he didn't have hers, but she could dangle it before him in the lure that he might receive it if only he was capable of jumping high enough. And in its pursuit, he would've done anything to please her. He would've pulverised this island to tiny pieces and fed it to her crumb by crumb.

That had changed once Laila entered the picture. He was no longer as pliant to Katerina's games, no longer so obedient. The hunger for her that had once ached inside him had switched palates to a newer flavour. She couldn't deny it stung her pride, if nothing else, but it also concerned her about his movements towards the Vidua Nocte. She feared he might truly set them aside, allowing the pride-wounded occassi to unleash their centuries of pent-up rage.

Katerina had enough of a taste for what occassi would do when their tempers and passions were stirred after her father had sold her off to become a courtesan. She was not eager to experience that sort of degradation again and would do anything to avoid it. Even if it meant waging warfare upon an innocent party.

She stopped once her infiltration led her into the inner quarters of the wing. She wasn't certain, at first, what had brought her into the bedchamber. It started off as mere curiosity to discover more about the elusive and beautiful solarite as Katerina tinkered around with her jewellery and rummaged through her wardrobe. This progressed to opening her toiletries and sniffing her perfume, borrowing both so she could imagine what it was to be her. To smell like her. What must it be like to be something so pure, light, and good?

Katerina sat at her vanity and ran her fingers along the unicorn bristles of her brush. Some of Laila's curls were still tangled up in them, and so she cleaned them out. She'd always envied the solarite's hair, bouncy and bright compared to her own sable sleekness. She rolled the strands into a ball and fiddled with them.

"What are you doing in my room?" Laila stood at the doorway, lips parted in surprise.

Katerina did not jump up from her audacious repose, nor did she go for an excuse. "Waiting for you."

"Well, I don't want you here." Laila huffed through her nose. "Leave now or I'll have the guards escort you."

"Don't be so discourteous," Katerina crooned with mocking softness. "Is this how you treat all that come to visit?"

"If you wanted to visit me you would've gone through the proper channels."

"And you would've refused. Quite rightly so." Katerina continued to bat the ball of Laila's curls around, to the regina's clear growing unease. "Then I wouldn't have had a chance to congratulate you."

Laila wondered how soon she could get a guard to come before Katerina performed any ritual with ill intent. She sagged in defeat, and approached her with a smile. "If that's all you came for then I give you my thanks. Now—" She gestured for the door.

Katerina glanced at the colourful assortment of toiletry bottles once more and picked one up, tracing the glass hummingbird stopper. "This is pretty."

Laila twitched in discomfort.

"You always have such fine things..." Katerina's amber eyes exuded warmth.

Laila moved towards the vanity and removed her kokoshnik. "Would you like to know what's in them?" She flexed her neck muscles and massaged her nape. This was the last way she wanted to spend her evening, but anything that got Katerina out of her sight and away from her hair was fine by her.

Katerina counted the gemstones that studded the headdress, likely forming the majority of its weight. "Why not?"

Laila held out her hand for the bottle.

Katerina placed it in her palm.

"This paste is made from gold dust and solar rays." Laila removed the topper to reveal a brush coated in paste. "You can either layer it on thick or spread it lightly for a glowing gold shimmer. Lasts hours especially if you stay in the sun to recharge it." She picked up a smaller pot next. "This is moon powder. A lot lighter than the sun rays but it gives you a pretty iridescent sheen." She unscrewed it and circled her finger over the contents a few times to display the rainbow shimmer.

"Ah! This is one of my favourites." Laila picked up a thin bottle and pulled out the brush. "Made from mermaid scales. Comes in a variety of blended colours but I think this blue and purple hue would suit you well. I use it around my eyes occasionally but sometimes I paint my brows and lashes too." She applied the paint to Katerina's lashes and brows, streaking her dark hair with a luminous highlight. "There you are."

Katerina glanced past her at the mirror and acknowledged how the enchanted paints transformed her. No longer was she a cast-off turned maligned sorceress but rather a beguiling creature with a history of her own design.

"If you want to take my things, Katerina, you may help yourself to whatever you like. Everything here is replaceable." A light sparked in her eyes. "Except my husband."

"I don't want him."

"Then why are you here?"

"To warn you of others who might. Particularly when they learn of your... deficiencies."

Laila's pulse skittered. "What are you talking about?"

"Something interesting I've noticed about you solarites is that there are no males among you. At first I thought you were like us and were hiding from them. But then after Dominus did what he did I realised it no longer made any sense."

Laila's breath hitched as Dominus's frail state after he'd exploded himself niggled its way back into her mind. She banished it. She would not, could not, be forced to confront that now.

"So then I wonder... perhaps you have no males. And how could that be?" Katerina rose from the chair to loom over her. "Unless... you had other ways to multiply."

Tension crackled between them, and Katerina was electrified by the way it jump-started the sound of Laila's frantic rabbit heart.

"I don't quite know how you do it but I gather it won't be long before people start to wonder why you haven't swelled with child. And once they do... well. You'll be in a spot of trouble."

"Why are you telling me this?"

"I'm just trying to prepare you for what's to come your way." Katerina reached out to cup her chin affectionately. "Many reginas have fallen to poison for less."

"Get out." Laila shook her hand off.

Katerina exhaled a deep-throated chuckle. "Thank you for your hospitality."

Darius stretched over the War Room table, palms splayed on the cold map of Mortos painted onto the ironwood. He'd been moving silver pieces about the board to represent his enforcers, musing on the most strategic places to commit units to best quell some of the wildlife.

His father had always employed a lax policy, believing in retaining their bestial roots as much as possible by allowing the country to remain largely untamed. Those who weren't fit to survive its perils would be fitting game for its beasts. Yet another mess Darius was forced to untangle.

He rubbed the nape of his neck. Tension burrowed deep within his shoulders. What with the stressors of the day and the night terrors disrupting his rest, it was a wonder he still had the energy to stand.

He decided to take a seat down at the table for a pause. Laila's scent permeated the room long before she entered in a light padding of steps.

"Ah, I was wondering why you hadn't come to bed yet." Her lips curled playfully as she approached. "Should've known you'd be distracted by your second-greatest love."

She plopped herself onto his lap and encircled his neck. Her flimsy nightgown rippled along her body in a way that immediately erased his tiredness. Sheer silk chiffon with a dangerously tapered neckline descended to a point at her sternum, finished with lace and a pink bow.

"Well now my first greatest love is distracting me from the second." Darius's mouth inched up wryly on one side as he rested a hand on her thigh. "I was on my way to bed, I promise."

Laila hummed and hiked up her skirt so that she could straddle him. "I believe you."

With her this close he discovered just how frail this garment was. A purposeful choice, of course, to have him see what he'd left waiting.

His smile grew more fiendish as he stroked along her thigh. "Why'd you decide to come fetch me?"

"I was thinking about your mother today."

Darius didn't think it possible for anything to kill his mood quicker.

"Don't look at me like that." Laila frowned. "She's been on my mind ever since our talk. I'm just wondering how we could possibly get her on our side."

"I hate to say it, but that may be a futile wish."

Laila sighed as she ran her fingers through the ends of his hair. "What if I tried harder... to make her see me as less of an obstacle? If we let her have the Widowlands—"

"My mother cares nothing for this country other than herself and her narrow circle." Darius said. "I suppose we have that in common. Give her what she wants, however, and she has even less reason to invest in the country's betterment. She'll simply keep cordoning herself off in the wilderness with her chosen few, and that will have far-reaching consequences for more than just us."

Laila sighed, unable to argue with his logic.

"Though I question your eagerness to befriend her when she tried to murder you."

"It's not as if I can pass judgement now, is it?" Laila's lips twisted in bitter mirth as she recalled Dominus disintegrating at her hand. "Being a murderer myself."

"Laila—"

"It's all right." She snuffed the conversation before it could continue. "You understood and you forgave me, and... and I loved you for that. It's only fair that I return the gesture."

He kissed her neck, nuzzling into her shoulder. Her clemency always coaxed something soft in him, made his chest light with the hope that perhaps she could forgive and understand him too. He clung to it like a star-spoken wish.

"In light of that," she said, "I wanted to know your thoughts on my intentions to create a Regina Council."

"A Regina Council?"

"Yes, I was thinking I would have representatives not just from occasselle but qarninas and lupari women as well. And... someone from the Vidua Nocte." Laila assessed his face for a negative response.

He did not give one. Instead he only seemed contemplative. "If that's what you desire."

"It's just I didn't realise before what their history was. All those occasselle crying out for help and no one ever heard them. Not until they were forced to do the unthinkable."

"This country is cruellest to its weakest and most in need."

"I plan to change that," Laila vowed.

He couldn't help but admire her lofty ambition. "And I will help you." He loosened the sleeve of her nightgown until it slid down her shoulder. "Any way I can." He pressed his lips to her skin.

Laila muffled a sigh, trying not to get distracted. "Are you sure you're all right with that? I know it's your mother. Her organisation. I—" Her words cut off as Darius worked her nightgown down to her waist and cupped her breast, thumbing the nipple. "I wouldn't want to make you uncomfortable."

"The only thing making me uncomfortable is the fact that we're discussing my mother right now." Darius covered her breast and massaged it with his fingers.

Laila exhaled a noise. "Well it's not as if I invited you to start mauling me, is it?"

"After you strode in and plopped yourself on my lap wearing a nightgown like that." Darius leaned back to regard her with a quirked brow. "You knew precisely what you were in for."

"Perhaps I just wanted you to admire the lacework." Laila humphed and tossed her hair primly. "It is rather fine, you know."

"Really? Then I ought to take it off you to have a closer look."

Laila's face settled into a faux-unamused expression. "You're insufferable."

He brought her into a kiss, a chuckle vibrating into her mouth as he ensnared her waist. With a swipe of his other hand, the silver pieces scattered.

Laila held the sides of his face to keep him kissing her as he pressed her onto the table. Their lips parted slowly as she gazed into his eyes, her skin humming for his touch, their hearts beating in tandem. She wondered how she could ever not long to have this, to feel this, no matter how much ruination she'd suffered in order to keep it. She wondered if he felt it too.

"Why was it me?" Laila whispered. "I'm sure you had no shortage of past lovers to choose from. You could've married Katerina in a moment if you wished. Made *her* your regina and resolved this conflict. So why was it me?"

A beat passed between them before he answered. "I didn't like who I was when I was with her."

Laila raised herself up to her elbows. "And with me?"

"Probably the only time I've liked myself is when I was with you. It's probably the only time I became someone worthy of liking."

"As flattering as that may seem... it betrays a certain worrying mindset."

"So focus on being flattered."

That should've been enough for her, but it wasn't. She traced a figure of eight along his chest before speaking again. "What was she like? In bed, I mean."

"Who? Katerina?" Darius's brow furrowed in wariness as if he were about to step into a trap. "Should we be discussing this?"

"I want to know."

Darius sighed. "Well she was... adventurous. Commanding. She would regularly test my limits and force me to test hers."

"In comparison to me, you mean?" Laila tried not to sound

indignant or affronted, but she couldn't help it. His recollection made her feel nauseated.

"I don't compare. You two are different lovers entirely. Katerina was always... a tussle of wills. I could either obey her or battle her, and she would often try her best to break me. With you there's more tenderness."

"And is that..." she started, bringing her knees up to her chest. "Do you find that boring?"

"Laila." Darius brought her down between his legs.

Laila gasped softly at the seamless manoeuvre as he leaned in close to touch their noses together.

"I have been alive for centuries. I've seen it all and I've done it all. And yes, while nothing we do together has been particularly shocking, no amount of wild, debauched sex measures up to the way I feel when I'm with you. Exploring you. Getting to know you. All the little reactions and responses you give me... that's the interesting part." His eyes grew hooded as they peered into hers.

She could feel a blush warming her cheeks the further he continued, provoking a knowing smirk.

"It's not about the acts we perform or the positions we're in. It's about the way we connect... and I connect with you far better than with anyone else."

XIV

LYRA SPENT DAYS DRIFTING IN AND OUT OF consciousness, still fighting off the apparitions that crowded her mind and begged for acknowledgement. Her limbs strained against the limited space of the silk cocoon she'd been placed in, a slow-healing sap seeping through the pores of her skin.

She murmured undiscernible croaks in her sleep as Aurélie parted the folds of her chrysalis to place a bowl of broth to her lips.

"Drink."

Lyra groaned as she obeyed and tasted dew sweetened with honey. Aurélie supported Lyra's neck gently, taking care not to choke her as she drank what she could, before sealing her back into her cocoon.

She slept on until she finally roused to a body fully nourished back to health.

Little by little, the weight of fatigue lifted, and Lyra stretched herself out until the cocoon's lip opened to spit her out into a puddle of slime.

Grunting, Lyra pushed herself up to shake a flurry of droplets from her hair and skin. "Where... am I?"

Wonder prodded her to investigate as Lyra glanced down at pearlescent film coating her and then up at the cocoon she had fallen from. The sap was warm and soothing on her skin, giving off a caramel fragrance. She swiped some of the ooze and rubbed it between her fingertips before deciding it was of no harm.

Her gaze panned across the unfamiliar terrain and discovered a world softened by a roseate haze—a plain of pink velvet grass cradling the warm peach sky above. There were other pods too, hanging low from the shimmering braided stems of tall plants, though they'd long shrivelled from the absence of a body.

By then, Aurélie had returned to give Lyra another bowl of steaming dew. Upon seeing her awake, she paused, her expression inscrutable behind the bejewelled glimmer of her veil. "Well. You've awoken."

"What is this place?" Lyra asked. A butterfly sailed past her with wings of intricate lace and settled on the tip of her nose before she nudged it away.

"I have transported you to the centre of the world." Aurélie gestured to all that encompassed them with her free hand. "The place where all aether sits."

Lyra looked around to take it all in. "How does this all work? How did I get here?"

"Think of this as a basin." Aurélie sat down cross-legged and placed the bowl in her lap. "A protective outer layer where the flow of aether is held in place. Protected." She wrapped her knuckles against the porcelain. "Nothing can pass through it. Over time the aether will evaporate, disperse through the atmosphere and infuse the world with magic. Until the Phoenix returns again to fill the bowl." She puffed the steam away before offering it to Lyra.

She accepted and took light, birdlike sips to keep from overwhelming her stomach. "And the pods?"

"You did well to reach here. Many sprites before you have perished for the effort. I wanted to test your resilience and see what was within your heart and whether you'd be able to withstand the conflict rooted at the centre. The pods here are all children of the Setâre Tree and infused with its sap. We stored you in it in order to heal you."

Lyra raised up her once scorched hands and twisted them, palm to back. "What do you mean by conflict?"

Aurélie gave her an obscure look. "Finish it until the very last drop." She got up and handed Lyra the bowl. "And then come and find me."

Lyra stared into her reflection in the iridescent liquid before tipping the bowl towards her lips and draining it. After she'd finished her drink, she got up to go find Aurélie.

Along her journey, she discovered several masked disciples of the Phoenix standing together, weaving golden strings of ethereal light through their bodies.

They were learning how to direct the flow of aether in order to strengthen their connection and enter the trancelike state to phase between the Astral and Material realms. If one mastered it, then they unlocked abilities only the most distinguished of sprites knew.

It wasn't what she was here for, but the thought of learning enticed her.

However, before she could approach a pair of disciples, a breeze swept along her skin and Aurélie appeared beside her. "You are walking along the wrong path."

Lyra leapt back, wondering where she could've come from.

"This way, please." She inclined her head. "There will be ample time for Enlightenment." With that, she turned on her heel and started to walk, leaving Lyra little choice but to follow her.

She trailed along behind the flower-plaited train of Aurélie's dress as it rained petals inside her footprints. An urge to inquire where they were going grew the longer they trekked, but the question died on her lips when she saw the bole of a tree in the distance.

The Setâre Tree was just as wondrous as she had imagined.

An impressive trunk of deep cerise coiled into curlicue branches, adorned with star-shaped leaves in matching hue. Age had enriched the vibrancy of its pigment, bestowing it a dignified grace against the blushing pinks of the realm.

"Oh..." Lyra drew in a breath, mesmerised, her feet carrying her forward to touch it.

Aurélie seized her wrist to keep her still. "That is quite far enough."

Her reverie broken, Lyra blinked herself back to lucidity.

"You'll notice there are ten branches." Aurélie gestured to each of them. "Every branch represents the dynasties of a solarite and her descendants. The leaves are what remain of their souls in the Physical Realm when they crossover into the Astral." She flicked her wrist and summoned a leaf to swirl through the wind and land on her palm. "This one represents Esterre."

Lyra's eyes bulged.

"Why look so shocked?" Aurélie offered a smile of tender knowing. "This is what you came here for, is it not?"

There was a sinking in her chest. "You were expecting me."

"We've been awaiting you for a very long time, Lyra. Born in the bluebell village of Lis. There is a reason why you were sent here."

The unease plummeted towards her stomach upon hearing her name. "What reason?" Anger flared inside her. "And if there was something I needed to do, something important, why wait for me to come here? Why not come to me?"

"Look at the Setâre Tree." Aurélie pointed a finger as blades of sunlight pierced through the gaps in the leaves. "Beautiful, isn't she? She will last all through Spring Equinox only to perish in Autumn. And do you know why? She is the only thing standing between us and the Abyss that threatens to swallow us whole. Yet cracks of it still manage to seep in, here and there. Calante. Mortos. His creations."

Lyra jolted at each word.

"She keeps the worst at bay but at great cost to her own life by consuming all of its darkness and allowing it to destroy her, yet in the end she prevails through strength and perseverance. Such is the essence of the equinox: the constant dance between chaos and creation. Light and dark, life and death... each seeking to conquer the other."

"I don't understand."

"These are forces beyond our power and scope, Lyra. And we have been preparing for a battle. In order for it to work we've had to move covertly, without alerting our enemy to any strategies in place. We cannot intervene, we can only influence and hope the seeds we plant shall grow fruitful."

Lyra grunted in frustration. "Can't you stop speaking in riddles for one moment!"

"We are aware of everything. We know about Lucrèce Mielette. We know of the Mountain. We even know of my granddaughter, who has a role to play herself. But she cannot know of it. She, however, is the key to preventing Calante's reign of blood and chaos. And rest assured, if he gets free then he will unlock the gates to the Nether Realm with him, and this world shall be flooded in unspeakable horrors. This wasn't to be her destiny, but Calante has put his designs on her now."

"What..." Lyra's voice degraded to a whisper. "What do you mean?"

"He has been languishing in his prison for millennia. And he wants out. But to become free he requires a vessel he can use to anchor himself to the Physical Realm. A descendant of his own blood. Before we encountered Mortos, there were three potential vessels. When Amira defeated Lanius, there were two. After Laila did away with Dominus... that left one. However, he cannot fully possess that vessel unless they are completely under his thrall... unless they've fallen so deeply into irreparable despair that they welcome him willingly."

All this effort... just to ruin my own chance at happiness...

"No," Lyra said with a slow sinking realisation. Her hands went to her hair, fingers raking along her scalp. "No, not that. Please, not that."

"And therein lies your dilemma. The wisdom at the end of your journey."

Her cheeks flushed in outrage. "You've been using Laila... as a *buffer* between them?"

"Not intentionally. It just so happens that was where the tides of fate took us. We were unfortunate in the sense that love is such a precarious beast by nature that we are unable to leash it. And now... we cannot interfere with them."

"No, no, no, no." Lyra kept shaking her head. Kept refusing the rationale. She couldn't let herself buy into a logic that treated Laila so expendably. "Not Laila. You can't just... you can't just *leave* her at his mercy. You don't know that this will last. You can't know his love will remain. What happens if...." Tears sprang to her eyes. "What if he *stops* loving her?"

"Until we have indication such is the case, we shall not intervene. And neither shall Esterre. I am afraid this is where you must ask yourself: Will you allow the one you love to fulfil her destiny or will you leave the world broken and in the clutches of chaos to restore your own connection to her?"

Lyra sank to her knees as a sob racked through her chest. "There *has* to be another way. There *must* be."

Aurélie observed her hysterics with an impassive silence, but behind her veil her face was written with sadness. "There is."

A sheen of hope glistened through Lyra's tears.

"However, it requires Laila to be willing to turn against her love. Do you believe that she would? Has she given you any indication that, should the choice be put to her, she would desert his side?"

Lyra exhaled tremulously.

"I think you know the answer."

"So, that's it?" Lyra asked in a diminished voice. "I came here for... for nothing?"

"I am sorry, Ser de Lis."

"It's not fair..." She sank her fingers into the grass, tearing it out in chunks. "It's... n-not fair." Her dirt-stained fingers curled into fists as she began to pound the soil. "It's not *fair. It's not fair.* Damn the gods! Curse Asemani to the Abyss!" She craned her neck up at the sky, seething with tear-streaked cheeks. "What have I ever done but *serve you?*"

Aurélie observed her grief with a gentle silence and allowed it to pass before she spoke again. "Serve you have... but I'll tell you something you do not know, Lyra de Lis, and it's that you may not be serving the right mistress."

Defeated as she was, it was a wonder Lyra could stomach yet another harrowing reveal. "What does that even mean?"

"Lucrèce hasn't been fully honest with you about the circumstances regarding Dominus's resurrection. And her part in it."

"Y-you can't be saying..." Lyra shook her head as more tears filled her eyes. "You can't be telling me she was responsible. For those sprite murders. For Aurea Park..." Her voice trailed into stunned silence.

"I am afraid it is so. Lucrèce has done well to mobilise your rage and point it where she wants it directed. But the reason I elucidate you is because I'd like for you to make a choice of your own." Aurélie held up the leaf in her hand and turned it into a pink feather, shimmering with the iridescent hues of holy fire.

"Is that...?"

"A flame of the Phoenix. I entrust it to you to offer to the solarite of your choosing. Take your newfound information and use it to your advantage."

The fabled feather of flame had been spoken of extensively in myth. Those who plucked it would be granted access to its immaculate power. Only a spark of it existed at the core of a living solarite; with an entire plume there was no telling how they might transcend.

"Why—why trust me with this? How can you know I'll make the right choice?"

"Because I see your heart is pure beyond the turmoil that governs it, Lyra de Lis. Esterre sees it too."

Lyra lifted her trembling hand and allowed the feather to flutter into her palm. With the lightest graze, it disappeared into her and left its foliate brand upon her skin, dormant and waiting.

XV

SABINA SAT DOWN AT HER HARPSICHORD AND PLACED a sheet of music on the stand. With a strenuous crack of her fingers she began to play one of the pieces she had written, closing her eyes in thought. Learning to play and write her own music had been skills Darius had taught her from youth. As a mathematician, he had instilled in her the concept that music was merely about timing, frequency, and sequences and that she should treat each bar as an equation to solve.

Since then she had dedicated herself to the craft, and being able to play a piece she'd written often served to calm her mind and allow for deeper thought. Such as the problem of murder. Her forehead creased as she thought back to the conversation she'd had with Serafina weeks ago. Occassi were creatures of chaos, designed to kill. Their purpose, according to the word of Calante, was to spread mayhem.

Yet Sabina couldn't help but wonder if there were situations where things could be taken too far. And if, perhaps, death might have been a sweeter mercy than living in torment. The thought of her father after he'd been delivered back to his cell made this internal dilemma more relevant than ever.

She paced around her mind. She couldn't stop thinking of the last time she saw her father—the blank slate of his face as he looked at her with just the faintest tinge of sadness. After the procedure, the only emotions that coloured his features were in the blandest of shades. Oh, how Sabina wanted to strike and shake him, to beg him to reprimand her for her betrayal. But yet all he gave—all he could give—was that loathsome silence. Whatever he once might have been before his heart was removed had shrunken inwards to a tiny, neglected corner no one could hear.

She had done that to him.

Her fingers prodded the keys of the instrument more harshly, and Sabina could hear the way some of them faltered, declaring a need to be finely tuned. As she played, Darius himself appeared at her chambers to listen to her.

He stood in the doorway with an expression of vague interest, as if he was trying to figure out what the music was to her.

"You seem to be in fine form," he said.

Sabina stiffened her shoulders. "Some of the keys need to be tuned."

"Well, that's easily done." He moved closer to sit beside her on the bench. "You know how to fix it. If only all things were so easy to mend."

Sabina knew he was referring to her father. "I was trying to compose a piece for him. He always loved my music. It was one of the few things I could do to coax a smile out of him."

"He treated you cruelly." Darius put a hand on her shoulder.

"I'd say we're the same in that now." Sabina returned to her harpsichord with the tuning wrench. "I hear the regina is holding her first meeting today." She twisted the turning pins to straighten the wires. "I can imagine the noble ladies are waiting in bated breath for what her goals and agenda for this gathering will be..."

"You are not attending?"

She shook her head. "Doesn't feel right." She hadn't been able to look Laila in the eye much lately. Laila's shows of sympathy for Sabina's ailing father had only been shrugged off as Sabina sought to avoid being where the regina was. It was easier that way. "Not as if much of it would be of interest to me."

"Suppose you've always been one to separate yourself from the herd," Darius said. "I should probably go see to ensure preparations are in order."

"Darius—"

He paused mid-rise. "Yes?"

"Is he... always going to be like that?" Sabina worked her jaw. "Just... gone?"

"My mother shall continue to see to him," Darius assured her, "but in the meantime... enjoy the perks of having taken his place as prime prefect. It's a once in a lifetime opportunity you've been given."

He draped a prideful hand on her shoulder. She tensed in spite of herself.

Laila's first Regina Council would be in her antechamber for the maximum comfort of her guests. She wanted them to feel free to loosen their tongues and relax their guards in the knowledge that no male onlookers would be around to dissuade them from frank testimony.

On the day of the meeting she had ushered in several maidservants to serve hot drinking chocolate infused with hazelnut, followed by trays of acorn-shaped hand pies dangling from a makeshift tree. The gingerbread cookies came next, coated with icing to resemble deer and mushrooms. The final arrival brought the honey cake coated in a layer of caramelised rowan berries and decorated with eagle skulls shaped from marzipan.

Laila arranged all the food on the table and folded her hands together against her cheek with a satisfied sigh. She couldn't have been more pleased with her presentation.

Serafina was the first of her attendees to arrive, and she wrinkled her nose at the table. "I thought this was meant to be a Council meeting? This looks to be more of a glorified tea party to me."

"Why, it's my *first* Council meeting!" Laila declared as though Serafina's observation was ludicrous. "I could hardly allow such a momentous occasion to pass without a plentiful feast in its honour." She took up a knife, cut a slice of honey cake, and offered it to Serafina on a plate. "Would you like some?"

Serafina's gaze made it plain that she would rather take up the knife and cut a portion out of Laila. "I don't like cake," she lied as she swept past the regina to take a seat on the divan.

Laila shrugged, unperturbed by this as she plucked a tiny portion off the corner to nibble. "A pity. You're missing out." She cut herself another piece and quietly hummed in pleasure before bounding towards her seat.

Serafina sighed heavily as Laila plopped into an armchair. There was a palpable frenetic energy in her voice and steps that resembled something of a squirrel; one could either be immediately charmed or aggravated by it. Serafina was the unfortunate latter.

Soon more arrivals were introduced into the room by her maidservants. First, the elderly qarnina by the name of Anya, followed by a lupara with a snow white pelt named Galina. Last among them was none other than Domitia Orlovia, who bristled the moment her eyes fell upon Serafina.

She peered down her nose at the blood sorceress as if she were a dish she had not ordered. "Well, I can see we're allowing any old tramp off the street to attend this meeting."

"Really, Domitia." Serafina snorted. "Here before me stand a qarnina and a lupara and it is *my* presence you question?"

"What is she doing here?" Domitia turned to Laila. It was clear her intent in bringing it up at all was in the hopes of having Serafina extracted from the room.

"Now, ladies." Laila raised her hands and gestured to the chairs. "I express my gratitude for your attendance. Please take your seats so I can discuss my intentions."

The ladies of the room did so, though not without animosity written into their faces. Galina and Serafina seemed the least tense of the members, sitting side by side, something Laila took careful note of.

"I have gathered you all today for a specific purpose. I find it troubling that for thousands of years the specific needs and desires of female citizens have been so overlooked. With this Council I have decided to remedy this—"

"Well, I would have to say I am honoured, Your Majesty," Domitia inserted, stroking her hand down her golden owl medal. "Though my husband and sons see to my needs quite sufficiently."

Serafina stifled a noise into her cup of drinking chocolate.

"And what could *this* hag possibly contribute?" Domitia sounded aggrieved. "I can assure you we don't need to hear any of her venom-spewing."

"I don't quite agree. As regina I desire to listen to each and every female voice under my care, no matter their background or allegiance." Laila picked up her cup of hot chocolate. "Plus, I feel we'll have quite a bit to learn from each other."

Domitia sniffed. "Hmph. I can't imagine that."

"We'll see." Laila sipped her beverage. "However, for this to work we shall all have to be cordial. Can I count on your behaviour?"

Domitia bared a smile, all fangs. "But of course."

Laila nodded in acceptance. "Why don't we start with hearing from you, Galina? You were good enough to travel here all the way from the coast. Please tell us what you feel most ails the womenfolk of your kind."

Galina made a soft rumble at the back of her throat. "My pack en't concerned about nothing 'cept keeping our land. We been driven to becoming wa'er people. Constantly on the move after centuries of being hunted. You promise to keep your grubby paws off'a our beaches, and we en't got no troubles."

"Please." Domitia rolled her eyes. "Spare us your victim screed. Your kind has been nothing but a menace on the coasts, exerting dominance over the fisheries in times of famine."

"What choice did we 'ave when it was *your* kind who drove us off?" Galina's lips peeled back to bare her jagged teeth. "We lupes use'ta pride ourselves on hunting game, same as you. We became fish ea'ers to survive after centuries of purges. Only decent ones o' you savages are the Vidua Nocte who 'elped keep us fed."

Serafina sat up proudly. "We blood sorceresses know well what it means to be expelled from society."

"*Expelled*? Don't make me laugh. You *abandoned* your society," Domitia sneered. "And for what? Dissatisfaction with your suitors? Ungrateful little girls that you are. I hope living the peasant life was worth it. At the end of the day, while you were all running off into the woods, *I* was enjoying a life of luxury filled with silks and jewels."

"As long as you keep letting your husband fuck you," Serafina shot back. "I wonder, what is the difference between you and a whore but a fancy necklace and empty title?"

"Ladies." Laila tapped the side of her cup with a spoon. "I believe I asked for cordial, did I not?"

Domitia and Serafina composed their faces, which had started to degrade into revealing their true monster visage.

"I can see there are many tensions here. Much to discuss." Laila pressed her lips together in thought. "Anya, we've not yet heard from you. Why don't you tell us about the issues most facing qarninas?"

Anya stood with the aid of a cane, her knees cracking like twigs. "I've got nothing to add, Your Majesty."

"Nothing?" Laila's brows furrowed.

"I only came here to say how cruel I think this was. Calling me to plead the ills of my kind to their slaughterers." She extended a knobbled finger to the other members. "Each and every one of you demons has hands soaked with qarna blood, and yet you think I should unburden my pain to them? Tch. I don't want equality with the occassi, a chance to seat myself at the table of your carnage. I want *freedom* from them."

By the end of her speech she'd left the occasselle in the room imbued with a savage rage. Only Laila remained humbled, cheeks tinged scarlet with embarrassment.

"Don't listen to her, Your Majesty." Domitia outstretched a hand in assurance. "Say the word and I'll have that upstart severely disciplined."

"I shall see no harm come to her." Laila's reply was sharp. "The way I see it, we are all squabbling about the same root cause. The occassi. In particular, the legacy of occasso dominance inflicted upon the island.

We've all been impacted, in various ways, with different consequences, and I don't mean to minimise the pain of anyone present—"

"*You*, Your Majesty?" Domitia asked. "What ills do you have to speak of? You have a loving husband at your side willing to put his own reputation on the line to elevate you in station. Your country *thwarted* Mortos's aims. I can be certain you've not tasted the violence inflicted by an occasso at full strength."

"I may have all of that. Yes. But it has not spared me." Laila thought back to Dominus biting into her shoulder with a shudder. "And for all that Darius Rex loves me, I do not consider him beyond reproach. I have taken him to task for many of his misdeeds in the past, and I would again. He is very much a part of what I am attempting to discuss."

Serafina arched a brow at her. She had not expected this much insight to be hiding beneath all that cotton stuffing.

"How about we end here for today? Help yourself to cake and cookies, and we can reconvene next week for a more civil discussion."

Darius made his way to the Regina Wing and passed by Yula carrying a tray of steaming milk and honey.

He traced the servant's walk as she pivoted into a room, and a chorus of light giggles soon followed. Darius recognised the girlish symphony as belonging to Laila. Creeping towards the doorway, he peered inside and found Laila and Yula huddled together over a book.

Judging by their muffled giggles and hushed whispers, it was clear the novel held scandalous contents, but due to Yula's lack of literacy, Laila was narrating in an exaggerated fashion, keeping her volume muted so more sensitive ears didn't overhear.

"Honestly, Your Majesty!" Yula scoffed in dismissal once she decided she'd heard enough. She picked up a hand pie and took a hearty bite. "I don't know how you can tear through so many of these books. They're all the same!"

"Oh, Yula." Laila poked her lightly on the nose. "You just hate joy."

"No, I like good stories."

"Now, what are you reading?" Darius asked.

Yula leapt up with a start. "Why, Your Majesty!" Her hands fiddled with her sarafan.

Laila shut the book immediately with a loud clap. She covered the title with her hand. "You certainly arrived quietly. Yula and I were just enjoying some leisurely reading."

"Must be an engrossing narrative."

"It is."

Yula's cheeks pinked as she picked up her tray. "I'll return this to the kitchens."

Laila didn't fight for her to stay. She'd come to realise how fearful Yula grew in the presence of occassi and didn't push for her to overcome it.

Once Yula left she resumed where she'd earlier left off, barely looking up from her page as Darius sat down next to her on the divan. Her brow furrowed. It creased further in concentration as he sidled closer, until his warmth radiated at her side.

Darius leaned nearer to slide his arm around her, placing his hand on her thigh. The weight of his palm was a comforting addition, but one that slightly agitated her. It wasn't until he kissed her bare shoulder that she realised he'd disrupted her ambience.

She sighed in mock frustration. "Well, now you're distracting me."

"Ah, my apologies." He started to draw his hand away.

"No, I—" She seized his hand and returned it to her thigh. "I didn't mean I wanted you to stop."

"Of course." He returned his lips to her shoulder, and she could feel the smirk on them.

She sighed again but this time much softer, allowing herself to nuzzle into him as she reclined against his chest.

He moved his lips from her shoulder to the crown of her head as she did so. "What is it that has so enraptured your attention?"

Laila lifted the book closer to hide her blush. "I'm not going to tell you because you will only laugh at me."

"Oh?" He sounded amused. "Try me."

"It's—I..." Her cheeks were inflamed and she could barely find the courage to glance at him. "I found a stash of these in the library one day." When he didn't speak immediately she forced herself to speak further. "They're very... interesting tales involving dashing lords and swashbuckling warriors."

"Oh, you mean one of those heroic epics?" Darius couldn't disguise his derision. "Yes, they're rather plentiful, though I've always found them to be dull, self-congratulatory reads."

"Well these are..." Laila nibbled on her bottom lip. "Not quite concerned with escapades in battle, so to speak."

"What do you—" He stopped to chuckle, and Laila realised with some mortification that he'd finally understood. "Ah. I see. You've been indoctrinated into a noble lady's secret thrill, have you?"

"I knew you would laugh!"

"Not *at* you, per se," Darius protested. "Though I must ask... how many have you read?"

Laila blushed deeper, too embarrassed for words.

"Well... considering how much of your time they've taken I can only hope I haven't found myself replaced."

Laila scoffed at the absurdity of such a suggestion in spite of its intended humour. She shut her book and cast it aside as though whatever enchantment it had woven had long dissipated, throwing her arms around him instead.

"Is that a no, then?"

"Are you really so oblivious?" She answered him with a kiss, pressing herself against him tightly. "You have nothing to be concerned about." Her thumb skidded along his jawline. "Although... they may have given me more than a few... impractical ideas, shall we say?"

Darius arched a brow, lascivious intent scrawled into his smile. "In that case I'm all ears." He dropped his mouth on hers again and banished any thoughts of ruggedly handsome heroes. "How did your meeting go?"

"It was... interesting." Laila scrunched her nose. "Mostly I realised it's going to be a lot more difficult than I thought to make all of these factions see eye to eye after centuries of division."

"I did try to warn you."

"I know," Laila said, "but that doesn't mean I'm going to give up."

"I never anticipated otherwise." Darius stroked her hair fondly. "So, what's your plan of action?"

After witnessing the verbal sparring match between Serafina and Domitia, she'd come to a few realisations about the nature of occasselle—and it was that the two were standing at two opposing ends of a pipeline all girls of the race were being funnelled into. If she was going to see change at a more fundamental level, then she was going to have to intervene before another one of the aforementioned occassella could be churned out into the world.

"I want to mend the ostracism suffered by the Vidua Nocte and bring them back into high society."

Darius gave her a wry look. "I don't think Domitia is going to care much for you encroaching on her space."

"That's precisely why I must do it," Laila said. "As long as she is the primary matriarch indoctrinating the occasselle into her ways, nothing I'm trying to tackle will alter. I need to catch them young, while they still have a chance and before they become either her or..."

"My mother."

Laila nodded. "Have you ever considered... sitting down and talking with her about why she did what she did? Really, truly, asked?"

His face scrunched in disbelief. "You are joking?"

"I believe it may help you." Laila placed a hand to his chest, smoothing her palm along it. "To finally hash it out with her after all these centuries."

"No."

"Darius..." Laila groaned. "What harm could it possibly do?"

"Plenty," he retorted. "I see no reason why she should benefit from my forgiveness."

"I'm not asking you to forgive her, Darius. Only to... come to a mutual understanding with her. To put aside this animosity. You've been holding onto all this loathing inside of you because you feel she didn't love you enough to..."

"Stop." He held up a hand. "I know what this is, and this isn't about me and my mother. It's about you and yours."

Laila fell silent.

"I don't need to make amends with her the way you need to with Amira, Laila. And quite frankly, you give her far more regard than she deserves."

"How can one do otherwise when it's your mother?"

"That... creature"—he spoke as if he could strip her of her maternal tie to Laila's life—"tormented you for your entire life, and still you remain loyal. She made you feel as if you were inadequate and unworthy of her love. Her esteem. When in truth it was she who was never deserving of yours. I can never excuse her for that. I don't see how you can."

"Maybe I just think some people are worth a chance at betterment." A knowing look followed. "Oh, I know it will be an arduous task ahead of me, but if I could warm the cockles of even your black, shrivelled heart"—Laila bumped her nose against his playfully—"how hard can Serafina be?"

Darius sighed deeply. "If it means that much to you, then... fine. I will try my best to bury the hatchet."

XVI

A COLD WIND WHISTLED OVER BLANK WHITE SNOW drifts.

Sadik shuddered as he gathered his arms around his frozen body, stumbling through the impenetrable mounds of ice that refused to melt. He huffed at his ungloved hands, but no breath came to warm him. His skin had taken the ashen pallor of the dead, cracked and flaking from blisters.

It was enough to make him whimper, seeing the blemishes. Once, he'd been flawless—nourished from head to toe in the finest of scented lotions to the point where he gleamed like obsidian. That was before he had tarnished his soul with chaos and been exiled to whatever abyssal realm he now found himself within.

Sadik thought of calling out but knew better than to expect anyone to be here with him. These dreams weren't anything like his other ones. They'd always taken place in hot tropical settings before a dark shadow swept over them. The last time he'd felt dreadful cold like this was when he had been in Mortos, and the one experience had been ghastly enough he'd been in no hurry to return.

He continued to walk, even though the aching tremors of his muscles and his rigid skin made each step unbearable. He continued to walk until he saw a copse of dead trees in the distance, and he sped his pace until he encountered what he'd longed desired but gave up expecting to find. A figure.

Through the veil of snow was a skeletal creature coated with an ashen film of frost. Sadik at first thought she was dead, yet as he grew closer he could see ripples of motion from behind her endless span of matted black hair.

Sadik realised she was human in shape but not quite, and she was naked, huddled over in pain. Her limbs spanned longer than they had any right to for her tiny body, and knobbles of bone protruded from ravaged skin that sagged limply from her frame with no meat or muscle to pad it.

"Oh, Goddess..." He smothered a retching noise. *Was that why I was sent here? Was that meant to be me?* The thought was so sickening he staggered backwards and, in his desperation to escape, snapped a stray twig.

Emica Hariken's head shot upwards and her neck, long as an ostrich's, made a full rotation to point in his direction. Streaks of black tears trickled from her eyes, and her lips widened into a smile of long-belated relief. "Finally..."

"W-wait..." Sadik threw up his hands to defend himself. "Don't hurt me!"

Emica blinked at him in confusion and stretched out her neck to examine him closely. "Why wouldn't you be hurt here?" She wove around him like a snake. "That's all this place is for."

Sadik's stomach turned as he backed away from her.

Emica extended her neck and looped her head around him. "If you are here, then that means Calante has claimed your soul for harvesting."

"But I am not..." Sadik gulped. "I'm not dead."

"He doesn't need you dead to have your soul in his teeth. He wants you to have hope you can escape. It's no fun for him if you do not hope." Her eyes brimmed with chaotic sludge.

"Oh," Sadik said softly.

"He"—Emica shuddered as she regarded her husk of a body—"uses me to spread his filth."

"I'm very sorry," Sadik said, wishing he could do more, say more.

Emica sniffled back tears. After two decades alone she'd forgotten what a soothing balm a show of kindness could be. It made her remember how alone she was. "That's why you need to... you need..." Her eyes bulged in terror. "No... no no no no no... it's happening again... it's happening again..." She started to dash her head onto the hard ground, violently, until wounds burst open and bled trenches down the frail skin on her cheeks. "Get out!" Her lips curled into a feral snarl smeared with her blood. "Out! Out! Out!"

Her cry of pain racked through Sadik's body like a shockwave and sent him tumbling head over heels on the snow. Weakened, he pulled himself onto his hands to see a gush of blackness explode around her.

Sadik withheld the urge to go to her—it—whatever origins this creature could claim—and, instead, chose to watch as the geyser of black matter took life fully matured.

Sweat dribbled down Sadik's back and hardened to icicles as he scrambled away from the chimera. The mutant clawed forward on raw stumps as appendages spiked with talons burgeoned from its wings.

Pulse pounding his ribs raw, Sadik wondered if this was how he was to meet his end. He found himself thinking about Elina and whether she was watching now, seated beside that stony-eyed doctor. He hoped that she wouldn't look. He'd always dreamed that when the time came for fate to catch him it would be a pretty sight he'd leave for her to mourn.

Sadik coughed a weak laugh. "Sorry, honeybee." He closed his eyes, fully prepared to accept his fate.

However, the creature did not intend violence. Its movements, while frantic, were random and uncertain as it attempted to birth itself. A watery gurgle spurted black phlegm from its headless hole as a new cranium began to push through. With a final sneeze of the neck hole, a face was expelled and the lizard-eagle shook off acidic droplets that melted the snow.

"Fuck..." Sadik exhaled, wanting nothing more than to reach out and feel along the black prismatic scales. The chimera snarled in response before melting away through a black puddle. For so many years he'd aspired to trick and talk his way into the viewing of a chimera. He never would've guessed the atrocity sealed inside Darius's vault of secrets was a woman driven mad from loneliness.

Emica wailed in agony, face bloodied and tear-streaked. "No! I won't let you make another! I *refuse* to allow another one of you wretched fiends to pass through the gates of oblivion—" She curled her fists and started to beat herself until her knuckles purpled. "*Argh*. Kill me! *Kill me*. Free me from this torment!"

Fear unfroze its grip from Sadik when he realised the mutant was docile. He turned his attention towards the distressed Emica and reached towards to take her hands. "Stop. Please. You have to stop hurting yourself."

"No!" Emica snarled, sinking her teeth into Sadik's thumb and raking it along before she spat blood.

"Hey!" Sadik snatched his hand back.

"Do you see now? Do you see this is the eternity outstretched before you? Emptiness and malaise and tedium with no end! And he doesn't have to kill you to achieve it. He takes you whole, fresh, and vibrant and squeezes you until he's able to feed on the fat of your pulp to sustain himself. *Do you see?*"

"I see, now," Sadik said softly, and without thinking he put his arms around her ungainly neck and attempted to pet her head. "I see."

Emica convulsed with a sob before going malleable in his hold. She hadn't felt the warmth of another human touch in so long.

"Hey... listen," Sadik said, unable to repress his discomfort. "Can you tell me your name?"

"It's..." She realised she had very nearly forgotten it. With no one around her it had become a set of sounds no more meaningful than a dog's bark. What use was having a name when there was no one to call for you? "It's Emica."

"Pleasure to meet you, Emica. My name is Sadik." His eyes creased with warmth. "So you see. You're not alone anymore."

And for the first time in twenty years, her cheeks streaked with chaos, Emica Hariken felt the strange but familiar tug of a smile on her mouth. "Thank you."

"How long have you been trapped here?"

"There is no time here. There is no length. There is only this." She waved at the landscape incarcerated in frost before them. "A long time ago... I learned about decomposition of the body. How if one were to perish under certain temperatures the body remains and doesn't rot. Nothing can thrive enough to start decaying it. So it simply lies there, stiff, suspended in time. Forgotten. And that's what I realised this is." She scrubbed away at the snow until it revealed a patch of blackness beneath.

Grass, Sadik assumed at first thought until he realised the texture, the animalic scent. *Fur*.

"This is Calante, a corpse preserved through the cold. So what does he do? He tries to bring in those with the heat of life in them. Something he can feed off of."

"To what end?"

"So he can come back. This is a war we cannot see. One for the spirit. One for the soul. He takes us and he strips us down until we can only fulfil one utility. Breeder and killer. A complementary pair. We multiply and destroy everything in our path until only his creed remains to plague the physical world. Mould slipping through the cracks in the walls until the entire house has crumbled."

"But we can stop him?" Sadik asked, his hope a relentless beacon even entrenched as he was in the clutches of the Nether. "We must be able to stop him?"

Emica fell silent before her neck withdrew towards her hunched shoulders. "You must... kill me."

"*How?*" The thought horrified him. "How is that even possible here?"

"There are ways that you can snuff a spirit out if you have sufficient will to do it." Her eyes cast over her mangled body, frail as a woodchip, encircled in a glowing ring of ancient runes. "I've tried... but..."

Sadik could tell from inference alone her injured state was likely the result of her many failed attempts.

"It is the only way. Please... end my suffering."

His heart clenched from the pain in her voice, from the stark view of her torturous existence, and yet he still couldn't bring himself to want to end her life. Not without knowing the cost. "If I kill you... what happens to me? What will it do to my soul? Will I replace you?"

Will I be left alone here?

He knew it was selfish to start thinking of the consequences for himself, even more so than his reluctance to harm someone so snivelling and defenceless. Perhaps it was why he had been the one to be led here, to be taunted with the cruelty of his own self-interest, so Calante could weigh the unworthiness of his spirit before claiming it for keeps.

Emica seemed to sense this internal battle in him and shook her head at it. "What does it matter? You're doomed regardless of whether you end me or not." It was not said unkindly, more as a resigned truth she had likely had to resist, bargain with, and accept several times over before he had ever encountered her. And that alone was enough to move him to a sob.

"Kill me... please," Emica cried. "You must kill me."

"I can't." Sadik shook his head. "Don't make me do this."

At his refusal, something morphed in her face. "If you won't kill me... then you can at least set me free."

Sadik cried out as Emica roped her neck around him until he was ensnared and merged her face into his. He struggled from her spirit-stealing kiss as she attempted to scrape his mind from his body, putting a padlock on his personhood even as his limbs fell flaccid at his sides.

He would not relent.

He couldn't.

XVII

LAILA PLUCKED AN ICE-BLUE ROSE FROM A BUSH and sniffed it delicately before tucking it into her curls. Its sweetness lingered, echoing the thousands of olfactory memories of where she'd scented it last. It brought her to another time. Another life. One of stifled shared giggles and intoxicating midnight conversations that never seemed real the next morning. How swiftly she'd lost it all when she turned away from the comfort of her mother's bosom and the trappings that came with it.

A sadness overcame her until she traced her fingers along Fleur's silken fur, and the bunny nibbled on a fat strawberry peeking out from Laila's skirts. She'd uncovered a treasure trove of them glistening like rubies among the leaves when she arrived and lined her skirts in shiny-eyed avarice.

Laila shooed Fleur away to the fringes with a giggle before she sampled the roundest and ripest fruit, bleeding juice onto her fingers.

As she helped herself to another, Sabina wormed her way around the yellow rose bushes to present herself. Laila had invited her here for a private discussion away from the prying eyes of Darius's prefects and could think of no better setting than this rosarium to host it.

"Well," Sabina exclaimed, as though she'd taken a long drink of the scenery and was exhaling in satiation. "I'd heard of this place, but nothing quite compares to seeing it in person."

One could see how it blossomed from the breadth of Darius's passion. How the golden tint from the aetherglass nestled an adoring halo around Laila's flaxen hair.

"He has his moments." Laila's cheeks pinked from flattery. "I thought it might be nice if we spoke here." She patted the empty space next to her on the bench.

Sabina eyed her hesitantly.

"You can stand if you prefer," Laila offered.

Sabina placed a hand in her pocket. "I think I might."

Laila frowned. "Have I done something to offend you, Sabina?"

"No, it's..." She'd decided long ago that she could not have an even split of allegiance between the rex and his bride, not when their aims so differed, and keeping her distance was the best way to enforce her boundaries. "I'd just prefer to stand."

"Very well." Laila picked up a strawberry and took a dainty bite. "I wanted to talk to you away from all of the other prefects for a moment. Since you are now acting prime prefect, I believe this sort of discussion should be kept to the innermost circle."

"What's this about?"

"I have a way to restore a lifeline of trade between Soleterea and Mortos. We shall need it if I am to import the aetherglass successfully."

Laila hid behind a mask of a smile. "I might have once called upon my mother. However, since the calamity in Aurea Park... my name is unfortunately mud."

"How do you suppose we might persuade them?"

"I have invited Oriel Guillory, one of my protégées, for a visit. I would like you to escort her and get her settled at Drakalyk. Tell no one of this."

"Certainly, Your Majesty." Sabina tucked her hand on her middle and bowed.

"And also... give her a gift from me. Mortos has a thriving pearl industry at the coasts. I know our reserves are diminishing in Soleterea. The Guillory dynasty has always held a monopoly on precious gems, but they struggle to fish for them without encroaching on mermaid territory."

"I see," Sabina said. "So you're hoping to dazzle them with pretty baubles."

"Solarites have always been connoisseurs of beauty." A lilac butterfly came to nestle atop the rose in Laila's hair as she spoke. She slipped a berry into her mouth and chewed in consideration. "There's something else I'd like your help with if there's not too much trouble. I have a tincture recipe to relieve moongrass dependency. I'd like for it to be safely delivered to the qarnina Anya. Since you once held ties with the enforcers..."

"I can do it," Sabina said, "though I'd have to warn you I don't think it will help much."

A flicker of concern crossed her features. "Why?"

"The more you attempt to legislate cruelty out of existence, the more they'll only craft ways to evade it."

"So what should I do, leave them to it?"

Sabina wished for a moment Laila could stop being so irksomely virtuous. "No. I am saying if you want this to be taken seriously you're going to have to enforce your will. Helping the qarna is honourable on its own. But you'll need to whip the occassi in line first if you want it to last."

Laila's lips pursed in dissatisfaction. "Thank you for your counsel." She hadn't bloodied her hands since Dominus but knew the moment would come around again when she'd have to bear up and hold the axe. The question was, how many heads would she have to slash before she devolved into becoming just as much a terror as those she condemned?

A crimson moon bled through the window as Darius leaned against the frame to sip from his polugar glass. He stepped away from the view overlooking his kingdom and went to oversee a document still laid out on his desk pertaining to the status of the Vidua Nocte. He and Laila had gone over the accords back and forth until reaching an equilibrium that was ultimately to their liking.

Darius thought the terms to be more than fair but knew his mother never spared an opportunity to take insult where there was none. To be discordant was her lifeblood. Such was why he wanted to wait for the chance to confront her alone and spare Laila any unnecessary ugliness.

He took another sip from his glass, tapping his ringed knuckles against his desk in wait before he heard his mother escorted in.

"I hear your regina is causing quite the stir across the kingdom." Serafina prowled inside with the esteem of a tigress and flashed him a smile. "Upsetting Domitia Orlovia never goes well for anyone. Ask your father. I'd take care to see that she was well watched."

"Laila will manage." Darius stood from his seat, muscles loose in spite of the agitation she inspired. He was unwilling to let his mother ruffle him. "Whilst we're on the subject of my wife, she has suggested you and I ought to have a talk."

"About what?"

"Burying the hatchet. Setting aside past grievances. Ambitious though it may be."

Serafina's brow furrowed. "I'm not sure I follow."

"You have made various attempts to connect with me over the centuries. And I always refused it. Until now. Because of Laila. And it is also because of Laila that I feel the need to grant her this one request... to try to forgive you."

Serafina's confusion migrated to bewilderment. "You want to *forgive* me?"

"Yes, and I'd like to start by offering you this. I have drawn up the accords for you to sign." He picked up the parchment made from qarnun vellum—an ancient practice. "I trust you shall find the conditions to your liking."

Serafina snatched the contract with narrowed eyes and unfurled it. She stifled a derisive chortle into a snort. "I see you still insist on claiming your tree tax."

"If you want to be recognised as an official landowner then you pay your dues along with the rest of them." Darius leaned his hip on the edge of his desk, arms folded.

"And the registry?"

"A simple matter of record-keeping. I intend to make it my business to know who takes refuge in the Widowlands."

Serafina rolled up the parchment. "I can't agree to this."

"You can," Darius corrected. "And you will. I don't see how you have any choice in the matter. I'm being far more generous towards you than any other rex has been or would be. You won't get another chance like this, Mother. Don't squander it."

"You think you're the one with the upper hand?" Serafina gave him a pitiful look. "We've been turning the tides of famine long before you were even a twinkle in your father's eye. It is us who makes and sets the terms." She paused, and her amber eyes glowered. "Or need I remind you who is keeping your dirty little secrets from unravelling your marriage. Keep testing me, Darius, and that could soon change."

Darius heaved a deep sigh, having expected this. He went towards the door to check there were no other ears in the vicinity before locking it twice behind him.

Serafina steeled against the impulse to flinch from the near deafening sound of jangling metal, the gesture unearthing something deeply buried. She stamped out whatever residual flicker it was and met Darius's gaze undaunted as he turned to her with a slow pivot.

"Go ahead. Tell Laila. Of course she'll leave me, but then I'll be freed from the pretence of having to maintain my civility towards you. And would you like to know what happens after?" He paced towards her with an ease, a calmness, but the impassioned hue of his eyes betrayed him. Beneath the thin glaze of his composure was a maniacal glee that simmered with contempt. "I'll exact my revenge by wiping every last blood sorceress off of this accursed map."

"You wouldn't dare." Serafina's lip curled, fangs edging out.

"Oh, but I would. You see, Mother, my chimeras are not corporeal. Their forms are made of inorganic matter. And the thing about inorganic matter is—?" He made a theatrical gesture with his hand as if to beckon her answer.

She refused to give him the satisfaction.

"It's impervious to blood sorcery." Darius foisted himself upon her until their faces were near, voice lowered to a silken whisper. "I could have your Viduas torn limb from limb right in front of you. For sheer amusement. And it wouldn't cost me a soul."

Serafina suppressed the snarl that threatened to come at his words until it was a tiny rumble in the back of her throat. She would not let him rattle her. Nor allow the tiny kernel of fear he'd embedded in her chest to sprout.

"However, I would rather it not come to that. It would bring me much greater pleasure to have us all work towards creating a better, stronger Mortos than the one that it once was. All I ask in return is to be allowed my one true source of pure happiness. If you take her away from me, well... the amount of blood I would have to spill to rinse away the outpouring of my grief would be immense, to say the least." A brief flicker of naked savagery bled through the façade, gone in a blink. "But if you'd sooner see me lose what I hold most dear, please—" He took a step back and raised his hand towards the door, offering escape. "Tell her."

Serafina let herself go statuesque with rage. Her only movement was the tremor of anger rippling through her as her gaze burrowed right through his skull. He had her at an impasse and she knew it. Resented it.

"No?" Darius cocked his head to one side. "Don't quite fancy it? Well then, I suppose this marks the end of this discussion, doesn't it?" He picked up a sharpened quill pen and held it out to her. "Sign."

Serafina's nostrils flared. She wanted nothing more than to let down her fangs and sink them into his cheek, tearing flesh and muscles from bone, but she took the pen and pricked her wrist with its sharpened edge, adding her signature in blood.

"Congratulations on becoming the official owner of the Widowlands." Darius tore the parchment from her grip and filed it away on his desk. "May your venture be ever prosperous."

Serafina seethed, her gaze near murderous. "This isn't over, Darius."

His smile bled shadows into the crevices of his cheeks and eyes until only the blue of his irises remained.

Even gazing upon his fiendish expression, Serafina couldn't quite conjure fear, only a reconciliation with the loss she'd long nursed to her chest. "Before we part ways tonight you should know something. The truth. Not whatever poisoned swill Lanius dribbled in your ear—and it's that I've always loved you."

That was enough to get the malevolent glee on his face to fade. Then his lips started to quiver, boyishly, before he was able to halt it.

"I love you. And I wanted you. I keep thinking, if only I'd had the courage, the selflessness, and the foresight to carry you away in my arms so that you and I could build some semblance of a life together." Sorrow bled into her voice as it lowered to a whisper. "Perhaps I could have stopped you from turning into this."

XVIII

MOTH-EATEN CURTAINS PEELED BACK AS SERAFINA watched Laila and Darius frolic in the courtyard. The two were clasped together like strangling vines, the intimacy of their embrace making it almost intrusive to look upon.

But that was typical of them. Having private moments in the midst of a crowd, marinating in the saccharine nectar of their love. It would be sickening if it weren't also somehow heartfelt to see two souls so completely and utterly lost in each other.

Serafina remained unmoved by it, her eyes narrowing before she let the curtain fall and relieved herself from playing witness to their overwrought exhibit.

There were other matters that required her attention now.

She knew that something needed to be done about those chimeras.

The question was what, and whether it would be within her capabilities when there was so much about them she still didn't know. She'd never encountered magic like this in all her four centuries—only a mind equal parts brilliant and baffling could've orchestrated it.

Until then she kept her attention on undermining the regina at court. And a rumour about her ineligibility to serve as a consort was the most fertile ground. All it took was a little whisper here, some gossip spread there, and soon the absence of an heir would be on the lips of the courtiers.

She ended up being the last to arrive at the next regina meeting. She strolled in to find Laila standing at the head of the table and picking up a sugar-coated strawberry from a crystal bowl.

"Please be seated." Laila outstretched her hand towards the final remaining chair. Once Serafina had taken it, she cleared her throat. "The rex and I have been convening regarding future steps since I began my Regina Council. Steps I'd like to share with you all." She gestured to the bowl of strawberries before her. "As you are aware, we have been putting together our aetherglass initiative as a way of revitalising agriculture in Mortos. We are very close to making moves on this initiative, but we require a diplomat to smooth over relations between ourselves and Soleterea. Thankfully, Prime Sabina Levitia has volunteered to be this diplomat.

Now I am aware you might all be concerned on how this affects you, but the rex and I have discussed ways in which this can benefit you all. Lupari will continue to have refuge at the coasts unhindered by occassi interference. Qarna will have greater access to crops. And the Vidua Nocte... will have their ownership of the Widowlands enshrined in law."

Serafina rolled her eyes.

"This will not remedy all the ills of the kingdom, but I am hopeful that it can be a motion for reform."

"All these prizes being doled out, and yet what do *we* stand to gain from this?" Domitia asked.

"I was coming to that." Laila strained for a smile. "I have decided that more resources need to be allocated to the budding development of girls in the kingdom."

Domitia grunted in disapproval. "What possible use could this have? Occasselle have charmed lives, with little concern other than whom they are to marry."

Serafina's eyes narrowed in suspicion as she tried to decipher Laila's motives. She could not allow herself to accept that Laila might be acting out of some authentic innate goodness. No, there were dark corners within every heart. Especially the pious ones. And Serafina was certain she would coax them out in due time.

"Yes, many occasselle such as yourself happen to thrive in their environments, but there is discord in many households that gets left unseen until drastic actions are taken. To avoid this I want to set up a charitable estate where occasselle might seek shelter from mistreatment and where they might be educated on matters of their bodies and expectations in marriage."

"I already educate girls on matters of religious piety, ladyship, and all other subjects pertaining to becoming wives and mothers to the nation," Domitia protested.

"That's precisely my point," Laila said. "I believe there are gaps in this that you are not overseeing. I mean no disrespect to you, of course—the work you do for the kingdom is vital. However... I believe occasselle need more support in the case of where things go wrong."

"Ah," Serafina said, realising her play. "You want to prevent more blood sorceresses."

Domitia chuckled. "Not an agenda one could argue against, I'm sure."

"Please, don't misunderstand me, Serafina Blackwood. What I would like is to alleviate the conditions that end up pushing desperate occasselle to the brink. Surely you can... find some merit in there being fewer battered wives. Fewer mistreated little girls."

Serafina scoffed. "How noble of you."

"I don't wish for us to be enemies on this matter. If anything I would like your help on this. You and the rest of the Vidua Nocte. I want to appoint you to help me manage this estate."

"*What?*" Domitia wheezed.

Though Serafina still held her reservations for the altruism behind the request, she almost had to consider whether it was worth seeing the rest of the room choke on their shock. "Truly?"

"We could use a blood sorceress in the ladies' realm. A seasoned one. And the others, well... they're not likely to accept." Laila tinkered with a gracious smile on her lips. "So I extend my hand to you. Not to extinguish your faction but to embrace it. We could all do with a little less division in this country."

Serafina contemplated the offer and wondered what to make of it. As was often the case, Laila had used her finely-tuned instincts to hone in on a cause her opponent held most dear. To accept it would be a gamble on Serafina's end, one she could not determine the result of. "I am willing to let bygones be bygones."

Anything to lessen the stranglehold Domitia had on society. She knew how these occasselle played. Their games and schemes.

"This is ridiculous." Domitia exploded from her chair. "I hardly think the regina is fit to declare what young occasselle need to thrive in this kingdom. Especially when—"

Laila's expression clouded. "When?"

"Especially when said regina has yet to produce an heir."

Laila's breath caught in her throat.

Serafina knew this would come eventually. Mortesians did not mince words. Yet even a soul as rotten through with spite as hers couldn't help but suffer a measure of guilt from Laila's crestfallen face.

She was quick to brush it off. "The rex and I have not even been wed a year yet."

"Yes, but due to the unusual nature of your coupling, I can see why it might become cause for conversation. And subsequent conspiracy. Many occasselle already took insult when the rex refused them in favour of a solarite, Your Majesty," said Domitia. "If they find out about your incompatibility in the marriage bed, then that insult grows more grave but also sparks opportunism for people to try sneaking their daughters into his bed."

Laila stuttered but knew she could say nothing to refute Domitia's claims. Nothing more than affirming her own desire for fidelity. But she knew such sentiments would seem mawkish before her Council.

"There is a way out of this," Domitia said, having grown more confident by the second. "The rex may take up a concubine. If you choose an eligible bearer from one of the noble families—"

Laila made a tremulous sound as tears pricked in her eyes.

Serafina shifted in her seat. She believed herself to have wanted this—until she saw the sharks go in for blood and leave nothing spared. *Calante's wrath, Domitia's ravaging the poor girl.*

"This could both settle tensions and lessen the weight of your burden."

"We are not discussing this."

"You won't be doing yourself any favours in the long haul, Your Majesty. You'll only continue to be out of place among the ladies whose favour you are so desperate to court." Domitia huffed. "All reginas come with shortcomings, but this particular one is impossible to overlook."

Laila had heard enough by that point. She stood from her seat and rushed from the room.

Serafina sighed as she withdrew from her chair and chased her down the hall. "Laila Regina," she called. "Laila!"

The sound of her name on Serafina's lips startled her into slowing her pace, but she kept walking forward. "Leave me in peace."

"Laila…" Serafina reached out to touch her shoulder.

She snatched it away. "How does Domitia know about the our infertility?"

"Doubtless she's heard gossip. It's hardly a difficult leap to make what with your… conflicting natures."

"But no one ever knew for certain. There was never anything conclusive." Laila placed her hands on her hips, eyes narrowed. "Someone must have said *something* for her to know about it."

Serafina swallowed, knowing her chance to escape culpability was slim. "I may have, but surely you didn't think no one else would come to the same conclusions."

"Why?" Laila asked. "Why would you do this to me?"

"Don't act innocent. You threw the first strike by conspiring with Darius to give me that botched Widowlands contract."

"That was never devised with ill intent! We *have* to put forth that we are not encouraging membership for the good of the kingdom."

"You say it isn't personal? Well neither is this."

"*Humiliating* me isn't personal? I thought you stood for the betterment of female rights throughout *all* the kingdom. Am I not considered one of them? Or does my race deem me unworthy of the courtesy of your protection?"

Serafina gaped, speechless.

Laila turned on her heel and stormed away.

One of the numerous benefits to marriage was the promise of stability. Darius could retire to his kingly chambers sure he would find Laila inside of them either sprawled across a divan with a book in hand, forehead delicately wrinkled in concentration, or idly muttering Soltongue to herself in that sweet, melodious cadence he'd come to find a source of calm.

No longer did he have to contend with the apprehension her prior flighty nature induced in him. The feline instinct he had to ensnare her with his claws so she might not flee like a bird from his grip.

Sadly for Darius, tonight was a return to form as he entered the rooms to find his regina was absent. And not only that, she had taken many of her nightclothes and toiletries and presumably moved them over to the Regina Wing. Malaise settled into him as he recognised the pointed gesture she was trying to make.

With a sigh he pivoted towards her quarters, sifting through the correct words he could muster to make amends. In the end he didn't end up finding her there, but instead traced her to the library, where she was poring over one of the torrid romance novels she had found a stash of and been addicted to ever since.

She did not stir when she heard Darius enter. She didn't acknowledge him at all. Rather, she sharply turned a page in irritation with an audible scrape of paper.

"I can see you've chosen to retire in the regina quarters tonight." Darius leaned against a bookcase in a display of nonchalance. He felt anything but.

"Yes, I should like to have some alone time this evening." Laila loudly flipped another page. "I hope you don't mind the lack of my company. Though if need be you can always replace it."

"Laila," Darius said softly.

It reached something in her enough for her to flinch. Still she carried on with her reading.

Darius lifted himself off of the bookcase to approach her side. "Talk to me."

Laila closed her eyes, breathing out slowly. "They know. Domitia knows. You should've heard them talk about me. It's as though I am defective."

"You know full well I don't think of you like that."

"It doesn't matter what you think." Laila slammed down her book. Then she settled her temper. "What matters is that as a consort I have a duty. One main duty. And I cannot fulfil it. Regardless of any love you show me, they're always going to look upon you with pity and think you've been saddled with something insufficient."

He grabbed her hand before she could pick up the book again, pressing it to his lips. "I apologise that they made you feel that way."

Laila's shoulders sagged before she glanced up at him with vulnerability widening her eyes. "I don't want you to sire an heir." She paused to swallow before rushing to expel the rest of her thoughts. "I know that's selfish of me. I know it's not... the most politically sound decision. I understand that as regina I have a duty to Mortos. But I am also a wife. And you have no idea how maddening it was to sit there and hear them talk of you taking some occassella to bed. All I could envision was her in your arms, you kissing and touching her the way you've done with me. Having to see the proof of it swelling her with child. Your child. It made me feel like I was being gutted."

Darius nodded as she spoke, stroking her backhand with both thumbs. "Then I won't do it."

"You know it's not that simple."

"There are alternative routes to gaining an heir without me siring one, Laila. It might not be in line with tradition, but there's been nothing quite traditional about any of this, has there?" The corner of his mouth lifted wryly.

Laila found her own lips perking up in return. "What are you suggesting?"

"In the vaults of the Abbakon Cathedral there is a tome known as the *Sanguis Vinetum*. Occassi have been using it for generations to trace our bloodlines. Past rexes have also used it to exterminate any potential threats to the throne. But there are still far removed descendants of Calante through female lines who I am sure would leap at the chance to have a taste of legitimacy."

Laila scrunched her lips to one side. "You're proposing to choose an heir from another line?"

"Same as the bridal pageants rexes have hosted in the past." Darius's eyes flashed with cunning intent. "If I pick a daughter and legitimise her as my own I can make the other nobles swear fealty by having them compete for her hand. These families will be too busy trying to ingratiate themselves to me in the hopes I might choose them to care for the preservation of my own line. Though such a thing comes with its own risks, should we open that door. Rest assured, I have contingencies in place for that. All I need is your approval."

Laila swivelled round in her seat to take his hands in hers. "I'll support you anyway I can."

"As for any talk of me taking another to my bed, put that out of your mind. You're the only one for me. There might have been many before you but there will certainly be none after you. I don't even see their faces."

His words paired with the bright blue intensity of his gaze caused a wild flutter in the pit of her stomach. Before she knew it she had sprung from her seat to pull him into a kiss, her hands clasping the sides of his face to meld their mouths together. She lunged back from the shock of her action.

Darius spared not even a moment to drag her once more into the embrace, kissing her until she sighed.

"We should probably discuss more of this—" she started to protest between the kisses, a shiver prickling her spine as he slid his hands down it.

"Oh, that can wait," he told her firmly, pulling her back into a kiss. He didn't manage to embrace her for long before she disappeared in his arms, having used an enchantment to turn herself invisible.

Darius's eyes flew open when he realised he was grasping air, then his head whipped round to locate her.

A beguiling giggle floated through the library's draught. "You didn't think it would be that easy, did you?"

He couldn't help but chuckle in response as he folded his hands behind his back and started to prowl for her. "Now if you don't get back here right now... I will be forced to hunt you down."

She went notably quiet after that. "Tell you what—"

Darius pivoted sharply as her voice came from another direction.

"If you can catch me... you can have me."

The offer stirred his blood, the arousal of a chase providing an alchemical high. He started to move with more purpose, gripping a shelf and poking his head behind it where he thought he'd heard her last. He only found her shoes, but he knew it put him on the right path.

"Laila..." Darius traversed down the aisle of bookcases. "Do you really think you can hide from me for long?" He moved three aisles following her scent before he found his next clue—Laila's filmy undergarments deposited on the ground. He snuffed a laugh as he picked up the lace-edged fabric. "Oh, so it's this sort of game you're playing."

Another giggle sounded from far off.

Darius narrowed his eyes, pausing in thought. Then he analysed his surroundings for markers of where she might be. He heard the bats getting agitated in a particular area and went there next, stalking forward in near silent footsteps.

There he found her nightgown among the cacophony of their flapping wings and whiny screeches. He bit his lip, now even more frantic to find her as his canines itched to descend.

While her invisibility shield was strong, it was not entirely imperceptible, a faint shimmer could be seen from the outline of her body if one were to look with keen enough sight.

That was eventually how he managed to snag her by the wrist, breaking through her enchantment as he shoved her naked form up against a shelf.

Laila yelped in surprise as he pinned her wrists above her head in one hand.

"Well, now that I've caught you," he said against her lips, "I can finally have what I want."

"No..." Laila whined in defeat, attempting to squirm free of him. This had not been the initial plan on how to spend her evening, but when she felt the scrape of Darius's fangs against that one sensitive spot beneath her jaw she couldn't stop the shudder going through her. The desire coiled tight in her core.

She managed to wriggle her wrists out of his grip to try and flee, but that only provoked the hunter in his blood. Within moments, he had her pinned up against the shelves and his stiff arousal pressed against her from behind. Something feral took hold in him as he latched his teeth into her shoulder—a gesture intended to subdue her—followed by a gentle flicker of his tongue.

A strangled whimper caught in Laila's throat as her body arched into his, seeking the heat of him through his clothes. She continued to tussle with all her playful might to resist his capture as Darius slid his hand between her thighs. He could feel just how excited this had left her, along with the way her bosom heaved in shallow pants he fondled her clit with the pads of his fingers.

Laila writhed at his touch and ground against him with desperate hips, eager for more. Her frenzied pace provoked a measured exhale from him as his arousal pulsed and throbbed from the contact. She sped up her movements, wanting him as frantic for her as she was for him.

But Darius kept tracing her lazily, his thumb soft over her clit. Laila whispered his name, putting her hand atop of his to dip his fingers inside her. He teased her open with slow pumps from his fingers, her spine going rigid as he curled them inside her enough to have the pit of her stomach tingling and her legs weak.

Gods, he knows my body so well, she thought as her toes curled. And what dangerous knowledge it was in the palm of his hand. To be able to make her yield to him with a single well-placed touch. She could feel her climax beckoning the more he continued and she knew it wouldn't be long for her now. A heat ran up her spine, spreading through her like a fever. She clutched the bookshelves to steady herself as her legs went numb.

Darius started to unbutton his trousers, and Laila, once more, made a futile bid to stagger away from him now he was distracted. He caught her with laughable ease, swinging her around to throw her on top of a nearby table.

"You ought to know by now you've been outmanoeuvred," he taunted, hand encasing her throat to keep her pinned to the table. "Struggle all you want... I'm not letting you get away."

Seeing no other move to make, Laila took a fistful of his shirt and pulled him into a kiss. His hand curved around the small of her back as their mouths collided with intensity, a moan of yearning shared between them. Then she removed his kaftan, unbuttoned his shirt, and wrapped an arm around his neck to compress their chests together as she took his shaft in hand.

The kiss broke with a ragged breath as Darius hummed in satisfaction, her fingers encircling his girth and gripping firmly. She kissed the bulge in his throat before trailing her lips along the sharp incline of his jawline down to his chin.

"Remember you're mine," she said, smiling serenely. He'd never truly grown accustomed to that. The way she looked at him. "I don't want you doing this with anyone else."

"Trust me, I'm all yours," Darius vowed, his mouth curling with mischievous intent. "Every inch of me."

"Good." She rolled the head of his cock between her thumb and fingers until he moaned. "Because if I have to share, then things might start to get ugly."

His breath hitched as she ran the fat end of her palm along his head, causing the foreskin to shift from the friction. Hearing her stake claim on him so possessively made him that much harder than before. "We definitely wouldn't want that."

She tightened her legs around his waist, twirling them round so that it was him flipped over on the table with her nestling on his lap. A look of mischievous intent winked in her eyes as she stroked the head of his cock along her before she sank down on him, palms splayed against his chest for purchase as she drove her hips forth.

Soon they were both sighing as she rode out her earlier frustration on him frantically enough to make his neck arch from swooning. Darius clutched the table as it started to rock from the vigour of her movements. The books rattled on the shelves behind them, but they were too immersed to care.

"Laila—" He grunted in that desperate way he did when he was reaching his limit.

Laila sank her nails into his shoulders to drag until she drew blood, despairing at the thought it might heal. She wanted to leave a brand on him as he had branded her. A public display of her claim.

The sharpness of the pain was enough to make him come, and she kept riding him until he went soft before letting out a short, little pant. "I suppose that was better than sleeping alone."

"You suppose?" he echoed in disbelief.

"Can't let your ego grow too large." Laila wrinkled her nose in amusement as she cupped his cheek, stroking it with her thumb. "Though I hope you realise I meant what I said. No one is to have you like this but me. I'll be the ruin of anyone else you touch."

"You already have been." He traced his knuckles along her taut stomach that would never swell with child for him.

She caught his hand and held it to her. "Do you ever... wish we could have a child together?"

The question surprised him enough it brought him to silence. "Do you?"

"It sounds silly, but I never thought about it before I met you. It's not really how we do it. But when we wed I found myself thinking of what it might be like to have something of you in my daughter... perhaps she'd have your dimples." She slid her thumb along his cheek. "Or the shade of your eyes."

"And now?"

Laila shook her head and nestled on his chest. "I'm content having you all to myself. Part of me just... worries that I'm proving inadequate. That there are things you might want—things that are natural to want—that I cannot give you."

"I'm holding all the family I could want in my arms right now." He wrapped his arms tightly around her. "No amount of petty squabbling among the nobles could change that. Now onto other matters... such as how I might punish Domitia for her insult against you."

"Darius." Laila sighed heavily, taking his hand and resting his palm against her cheek. "I know you love me. And I treasure how much you desire to shield me from harm, wherever source it comes from... but I don't want you to torture people in my name."

"I understand," Darius said. "You have a gentle heart and I cherish you for it. But the people here—my people—they don't respond to kind words, and graces, and attempts at understanding. They respond to action, violent action, if necessary. I am only trying to ascertain that you are not taken advantage of."

"Have you ever tried mercy? Perhaps they might surprise you if you did."

"Even in the event there might be some miniscule benefit..." Darius stopped to consider it before shaking his head. "The costs, if it fails, would be far greater."

"Promise me something." She brought him close in an embrace. "Try it my way. Just this once. And if it fails... I'll be open to anything you suggest."

His brow furrowed in hesitation.

"Please," she said softly, pecking him on the lips. "This is what I want from you. Please love me the way I wish to be loved."

"All right. If that's what you wish of me, then I shall grant it."

Yula cursed under her breath as a group of wine bottles tumbled from her hands onto a thankfully rug-covered floor. With a sigh, she gathered them back up to tuck beneath her arms and carried on down into the cellars, where she placed them all into their empty racks.

She snorted as she wondered what they could possibly want with so much wine. And in so many varying flavours and bouquets. She thought about the times she would sample a few of them at Domitia's estate. Each one had their own quality—from the high sour-sweet notes and to rich, full-bodied basses.

A cup or two would often be enough to coast her through an evening. The servants would top up the bottles with water after, praying that the occassi didn't perceive the trick. She felt tempted by the prospect, but she thought better of it with her venom addiction still lurking in her veins, ready to seize hold of her.

She slotted the last bottle and prepared to leave when a clink sounded behind her. Yula turned instantly, her pulse thrumming. Seeing nothing, she put a hand on her chest to settle herself.

"Just hearing things," she said to herself, walking towards the door. Then it happened again. The rustle of a draught along a row of bottles made her halt in her tracks. "H-hello...?" Yula swallowed as her eyes darted around. "Is someone there?" She withdrew a bottle from one of the rows and readied it to strike.

A hand seized her by the wrist and twisted it painfully while another shoved her up against the racks.

Yula cried out as her grip slackened on the bottleneck, and it burst into a puddle on the floor.

Katerina tutted. "What a mess you've made."

"Please—don't—"

Katerina's hand clapped over Yula's pitiful wail as she shushed her. "Listen to me very carefully. I have a job for you and you'd best not screw it up. Or"—she bared her fangs with a sharp hiss—"I'll hex you to murder every single person with your blood running through their veins. And then yourself."

Yula gave a frantic whine of acquiescence and nodded.

"Good." Katerina took a moment to neaten her hair. "I know you're serving the regina personally. So you ought to know some of her secrets. Tell me... how close is she to attaining aetherglass?"

"I don't know. I—"

Katerina clenched her fist around Yula's throat, siphoning off her air. "Don't lie to me... You'd do well not to make me upset."

"Please—" Yula croaked, tears springing into her eyes. "Please—"

Katerina loosened her hold and let her stagger backwards, wheezing to drag life back into her lungs.

"All... I know... is that she is going to be receiving a visitor soon. From"—Yula coughed up the dust-filled musk of the cellar—"Soleterea."

"Good girl." Katerina reached out to pet her on the head before Yula flinched from her touch. "You've done very well for me. Now, I want you to tell this bit of information to Domitia Orlovia. Understand? If you are caught... you and I never once spoke."

Yula sniffled a dangle of snot back into her nose, nodding. Then she lifted the skirt of her dress to dry her face. "Wait. But—" She looked up to find Katerina was already gone.

XIX

FTER SHE'D SLIPPED BACK INTO HER BODY FROM THE Astral Realm, Lyra fled from Setâre and didn't look back. She stole away in the night with nothing but the clothes on her back and rejected the numerous buzzings of her compact mirror as Lucrèce tried in vain to contact her.

She knew the consequences she would reap for her abrupt departure. She didn't care about any of them. All she knew now was that she needed to return home. To Soleterea. To the sole person with enough rank and influence to turn the tides of destiny in the direction she needed them to go.

A scent trail of warm, fresh pastries wafted from the ovens of Le Creissant, mingling with the sweetness of wisteria-covered storefronts. Windchimes tinkled as customers wove in and out of their boutiques with delicious wares in hand, lovingly baked and hand-painted with flourishes of frosting.

Lyra's stomach clenched the moment she caught a whiff of it and was struck hard by a crippling pang of nostalgia. It'd been so long since she'd been among these streets. Too long. Yet they were still as welcoming as ever. She had to fight her tears when she heard the soft coo of the doves overhead, heralded by the diaphanous rain of their iridescent feathers.

She came here on horseback so she could immerse herself fully in the sights and sounds and smells. Part of her wanted to click her ankles into her steed and dismount, taking shade beneath the inviting frills of the parasols and helping herself to an ice cream wafer. Thankfully, she resisted the impulse, seeing it for the distraction it was, and continued on the sun-gilded road to the palace.

It was late enough in evening when she arrived for a chill to rest on her nape in spite of the sun still being upright. She prayed the guards would not bar her entry for, while she knew them by name, she'd seen them last when she'd handed in her uniform and took off for pastures new. Such a cowardly act. She realised that now. She'd run so far from duty with her head turned over her shoulder that she didn't realise she'd circled back.

"That you, Lyra?" Narcisse rubbed the dross from his eyes to get a better look. And sure enough, they had not deceived him.

"It's been a long time," Lyra said, a smile twitching on her lips. "You couldn't sneakily let me in, could you?"

"Of course!" He made haste to open the gates for her and Lyra rode through, leaping down from her horse in a swift movement.

"I'm entrusting him into your care." She handed the reins to him. "I must meet with the impératrice. Is she available?"

"She is taking in the sun in her garden. You know the way."

Lyra saluted him in thanks as she made her way through familiar marmoreal halls decorous with stucco, echoing the whispers of gossiping starlets. She paid them no mind as they halted in their tracks to gawk and point at her, each of them with the same question on their lips—their silver knight had returned to them. *Why here? And why now?*

In the garden itself, Amira was being fanned by alternating enchanted animated peacock feathers. She'd stretched comfortably to soak in as much as she could from the waning twilight, her cursed-blighted veins considerably healed from this continuous exposure.

While Amira had not fully mended, she was improving, and that was the best she could have hoped for with an injury that struck her so grievously. After so much suffering and torment, having a moment where she could lie in the sun with her pain reduced to a dull thud of what it once was gave her a peaceful visage.

"Hello, Lyra."

The sprite leapt in alarm, having not anticipated her voice. She assumed Amira was sleeping until she spoke. "Your Luminosity."

"So you have finally decided to return to your rightful place." Amira's lips twitched in amusement. "Did you have your fun with Lucrèce while it lasted?"

"You... knew I was with her?"

"I have my networks in Setâre." Amira heaved an exhausted sigh as if the answer should be obvious. "Particularly with... my mother. And I know you went to see her. Why?"

Lyra grimaced as she took a seat on a nearby log and laced her fingers together. "Lucrèce wishes to summon the Holy Phoenix."

Amira barked a laugh. "Of course she does." She removed her sunglasses and rested one handle on her bottom lip. "And what did my mother say?"

"What does it matter? You know it's not possible for another... five hundred years."

"Don't play coy with me, Lyra. I know you wouldn't be here if you didn't think there was something I could do about it."

Lyra skidded her thumb along the brand of the feather. She couldn't let Amira know of it, not yet. "Esterre was the first. That's how you... survived for so long after the tragedy in Aurea Park. Your bloodline and the Phoenix have a special connection. We thought we could sway Aurélie to join our forces in the hopes we could end chaos. However, she told us something else instead."

"What?"

"It's about Laila. The Elders are using her as a shield to ward off Calante."

"That's absurd." Amira snorted. "How could *Laila* possibly be used as a shield..." Her face darkened. "Ah. I see."

"Your Luminosity, you have to help me." Lyra fell to her knees. "If there's any part of you that can find it within your heart to forgive Laila after all she said—"

Amira raised her hand to silence her. "This is an entirely reckless plan. Placing the very thing that can extinguish Calante in the clutches of his potential vessel. What could they be thinking?"

"Laila stops him from taking hold. As long as she keeps Darius tethered to his soul, Calante cannot take over."

"Yes, so long as Darius proves gallant in his intentions." Amira twisted her lips. "I tried to capture the Phoenix once before. When I was younger and more foolish, I sent a sprite lover of mine to retrieve a feather. It ended... poorly." She winced as if disturbing the tenderness of an old wound. "After that, I set the goal aside from my mind and pursued it no further. With the information you bring to my attention, I have to wonder if there was a reason for it. My desperation. My failure. Perhaps that destiny wasn't meant for me..."

"And now?" Lyra asked.

"If it comes down to retrieving Laila from the clutches of that creature... I suppose as her mother, I must." There was no affection in her voice—merely a resigned sense of duty.

"You *suppose* you must?" Lyra scoffed.

"I am sensing condemnation in your tone."

"It's our fault this has reached the point that it has. Yours... and mine. Laila was hurting for so long right before my eyes and I didn't see it. I didn't let myself see it until she ran off with that—"

"I loved her. The same as you."

"And what does it say of us that this love was deemed so insufficient she thought *Darius's* was superior to it?"

"So you agree with her assessment? You believe *I* am the true monster?" It was not a difficult conclusion to reach with the ferity befitting a lion on her face. But Lyra had stared far worse beasts in the eye and came out of it scarless.

"That is not what I intend to say at all. But you cannot deny that Laila has sought to attain the impossible heights of perfection just so you might give her a crumb of praise. She doesn't have to do that with Darius because he is obsessed with her as she is. What use is it, then, to keep climbing the gauntlet for a glory that might never be realised if she can simply let herself fall into the possession of the wicked?"

Amira made a 'tch' sound through her teeth, but behind the curtain of dismissal, her mind had started to pull some strings. "Send for Lucrèce... It's time we had a discussion."

Dr Isuka picked up a sandwich from her lunch and took a hard crunch of a bite into cold salmon, cucumber, and juicy tomato. The bread had been shaped to resemble a rabbit—an endearing trait her beloved, Jun, had given all the lunches he'd prepared for her in the eighteen years they'd been together.

Thinking of him now made her wonder how she'd respond if she were in Elina's place. Of course, it was different for her and Jun than Sadik and Elina, for the latter had been separated for over a decade. And yet, Akira spent enough time in the lab for their love to be perfunctory at best. Something they'd fallen into out of habit and saw no reason to rid themselves of. In that regard, one couldn't say with any certainty how she might react to such a dismal circumstance. Would she ever forgive him for making such a choice? Would *he*?

Isuka scrubbed the thought from her mind and focused on finishing her sandwich. After that, she prepared to go through the footage of the dreams they'd extracted from Sadik's mind thus far. She picked up a remote controller and used it to scroll through reels of cloud-smudged darkness, natural for a slumbering mind before a dream could emerge, and then noticed the blink of an image skip by her so swiftly she thought she herself had conjured it.

Isuka paused the reel and rewound but found nothing. Whatever it had been had fizzled away like static, almost as if she'd watched it become actively erased from Sadik's subconscious as it happened. Her lips wrinkled with a scowl as she pushed forward again with the footage, pausing when it shifted to the pallid frost of Mortesian winter.

A shudder rippled down her spine at the mere sight of it, as if a coldness had reached out from the screen to seize her in its clutches. She took a sip of tea to warm herself and pressed play, following Sadik's journey through the desolate wilderness forked by black trees.

She hadn't known what she was hoping to find in his head and almost resigned herself to there being nothing at all of interest. As unpleasant as the setting was, she'd been expecting a lot more from it, considering the fuss Sadik had kicked up.

Then the figure came.

She'd been unprepared when it emerged, and its suddenness frightened her to alertness. The length of black hair was like moonlit ink down her spine, and she'd thought it was a river until its shape came further into view. Immediately, she paused to study it. Then she zoomed into it. Closer and closer. Until—

"Emica," Isuka whispered. The remote fell out of her hand and clattered on the hard stone flooring. *It couldn't be. It couldn't.*

For so long. Over twenty years. She had sought to scatter her long lost friend's ashes from her mind. But it was to no avail. There was far too much ash; so much of their lives had been entwined together that to bury Emica would be to bury half of herself, too.

She pushed forward in her chair, reaching out to palm Emica's tiny body as if doing so would render her physical enough to touch. "How?"

She scrambled for the fallen remote and fumbled over the buttons with trembling fingers until eventually she was able to press play again, eager to devour the contents of this encounter.

When the cry released from Emica's lungs, it pierced through the screen like the shrill caw of an eagle, cracking the glass. Isuka cried out in pain as she fell from her chair, the drums in her ears bursting and leaking trickles of warm blood down her cheeks. A low groan squeezed out of Isuka's chest as she lifted her eyes to the screen enough to see the misshapen lizard creature bearing down upon a trembling Sadik. *Familiar.* The sight made her recall the unidentifiable mutant pacing about its cage.

"Is this..." Dr Isuka composed herself enough to grow cold. Emica's sighting had fumbled her enough to lose her footing and she had to gain it back. "Is this how chimeras are made?"

She scrolled through hours and hours of footage, snipping them from Sadik's recorded dreams to dissect them frame by frame.

What was the connection? Her mind probed as she attempted to reassemble the jigsaw and fit the missing pieces. Twenty years ago, Dr Hariken took up communion with the cryptograph, after which she suffered debilitating nightmares and subliminal thoughts all the way up to her disappearance. About five years after that, the first of the chimeras arrived from an unknown source, pioneered by Darius as weapons of deterrence.

Emica had been that source. A fact which Akira now struggled to reconcile with. How could her beloved friend, who'd never even take up a hand to crush an insect, become the machine that orchestrated such destruction?

Emptiness and malaise and tedium with no end! Her friend's cry rattled around her skull like a coin before it dropped. *He takes you whole, fresh and vibrant, and squeezes you until he's able to feed on the fat of your pulp to sustain himself.*

That must be it then; Calante fed on her despair, her isolation, her spiritual agony, and twisted it into something wretched. And he would do the same with Sadik, in time.

The longer she sat with this inevitability, the deeper her frustration sank in her chest. Her hands bundled into fists as she slammed them down on the table, over and over and over until she sensed her bones starting to crack from the impact.

She hissed as she brought her throbbing hands up to her face and sank down into a chair. *This can't have been all for nothing!* Her gaze drifted over to Sadik Yilan, motionless under the fume of anaesthetic. He'd refused to end Emica out of concern for his own fate, but it wouldn't be enough to spare him.

They were two doomed souls clinging to each other as they surrendered to the bone-crunching tug of the Abyss. Who would emerge the victor?

A buzz from her compact mirror summoned her out of her dejection, and she hurried to answer it.

"Hello, Akira." Dr Mielette's face was sun-kissed radiance. Her time in Setâre had done wonders for her unearthly glow. "I'm afraid I have some unfortunate news."

"Truly, I am not sure how much more I can take…" Dr Isuka rubbed at her brows, thinking almost hysterically how much could've been averted if she'd chosen another line of work.

"Lyra de Lis has fled." Dr Mielette sighed. "I am assuming it can only be to the impératrice, which means it's not long before she is alerted to the entirety of our plot."

"*What?*" Dr Isuka shot upright.

"Worry not, we still have some time until then. For now I must ask you to continue as usual. What have you discovered for me?"

Dr Isuka relayed the contents of her discovery regarding the chimeras, Sadik, and Emica and watched as Dr Mielette's mirth migrated into something indistinct.

"I see." She paused for a beat. "This could be useful information to have up our sleeve. If we let the impératrice know, she may allow us to continue our operations."

Panic burned at her nape, but Akira did her best to retain her calmness. "And then…?"

"I do not know what Lyra was told. But whatever it was, it was distressing enough to make her abscond and seek Amira. I believe she would only do so if she thought Laila was in deep enough peril. *If* we find out what that information is…"

"I want Darius Calantis eliminated."

Lucrèce's voice sputtered out and her expression folded into her best approximation of condolence. "I understand your desire for vengeance, Akira. But I must ask we consider this rationally. Killing Darius when we have no idea of the control he has over Emica will not save her and it will not resolve our issue. We need to find another way."

"But... why?" Akira's voice had become the petulant whine of a child, and she loathed herself for it. "I thought you were supposed to protect us. To save us."

"We are saving you, Dr Isuka. However, in order to do so, we must take a stance of non-interference regarding Darius Calantis until we have all the information. He is the potential vessel, like we suspect. We cannot risk approaching them and setting off a sequence of events that allows Calante to gain a foothold. The consequences would be far too grave."

"Then... what was all of this for?"

"Take heart. You did a great deal for humanity in all your work. Expanded our knowledge of chaos magic by startling proportions." Lucrèce infused her tone with heartfelt gratitude. "This is not a failure, Dr Isuka. You should take pride in what you accomplished. I'll let you have a moment to compose yourself."

Akira discovered she had started trembling. Nausea congested her stomach and burned a trail up her throat. She put a hand to her mouth to stifle a retching as she thought to all the bodies zipped up in the morgue. To Elina's pallid face.

"I can't let this be over," she whispered to herself. "I can't."

She stumbled out of her chair on shaky legs and made her way towards the oneirometer where Sadik Yilan slumbered. As she watched the waxen stillness of his face she thought of what she had seen unfold on the screens recording his consciousness. It was then she understood what it was she had to do next.

With a few button presses the oneiromancer apparatus bleeped its conclusion and the lock on the door unlatched. Anaesthetic steam wafted from the glass as it retracted, and Sadik wheezed back into consciousness.

"Sadik?" Dr Isuka called to him as she took him by the shoulders and gave him a light shake. "Sadik? Can you hear me?"

Sadik let out a groan as the whites of his eyes bled entirely black. He looked at her with tear-filled relief, eyes shimmering with a fondness that sent a trickle down her spine. "Akira..."

"Yes, good." She sighed in relief. "Thank the stars your faculties are intact."

"It's been a long time... my old friend."

Her heart drew to a shuddering halt.

It can't be.

When Lucrèce Mielette learned of the impératrice's desire to parley, her first thought was how woefully overdue it was. The second was how best she could barter to attain the upper hand in the discussion. The little she had woven together of this complex tapestry of strife was that she was now unable to move any further without having the allegiance of the Rose dynasty. This made having to cede the election for the next impératrice to them a near certainty, and she doubted Amira would be so unpredictable as not to request it.

With this in mind, Lucrèce needed a way to secure a win for herself and her kin that did not completely erase them from the running, and she decided the truth of the chimeras needed to remain her trump card, tucked away for last resort.

The impératrice's arrival at the chateau was presaged by a shimmer of afternoon sunlight that polished the dining table's faded gilt marquetry. Lucrèce took that as auspicious as her maid brewed orange and vanilla tea and poured it with a dulcet tinkle into her teapot. Citrus and spice entwined into an oversweet perfume that Lucrèce hoped might be seen as ambient when Amira was shown into the room with Lyra alongside her.

"Thank you for meeting with us, Lucrèce," Amira said. "It's been a long time coming, wouldn't you agree?"

"Quite." Lucrèce poured a piping hot cup of tea. She elected to become the passenger in this conversation in the hopes of hearing everything Amira knew. "How would you like to start?"

"I've heard twittering that you've been snooping around regarding the Phoenix." Amira tutted at her and shook her head. "You ought to know better than that, Lucrèce. But since you've started down that path, you should be made aware that Esterre Rose has left certain precautions in place to ensure such power cannot be abused. It's a barrier very few can overcome. Not even myself. Though to be certain I've attempted it."

"But there is a method," Lucrèce deduced. "Lyra would not have fled so quickly had there not been."

The sprite shifted uncomfortably and busied her hands with a frosted madeleine.

"Say that there is," Amira said, "and I were to tell you, would you cease with these relentless attacks against my dynasty?"

Lucrèce's laugh was so enriched with joy it sounded of coins jingling. "I was wondering when we'd arrive at this point. You are quite efficient."

"I do all that I do in the name of preserving myself and my own. We are not so different in that regard. In spite of our division we all have the same aim: We want to put an end to this chaos disaster once and for all."

Lucrèce's mouth twitched in response. "Be that as it may... your conception of how this conflict ends and mine are vastly different."

"Regardless, it is clear you cannot accomplish anything without our allegiance."

"Perhaps... but I do know a secret of my own." A light of knowing cascaded across her lavender eyes. "I know how Darius Calantis creates his chimeras."

Amira ground her teeth together so firmly they screeched. "How?"

"Ah," Lucrèce said, "I think I'll keep that one to myself for now. So we both have something essential to offer one another."

"What is it that you want, Lucrèce? Spit it out and be done with it."

"You may have the crown if it so pleases you, Amira. I believe it may help persuade Laila back to our side. But in return I want Calantis. Dead or alive is of no consequence to me, but he will be mine."

Lyra's jaw tightened. She knew convincing Laila over to them alone would be a feat even without having to sway her into relinquishing Darius into Lucrèce's hands. "If this is to work then we'll need to give Laila something. Something more concrete than political favours as promises. Whether we like it or not, Darius is the one she loves and I highly doubt she would sit comfortably with this fate without cause."

"Yes, I am afraid she's correct," Amira said. "I overestimated my daughter's appetite for ambition when put against other forms of... sentiment. She'll not give up her beloved imp without a struggle. That is, unless you can offer something to convince us."

Lucrèce drummed her fingers along the linen tablecloth, deliberating how much she could breadcrumb the truth. "I can't tell you the full extent of it, but I can offer you a name..."

"Who?"

"Emica Hariken."

XX

PRAWLED ACROSS THE SEATS OF PLUMP RED LEATHER, Sabina twiddled a coin along her fingers as her carriage drew closer to the coast. She bounced an ankle on her knee, soothed by the steady rocking motions of a journey left uninhibited by monster attacks.

The strict guiding hand of Darius's leadership seemed to have done the unthinkable—Mortos had been *tamed*, its insurmountable horrors quelled and beaten back to the fringes, and a new skin had started healing over the scarred surface.

Perhaps this would be enough to silence the phantoms of doubt that had gotten purchase in her mind. Darius had brought a much needed change to Mortos. He had dragged this country kicking and screaming from Lanius's benighted reign into something of a dawning age, exposing stubborn minds to his enlightened principles little by little instead of removing the rock of tradition they had taken shelter under outright and sending them skittering.

Sabina had been rewarded enough from lending him her loyalty that she had to trust that whatever reservations she had of his more brutish plots would come round to some inspired outcome she simply could not see. She could not afford to believe otherwise.

Her coin flashed under the sun's radiance as she flipped it again, palm open to catch it, when a weight crashed against the carriage. The coin bounced off the walls, clattering to some unreachable corner beneath the seats.

"Sorry, miss," came the driver's sheepish mutter. "We're here."

Sabina grunted as she opened the door to the salt-laced air of the seaside and awaited the landing of an airship at the docks. She leaned against the carriage, one foot propped against the frame as the airship floated down from the sky and dispersed the clouds into swirling vapour.

Once it had docked the ramp descended, and then came the unexpected twinkle of Amira Rose, her diamond-encrusted cane tapping as she brought herself earthward. She'd swaddled herself against the cold in an ermine-trimmed woollen cape threaded with enough pearls to make it a firmament.

Her gaze met Sabina's with a politely poised smile neither dismissive or welcoming—it simply greeted and then awaited its next cue. "I assume you must be the Citadel envoy?"

Sabina grimaced, as she was unpractised in the speech of the solarite language. "Yes, I am here to deliver you to the embassy." She scratched behind her ear. This was not the solarite she'd been told to expect, and she was uncertain of how to broach the matter.

An entourage of silk-armoured sprites emerged from behind Amira, and one Sabina vaguely recognised from the wedding approached to whisper in her ear. Jewels chattered from Amira's hummingbird hairpiece as she pivoted her head to attention. "You may speak Mortesian to us," Amira said.

Thank Calante, Sabina thought. She switched tongues as she opened the door of the carriage for them. "If you'd like to follow me, I shall escort you to Drakalyk Castle."

The solarite entered first, perfuming the interior with her gourmand fragrance. Everything about her seemed to be, like Laila, an irresistible distraction for the senses. Sabina wasn't sure how they accomplished it. The idea of them could only have been concocted by a fanciful soul. Someone who spent more time dreaming than living.

"I'd first like to welcome you to Mortos," Sabina began once they'd each settled and the hippogriffs were whipped to charge forward. "You are not the one we had been told to expect. Laila Regina will be... most surprised you have chosen to visit."

"I'm sure," Amira replied curtly, glancing out of the window. It happened so quickly Sabina almost missed her true distaste flutter across her face. "In truth, I have always desired to travel here again. My time during the wedding was ever so brief, and the offer of your healing salts proved irresistible. And I wanted to see what country could give birth to such imposing figures."

"And?" Sabina brought her ankle to her knee. "What do you think?"

Amira pursed her lips at the staggering height of the trees, still looming above them even in flight. "The land here suits your nature."

A request for clarification perched on Sabina's lips before a crash sent the carriage swaying. "What in oblivion—?"

Darting past a gap in the drapes was the figure of a masked luparo bandit, a long curved obsidian blade in hand.

"Fuck!" Sabina threw herself atop Amira as the falcata came slicing through the body of the carriage, skimming a few precious platinum strands of hair. *They're here for her.*

And he didn't come solo.

More bandits on hippogriffs were rising up from the clouds, loading bone spikes into their rifles.

Amira's foremost sprite guard whipped out her pistol before they could take aim, shooting a lightning bolt straight through the neck of the first assailant. The luparo gurgled as his throat crackled and fizzed with dancing sparks.

Panic slithered down Sabina's spine as Amira writhed beneath her. "Stay low and don't let them see you!" With that, she threw the solarite to the floor and readied her wrist gauntlet filled with cursed poisons.

A good judgement, seeing as a series of jagged bones pierced through the carriage's wooden hide, sending splinters spraying.

Sabina pierced a dart through the eye of a luparo and watched him howl as his cornea ballooned and exploded a portion of his skull in a red mist. "Driver?!"

"Lightshields are not far behind," the qarnun responded, thrashing the reins to pick up speed. "Hold onto something tightly."

The three tumbled to the other end of the carriage from the turbulence as the driver attempted to outrun the spikes.

Sabina screamed as the force knocked the wind from her. A spike skimmed across her cheek, just missing her eye. She lifted her cane with shaking hands and took another shot at a bandit. A miss.

"Come on..." she grunted, cocking the staff to aim again. "*Shit—*" A spike hit her again. This time right through the shoulder. A sharp burst of pain made her arm droop as her hand went to seize the spike and tug it out.

Blood soaked her coat through and she tried raising her arm again, but it tingled too sorely to keep it upright. "Come on... please..."

Another luparo hovered in her line of sight, ready to spear her through the face. He bared his yellow teeth in a satisfied leer, and Sabina let her eyes sweep low.

A frizzle of lightning scraped her ears, and she realised the sprite had dived to cover her, slaughtering a few remaining bandits with quick, clean shots. The sprite's thumb jammed on the trigger and she cursed, realised she was empty, then dipped to reload.

She didn't see the luparo aiming for her, but Sabina did. She summoned a tendril of darkness to wrap around the bandit's throat and yanked his head from his shoulders. Black blood sputtered in a few vigorous pulsations before the body fell off of his hippogriff.

Sabina lunged forward, still cradling her bleeding arm to survey if the rest of the sky had been purged. "I think that's all of them." She slumped against the chair, smearing blood over the seats from her deadened arm. "It's all right now, madame. You don't need to hide there any longer."

Amira perked up like a daisy from the soil and dusted herself off, though with far more infirmness than typical due to her ailment. It took the sprite's aid to return her to her seat for the remainder of the journey.

The skies stayed clear on the path to Drakalyk, and once she had delivered Amira safely, Sabina fired a flare and waited for her reinforcements to appear.

"Prime Sabina." An enforcer approached, eager for further instruction.

"Scan the area and keep watch of the impératrice," she said. "Only the sprites are to remain."

"Understood."

Sabina leapt atop her hippogriff and clicked her heels, setting forth towards the Citadel. While astride, she thought back to the bandits she had killed. Part of her pondered whether the attack had been random opportunists or a calculated move to sabotage Laila's aims to distribute aetherglass. If the latter, she ought to be on alert for further signs of unrest, but for now she withheld judgement until she was able to talk it through with Darius.

Sabina galloped into the courtyard before she dismounted. At this hour she was likely to find Darius in his study, so she made her way there first, straightening an imaginary crease on her coat before she knocked and peered through the door.

"I come with urgent news."

Darius glanced up from the document holding his attention and waved her inside to sit on a cushioned velvet divan. "What is it?"

She slumped in exhaustion, taking a pose that would've earned her a few lashings from Domitia. "Things have not gone as we expected. Impératrice Amira has arrived and somebody attacked us while I was delivering her to Gravissia."

Darius flipped his folder shut. "Is she secure?"

"Yes."

"Do you know who attacked her?"

"They seemed like simple bandits at first glance. They were lupari armed with occassi weaponry. So either they stole it or they were hired."

"I'll send out some enforcers straight away." He got up from his chair. "I suppose it won't be long before Laila hears of this..." He pinched the bridge of his nose and sighed. "I'll have to prepare her for it. If someone knew about the visit, then we clearly have a spy in our midst... This could be troublesome."

"What should we do?"

Darius deliberated on his answer for a good long while. "The qarnina Laila rescued... have her sent to me. At once."

Domitia peered in suspicion at the parcel deposited on her dining table by one of her servants. Wrapped in black velvet and embossed with the platinum foil of a six-headed eagle crest, she knew it could only have originated from the rex himself.

"Open it."

The qarnun nodded and tugged the end of the red silk ribbon keeping the box bound. As it fell away, all sides of the box descended to display a miniaturised version of Mount Occassus. Upon reveal it ejected a hot spurt of imitation lava down the sides and onto the table, scrawling itself into an invitation for the annual Erupere Circus.

"Skilfully done." Domitia sighed in lament. Very little could be said against the royal couple's penchant for theatrics. "Yet they continue to host our rites with no respect for the traditions that uphold them." She drummed her fingers along the tablecloth with increasing impatience. "Do you believe that fair, Fedyor?"

The qarnun flinched in alarm. "I—you—I—?"

"Yes, *you*," Domitia snarled, "though I shouldn't expect a feeble-minded dimwit to have more to say than pleading for my venom." This would not prevent her from continuing on. "Ugh, that regina has proved rather irksome. *First* she interferes in how we choose to treat our lessers and *now* she has aims to poison the minds of the youth with her foreign notions." A dark thought cast a shadow on her features. "It's time I remove her." Before she could give weight to such a treasonous thought a knock came at the door.

"Come in."

A masked bandit entered, oozing blood from his throat. He cracked his neck with his hands to lodge his recently decapitated head back into place.

Fedyor's eyes bulged before he could help it. "Mistress..."

"Oh, dear." Domitia sighed at his sorry sight. "I assume since only one of you has returned, Ivan, you don't have good news."

Ivan frothed from his nose. "We were... unable to retrieve the cargo."

"Evidently," came Domitia's dry retort. "That cargo is the only thing standing between myself and increased taxes to the likes of..." She glared at her tremulous servant. "Can you at least tell me if you are the lone survivor?"

"Yes," Ivan said. "No one left but me."

"Good." She yanked him towards her, shushing him. "It's all right." Domitia brought him to rest against the cleft of her bosom and stroked her fingers down his neck. She sank her fangs into him, and Ivan moaned in ecstasy and anguish, wilting from the venom pouring into his veins until his body yielded to her. "Find the rest of your comrades and burn them."

Ivan nodded, dazed from her poisoned kiss as he went to fulfil her demand.

Domitia wiped her mouth with the back of her hand. There would be much for her to see to before the circus. She poured herself a goblet of wine and swirled the tart red liquor as it rippled from the force of her approaching sons. They had come unannounced and unsummoned, rumbling the ground beneath the hooves of their stampeding hippogriffs as they slowed to a crawl at her gates.

While their presence was an inconvenience, she knew better than to turn them away. She'd once learned, from her own mother, that a good matriarch should always have room on her bosom for her son's head to return to should he wish it. It kept those ties reinforced from the fray of separation and ensured he'd still keep her in his favour.

So there was little Domitia could do but to suck in a breath and prepare to apologise for the lack of meal preparation. What else could they expect due to short notice? Of course, she would soon whip her servants bloody to have the grandest feast prepared to greet them, as was befitting of her boys. Only the best would suit them.

She took the liberty of downing her wine whilst she still had a moment of calm before the servants showed her children into the sitting room, a look of disgruntlement upon each of their faces.

"My, what a sour look you all have for your mother." Domitia snorted and set her goblet aside.

"Well, we ought to!" exclaimed Antonius, her eldest. "What's all this about the aetherglass? I thought you were putting an end to it?"

Domitia massaged her temple. "There have been some... unforeseen impediments to my goal."

"Of what sort?"

"My attempt to halt the proceedings has failed." Domitia lifted her goblet for a refill. "Fow now."

"So that's it, then." Her son withdrew a letter from his coat. "And because of this we all have received orders from the Citadel to cede land for a communal greenhouse for qarna."

The rest of them revealed similar envelopes and held them out for Domitia to review.

Her face darkened. It was the worst indignity to be accosted by the brood she'd ejected to life between her very thighs as if *she* were reared to serve *them*. "Show your mother some respect," she snarled. "I will sort this out."

Back in the Citadel, Yula scurried towards the rex's antechamber with mouselike caution and little knowledge of what to expect. All she'd been informed of when Kirill had jerked her aside from the rest of the maidservants into a shadowed corner was that she'd been asked for. A faint tremor rippled down her spine at the recollection of his wispy voice and the vacuous stare that went on for too long without blinking.

Even though the end of the Culling had done away with the tradition of ghouls, there was a phantasmal quality to the remaining dead that still lingered in their pale eyes, cloudy and reflective as glass. It was as if their essence had been tipped empty and only a stained residue remained.

She gulped as she approached the doors emblazoned with cast iron chimerical figures, their jaws unhinged into a handle. Without knocking, she slid her lithe fingers into the teeth and pushed the door open a crack.

"You called for me, Your Majesty?"

Darius lounged on his divan, elegantly draped in shadow. The only light in the room other than the candles seemed to be the infernal flame of his blue-green eyes. When he saw Yula he flicked his wrist lazily to a nearby table. "Pour a drink for me, would you?"

Yula obeyed, approaching the tray of glasses and the decanter. It unnerved her to get so near to him, the muscles in her neck twinged with the sense of peril every time she heard the velvet cushions shift under his weight.

Darius swung his legs onto the floor and crossed them at the ankle. "I have a question for you, Yula."

She flinched in surprise. "Yes?"

"You used to serve on the Orlovis estate, did you not?"

"Yes..." She offered her answer unwillingly, and with immediate regret.

"See, I'm just trying to piece a few things together for my own peace of mind. I have a suspicion and I'd like you to help me through it."

"I'll... I'll do my best."

"Thank you." He bent his head, a deceptively graceful stance that made her no less comforted. For someone so large, he had a silent fluidity to his movements that made her not want to take her eyes off of him for too long a period. "It's come to my attention that we have a spy problem in the Citadel."

Yula continued to pour wine into the glass. "Oh, that's awful, Your Majesty."

"Yes, indeed. I've been trying to decipher who the spy might be so that they can be dealt with swiftly. I know judging from the information that it had to have been someone who is familiar with the Regina Wing and her inner quarters. Now I have vetted every servant in this Citadel personally. Barring one."

The more he spoke the less control she had on her grip, and the bottle in her hands seemed to become as slippery as an eel, sloshing liquid over the tray.

"You can stop pouring now."

Yula realised that in her fear she'd allowed the cup to overflow. She swallowed tremulously, realising it had been a trick to expose her nerves. "Your Majesty, I..."

"How long have you been spying on Domitia's behalf? Was your entire damsel act a ploy to get into the Citadel quarters?"

Yula's face whitened. Tremors broke out over her body as her lips parted to deny. "No, Your Majesty... please. I—I swear I had no choice."

"There is always a choice, Yula. And I'll be giving you one now."

Her mind leapt to the worst conclusion. "Are you going to kill me?"

He looked at ease, but she could tell he'd be on her with one spring of his limbs. "No."

She had but a moment of calm before she considered something worse. "Are you going to tell the regina?"

"Also no. She's suffered enough betrayal and heartbreak, and I have no desire to add to it. Though I must wonder why you'd act in such a callous manner after how good she'd been to you."

"I..." Yula hung her head low. "I... I apologise, Your Majesty."

"There is still a chance to make it right. You can either swear allegiance to me now from this point forth or you can return to the service of Domitia in disgrace. What's it to be?"

It seemed strange to think now, of all moments, to Kirill's vacant eyes. When facing the rex, she could imagine how serving him for such an extended amount of time could cause one's soul to condense away into vapour. Perhaps he himself had been the one to suck them dry.

Yula knew she had to consider her options carefully now. If she gave up Katerina there was no telling what the blood sorceress would do to repay her, but she couldn't refuse the rex's wishes. Her best chance and perhaps the one with the least bloody outcome for her was to give over Domitia like he suspected. "I am yours, Your Majesty."

XXI

PIQUANT SMOKE FROM BURNT CARAMEL WAFTED from the Erupere Circus—a one-night occasion to celebrate the day the occassi first emerged from the volcano's fiery pit and onto the snowy plains of Mortos.

Darius observed all of the commotion with a faint smile on his lips, the carnal odour of monsters attuning him to the bestial instincts that always remained dormant beneath his skin. And with the plan he'd set in motion to ensnare Domitia, he knew no more opportune time to awaken them.

A lecherous breeze swept upskirt of the striped circus tents, rustling them through its cold fingers to tease at the attractions awaiting inside. The performers were varied in their offerings, from the bone contortionists who snapped themselves into impossible shapes, to the escape artists who incarcerated themselves in deadly traps under the threat of dismemberment, to the shadow puppeteers rendering traditional folktales under beams of thermal light.

He checked his watch idly before pocketing it and peered up at the slumbering crater of Mount Occassus, guarded by occassi so ancient they had degraded into something purely bestial.

Few saw Elder Occassi outside of Erupere, for those fortunate to live long enough to grasp the honour would take their eternal pilgrimage to the unholy city buried in the mountain where water ran backwards. They were instantly recognisable from their coal-charred skin, the unearthly gleam of their flaming eyes, and their elongated phalanges into scythe-like claws. Leathery bat wings were kept retracted at their spines, making an appearance only when they were given a sacrificial offering, after which they would take flight to deposit it into the waiting mouth of Occassus.

It was a custom of this night to send a sacrifice to Calante. An individual would carve their greatest sin into the hide of an animal (later it would become a decorated wooden substitute) and send it off to the underworld to nourish their god for another year of perdition.

Many saw this as an excuse to engage in an act of confession, safe in the knowledge that their blackest misdeed would go up in flames and aid their maker in improving his strength. Not many Calantists still actively believed in the Ascension—that Calante would come to the earth again with a royal vessel to reconquer the world he had lost—but it was woven enough into the fabric of their religion that such traditions stayed upheld.

Darius brought out a figurine of a brass-plated wolf and traced his fingers along his sin. A name. *Delanus.* Eventually, he found his way to Laila through the pale glimmer of her dress. A billowing skirt of swan feathers studded with diamonds flared around her legs, whereas Darius's black eagle-feather cloak was tipped with gold.

"And how are you this evening?" He slipped his arms around her and kissed the side of her head.

"I must say I'm impressed with the creativity on display here," Laila said and produced a bauble of a solid gold bird in a glass cage. "Did you make this one for me?"

"I thought it suited you," Darius said. "And also that it would be symbolic of allowing yourself to finally unburden the guilt you've been holding onto and let it take flight."

Laila's smile flickered, knowing he was referring to the confession she'd sealed in her bauble. Her murder of Dominus. "I'm not sure if that should ever leave me." She met his gaze. "I... I don't want to forget. I don't want to let myself become unburdened by it. I fear I... if I don't recall how awful it felt then—"

"You might do something worse?" Darius took her hand and raised it to his lips. "These are still the hands that have tended to, raised up, and reached out towards so many. One kill doesn't change that."

"Perhaps not," Laila conceded, "but it's all the more reason for me to keep that number low."

Darius cupped her face, sliding his thumb down her cheek. "Then we'll keep it low." He was more than happy to sully his own hands in her stead, after all.

She drew in a feathery breath and leaned in to press her forehead against his. Had it not been for Mortesian reticence against public displays of affection, she might have kissed him then.

Part of her still longed to when a voice drew her attention. "Laila?"

She turned to the call and saw it was her mother, entwined in layers of coral pink like the corolla of a lily. Her face was smoothed down as stone.

"Maman." Laila acknowledged her with a hesitant smile, a pinch of discomfort tightening at the nape of her neck. "Thank you so much for coming tonight. Truly." She tucked a curl behind her ear. "I do want to apologise for the terrible journey you've suffered—"

Amira raised a hand to halt her. "We shall speak no more of it. This is…" Her eyes swept around in search of the right word. "An interesting event. I am pleased to have gotten the chance to see it."

"We are honoured to welcome you back to Mortos." Darius appeared to twirl Laila into the security of his arms, as if sensing her discomfort. "Hopefully this might be the return to form in regards to diplomacy."

"Perhaps." Whatever geniality held in Amira's tone sifted when directed at him. "Laila, might we discuss things in private?"

"Of course." She parted Darius's arms from her and gave him an affirming smile. "We'll be back in a moment." She kissed his cheek and departed to join Amira's side. "I must admit I did not expect you to ever step foot in this country again, Maman."

"After word came to me of your offer I knew I had to see to it. Personally." Amira rolled her tender joints with a muted hiss of pain. The dark strains of chaos magic in her blood had largely faded but the pangs of discomfort still struck sharp. "In fact, I've already felt immensely better after being treated in your salt baths."

"Well, there's certainly more where that came from." A slyness edged into Laila's voice as she slipped into familiar patterns. "If you're open to discussing terms…"

Amira fell silent for a beat. "Laila, I want you to know I am not here to haggle with you over goods."

"Then why *did* you come?" Laila sighed, exhausted. "Because after I didn't hear from you since my wedding night I expected that was it for us."

Anger flashed in Amira's eyes. "You know full well what you were doing when you dangled the hope of treatment under my nose."

"Which you still have yet to repay us for," Laila countered. "Well?"

Never did Amira ever think she would be in receipt of such a cold, mercantile attitude. She realised something had altered between them, something irreparable. The starry-eyed reverence Laila once beheld her mother with had dulled into something grudging and resentful. A respect reluctantly given for no other reason than because her title commanded it, not because she *believed*.

Amira parted her lips at her daughter, no longer seeing the fledgling princess she'd kept smothered under her wing but a queen fully matured and in rule of her own roost. And for once in her life, she struggled with what to say to her.

"I think it's time I took the helm from here."

Laila went stiff as a voice she knew almost as well as her own emerged from behind an empty tent and its owner held up the fabric for entrance.

"Lyra."

Carriages landed by the circus in heavy thumps, drawn in by hippogriffs from the farthest reaches of the kingdom.

Within one carriage, two familiar faces appeared. Katerina reclined in a red velvet gown trimmed with gold tassels, so devastatingly striking she slipped like a dagger between one's ribs. The garment made her ghostly pallor even starker and brought out the rustic sheen in her winter gold hair. Tonight, she looked nothing like a blood sorceress. She looked to be Mortos's finest, bred to dangle off the arm of a king.

"How's our plan coming along?"

Serafina huffed as she picked lint off of a floral-patterned puff sleeve of her gown. "We may require a new one."

"Oh?" Katerina frowned. "Why so?"

"The regina has asked for us to create a new estate for young occasselle and remove Domitia from her pedestal. Do you know what this means? We'll have access... to the youth."

A trick, Katerina all but voiced. "You don't believe her... do you? She's merely trying to flatter you, Serafina."

"Perhaps," Serafina conceded. "However, I shall take the offer anyhow."

"May I ask what's brought on this tactic?"

"Darius has unfortunately managed to remain a step ahead. I thought pointing out his heirless state would fumble him, but he has an answer to that... however daring it may be. So I'm shifting my aims. Rather than trying to get rid of the regina, I think we may well be able to work alongside one another—provided I can get her to see my way of things."

"Why, I'm *surprised*, Serafina. You're not going soft on the little firefly?"

Serafina knew Katerina well enough to detect the ember of jealousy in her tone, however minute. She cupped her mentee's chin in her palm. "I am not Darius. You shall always be my favourite." She placed a light kiss on her forehead. "However, I will admit to my perspective on our star queen having altered slightly. I was wrong to think her a threat; in truth she's just as much a pawn in Darius's games as the rest of us. Worse still, the poor little lamb is too blinded by love to see it. You almost have to feel sorry for the thing."

Katerina sniffed. "If you say so."

The sudden change left her in a foul mood. It had been the last thing she wanted to work with Laila Regina, and yet she could see clearly enough that Serafina had already been compromised. As she fiddled with the vial of a potion stowed between her breasts she considered if it might be time to go rogue.

"I'm going to take in the sights," she said, slipping out of the carriage in search of Yula. She entered one tent and saw a bone contortionist shaping herself to fit inside of a fishbowl, then went into another where she found the servant watching as a monster charmer reduced a salivating beast's temperament to that of a playful kitten, pliantly frolicking along with the tune of her flute.

Katerina hummed softly along to it, the music sounding of the wind's forgotten tongue. She tapped Yula on the shoulder, smirking as the qarnina leapt in fear. "Only me."

"*What are you doing here?*" Yula failed to compose herself, fiddling nervously with the ends of her white woollen curls. "The rex knows. He—"

Katerina clapped her hand over the girl's mouth and dragged her off into a black corner. "What does he know?"

"He *knows* about Domitia." Yula's chin wobbled as tears moistened her pigeon-grey eyes. "He knows I told her things... private things. And now..."

Katerina shushed her, taking this moment to come to a realisation. "You didn't give me up." She sounded almost impressed by it.

Yula drooped her head, unable to meet her gaze. She elected not to tell her that Darius requested her to aid him instead.

"You're smarter than you look," Katerina commended, with a short sputter of laughter. "Well, now... since he knows to suspect Domitia I can use this to my advantage." She produced a vial from between her breasts, its liquid gleaming red before settling into a dark maroon that resembled wine. "I was going to make you put this in the regina's drink."

"*What?*" Yula's voice rose so high it practically squeaked. "How do you expect me to—"

"Now, though, I believe things can be made *far* more interesting." Katerina twiddled the vial between her fingers. "So, here's what you shall do instead. You're going to hand this over to him like a good little servant, and he will suspect Domitia was behind it. That way, you get your commendation and *I* get to see a much livelier act unfold tonight."

"You're... wicked."

Katerina curled the corner of her mouth. "Let's not pretend Domitia was any friend to you." She plopped the bottle into Yula's palm and turned away.

⸎

"What are you doing here, Lyra?"

Her former friend tilted her head inside of the empty tent. "We need to talk."

Laila glanced at Amira in concern before taking the first steps inside of the tent. Once all three had entered Lyra rolled down the flap and cracked open a piece of ætherald to light a lantern.

"What is this about?" Laila swivelled round to face her. "I haven't heard from you since you left at my mother's side... and now you're here..." She didn't dare to hope this was an attempt to repair the bridge between them, that Lyra had chosen to defect to her side. Too many holes had been worn into her once immaculate veil of naïveté.

"I'm here to warn you, Laila." Lyra traded a glance with Amira. "We both are."

"Warn me of what?"

"Darius."

Laila already anticipated the answer before it came. Exhausted, she spun on her heel to exit the tent.

"Wait—" Lyra called after her. "Just listen. Please."

Laila stifled a huff. "To what, Lyra? More of your unbridled vitriol towards the one I love? Because I think I've heard enough of that. You've made your thoughts quite clear."

"You need to listen to me, Laila. Because this is serious. Far more grave than anything you could have possibly imagined. It involves *Emica Hariken.*"

The urgency in Lyra's voice stilled her before she could make her grand retreat. Then a sense of confusion overcame Laila that settled into fright when she realised she hadn't thought of that name for decades. "Dr Hariken?"

"Yes." Lyra didn't know where to start.

"The scholar who drowned in the shipwreck over twenty years ago? That Dr Hariken?" Laila's brow furrowed. "Because if this is about the *Great Northern*, then he's already confessed to that."

"Did he also confess that she never died on that ship?"

Laila froze. "What?"

"It's true. She wasn't on the ship when it wrecked, Laila. She escaped on a lifeboat. And then he took her, and he finished her off but not before using her to..."

Laila shook her head. "To what?"

"To make his chimeras."

Laila allowed her words to hang in the air, as if to soak in the absurdity of them. Because she regarded this claim with such ridicule that she burst into laughter. "Really, Lyra?"

Lyra flinched, having anticipated any reaction but that. "It's... it's true... it's..." Yet the more Laila laughed the more convincing it was for the accusation to seem a farcical act of spite.

"I must admit..." Laila clenched her stomach as she attempted to recover herself. "You truly had me worried there for a moment. Of all the stories you could've plied me with, this one is... it's certainly inventive. I'll give you that."

"She is telling the truth, Laila," Amira said.

"Dr Emica Hariken drowned on the Great Northern over twenty years ago." Laila recited it as an indelible fact. "It was a great misfortune that Darius was, indeed, responsible for. But he has answered for such a crime, and I don't think it fair to keep dredging up his past sins."

"Laila, *for the love of Asemani*—" Lyra lost her temper. "Open your eyes! Do you really believe I would travel across the ocean simply to deliver a lie of this nature? If it's not true, then tell me this. Tell me how *does* he craft his chimeras? Do you know? Has he ever shown you?"

Flustered, Laila said, "I am hardly a scientist, Lyra."

"So then you don't know enough to refute it?"

"Perhaps not." Her face hardened. "But let's say I were to believe you... from what source did you uncover this information?"

"It was Lucrèce Mielette, who discovered it from Akira Isuka."

"Isuka..." Laila's stomach clenched from a different form of emotion. "Why? Why would Lucrèce tell you this?"

"Because we need your help to put a stop to it, Laila. You must return to Soleterea with us at once. Make up some excuse to Darius, but get away from him. Tonight. I can explain the rest when we leave."

"Absolutely not."

"Laila..."

"No, Lyra. You cannot come here and upend my life by telling me my husband has been keeping a secret of such magnitude and then expect me to remain in the dark."

"It's... it's complicated, Laila! All right? Lucrèce has this plan in place for how we might be able to stop whatever he's doing to her. But it involves you having to come back so we can access your ancestral plane in the Astral Realm. So we can reach Esterre."

"And then?" Laila asked. "What happens after? To Darius?"

"Never mind him," Lyra said cautiously. "If this happens, then the Mielettes are willing to cede the election and vote for you. You'll become impératrice."

Those words conjured a nostalgic ache for the lonely girl she had once been, who believed that with a heavy crown and a high throne she could slake her thirst for love with adulation. She shed a single tear on behalf of that girl, mourning her for what she once was and what she could have become.

"Lyra... tell me what's going to happen to Darius."

It was then Lyra knew her friend was lost. "Lucrèce wants him. Dead or alive."

Laila patted her tears with one hand. It was all she needed to hear to cast the veracity of the claims into doubt. "Then I need to think about this."

"You cannot be serious? After everything I've just told you?"

"You cannot expect me to leave without speaking to him first. I must let him have his say. This is my husband. This is my country. I have duties and obligations here."

"And what of your obligations to *us*, Laila?" Amira retorted. "You abandoned us in the time when we needed you most. When we needed you to stand with us as our princess, you fled into the arms of your monstrous king and you deserted us."

"Maman..." Laila swallowed.

"It's not too late to make it right. You have a chance to make it up to us now. All you have to do is leave with us tonight. Come *home* to us, Laila."

"I am home." Laila drew her arms back to cradle herself. "Darius is my home. And there is no crown, no throne, no country that I would *ever* give him to you for."

⸎

Darius tapped his ringed fingers on the arm of the wooden throne he'd been given to sit in as he waited for Laila to return.

"Your Majesty?" Yula scuttled over with a tray rattling in her shaking hands. Snail-stuffed mushrooms and spiked sea urchins filled with caviar arrived to soothe empty stomachs, paired with goblets of black raspberry wine.

"What is it, Yula?"

"Domitia Orlovia sends her regards..." She gestured to a goblet. "She requested this wine be gifted to the regina."

"How gracious," Darius said, deciphering the words behind the words. He accepted the goblet and raised it to his lips to inhale the scent. "Hm, smells of black fright. Do you know of it?"

Yula shook her head.

"It's a flower. They grow in very sparse parts of the country, quite indistinct when mixed with other flavours, but there's a faint metallic tinge to those who are accustomed to working with poisons."

Yula swallowed. "I see."

"Do you want to know a common trait of this flower? Inducing fatal heart palpitations through sheer terror. Starts off with sweating. Chest pains. Shortness of breath. Ordinary signs of mental distress and then slowly... it claims you."

"Sounds truly awful, Your Majesty."

"It does, doesn't it?" His sarcasm was palpable, a cold light strobed his eyes. "Tell Domina Orlovia I wish to speak with her."

Yula bowed and departed from him with a shudder. Nausea

sprouted like weeds in her stomach as she sought Domitia's silhouette among the multitude of occassi. She could be found with a round-cheeked infant occasso in her arms. A grandson. They were watching to see if an escape artist could free himself of his chains and exit the tank before he succumbed to asphyxiation.

Yula struggled not to retch at the sight of the occasso clapping his chubby hands in delight as Domitia nuzzled him to her breast. "M'lady?"

Domitia's eyes grew hooded upon sight of her. "Well, aren't you a sorry sight? It's been quite a while, Yula. You're trembling like a leaf. Surely I can't be so frightening."

"Cold," she said evasively. "The rex would like a word, m'lady."

"Hmph." Domitia snorted. "Take him off my hands. His mother should be about."

"Oh, I—" The bundle was deposited in her hands before she could protest and writhing in her arms. Yula gazed down into the face of the grinning occasso, toothless except for the hint of his growing fangs. Her eyes started to moisten with regretful tears as she trailed Domitia's path towards her doom.

"I hear you were calling for me, Your Majesty." Domitia curtseyed before eyeing the empty throne beside him.

"Please, sit." Darius's lips crooked into a roguish smirk. "Have a toast with me tonight."

"To what occasion?" Domitia picked up the goblet on offer.

"To the future of Mortos." He clanked his goblet against her. "May she be ever prosperous and evolving." He followed it with a lengthy sip, paying close attention as Domitia took her own.

"It is rather astounding what you've accomplished." Domitia licked her lips to savour the taste. "I never would've imagined after aiding your coup that this is quite where it would lead."

"I assume you have criticisms."

"Plenty." Domitia shrugged. "But some praise, too. I was there for your father from the start, you see. And his father before him. So I got to observe both the highs and the lows of their reigns. And your impression on Mortos was stamped in far fewer decades than either of theirs. I would say, whether I approve or not, that is an accomplishment to cherish."

"Fair play."

"I would caution you, however... Your Majesty. We see few mavericks stand the test of time for a reason. At least in positions of power. This is a stormy sea you are sailing, and I do wonder if you'll see yourself shipwrecked before the waters can straighten out."

"I seem to be sailing smoothly so far."

"Pride goes before a fall... and your triumph was borrowed. Soleterea may soon come to collect on that payment. I'd be wary of that. Perhaps you might consider finishing what your father was too foolish to start and embark on building your empire."

Darius couldn't help but chuckle, for that doomed pursuit was one he had all but forgotten about. "You forget I am a married occasso now, Domina Orlovia. Why should I take Soleterea through force when I can support my wife's ascendancy to the same ends?"

"Ah, and here I was wondering why you'd bothered to take a wife outside of the race. I feared you'd turned sentimental."

"There's a little of that, too." Darius took another sip. "Never let it be said I am a creature of singular aims."

Domitia's smile faded, forehead creasing as she put a hand to her chest.

"Something the matter?"

"I'm feeling a bit..." Her chest tightened, heart beating rapidly within it. A gauntness ravaged her already sharp cheeks—she looked as if she'd sighted Death in his midst. "I'm fine." Domitia attempted to shake off whatever strangeness had taken hold of her.

"You don't look it."

Domitia's heart was racing as if she were in near peril, throbbing at such a speed she thought it might puncture through her ribs. Her lungs burned, igniting a searing pain each time she inhaled. "What... was in that wine?"

"You should know," Darius said. "You were the one who asked Yula to poison it."

"No..."

"You miscalculated, Domitia." Darius gestured in the direction of the sun who kept him in orbit, the loss of which would've cast him hopelessly adrift. "Laila wouldn't have known about the fright flower and would've perished long before she had a chance. I, on the other hand..."

"I didn't..."

"There's no point in denying it. The truth shan't save you, but you can at least still reach your sons before you perish."

"Well." Domitia threw her head back and cackled. When her head rose again her eyes were crazed. Her composure was faltering; she was scared in spite of her best efforts to conceal it. "You've certainly stepped into the large shoes left by your father and surpassed them."

"Oh, I'm not my father. See, my father would've enacted the old punishment of dynastic blood purge for treason. I, however, would like to be fair. Yula has already attested to your guilt. All that is required now is for you to confess."

"I will confess to *nothing*. All you have to prove my guilt is suspicion and hearsay. Nothing more."

"You're right." Darius granted with an appeasing tilt of his head. "But what do *you* have, Domitia? Do you have anyone willing to attest to your whereabouts the night Impératrice Amira was attacked? One of your sons, perhaps?"

Horror flowered in the pit of Domitia's stomach. She could sense the tides were turning somewhere she didn't care to travel. "Your Majesty..." She reached for him, but he already sidled out of her grip.

His eyes scanned across the seven of them. "How about Marcus? After all, you did say he was the most disposable."

"I never said that!" Domitia snarled.

"No?" Darius countered. "That's not how I recall it. Seems you have a habit of lying..."

Domitia had become too hollowed for anger. Her cheeks flared with the humiliation that this was to be her fate, sold out by the likes of a qarnina for a crime she did not commit. "I suppose that's that, then. Isn't it?"

"Indeed. Domitia Orlovia, I hereby sentence you... to death."

Her vision was starting to double, quadruple, and she didn't think she would make it far enough to reach her kin before she collapsed. "Let me warn you of you this, Darius Calantis. Erasing me from existence won't be enough to save her. There are more where that came from. How far will you go? Will you raze your kingdom to the ground for your little star queen?"

"All that," he said quietly, "and more."

He shoved her off the throne, and Domitia staggered forward on her dying legs, streaks of blood seeping down from her eyes and nose. A series of jeers made Domitia's head dart round. Her face went ashen as she realised her disgrace was about to be witnessed.

And the crowd, oh, how they relished it. Qarna distorted into flesh-melted skulls seemed to be pointing and laughing as their almighty mistress was reduced into a pitiful echo of her once greatness. What sweet revenge it was, delivered to them by their rex, to see the predator become the prey.

The occassella closed her eyes and let out one final meek snuffle before she toppled over, heartbeat slowing to a crawl. And then a ceaseless slumber.

A mournful wail broke out among her grieving sons, overtaken by the crowd's jubilant cheer from the demise of their cruel oppressor. Yula covered her mouth to stifle the tidal wave of nausea that threatened to empty her stomach.

Bodies bent like stalks of grass as Laila pushed her way forward through the masses until she was faced with Domitia's haemorrhaging body. Then her eyes went to Darius's face—his cruel smile, the vacancy in his gaze, the way he beckoned the crowd for an ovation.

XXII

SLAM OF THE CITADEL'S COLOSSAL BRONZE DOORS made the ancient walls shudder, sending a mischief of mice scurrying out from the crevices with panicked squeaks. Darius's footsteps echoed up the grand staircase soon after and frightened the mice into a sharp retreat to their eroding sanctuary to await his passing.

He could hear Laila's frantic sprint after him on the stone steps. "You lied to me!"

"You wanted me to show mercy, Laila. And I did." He stopped to swivel on his heel, and his shadow flooded over her body with the strength of a wave. "I was willing to pardon Yula for her part in the conspiracy, but Domitia had to die tonight."

He continued onwards into his antechamber and poured himself a drink in typical elegant fashion. It was the drink that did it. The flagrant lack of remorse he demonstrated by going about as though he intended to retire from a laborious day's work.

"Public execution is not the way we agreed to run this country!" Laila quivered in fury as she closed the door behind her. "You murdered a noble lady in the most undignified manner possible. That is not justice, Darius. If she had to be punished, so be it... but you could've at least allowed her children the dignity of not becoming a spectacle for your vengeance. We have to lead by example on this. Domitia deserved a fair trial."

"Oh, you mean like Dominus had?"

Laila recoiled with a gasp, taken aback by the verbal slap. Then her expression took a turn. "You know I regret that. Every single day."

"Yes. And you also know that I forgave you. I've seen you at your darkest hour, and I never once turned away. Is it so wrong of me to ask the same of you?"

"How dare you? I have bent and bent and bent for your sake. Over and over. I abandoned my loved ones, my country, my entire... people. All of this. Just to be with you. Because I saw the monster you are and still believed there was something to salvage."

Their eyes aligned, gazes transfixed. He could see that whatever allowances she'd made for his prior brutality would not stretch this far.

"Please understand, Laila, Domitia had to be taught a lesson. Not only her but the rest of them too. Her demise, mortifyingly public a display that it was, served to warn the others of what will come their way if they continue to trifle as she did."

"What you did to her..." Laila's voice splintered as if she needed to prepare to speak it. "Was barbaric. Do you not feel anything at all?"

"I do." Darius took a sip and set his glass down. "I feel *vindication* that justice has been served to the one who threatened the woman I love."

Laila's breath rattled at his confession. She had come here to scold, to condemn, but the passionate tone with which he delivered his speech had unsteadied her.

"And I'd do it again. I'd do worse. If it ensures your safety."

"Darius—"

"You told me you'd love me whether I deserve it or not. And I don't deserve it, but I have it. So allow me this one misdeed, Laila." He caged her hands inside his own, cradling them like precious jewels to be cordoned from defilement. "One more pardonable sin."

Lyra's words reverberated in her mind, then, and she wondered just how numerous the sins were that preceded the current. The ones she did not know. "I can't." Tears filled her eyes as she shook her head. She couldn't allow herself to have her conscience swept away by the voracity of his love. No matter how much of a monstrous appetite she'd developed for his affection.

"Domitia got what she deserved and you know it." Darius cupped the side of her face. "Do not spare her a thought any longer. All I want, all I care about, is keeping you safe. And for that one thing, I'd commit all manner of atrocities." He slid his thumb down her cheek as he drew nearer. "At least forgive me for that." He whispered before dropping his lips to hers.

It was wrong to respond to it. Oh, she knew it was. To listen to him drip the sweetest poison in her ears and then throw her arms around him. To feel a shameful sense of *gratitude* kindle in her breast at knowing the lengths he would go to for her. Lengths no one had ever gone to before in her name alone. But she couldn't stop herself. Her knees buckled and she let out that weak, trembling breath, letting him know she was caught.

Darius's arms encased her back, gripping her close, and they collided against the desk in a strenuous kiss. He paused to throw her across it, keeping her anchored by his hips as he pushed up her dress and ripped her drawers off. Then his belt came free with a rustle of metal as he scrambled to take out his hard cock.

Unlike other times he didn't ease his way in or give her a chance to acclimate. In one smooth motion he was fully inside her, making her cry out from the suddenness of it. He spent a long time pinning her there, soaking in her heat, the suppleness of her body curving around his. Then when he moved, it was raw, carnal, animalistic.

"*Oh—*" Laila's exclamation came strangled as he went as deep and rough as he wished. Her muscles strained around him, but she could feel herself growing slicker between her thighs to counter it. Her hands clutched the edge of the desk for purchase. A soft whimper escaped her from the painful dig of his fingers into her hips as he increased the speed, latching his fangs into her neck until she bled.

Darius gripped her so tight that he had the full breadth of control over every thrust. There was no escaping this. She couldn't budge an inch. Only surrender as her body moulded itself to his girth, loosening and stretching to receive him.

With each stroke Laila could feel her resistance waning, supplanted by the indescribable ecstasy he always brought her to. She fought against it. She fought her body's impulse to clamp around him and intensify that delectable friction shooting tingles up her stomach. She fought the waves of pleasure clouding her judgement. She fought the moan cresting in her mouth as his hips rolled in continuous circles.

It was all to no avail. He knew too well how to make her body yield. She didn't resist when he kissed her and slowed his pace to lengthier thrusts to delay the inevitable climax. Hearing his sigh of relief as he lost himself in her only gratified her more. He'd already left her sore and aching, legs trembling and weak, but she couldn't make herself tell him to stop.

Laila gasped as he continued with more punishing thrusts. He unsheathed his claws and used them to slice off her dress until she lay shivering and bare beneath him. He ran his claws down her breasts to the sensitive tips of her nipples, drawing pricks of blood that made her tingle all over. He dragged his hands down her stomach, her waist, scraping and grazing along her hips and thighs and leaving the trail marks of his journey.

"Darius…" The wood crackled from the collision of their bodies and she almost feared it might break apart beneath them. She wasn't sure how much more she could bear without some form of relief. This was precisely the kind of ravishing she'd feared, wanted, and a little more than she'd bargained for. "I can't. Please, I can't take any more—" The soft protest was all it took for him to desist.

He withdrew from her, shoving himself between her legs. "You can condemn me as a monster if it pleases you, Laila. If it soothes your guilt. I won't deny that I am one. But what I also am is *your* monster to do with as you wish." A torrid storm of emotion suffused his clear blue eyes. "So will you condemn me or will you use me, Laila?"

It was too hard for her to think straight with his cock nestled into the crook of her thigh, with the immediacy of how he'd felt inside her. It was clear he knew that and was counting on it to influence her next words.

Laila's breaths shallowed in recognition that, in spite of the strength he used to keep her subdued beneath him, his voice was rippling vulnerability. His transition between the faces of brutality and weakness was so seamless that there was no telling which of them was true. Perhaps the answer, as immeasurably complicated as it was to parse, was that he was both at once.

"Say you still love me," he murmured against her lips. "Say it."

"I do." The words came harsh and ragged, pried from her unwilling lungs.

A flash strobed his eyes like lightning. Then he grasped her buttocks, threw her legs over his shoulders, and delved between them.

Laila arched her neck and breathed out. Her heels dug into his back for balance as Darius glided his skilful tongue along her in swirls, his nose against her clit. She braced her hands on the desk for enough leverage to push back against him. It was a struggle to keep her breathing steady, and her nails scraped splinters out of ageless wood as she rode his face.

Her vigour only encouraged him as he took her clit into his mouth and sucked hard enough to make her legs turn numb. He was determinedly savage, almost as if he sought to devour her whole.

Laila's legs spasmed around his shoulders, her toes curling as he continued to run his tongue along her clit until she was on the brink again, and when she had sufficiently wilted as a flower trampled underfoot, he stood and thrust inside her.

"O-oh, *gods*—" Laila cried out.

Darius moaned in response as his hips pumped against her with a vigour that sent them both over the edge, succumbing to their lust.

They somehow made it to his chambers through the trail of debris they created in their path, their lust as yet unsated. Strewn clothes, toppled furniture, and uneven paintings were some of the many unfortunates to get swept up in their fervour.

When Laila awoke in the middle of the night she found her skin grafted to Darius's embrace, with him still soft inside her. It was foolish of her to take comfort in his presence, reckless even, that she would make passionate love to a demon and then feel safe in his bed. But she never could train herself to view him as the remorseless killer he so clearly was when he so appealingly filled in the armour of a stalwart protector.

And within this land, among these creatures, was the distinction so immutable as to even matter?

She turned over to press her palm on his slumbering cheek and trace her fingers down to his chin. If only she could gather the courage to use her power to dreamwalk. To slip into his mind and expose herself to the illimitable horrors that dwelled there. Then she would see him stripped of his princely disguise to the beast that snarled beneath.

He would know then, however, that she had reason to suspect. And she had come to cherish this nuptial home they had pieced together from the wreckage of their childhoods, flimsy as it was on these corrosive foundations. She wouldn't knock it down just yet. Not without concrete and inarguable proof.

She started to disentangle from him with slow and measured movements, knowing that his post-coital slumbers were the ones where he slept the soundest. Once she was free of the bed she turned back to glimpse his face, peaceful as it was with a crook of a smile on his lips. A state he had only ever shown her. Part of her treasured that she alone had been granted a private viewing to this deeply buried jewel. This vulnerable facet to him he'd been forced to keep secreted away from the public eye, lest they exploit him for it.

It made her upcoming treachery come as an even guiltier blow to her stomach when she decided to leave the bed.

She slipped on her nightgown before drifting out the door and into the passageway, retracing the steps she'd walked in one of her earliest visits to the Citadel over two decades prior. When the ghost of Dr Hariken summoned her and she'd neglected to fully answer, having taken the hand of a demon to shake instead. What might have happened had she not agreed to the deal? Had pushed further? Just what had that weary soul been trying to warn her of before Laila had abandoned her in pursuit of more pressing political matters?

Tonight is the night I reach the bottom of it, she decided. She could only hope Serafina would not provide too much of an obstruction to her investigation.

With an enchantment she rendered herself invisible once more and descended into the old chambers of Darius where he had dwelled during his time on the lower rungs of the Citadel social ladder. Not much of the room had changed other than the colourful, antique decor of Serafina's tastes. The desk she had once tried and failed to rummage through still lingered. And so did the bookcase.

Laila closed her eyes and tried to recount her movements to the best of her ability. What was it that Dr Hariken had wanted her to see here? She approached the bookcase and swept her hand along the tomes to see if there was one that leapt out at her in recognition. At first, there was nothing, but then a conspicuous detail emerged, and it was that all texts with the mention of chimeras had been removed.

A swell formed in her throat, which she swallowed with the simple justification that once his research had expanded he would've been likely to take his studies elsewhere. But with that reasoning came disappointment that she would never know the clue that had been sitting in between those pages, waiting for her prying gaze.

She was about to turn away when she heard a creak in the room, followed by footsteps. Her pulse stammered as she turned to the bedchamber, expecting Serafina's presence. Then she realised that the sound was not coming from the direction she anticipated. It was instead coming from *behind* her, behind the bookcase where she had just searched.

Laila turned to a statue, waiting for whatever would emerge with pinpricks of sweat tingling down her back. She didn't know what she was to expect, but the last thing was for Serafina herself to throw open the bookcase like she'd stumbled in from a hard day's labour with a yawn and a stretch before quietly closing it again.

The shock of it was so grand that she almost lost composure, along with control of her enchantment, but thankfully contained herself enough to calculate her next movement. Her instinct for immediate confrontation was tempered by logic that she might discover more if she approached differently. Thus, she let the sorceress sweep past her on her way into the bedroom and pushed onwards to uncover more of what she encountered.

There was no sign that the bookcase was anything more than its solid oak frame. No hidden handle. No conspicuous grooves in the walls. She decided it must be the books where she would find her answer and started rifling through them, one by one, trying to maintain a silence to her trembling, unsteady hands. Before she could get far she heard footsteps entering the room again and, in her panic, allowed herself to materialise in full.

"Calante's wrath..." Serafina cursed in the vicinity of the antechamber. Her copper eyes glinted like coins. "Now what are you doing out of bed so late?"

"I..." Laila fought to stifle her shame at intruding. "I could ask *you* the same question."

"You are in my quarters," she said flatly. "I must ask that you come at a more reasonable hour if the rest of the conversation you have to offer will be this charming."

"Wait, I..." Laila reached for whatever contrivance she could use. "I wanted to talk to someone. About... tonight."

Serafina's face migrated to wary interest.

"I can't stop thinking about Domitia. I feel as if I should've stopped him. I should've done more."

Serafina's expression remained stiff before gentling as she pointed at her divan. "Why don't you sit down?"

Laila accepted the invitation with relief. "I just don't understand. He wasn't like this before."

"Wasn't he?"

"I knew he could be cruel. Violent, even. But never to the extent where I feared I couldn't make him see reason."

"Nothing you could have said or done would've impeded him from this," Serafina said. "He's doing all of it for you, you know?"

"That's what sickens me so much! I never wanted... this. Any of it. I never would have stayed if I thought it would become like this. And yet, every time, just when I thought I was through with him, he would do something or say something. Something small. And it would give me hope I could—"

"Save him? Make him see the error of his ways with your scintillating goodness?" Serafina exhaled a scornful laugh. "Oh, you dear little lamb. I'm afraid he only cared to exhibit as much goodness as it would take for you to love him, and no more than that."

Laila floundered, wanting nothing more than to argue back but unable to muster any counter. So instead she hung her head. Anything to keep from facing Serafina and the veracity of her claim. "I can't have done all this for nothing."

It was a sorrowful remark, spoken quietly, yet still audible enough for Serafina to feel uncomfortable for overhearing it. "Why were you in here *really*, Laila?"

It was the first time she had used her name and enough to make her jolt.

"What sort of answer were you hoping would ease your turmoil?"

The question still eluded her, or perhaps she knew she still wasn't ready to confront it. "I've always wondered... How does someone like you end up involved with someone like Lanius?"

Serafina reclined into her seat with an inhale, as if winded by the topic. "Well, he was different back then. Not softer but... intense in a different way than he ended up. I remember when I first met him. He had only just been crowned rex and was full of vigour. I was attracted to him. The moment I saw him, in fact. Always hated myself for that. That weakness." Her eyes had taken on a sheen of distance. "I thought I could control it. Resist it. Until I couldn't anymore. He wanted to get married. I didn't. We fought. I left. I always knew that he was going to come after me eventually. Someone like that never just... stops. So I hid in the Widowlands until I had Darius and, well, Darius told you the rest."

"Sounds familiar," Laila said. It startled her to recognise herself in this black mirror.

Serafina gave her a rueful smile. "It wasn't all bad, with us. With him. There were times when I thought he would do anything for me. He even passed laws on my behalf. I got him to stop that barbaric practice of mutilation and blood purges of honour, for one... but I knew it would never be enough to rely on the precariousness of his affection. That eventually he would come to demand something of me that I could not give and he had no right to ask for. That's the balance you have to strike with a powerful male figure. You might be able to take the reins, to steer him where you ought to think he should go, but you should never forget the ferity inherent to his true nature."

Laila swallowed softly in acknowledgement. "What if I think I've... lost control? Not only of him"—she steadied her wobbling jaw—"but of myself?"

An awkwardness struck Serafina as she realised she too had found herself reflected in the youthful glimmer of the solarite. In her distaste, she rooted around for another subject to switch to but found that she couldn't. Her capacity for lies had reached its limit. "There's something I need you to see."

"What?"

Serafina walked over to the bookcase and shifted the correct tome to open the hidden tunnel.

"What is that?"

"Your husband's secret laboratory." Serafina leaned her hip against the open doorway.

Laila shook her head, as if by doing so it would wake her from a dream. "This is... I... this is insane. Secret lab? How—when—?" She took a few paces towards the threshold before stopping.

"It used to be mine before it became his. But I assure you it's been well used since then."

Deep in the bowels of that cavern were revelations capable of rupturing the birdcage Darius had crafted with his cosy deceptions and lured her into for safekeeping. Laila did not want to admit she'd grown comfortable in that cage, had taken shelter in it, ignoring the gilded bars every time Darius sought to distract her with offerings of treats and toys. She did not want to leave that cage. She'd paid her ignorance in full for the seductive premise of its safety, and without it she knew she would have nothing left. Nothing but the truth and its cold, hard apathy.

"What's down there?"

Serafina had already started descending. "Come with me and you'll see."

She glanced down at Serafina's expectant face, already halfway obscured in darkness. Then she sighed and put her foot down on the first rung of the ladder.

After she followed Serafina into the lugubrious gloom of the tunnel winding through to the sterile confines of the laboratory, the first reaction she had, with her heart in her throat and her legs aquiver, was certain relief at its normalcy.

She wasn't sure what instruments of evil she expected to reside here but there appeared to be nothing of consequence except polished beakers and lab equipment giving off an innocuous shine. Then bookcases with rows of leatherbound volumes all in impeccable order, doused with petroleum and peppermint oil to preserve the pages from the elements.

That was before she noticed the catafalque.

She staggered backwards the instant her eyes fell on it. The body it cradled was veiled with a thin white sheet, but she could still make the impression of a male figure laid upon its varnished yew.

"Who is that?" Her pulse thrummed in her ears so loudly she could barely conjure a thought.

"Haven't you ever wondered what happened to Delanus?" Serafina gave her a wry look. Then she removed the sheet to uncover his vacant slumber, arms crossed to provide some modesty over his gaping chest wound.

Laila shielded her mouth as a rattled breath escaped her. All this time she'd been blissfully ignorant, thinking he'd been remanded in the dungeons to serve his sentence while he suffered this agonising torture right underneath her feet.

Serafina took out a tome and threw it open-paged onto the table to reveal her heartless research. "We'd been going over it together. Hoping to refine it. Delanus was... an unfortunate test failure."

"No..." Laila took a step back. "This is absurd." She released a shaky laugh. "This is absurd. You can't possibly expect me to believe I don't know what you're doing."

Serafina had to force herself to hide the pang of pain that caused her. The immediate disbelief. "And what am I doing?"

"Oh, I'm so foolish." Laila put her hands through her hair and laughed maniacally, wracked by full body trembles. "All this time I thought we might be becoming closer. That we were mending the bridge. But this is what you'd been planning all along, isn't it? To drive a wedge between Darius and me."

"I think you know that's not true."

"No, I don't believe you. I won't. Because the alternative is for Darius to have been lying to me this entire time, and Darius wouldn't do that—" Her voice wavered. Yet it was the only explanation she would accept. Could accept. To allow the alternative to take root and sprout its truth in her heart—that she'd been hoodwinked, manipulated, struck blind by her affections from her very wedding night, and perhaps even before—that might be her undoing. No, it was Serafina's duplicity she must cling to. And with the conviction of her deception now strengthened, she couldn't even look at her without sparks spitting from her skin.

"You're lying to me. This isn't his laboratory. It's yours. And you've... you've schemed to exploit my vulnerability as a means to cover up your own sins. Admit it." She advanced upon her. "Admit it, Serafina."

Serafina did not back down, no matter how potent her fury. Nor how closely Laila leered with a threat of violence both knew she would not act upon. She merely stared at her daughter-in-law with a steadfast sympathy she had long thought was beyond her. "If you don't believe me, why don't you ask him? Ask your husband to tell you the truth. You won't, however, because you know there was something he was hiding. All those late night disappearances? The vague misdirections? You blinded yourself because it was easier than to ask questions, but you can't hide from it any longer, Laila." She attempted a pitiful mimicry of maternal softness. "You deserve to know who he really is."

Whatever brittle shield Laila had been hiding behind crumbled. She took a step back and drew in a shaky breath, tears misting her gaze. Her voice had snuffed itself to a frail wisp. "Please... tell me it's not true."

Now she'd grown desperate—clinging for dear life to this comforting blanket of falsehood before the truth unravelled it. "Tell me it's all a lie. *Please*. I need you to—" She couldn't finish before her throat sealed and her hand went to cradle her knotting stomach. It had gotten too hard for her to breathe, to speak, to do anything other than violently retch on a sob as she sank down to her knees, finding them too weak to stand on.

XXIII

DAWN FLOODED THE ROSARIUM WITH ITS unearthly pallor as Darius sat down to tea. He poured a floral brew for himself and Laila in her favourite tea set and sat back to admire the rose-embossed porcelain with its hand-painted gold rims. A wedding gift. And a reminder that their first anniversary of marriage was briskly approaching.

He hoped to create a peaceful setting for the two of them to make amends for last night's conflict after he had awoken to find her absent from his bed. He'd even had a plate of her favourite sugar-powdered strawberry tarts prepared, exercising the necessary self-control not to devour them while he awaited her.

A cosier setting could not have been envisioned.

So when a cold finger of dread raked down his spine he could not have guessed whence it originated. All he knew was that this idle moment of sipping tea and planning parties in his mind had become irreparably spoiled, and he felt certain something worse was to follow it.

He sighed as he glanced at the dwindling steam coming from the teapot. He'd been sitting here for an hour since he'd sent for Laila, and she had not come. He debated if it might be better to seek her out in person but thought better of it. If she did not come by his summons, then it was likely she didn't want to see him at all.

Darius drummed his fingers against the linen tablecloth as his anxieties rose. There was so much he wanted to tell her. So much he desired to explain. If only she might see him, features gaunt from the fear he had pushed her too far with the act he'd so callously committed. He needed her before him so he might throw himself upon his knees and plead his remorse to her. He was a rotten wretch—incorrigible to the bone. He longed to be scalded by her righteous incandescent rage, judging him in a way he couldn't be beholden to by his subjects.

Alas, Laila did not come, and he remained tormented by her absence. He almost thought about retiring to his rooms for the afternoon when the sound of stumbling footsteps alerted him.

He stood immediately and turned. And there she was.

"You asked for me." She came forward, enamelled with a decorative veneer of cordiality.

"I..." He rubbed the bridge of his nose nervously. "I woke up and you were gone." He sheathed his fidgeting hands into his pocket. "Last night, we... well. I assume there are things we left unresolved."

"I needed time to myself." Laila raised a hand to rub at her purpled eyes. "To think about things, you see. I couldn't do that last night. When you're near me, I lose my centre. It's like gravity. Everything pulls me towards you."

"And now?" He took a cautious step nearer. "Which direction are you being tugged?"

"Stay where you are, please." Laila raised a defensive hand to ward him off, staggering backwards against the wall.

Darius halted in his tracks. "Come now... You can't possibly be afraid of me? You know I'd never hurt you. I never have and I never will." He took another small step forward. "Laila—"

"That is close enough."

He flinched, the nape of his neck burning. He couldn't stand to see her look at him like this. Never before did Darius imagine she would approach him with the naked terror of having encountered a stranger. Yet, all the prior comfort and familiarity she'd come to associate with him had been scrubbed from her features.

"You're trembling." He observed this with a wave of shame and gestured to the table behind them. "If you'd sit with me, you can have a cup of tea to calm your nerves and then we can talk."

Laila scoffed. "I really don't think tea is going to remedy this."

"Then what?" Darius threw a hand up in exasperation. "Tell me, Laila. I need to know how to fix this."

"I think you and I need some time apart."

Darius still stood in a daze, hand lifted in mid-air. Then he dropped a hand into his pocket. "As you can see I've laid out your favourite tarts." He placed one of the sugar-dusted goods onto a plate and offered it to her. "Perhaps you might have one? It might make you feel better."

"Have you listened to a word I said?"

He clutched the plate in his hands until a tiny fissure appeared, the first chink in his composure. "What am I meant to say to this request? Where could you possibly go?"

"I don't know! Somewhere away from here. Away from you."

He recoiled from the words and the fury with which she spat them. "If you'd come here and sit we can discuss this—"

"Have I not made myself clear? I don't want tea. I don't want pastries. I don't *want to be around you!*" Her voice had risen into a shout, chest shuddering with heavy breaths. She fixed her stare upon him, daring him to let the mask slip and release the fiend from his disguise. Would he finally uncloak himself in all his malevolent glory as her nemesis and give permission for this loathing burbling inside her to manifest?

He didn't, of course. His gaze contained nothing but the crestfallen look of a husband who'd had his heart shattered by the object of his love. "Laila..."

"I'm making preparations today." She wiped away a tear that had treacherously escaped down her cheek. "Don't try to stop me."

Laila ran upstairs to her quarters and hauled a trunk onto the bed, filling it with anything she could carry. She didn't bother calling for a maid in fear that any witnesses would likely double as informants for Darius. She didn't want him to know where she was going or what she intended to do. She didn't even know it herself. She just needed out.

"When you said time apart I didn't expect you'd be taking any luggage with you."

His voice brought everything to a standstill. She turned to see him leaning against the wall, arms folded.

"Where are you going?"

She clutched the garment in her trembling hands and brought it to her chest for comfort.

"I asked you... a question." He was moving closer to her now but she couldn't make herself move. Her breaths, her joints, her pulse, all of her was frozen in the moment he closed the door and locked it behind her.

"I'd like to take my leave at Drakalyk Castle for a while."

"No."

"I wasn't asking your permission." Defiance flared in her eyes as she folded the garment and tossed it into the trunk in a deliberate gesture.

That was all it took for him to advance on her. He snatched her wrist hard enough to leave an indent of bruises from his fingers.

"Darius, get *off* me."

"Not until we've had a chance to talk this through." He picked her up by the arms and walked her into a nearby chair, arching over her with his hands on either side.

Laila met his stare with a brazen ferocity, sparks crackling across her skin as a defensive shield. "There is nothing for us to talk about."

"So that's it? Your mind is made up? I'm supposed to stand idly by while you pack your bags to desert me, is that it? I don't get a say in this?"

"There is nothing you can possibly do unless you're intent on forcing me to stay." She stood up from the chair.

He caught her shoulders and shoved her back down. "And suppose I was? Suppose I used a curse to seal you into this room at this very moment? Then what do you intend?"

"You would really do that?" Laila asked him. "Lock me up? Bar my exit with curses? Is this the monster to whom I have pledged my love?"

His gaze grew pained but he didn't relent. "If your aim is to punish me for my brutality, then do so at my side. I welcome your scorn. I accept your judgement. Only... do not leave me, Laila. That is the one thing I ask. I have experienced what my life is without you in it, and I can't return to it. I can't..." He reached out to touch her hair and sighed when she shrank back from him. "Do you really think abandoning me is going to motivate me to anything but wallowing into a deeper pit of despair? I *need* you, Laila. Any monster you think I am now will only worsen in your absence."

Laila's expression gave way to softness. Try as she might, she could not remain unmoved by his grief. She held out her hand to cup his cheek and let him burrow into it. "I love you, Darius. In spite of it all... I still love you." She stroked her thumb along his cheek. "I just can't be with you, right now. Please understand. I need... I need time."

Darius enclosed her hand in both his own and pressed his lips to it.

Laila had to struggle not to flinch when she felt it. She hated him for how much the same he was, thinking he still had a right to hold her like he loved her. She hated that she was still able to feel soothed by it until she recalled, with a sickening roil in her stomach, the dead and rotting body of Delanus in his laboratory. He'd had his elbows deep in Delanus's innards and yet the gentleness that infused his palms made him seem incapable of harm.

"You need to let me go."

He glanced up at her, head shaking slightly. "No, I can't."

"I used to think there was enough love in me to withstand any lows you might sink to. Now I think... perhaps I was fooling myself."

He swallowed, tears filling his eyes. "That's not true."

"It is."

A fury now blazed through the sheen of his tears. He yanked her out of the chair and pulled her flush against him. "Do you really expect me to accept that? Where do you think you might escape to that I won't find you? This is my kingdom and you are my regina. There is nowhere for you to turn that is ungoverned by me."

Laila's heart hammered against his chest. "Darius." She let out a tremulous sound. "Do you want to hurt me?"

His fingers sprang free of her in an instant. "No. Never... I would never. How could you ask me that?"

"You didn't see the way you looked at me just then," Laila whispered, so timid and so quiet. She sniffled and wiped her face with her sleeve.

"I—" He started to speak before a trail of blood slithered down from his scalp. He leaned up to touch it, rubbing his fingers together in shock before falling to his knees with a low groan as blood spurted from his eyes, ears, and nose. "This is... blood magic..."

Serafina entered with her hands outstretched, murmuring a continuous chant that made Darius slump to the floor. "Well, that ought to take care of him for a while."

"How did you..." Laila's eyes bulged. "He didn't have a rune on him."

"Don't need one when he is of my own bloodline." Serafina tutted as she glanced him over. "Come along. You'll be staying with me."

"Where will we go?"

"To the Widowlands." Serafina picked up the stray objects scattered across the bed and put them into their designated trunks. "It seems the appropriate refuge for someone in your state."

"You know that won't stop him," Laila said quietly, stroking the marks appearing on her arm.

"It'll do enough." Serafina snapped the lid shut. "Don't allow him to bully you into staying now. He's emotional. He'll only grow more volatile when he wakes up."

"But when he finds me gone—"

"That is not for you to worry about." Serafina moved closer. "Laila, listen to me. You are smart to consider putting distance between the two of you while you have no means to confront him. However you wish for it to occur. But right now you cannot allow yourself to falter. Do you understand me?"

Laila let her gaze wander over to Darius's bloodied form. "I... can't."

"What do you mean?"

"I can't... do it." She hiccupped, tears streaming in rivulets down her cheeks. "I can't turn against him. I can't leave him. I can't—"

"What are you saying?" Serafina asked. "You're going to stay with him now, after all of this? After everything he's done? All these lies? You're willing to let him make a mockery of you with your eyes open, is that what you want?"

"Do you believe it gives me pleasure to admit I was a fool? That I will receive sympathy? If I were to return home right now it would be to a mother who would laugh in my face and a friend who couldn't wait to shame me. No kindness. No coddling. There are no such things in store for the deceived. Only superiority and scorn." Laila broke into a sob and cradled her face in her hands. "Do you understand? Darius is all I have. He's the only one who truly loves me. I can't leave him."

All this time. So many moments. He'd been kissing her, caressing her, holding her in his arms while knowing how she would've cringed from his touch if she understood the full extent of what he was. She thought she'd been prepared to make peace with loving the worst parts of him, but could she? Could she *really*? When he'd gone above and beyond to keep his gravest sins cloaked from her view? Who even was he to her now beneath this doting husband disguise he'd craftily tailored to deceive her?

The truth was she didn't know. She didn't know. And the inner duel was rending her mind in two.

Laila palmed the wall for balance, her body shuddering as she collapsed against it, retching and sobbing until her stomach ached.

Serafina's lips thinned into a line upon seeing her distress. Then she reached a hand out to rub her back. "That's right. Let it all out."

"Get me out of here." A shaky plea, barely comprehensible. "Get me *out* of here."

Sabina wandered into the ransacked chambers of the regina long after the commotion had come to pass. She'd heard word that Laila and Serafina had left with bags of luggage in tow and drawn her own conclusions. Her incisive eyes made a quick scan of the room to see if she could recreate the scene that had led to this dishevelment before she sighed in lament.

She'd arrived too late. Serafina had made a bloody mess of most of the guards to this point and successfully whisked away her captive. Now all that remained was her sovereign slumped before her on the floor.

"Darius?" Sabina put a hand on his shoulder and gave it a firm shake. "Darius?"

A soft grunt emerged from his lips as he dragged himself upwards. "Where is she...?"

"Laila?"

"My mother," he clarified. "Tell me where she is so I can kill her."

Sabina raised her hands to steady him as he staggered forward. "I don't think you're in any killing shape."

Darius swiped a coating of congealed blood from his eyes and smoothed it between his fingers. "She got me good this time." He acknowledged it with a wry chuckle and wag of his brows. "I'll have to deliver my commendations personally."

"You believe that's wise?" Sabina asked. "Considering...."

"Considering?"

"Your wife has just left you. To go with her."

"Laila isn't thinking clearly right now. If I could just speak with her—"

"That's precisely my point. If you go in now angered by the altercation with Serafina, it will only alienate her more. You need to stay calm, Darius. Take a few days and think about your next moves."

"You have become the spitting voice of your father." Darius cast her a sardonic look before slowly rising to his feet. "However, your logic is sound enough that I shall take heed of it." He collapsed against the bed and massaged his forehead, trying to orient himself after the pangs of his haemorrhage faded.

Now that the heaviness was lifting from his brain he was able to decipher more of his immediate surroundings. What had occurred just before he lost consciousness.

His jaw clenched as he noticed the stray nightgown Laila had left behind in her scramble to abandon him. He picked up the frail garment and ran the delicate silk through his fingers. It still had her scent.

"Do you think…?" His throat tightened, a burn forming behind his eyes. "Do you think she's gone for good?"

He couldn't erase the look of fear in her eyes when he'd grabbed her and pulled her to him. *Why did I do that?* He regarded his offending hands with loathing. He hadn't wanted to hurt her. Much less scare her. All he'd wanted was to hold her tight enough to him so she wouldn't flee. It seemed all he'd been trying and failing to do since they'd met was catch enough of a grasp on her to keep her by his side, but she kept on drifting away from him.

"Give her time," Sabina said, a stock phrase for lack of anything better to say.

The faint echo of his father's laughter wormed in his ear along with the taunt he'd long kept buried. *There is a rot deep in the core of you…* He'd been so convinced of his superiority to his predecessor and yet, look what he'd become. Alone, surrounded by the enabling voices of sycophants, having driven those he once held most dear to the fringes of the country to escape his oppression.

"How much time?" he asked.

"A few days at least." Sabina took note of his reluctance. "Enough for the initial shock to pass over. In the meantime, the realm needs your focus, Darius Rex. You must see to all of this." By *this* she meant the aftermath of Domitia's execution, of course.

"Right." Darius gently laid the nightgown to one side. "Let's get started, then."

⁐

Serafina took Laila home to her izba in the Widowlands, where she remained sequestered in a spare room for days on end. Not leaving. Not eating. Not drinking.

She had left her to it, wanting Laila to come to terms with her loss in her own way. The Widowlands were built to shelter vulnerable, wide-eyed girls like her from the machinations of their husbands. However, not all of them saw it as a haven, but rather a respite until they were ready to flee back into the arms of their doomed love.

Serafina knew, in these crucial early days, that she could expect Laila to come with her doubts, her desires of going back, her questions of whether she'd acted in haste. She awaited it each time she brought offerings of food to her only to be turned away. Until one evening, finally, when she'd taken a tray of warm milk and lingonberry cookies, Laila's voice had croaked in acceptance.

She turned the knob at the door and set the tray of cookies at the end of the bed. Laila was scrunched up in a ball on the other end of it, knees hugged to her chin, back straight against the wall. She looked like she hadn't slept in a week.

Serafina glanced over at her law-given daughter, finding herself at a loss for words. What could one even think to say in the event of a star collapsing?

Laila had been their star. She had been at the centrepoint of the Citadel's orbit, breathing life and energy into its halls. Serafina hadn't realised how much they would lack for light once again now she had been snuffed. Now all the joy, the hope, and the wonder in her eyes had been dimmed to a wisping trail of smoke, soon to dissipate.

It was not in Serafina's nature to feel remorse, to look back and want to alter her actions. Such impulses had always seemed useless to her. But when she gazed upon Laila's wan features, her fixed and immovable eyes, there was *something* deeply buried that scraped inside her chest.

"Laila?" Serafina lifted a hand to her before she thought better of it.

"I'm fine." Laila slid a hand down her dry cheek. Her eyes were warm and red-rimmed, though she hadn't cried in days. She was too empty for that now. "You know when you first told me the truth of Darius... part of me had already known. I'd always known. I just didn't want to allow myself to believe that I could be fooled by someone who was so repugnant. Who could do so many awful things." Her eyes were misting again but she was too withered for tears. "That he could look me in the eye and lie when he said he loved me."

"He does love you," Serafina insisted.

"Does he?" Laila smiled bitterly. "Is this what you do to someone you love? If that's the case then I don't know what's worse... believing it was all a lie or that he could be this monstrous."

"He wanted to protect you," Serafina said, swallowing down the scoff it provoked in her even now. "He never wanted you to see that part of himself. He thought if he hid it then he could keep you safe. Happy. Trapped in your little glass bauble none the wiser."

"Well, the bauble has shattered now, hasn't it?" Laila breathed a scornful laugh. "And what am I left with but this... sham of a marriage?" She closed her eyes and exhaled. "It's as if he's died. I feel as though I'm mourning him. And yet, he's not gone. I've just... I've lost him." She breathed deeply as the tears rolled hotly down her cheek. "I thought I'd be ready to. Now everything is clear to me. But now I see that instead...

it's me who's dying. Because this is killing me. I can feel it. It's killing me."

Serafina made a soft sound of sympathy and leaned towards her despite herself.

"Please, don't." Laila flinched back, wiping away her tears. She moistened her lips. "You know, it's ironic how desperate Darius was to preserve his ability to feel upon becoming heartless. Because right now, at this very moment, I think I'd do anything never to feel again."

Serafina knew it was a plea spoken in heartbreak, but the words kindled an idea in her. A temporary measure to ease her of the pain she felt. "I can help you with that. If that's truly what you want."

Laila's head whipped around to her, bewildered and suddenly hopeful.

"But I would think very carefully before agreeing to something so drastic—"

Laila snatched her hands and held them with fierceness. "Take it. Please. Take all of it. Something must give. Because if it doesn't... I honestly don't believe I'm going to be able to survive this."

Serafina looked into her eyes. A shine had returned to them, but it was not the light she hoped for. Instead it was the gloss of a polished window. Vacant. Hollow. "All right." She stroked the side of Laila's face. "I'll take it all away."

Volume VIII

Dawn of the
Phoenix

"The Age of Summer ushers
in a world in which Chaos is
diminished, but not destroyed—
its black wildfire tamed through
collision with an immaculate
counterpart"
— The Solaribus

XXIV

A soft grunt escaped Dr Isuka as she hefted the weight of the chimera's arm onto the operating table. The stubs of its fingers flexed as she laid it to rest, having been cut off to protect her from the lethal threat of its claws. She had tried just about anything fathomable she could to put the beast to rest so she could study it further. Yet the fiend supped on poison like it was nectar and seemed impervious to the use of anaesthetics. Alas, nothing remained permanent until she decided to simply dismember it and take the disembodied limb for examination.

She picked up a knife carved out of fine unicorn horn and slit an incision from its elbow to its palm. The 'flesh' gave little resistance to the blade, having no more consistency than that of congealed soup. It squelched as she peeled back the folds of dark matter to reveal a stringy substance clasping it together. There was no blood within it but rather a murky sludge that puddled at its core and belched a pungent odour.

"Ugh!" Dr Isuka dropped the flap in her hand and held her nose. Then she pressed the record button on her audiotape. "Subject is devoid of any recognisable circulatory system or musculoskeletal frame that distinguishes it as a vertebrate in spite of its mimicry."

With caution she picked up some forceps and plucked a tiny sliver of chaotic sludge, holding it up to inspect. The sludge coiled and writhed in response, as if beckoning for escape. "Subject seems... conscious. It's not alive and it's not undead. It runs on... something. Something I cannot understand."

It was impossible. It was chaos. And yet... some part of it was born of Emica. And Isuka knew her better than she knew anything else in the world.

"Come on, Emica, give me some guidance. Tell me how to save you." She'd had the recordings of conversation between Sadik and Emica turning in her mind for days, but she couldn't accept the conclusion. There had to be some way to retrieve her friend's body and soul without theft of another, or her untimely end.

Isuka reached for a bottle of undiluted liquid from the Rejuvenation Pit and poured it onto the creature's limb. That seemed to have an effect. Like bleach to a stain, the viscous substance that composed it lit up in a rainbow and steamed until total erasure.

"Subject seemed to respond to the embers of phoenix fire in a solarite's remains. There is a high chance of fatality in direct exposure to a human body, but perhaps if I could synthesise a remedy from a cured occasso..."

If only she'd have Darius Calantis delivered to her as she demanded! Then it would be him she'd have spread out on the table to hack up as she required. No less than he deserved after the reign of sadism he'd wrought for his entire tenure. Still, she had solved one piece of the puzzle. She had some idea of how she could free her friend of this ceaseless torment, and that would be a victory she could cling to.

Emica used the hand of Sadik Yilan to take a peach mochi into her mouth, savouring the bite. She'd wept copiously the first time she tasted it, as she had with the other simple pleasures she'd been permitted since her imprisonment. A sip of tea, the nibble of a rice cake, all had been enough to reduce her to tears. She'd spent much of her newfound liberation on a binge of decadence, exercising Lucrèce's magnanimity to the fullest extent.

Once she'd gorged herself into a stupor she would sleep for half a day, rise, and repeat the cycle. Eating, weeping, sleeping—in that continuous pattern.

"I don't know what to do with her." Lucrèce shook her head with a sigh before looking to Keiko, an assistant scientist. "She's spoken nary a word to me ever since we found out about this development. We've no idea if this is to remain or if Yilan is still alive..."

"Dr Isuka?"

"Still barricading herself in the Bestiary. I don't think she's ready to face this conundrum just yet. And truly, who could blame her."

Ever since Sadik opened his eyes with the spirit of Emica Hariken inside of him, Dr Isuka had fled down into the Bestiary rather than come to face the creature that started it all.

"Shall I fetch her?" Keiko inquired.

"No need." Lucrèce canted her head. "I hear her coming."

Footsteps tapped in the distance as Dr Isuka marched forward with resolve in her step. "I need Darius Calantis. I don't care how and I don't care when. But I need him."

Lucrèce nodded. "It is our aim to deliver him to you. The impératrice and Lyra de Lis have gone to make good on just that."

Dr Isuka stiffened, still unsatisfied.

"I only require a little more patience from you, Akira." Lucrèce placed a hand on her shoulder. "Please."

Isuka deflated in response, then glanced through the observation window into Sadik Yilan's cell. "How is... she?"

"The same as before. She still occupies the body, piloting it as her own. We are unsure for how long this condition may last."

Dr Isuka pursed her lips as her friend gorged herself on treats and blinked back an onset of tears.

"You should speak with her," Lucrèce said. "You're the only one to whom she responds."

"I don't know what to say to her."

"You do. You've known for twenty years. You just need to recall the words."

Dr Isuka swallowed thickly before bracing herself to enter the room. She took a seat beside the bed Sadik Yilan lay in and looked into the eyes of her long-lost friend, who looked back at her through the man whose body she'd stolen. "Emica..."

Emica gulped down the last of her treat. "I'd forgotten how delicious these were. How cold. How chewy. How sweet. They taste different on this tongue than they did on mine, but the power of memory"—she closed her eyes and smacked her lips—"accounts for a lot, to be certain."

"Emica..." Dr Isuka's tongue tripped over decades of words unspoken. "We need to talk about Sadik Yilan."

Emica paused, a wavering look of guilt settling on her stolen face.

"He's not dead. That's what you want me to answer, isn't it? His soul is stashed away for now, but I still feel him. Fighting. He's fighting me."

"You should give him back."

"I can't." Emica shook her head. "I can't... I can't go back. I... You should be happy. I thought you would've wanted this. Wanted me returned to you."

"Oh, Emica." Isuka smothered a hand over her mouth. "For over twenty years I have done nothing but work in the pursuit of avenging your loss, but... you know we can't have it like this. Not at the expense of an innocent man."

"I can't go back. I won't. Listen... as long as I'm free the chimeras are vulnerable. They are powered through the force of my connection to the Nether, but I am not *in* the Nether. Not anymore. I am his weakness. *Use* me."

Dr Isuka sighed heavily, knowing without looking that Lucrèce was scrutinising every word from behind the glass. Calculating.

"I know it's... wrong. What I'm doing. I know I can't come back like this. I wouldn't *want* to come back like this. I'm only asking for a little more time. Please. Let me stay." Emica reached forward to take Isuka's hand. "At least until we put that monster to rest." Her voice rattled with a rage that seemed to lodge like jagged glass in her throat as she spoke of her tormentor.

Isuka knew that so long as this gave them an advantage that Calantis couldn't see, Lucrèce wouldn't hesitate to exploit it. No matter the cost. "As you wish... but could you please grant me this one request?"

"Anything."

"Let me speak with him. With Yilan. For only a moment. I need to be certain what's become of him."

Emica took a moment to deliberate the request before she nodded and slowly let her eyes roll back. A hoarse cough escaped her not long after as Sadik glanced around frantically at his surroundings. "You..." He slurred over his words. "You... brought me out."

"Yes," Dr Isuka said, stiff and formal. "Though releasing you shall do little in the grand scheme. You're still at Calante's whims to be sucked back in whenever he desires. Thankfully, you still have use to us."

That combination of words seemed to be the very thing to infuse vitality back into Sadik's half-conscious form. "Fuck off to oblivion."

Dr Isuka stiffened, considering, *hoping*, that she had misheard and that such flagrant disrespect had not left his lips in her presence. "What did you say?"

"I ain't helping with you a Goddess-damned thing until you start treating me with respect!" he snarled. "Do you have *any* idea what I've gone through? What I've experienced? How could you put me there and leave me dangling without any hope of opening my eyes again? You can't just treat me... treat us... like pawns. We are not your pawns. In what way are you remotely superior to the monsters you are fighting?"

Isuka's face drained. "I—"

"Well?"

"Mr Yilan," Lucrèce called over the speakers. "I suggest you mind yourself considering the precarious situation we are currently in. Now is not the time to waste your precious minutes arguing."

Sadik huffed as he looked at Isuka. "She's going to come back. I can feel it... feel her."

"We *need* her, Sadik. At least for the moment. I promise you your body will be yours again once we have Calantis in hand, but until that moment..."

"Nuh uh. No way." He shook his head. "Already got out of that place once. And you want me to go *back*?"

"You misunderstand me," Dr Isuka said. "I don't *want* you to return. I simply require your cursed soul to act as an anchor whilst I make contact with... Emica's spirit." She shut her eyes at the possibility that reunion with her long-mourned friend would be so short-lived.

"I don't mean to be rude, doctor," Sadik said, rubbing at his stinging eye. "But you can see why I don't quite trust you, right?"

She could barely tamp down on her impatience in response. "Do you want to help me or not?" The clock was ticking, and she had neither the time nor the desire to persuade this selfish, near-sighted man why his actions were required for a greater good than his own immediate needs. Such was the nature of the average human; it was no wonder she'd taken more to the company of immortals. "Do you want to help *Elina* or not?"

A splinter of sorrow cracked down his face.

"Let me tell you something—something I'm sure you do not know." Dr Isuka sighed. "You and I are not quite so different, you know? I too have someone I love dearly I am trying to free. And her name... is Emica Hariken."

Sadik's eyes widened.

"She was a friend of mine. One I thought I lost to our research into chaos magic. Until you found her again. It... it anguishes me to know she's been suffering all this time, right under my nose. And I didn't see it. Now I know I have an opportunity to free her, I can't just stand back. I can't squander it. You can understand, can't you?"

Sadik could see now this was precisely what he'd needed. To see her stone casing disintegrated to reveal the pulsing, loving, warm heart of the human at the core of it. "You're sure this will work?"

"I'm sure that it must."

Sadik ran a hand down his face. "I want to help you, Dr Isuka. But for *Elina's* sake. No one else's. The rest of you can rot under Calante's reign for all I care. But first I want a hot shower, a change of clothes, and to eat some *Goddess*-damned food."

Sadik would barely hear of her plans for several days after. But she let him have free rein of the facilities as he partook in all the rituals required to return to a sense of humanity. Once he had sufficiently gorged his appetites of food and wine, rested, and had an indulgent shower, his final request before his departure was to enter Elina's room to visit her for a brief moment.

His former beloved had not been faring well in his absence, and her condition had reached a point where she could no longer wrestle off the intense bouts of fatigue whenever she was laid to rest. It pained him to know he'd put her there, that he might need to look into the sweet, longing eyes of his daughter one day and explain why her mother would never return.

"Hey, honeybee." Sadik sat down at the edge of her bed and took her clammy hand in his. Then he brought it to his lips to kiss it. "Goddess, I've missed that face."

He watched as Elina's chest continued its rhythmic rise and fall.

"Doc says there's a way for me to help you, but it means I'm... gonna have to leave you for a little while." He stroked her hand with his thumb. "I suppose I've already been away from you long enough, haven't I? What's a little more time, eh? Especially if it means I get to see those pretty brown eyes again." His bottom lip trembled as he thought back to the first time he'd seen them.

"You know, when I was a boy growing up in a border town near Seraj, there was nothing in my life I wanted more than a firedrake. I'd go to bed every night before my birthday on my knees, praying, 'Give me a spark!' That's what we used to call it when someone would get fire powers."

He exhaled a laugh. "Broke my heart when I realised it weren't ever happening for me. I was a boy, so I lacked the spark. I could never be worthy to hold something so magnificent in my hands. I didn't think I'd ever feel that lowly again... until I met you. First time I saw you walk up in the Salt Ring when it was nothing more than a dinky little corner store. I thought to myself, 'That girl, I have to know her.' And there I was... praying on my knees like a little boy again to make myself seem worthy. I still ain't. Perhaps I'll never be." He breathed in deeply. "I'm sorry I had to cause you so much pain for me to see that."

Carefully, he lowered her hand back to her side before exiting the room and returning with sagged shoulders back to Dr Isuka.

"Are you ready?" she asked.

"Yeah, doc. I'm ready." And slowly Sadik let his eyes roll back.

XXV

LAILA SKIPPED MERRILY UP THE QUARTZ FOOTPATH, a tuneful hum in her throat.

It was something of a pleasant day, by Mortesian standards. The sun had found temporary release from the cloud's impermeable barrier and had graced them with its warmth. A filmy glow trickled in through the trees to the commune, bouncing off the oven-baked roof tiles that mirrored a coastal town from the Soleterean countryside. She stopped to stare, to breathe indulgently the herb-scented fragrance of her surroundings and observe the serenity of the village that was, admittedly, far from the nightmarish tableau she'd kept in her mind.

Even flowers sprouted along the brick walls of the Widowlands in lacy clusters—poisonous to eat but deceptively pretty to look at. Laila prodded a blossom or two with her fingers and rescued a little caterpillar before it could sink its teeth into a lethal meal. She wiggled her fingers as the insect clung to her skin, her smile fading into a state of blankness. Out of curiosity, she extended her hand back to the flowers to observe what it would do.

She kept her fingers steady as she awaited the caterpillar's choice—would it remain in safety or would it scurry back towards the flower to have that one forbidden nibble? In a moment of disappointment, the caterpillar crawled off the edge of her fingers towards the flower's sweet lure. She abandoned it to its fate. There was no saving a creature that wanted something that wasn't good for it.

Her exploration of the commune continued until she stopped outside of the dry-ageing salt chamber. Noises were vibrating against the walls. They sounded like groans and grunts.

Laila trailed in to investigate a room soaked with the scent of blood. She covered her nose with her sleeve to protect it from rows upon rows of meat sliced into fine cuttings prepared for storage, aged for a month by pink salt bricks. Much larger, unrefined slabs of meat swung from hooks behind them. Nothing was out of the ordinary. Besides the live occasso, bound, gagged, and writhing for release.

Laila's feet drew to a sudden halt when she saw him and his captor. Katerina stood before the swaying occasso, humming jovially, pushing the hooked end of a fire poker into his liver and twisting it with relish.

He squealed like a pig with each turn of the rod, his words muffled through his gag. "Stop! Please, stop! I'll never touch her again. I'll not even look at her. Please—"

Katerina tore out the poker. He screeched in pain.

Laila's head canted to one side in curiosity as if silently calculating whether she should make herself known or continue to observe. She didn't have to wait for long before Katerina twitched in alertness, aware of a new presence in the room.

"Well, now... who's this making the place smell so nice?" When she saw Laila, Katerina had the grace to look sheepish as she wiped her rod on her apron. "Well, well." Katerina tilted her head to one side. She made a mock-curtsey. "Had I known I was going to be in the presence of royalty I might have come better dressed."

Laila stiffened as Katerina swept close to her.

"Don't be shy. I won't bite. Not unless you ask," Katerina said, her smile ferocious. "Though your husband used to like a bit of rough handling."

Laila could tell she was sniffing for a weak spot. She wouldn't give her the satisfaction. "I heard noises outside."

Katerina mimed confusion. "Oh? Him?" She pointed her rod at her captive. "Don't mind him, Your Majesty. This is not a creature you want to extend your mercy towards." Katerina patted his face hard enough to leave a dark print. "He's scum of the earth. The country will be better off without him."

I'll take it all away, her mother-in-law had said, and oh, those were dangerous words to cast out to a person who was drowning. Laila had clung to that promise like a raft as Serafina extended a claw to scratch a rune above her left breast and cast a spell that rendered her heart to stone.

How freeing it had been to float back to the surface after feeling all that weight on her chest just drop within a single moment.

Now she could breathe again. Now she could *think*.

And what her thinking had led her to was this current state of apathy in the face of torture. "It's no business of mine. I was merely curious."

Katerina's eyes narrowed. "You're not about to reprimand me? I had thought you fled from Darius because he overdid it with Domitia

Orlovia." She made a mock salute in prayer. "May Calante guide her soul."

"Not at all." Laila shrugged. "Do as you like. It's not my place to scold."

Katerina prickled with irritation. This was not the fun she'd been expected to have, and Laila's apathy made her sullen. "What's with you today, anyhow?" She drew near, circling her like a vulture inspecting carrion for a twitch of life.

Laila stared ahead blankly.

"Oh, I see." Katerina's eyes flickered with recognition. "You let Serafina work her magic on you. Poor thing. Always told Darius you'd buckle under the pressure. But he'll be heartbroken. His chipper little songbird... stifled."

Laila stretched her lips into her most convincing smile. It came easily to her now, after so many decades of practice, to put on her cordial guise when she felt anything but. What difference did the act of performance make now she felt nothing at all? "Never liked the songbird that much anyway." Everyone else did far more than she.

"So... you truly don't care anymore? About... anything?" Katerina tapped a finger against her lips as she considered this. "Not even if I told you there were other forces behind Domitia's poisoning than her own self-interest?"

The minute spark of interest from her wasn't much, but it was enough for Katerina to seize it and attempt to ignite the flame.

"Apologies..." Katerina waggled her fingers. "I do believe it was my fault."

Laila stared at Katerina unblinkingly for some moments. Then in the next, she had her hand enclosed around the sorceress's throat, clenching tightly, infusing her with an illumination spell so powerful her entire neck ignited white. "Tell me what you did. The truth. All of it."

Katerina had not expected this display of violence from her. For instead of making use of her own arsenal of blood magic, she was so taken aback she flailed and clawed at her steaming throat. "I—you—" Hoarse coughs followed by puffs of smoke came. "You need to let go... of... my neck."

Laila released her and Katerina stumbled backwards to the floor, wheezing painfully as her hands cradled her scorched vocal cords. "Well?"

"The poison was..." Katerina rasped, "my idea. Not Domitia's... No intent to kill... her... It was meant to be you."

"So then you caused all of this." Laila tilted her head to one side. "Domitia's death. Darius's verdict of execution. That was all you. But then, that was what you wanted, wasn't it? This is precisely how you like him. Broken, corrupted—it's easier for you to get to him that way. The only inconvenience was that I was left alive."

Katerina's eyes narrowed but she did not deny it. The light scalding her throat rendered her unable to. "Yes."

"Was it worth it?" Laila's eyes were searching, curious. "Was he worth it?"

Katerina gave a little cough before glaring at her. "It was never about him. Always about who had the true influence over the throne. Because I saw you both... I saw what he was willing to do for you. And I wanted it too."

"Well, he wouldn't do that for you," Laila said, though she took no great delight in saying it. To her, it was simply factual. "Not while I'm alive." She pivoted on her heel.

Serafina spread feed among a herd of clucking chickens while awaiting Laila's return from her latest excursion.

Very little had been heard from Darius since their escape from the Citadel, and it was something that hovered in the back of Serafina's mind the more the days ticked on. In her mind, there could only be two reasons for his silence—one being that he was biding his time for an attack and the other that he was simply too heartbroken to act on her betrayal. Neither of which were favourable states for him to be in long-term. She had yet to broach the subject of next moves with Laila, wanting to give her space after granting her reckless request. One she already terribly regretted the moment she saw that stretched elastic smile upon her face.

Nothing good could come of this, she realised, but the spell had been binding. Only by Laila's own will could it be broken, and Serafina had her doubts on whether she was likely to want to anytime soon.

A door slammed in the distance, and she realised she'd gotten carried away with her chores. Treading carefully through the chickens, Serafina made her way back into her izba to find Laila already there awaiting her.

"I didn't hear you come in," Serafina said, using a rag to clean her dusty hands.

She'd seated herself with the utmost poise—ankles crossed and folded primly to one side, a lingonberry cookie delicately pinched between her fingers. Not a crumb appeared from each one of her perfect bites. The way she handled herself with immaculate precision was quite a disturbing sight, like relinquishing her emotions had honed her into something more mechanically efficient.

"You looked busy. I didn't want to disturb you." Laila carefully flipped a page of the pamphlet she was reading. "This is quite an engrossing read. You've got a gift."

Serafina knew instantly what she was reading. Her memoir. How she'd been led to the Vidua Nocte. "Where did you find that?"

"One of your widows handed it to me," Laila said, lowering it from her gaze. "I never quite understood the meaning behind the name, but reading this, it's truly clever. I understand you a lot more now. What you do here. Why you were so afraid of me."

Serafina opened her mouth to protest before immediately closing it. For at this point, what could she even say?

"And now." Laila closed the pamphlet. "I see that you were right. I should not have come here in an attempt to interfere. This place... I do not belong."

"So what will you do?" Serafina asked. "Return home?"

"I thought of that... but I know Darius won't let me leave so easily. That's why I'll need you to get out a message for me. To my former guard, Lyra. An embroidered message." Laila lifted up her completed design. The first thing she did, upon deciding the defeat of her husband had become an imminent concern, was take a seat by the fireplace and start stitching. Under her hand, the needlework blossomed into an immaculate garden heavy-laden with meaning in the various flowers she placed in it, no detail left unaccounted for.

"It's something we used to do when we were children. I'll need you to get it to Soleterea as soon as possible." She paused for a moment. "She may not listen, but... no, Lyra is too inquisitive; she won't be able to resist if she receives any hints of danger."

Serafina reached out to take it from her. "And then?"

"I bide my time. I need to consider my options. Until I hear from her, I cannot be confident on what moves I can and cannot make."

"I'll get this to where it needs to go."

XXVI

ARIUS LIFTED THE TOPPER FROM HIS DECANTER OF gold wine and poured himself a glass. He made sure the wine had been rigorously tested, as drinking so soon after his close encounter with poison had made him antsy. Heeding Sabina's advice to wait for Laila to come to him had left him anxious and impatient. And the more his mood darkened, the stronger the impulse grew to send out a chimera to fetch her himself.

His rational mind fought against it, knowing that sending such an aggressive gesture would be likely to harm his case more than it helped. Still, it whispered seductively in his ear as he sipped his liquor, and one of his infernal children let out a hollow gurgle of a purr before nudging its head against his fingers.

Darius allowed his fingers to glide along the chimera's cold, inky pelt as a display of affection as inches away from him Marcus Orlovis let out a meek snuffle on the ground. His face had been bitten and torn off, and his fresh blood still spattered Darius's blank features from when he had ordered the savage attack.

Shreds of his skin fluttered in the draught, his tongue lolling from his shattered skull. But still he was alive. His jaw flapped helplessly, attempting to form words as it dangled.

"You see, now, why it's best not to try and fight me?" He approached Marcus and, in a show of grim hospitality, tipped what remained of his glass into his open face.

Marcus's throat bobbled as he strained to swallow, grunting in discomfort.

"I'm willing to allow you to live through this, Marcus." Darius crouched down to his knees and laced his fingers together. "Provided you make sure the rest won't try their chances."

He could only make an indecipherable noise in response.

"We'll take that as a yes, then? Shall we?"

Gold eyes bulged as Marcus's head made the approximation of a nod.

"Good." He snapped his fingers to summon guards to drag him from the room, not turning back to look as Marcus's slumped legs squeaked away on the floor and abandoned Darius to silence. Alone. His chest tightened as the quiet settled and he knew it wouldn't be disturbed by the clear, sweet ring of her birdsong voice.

What a cold shadow she had left behind in the Citadel.

"I can see you're still resisting…"

Darius paused. His head whipped around. There was no sign of where the voice had come from, but he knew it was his father's.

"You know where I am," Lanius taunted. "I'm where I've always been."

A shadow spilled into the room. The shadow of an eagle bred to a wolf.

"You're not real..." Darius edged his way towards the mirror, knowing what he'd find there. "You're in prison."

His father's sneer edged into the mirror's view in the place of his own reflection. "Oh, I'm very real. I'm the dark thing that dwells deep inside of you, Darius. The part of me that you consumed."

Darius suppressed a memory as he remembered the feast he'd made of his father's heart. "What do you want?"

"*I want you...*" Lanius leaned his palms against the mirror's glass until it crackled beneath his weight. "*To let me out.*"

"No."

It could only have meant one thing, but he refused to hear of it then and still wouldn't now.

"Oh, come now... she doesn't even love you anymore. Do you really think if you crawled on your knees for her until they were bloody she would even give you a sideways glance?"

"You know nothing."

"I can see what's in your mind, Darius. What lies in the darkest corners of your heart. I know precisely what you are capable of. That, and so much worse. What you've done with Hariken is only the beginning. We could cloak the entire world in our shadow, reap the souls of the witches and make them birth our slaves."

"No..." Darius shook his head. That had never been what he wanted. He didn't seek to rule the world, only to cast a shield around his own.

"All you must do... is give in...give in to me..."

"No!" Darius punched the mirror, watching the glass shatter upon impact. Shards spilled along the floor and dispersed the image of Lanius's smiling face, leaving Darius in solitude.

Darius panted heavily and put a wounded hand through his hair, slumping over a chair to heave air into his lungs.

That was the pitiful state Sabina found him in when she entered, eyes sweeping over the destroyed mirror. "Now, what did that priceless antique ever do to you?" There was a quiver of concern in her tone.

He exhaled a short laugh as he flexed his fingers, composing himself. "What do you have for me?"

Sabina wanted to press further to inquire on his state of mind but thought better of it, longing to preserve the image of stoical steel she'd held of him and ignore the mental corrosion setting in. "She's still in the Widowlands. But there's been movement to Drakalyk. I believe one of them attempted to deliver something to a sprite."

His jaw stiffened as he understood who the sprite must be. "Find the sprite." He reached down to cradle his chimera's muzzle. "Figure out what she knows."

Sabina nodded, repressing her urge for questions. Though part of her wondered how he knew it was a she.

Lyra had always loathed embroidery. Any sprite soldier worth their title was expected to be a master of not only the sword but also the needle. It was expected that if you could wield the sort of discipline, steadiness, and precision to stitch a complex design then you'd extend those same traits to the battlefield as well.

But she had never quite gotten her head around it.

Those ruler-straight topstitches Laila sewed so effortlessly were an insurmountable feat for her. More than once she'd dashed and shorn fabric in the depths of her frustration, determined to rebuff this skill that refused to welcome her into its ranks.

Eventually, Laila had helped her through it, little by little. She'd pat an empty space beside her during one of her own embroidery sessions and mark a straight line with chalk, coaxing Lyra to follow along it over and over until she gained enough confidence to do it without.

After that they'd made their own little language together out of embroidered patterns. Whenever there was a crisis on either end that required an emergency gathering, one would send the other daisies to signify the private glade Léandre would always take them to during hikes.

Hence, when she received the intricate pattern of daisies at Drakalyk she knew it could only have originated from one source. Laila was trying to contact her, and the matter must be grave. A stew of conflicting emotions burbled in her—fear, dread, curiosity, and resentment, even now, that of course she would be the person Laila would come to in spite of everything that transpired between them.

Lyra suppressed these thoughts as she looked closer at the image and saw a white lioness resting among the tall grass. Her mother. It seemed clear the intent was for her to mediate between the estranged relatives and get them back in contact with one another.

"Are you going to go see her?" Amira floated down the stairs in a sheer lace peignoir efflorescing down her hips.

"I don't know if I should," Lyra admitted. She couldn't erase the disappointment she felt upon seeing Laila the night of the circus. The way she'd not even hesitated to go to Darius's side after seeing the newly felled corpse of one of his female subjects. If seeing the unbridled cruelty he enacted upon civilians of his country wasn't enough to turn her head, then nothing would. "Do you think I should?"

"I think... the Laila that we both knew and loved would never have hesitated to do what is best for her kind and country." Amira's lavender eyes set hard. "I didn't recognise that Laila the other night. However, this might be a sign she still lives."

Lyra studied the embroidery once more, inhaling a deep breath. "You think I should still try and reach her?"

"All I know is you are probably the only one who still can. The last time Laila was adrift was when you and she had split apart. She fled to Seraj for all that time and no one—no one—could bring her back except for you. You have always been her constant, Lyra. When she doesn't have you, I'm not certain she knows who she is."

Lyra still recalled with some shame how their relationship had fractured due to interference from the impératrice. Even though she knew her choices had been few, her hands tied, she couldn't rest until she'd made things right with Laila and brought her home to where she belonged.

Part of her knew, in spite of her show of resistance, that she wouldn't be able to stop herself from doing the same again.

"I'll get my horse ready." Lyra sighed. "Guess I'll be heading into the forests."

Autumn blazed through the trees of the forest in a series of bonfire colours, performing a mimicry of warmth that never quite reached through the frigidity of the evening.

Lyra had ventured far into the wilderness primarily to save time on the journey, but she had been expecting to encounter a fight. Had been aching for it, almost. It'd be a good way to blow off steam so she could approach her friend clear-headed. She couldn't stop her disappointment when she realised the woods seemed to have been nearly picked clean of monsters.

She'd come to understand this was not quite the same desolate wasteland she'd fled over twenty years ago. It had, in some ways, developed a softened edge for the ease and convenience of travellers who sought to brave through it. Against herself she started to see why Laila might have wanted to remain here, to witness her legacy of a domesticated Mortos reach full actualisation to the marvel of her sceptics and doubters.

Once she reached the Widowlands she slowed her horse to a canter, wary enough of her surroundings to take comfort in the proximity of her pistols. The charmingly quaint village did little to assure her that she had not wandered into an unfortunate fable of sorts. The blood sorceresses who lurked from behind the twitching curtains only added to the sense of foreboding.

There was no sign of Laila anywhere.

Then she heard something. A whisper as faint as a dandelion tuft on the breeze.

"Hello, old friend."

She pivoted sharply in its direction.

Laila stood behind her garbed in white velvet, a vacancy behind her eyes where her soul should be.

Horror quivered in Lyra at the sight of her. She didn't seem real. Some sculpted likeness had come to flesh and taken residence of her identity. "Laila…?"

"Come, sit." Laila gestured at a table and chairs positioned on the porch of one of the houses. "We have much to discuss." She pulled out her wrought iron chair and then picked up a porcelain teapot to fill matching cups with dark berry tea.

Something is wrong here, Lyra thought as she dismounted her horse and took her seat. She'd seen Laila in a state of performance many years before but there was always something beneath it. Now it seemed the enamelled mask had become her.

"I didn't think you would make contact," Laila said.

"You call, I come." Lyra shrugged. "That's always been how it worked between us."

She had seemingly no reaction to this, which made Lyra wonder more.

"Why did you call me?" Lyra's eyes darted around her. "And what is this place?"

"The Widowlands is a refuge created specifically to host occasselle fleeing the dangers of male violence. Often from a father... or a husband."

"Fleeing?" Lyra's face tightened as she sought for any signs of harm on Laila's person.

"After you visited your accusations upon him, I decided I could not rest until I did some investigations of my own into Darius. I discovered—"

"You discovered the truth of the chimeras," Lyra guessed.

"No." Laila raised her teacup for a dainty sip. "I discovered something just as grave, with implications that if this were true... then why not the rest."

"You seem to be taking this exceptionally well." Too well, by Lyra's estimation. She knew her former princess and the breadth of her feelings for Darius well enough to not have anticipated anything short of hysterics. "What are you on, right now, Laila? This is too calm to be fever. Don't tell me you've resorted to moongrass?"

Laila's mouth twitched as if her face lacked the elasticity to disrupt its serene poise. "I could never get one past you for long. I'm not taking any intoxicants, Lyra. However, I might have... requested some magical intervention as a form of precaution. To free me from the inhibitions of my foolish heart."

"*No*, Laila..." Lyra sucked in a breath. "Tell me this isn't permanent. Tell me you've at least thought that far ahead."

"I thought this is what you wanted?"

Lyra dropped her hands to the table, shaking her head in confusion.

"For it all to come crumbling down between him and me. For my heart to be broken and my life to be ruined." Laila's lips stretched into a marionette of a smile. "Come now, Lyra. I'm asking you because I know you're the only one who would never treat me like I'm made of glass. You were right. I was wrong. Here is your chance to gloat. Truly—" She placed her elbow on the table and rested her chin in her palm. "Let me have it. I'm prepared."

Lyra's lips stiffened. Her eyes flashed with defiance. "I didn't want it to be like this."

Laila tutted, giving a comical shake of her head. "That's a lie. We both know it." Her carefree sing-song tone was at clashing discordance with her insouciance.

Lyra sighed, eyes downcast, and tucked a loose white strand of hair behind her ear. "All right, I admit when you married him... I kept waiting for the moment when he inevitably showed his true colours. I wanted desperately to wish for your happiness, but I couldn't make myself do it. That was until—"

Laila arched her brow, passively curious. "Until?"

"Until I saw what it did to you, Laila." Lyra's voice swelled with the sorrow and guilt she'd been trying to keep tamped down. "I didn't want it to be like this. I didn't want this for you. I'm sorry that you found out this way. Truly, I am."

Laila's smile disappeared. Her deceptively sunny veneer grew overcast with something darker and more calculating. "You know, it's funny, having this side to you now when I can't even appreciate it." Then she shrugged, her smile sparking back to life on her lips like a pierce of sun between the clouds. "No matter. It's not much like I care either way. Just a pity you've deprived me of my lecture."

"And you've come to me... why?"

"Because whenever I've needed to be set right on my path, I always come to you. You're my compass, Lyra."

"So we leave now."

"We can't."

"Why not?"

"Right now he doesn't know the full extent of why I'm upset with him, and I intend to keep him in that state for as long as possible. The longer I can keep him from being on alert, the better. Besides, he has eyes everywhere, and he's doubtless watching me now."

"And so?"

"I go back. And I ask him to leave with me."

Lyra scoffed. "Are you out of your mind?"

"You forget that I know Darius. I know what makes him tick. I know what he wants. And more importantly... I know what he fears. You say Lucrèce wants him? Allow me to deliver him by hand. We have an opportunity to do this cleanly, Lyra. The last thing I want is for this to cause any unnecessary bloodshed."

Her final words ignited a flicker of hope. "It's still you in there, isn't it?" It gave her comfort to know she had not abandoned all her softness. She'd merely stored it away in this hard shell casing where the wrong parties could no longer have access. "All right. I'll trust your judgement."

"Thank you."

"And what about after?"

Laila blinked, wordless.

"After when the spell is broken and you have to face everything you've been putting off."

"I don't understand."

"You loved him, Laila. You were in love with him. You married him, for Asemani's sake. There will come a time when you have to reckon with that without any spells."

Something inside her seemed to switch off, to trample whatever fragile bloom of emotion had been taking root. "I will deal with that when the time comes."

"If you insist on staying, at least allow me to give you this." Lyra upturned her palm to reveal the Phoenix feather's brand.

Laila regarded its beauty vacantly. "What is it?"

"A flame of the Phoenix. Your grandmere bestowed it upon me to choose a worthy solarite to offer it to. I'm choosing you."

Laila traced around the rim of her cup. "Why?"

"Because I know you're going to need all the help you can get."

Laila held out her palm for the feather, cautious. She'd heard the tales enough to know the power imbued in it. Yet the moment their hands touched there was a fusion, a flicker, but nothing more. She did not feel the flame ignite its magic in her core as she expected. "Fascinating."

"Your curse is likely to prevent it from taking root," Lyra guessed. "If you want it you're going to have to embrace it... all of it."

Laila slid her thumb over the brand on her palm. "Thank you for your service. I'll be sure to give it use."

XXVII

YRA SMOOTHED HER TONGUE OVER HER LIPS TO savour the dying notes of cinnamon and ginger spiced gin before lifting the stem of her moongrass pipe. She sucked deep, exhaling a calligraphic spiral of smoke that tinted the room with an iridescent shimmer. While not her usual poison of choice, she couldn't deny its effectiveness. It gave the world the prettiest roseate haze and smoothed off its sharper edges. On moongrass everything was blissful. Which was a delusion Lyra so surely needed to quell the rabble of anxiety that grew louder with every step she took away from her cursed friend.

It took every ounce of willpower she had not to snatch Laila up and cart her away to safety. But where was safe in this treacherous terrain, governed by the very fiend they sought to thwart and capture? As much as she loathed it, Lyra couldn't deny that Laila's reasoning was sound. To outsmart Darius was the only avenue they could take to prevent harm coming their way. All Lyra could do is sit, wait, and be ready to offer muscle as and when needed.

She leaned her head back on a seat cushion and framed it with her arm. Taking in another puff to fill her lungs, she exhaled in relief. Lyra glanced up at the ceiling and watched the carvings of roses moulded into the ceiling bloom and retract in fluctuation. Her mind swarmed with moongrass smoke, which cloaked a dreamlike haze over her senses and thoughts.

A satisfied smile came to her lips as her muscles relinquished all tension, serenaded by the singing of the drug through her veins. Who would've thought Mortos capable of producing something worthy of being salvaged. She gave herself over to the warmth of her high and reclined in her booth. This dulled the blade of her huntress's senses without rendering them ineffective.

"Can I top you off?"

Lyra sleepily raised one eyelid to peer at her intruder. A red-haired occassella stood before her with a bottle of mulled gin in hand and gave it a slight wave for emphasis. Her eyes were a silvery blue, pale to the point of transparency. She seemed recognisable to Lyra in a way she couldn't place for now.

"Sure." She made a limp-wristed gesture to her empty glass.

The occassella popped open the cork and filled her glass, then took a swig for herself. "Don't suppose you're looking for company?"

Lyra regarded this with the arch of a brow. "An occassella requesting to fraternise with a sprite of all things? These must be desperate times."

"Well, you must've fallen far from your perch to end up wallowing in the gutter with the rest of us. No sprite comes to this neck of the woods if they still retain their honour."

"A logic I can't argue with." Lyra nodded to the empty seat across from her. "Sit."

The occassella instead nudged her way in the scant space beside her until she was practically in Lyra's lap and filled the air with the heavy scent of her cologne. She, like most of her race, was made of sinuous curves and firm muscle. A boastful figure that commanded notice.

Her warmth made Lyra startlingly aware of how long it'd been since she'd been close to a female body. She cleared her throat and willed herself to stay calm. "Not quite what I had in mind, but..."

"I'm Sabina." She inclined her head towards the moongrass pipe before she picked it up and inspected it. "May I?"

"You seem to enjoy asking permission while helping yourself nonetheless," Lyra replied flatly.

"In Mortos we learn to take what we want." Sabina took an indulgent drag and released a hum thick with pleasure. "Though that's a trait I didn't get to enjoy. Ironic, don't you think?"

"How so?" Lyra found herself sitting up in interest. "I can't say I ever imagined any impulse was barred."

"Let's just say I have certain proclivities as a female that aren't fruitful towards my motherland's aims." Sabina swivelled the pipe in her fingers. "So I learned to abstain and suppress. Even as I watched my male counterparts fuck to their heart's delight with no shame for what it wrought. There are many stories like mine, I'm sure you've heard."

The truth was Lyra had not, and such a naked display of vulnerability caused something to claw in her stomach. She soothed it away with a sip of gin, not willing to be mollified by this creature's docile façade. They only sprang when you let your guard down, after all.

"My sympathies," Lyra said, picking up the bottle of gin to refill her glass. She snatched her gaze away from Sabina with a shame she wouldn't be able to decipher the root of.

"It's good stock, this." Sabina's words seeped with smoke. She wrinkled her nose in critique. "But I think you might fancy something a little bit stronger."

A hint of alertness prickled down Lyra's spine to the point she had to keep from clenching. She feared Sabina would sense it if she coiled after being so serene. "Such as?"

Sabina bared her fangs with devious intent. Under the dimmed lighting, her slitted pupils gleamed like cave crystals. The veins beneath her eyes turned dark and writhing and flooded the whites of her sclera with black ichor. "Let me show you." She claimed Lyra's delicate chin within the pads of her fingers. "Come closer."

Her voice was a soft murmur in Lyra's ear, far too tender for the intent behind it. She suppressed her natural impulse to squirm and slap her away, allowing curiosity to take over. A part of her wanted to know the monster's bite.

Sabina started off with a few nibbles along Lyra's jawline before a breath slithered down her neck. Then she sank her teeth in enough to puncture through layers of skin and muscle, though with enough restraint to prevent a grievous tear.

Lyra tried not to jolt from Sabina and clutched the occassella's shoulder, letting her ease her way in before the venom spread. It was purer and stronger than any treated strain of moongrass, and her mind was instantly heady with it. Her lips parted with a groan as her tensed body crumpled. She wondered if this was how it felt for Laila. Would Darius melt her defences with his gaze upon her like she was a succulent lamb? Would he put his lips against her, like so, and drink her like she was fortified wine? She didn't think she was capable of understanding it until Sabina drew away from her, blood-stained lips broadened with glee as she lapped them clean.

"How about we advance this somewhere more privately?" Sabina skirted her fingers along the inseam of Lyra's thigh. "I've always been curious about you sprites, and once one has sipped from the chalice of the aether-touched... I've found there is nothing sweeter."

Lyra smiled back at her with a feral triumph, knowing her fate was sealed. "Lead the way."

Sabina led her from the bar to the urban sprawl of sangrestone townhouses encircled by spiked gates. Outside a couple of occassi were puffing luneleaf cigars like chimneys and murmuring Mortesian among themselves in their rough, guttural tongues.

Lyra tensed the moment she passed them, fingers flexing on the weapons she never kept far from her person. Thankfully the walk to Sabina's home was brisk, and the occassella opened the door for her with a few jiggles of a cursed knob. The house announced itself with broad masculine strokes and understated elegance from its silk-panelled walls, black lacquered wood, and cracked leather. The hearth of her jade fireplace was covered in soot and reeked of pine cones.

Sabina could barely wait until the door was locked before she was upon her. Lyra kissed her with a fierceness she didn't think herself capable of since Aurea Park went black and something within her turned black with it. The occassella responded with relish, devouring her lips with a carnal hunger and pushing her onto the gold-tassel cushions of her red velvet divan.

Lyra braced herself against the weight of the demoness on top of her, flipping them over with a fluid dexterity. Sabina slid her hands up her shirt, unbuttoning it as she went until the garment was discarded in a flutter of filmy fabric, revealing the small roundness of Lyra's breasts.

Then she put her hand on her knee, sliding it up to unbutton her trousers and push past her dampened undergarments, dipping her fingers inside. As a spritemaid, Lyra had an enlarged clit, which Sabina discovered with slight surprise as she fondled it with her fingers.

A shudder wracked through Lyra's body as, caught between lust and revulsion, she broke their lips apart with a gasp and stared down at Sabina with her chest heaving.

Sabina was gazing at her with a kind of wonderment she didn't think an abomination would be capable of. Something akin to the innocent bloom of an infatuation. "I... I haven't..."

No, this was far beyond what she could've prepared herself for this night. To go to bed with a demoness was one thing, but to *deflower* one was too farcical an event for her drug-addled mind.

"Aren't you going to kiss me again?" Sabina asked, coy and teasing with eyes aflutter.

"No, I think that's over now." Lyra jerked Sabina's hand away from her as a wave of disgust rinsed away her prior drunkenness. She swayed uneasily before crawling off of her lap.

"Wait." Sabina snatched her wrist. "You don't have to leave yet. We can just ta—"

Lyra smashed the fat of her palm against Sabina's nose. It had been an instinctual response, rather than one of loathing, but after Sabina flinched in surprise something primal took over.

"Well..." Sabina wrenched her mangled nose back into place. "I was hoping we could have a pleasant night of this. But if you want to play rough, that's fine with me, too."

Lyra's chest flared with the realisation that what she thought would've been a misguided tumble in the sheets had been orchestrated. She had been hunted, preyed upon. How stupid was she to let her guard down in such a manner?

It was then she remembered where she'd seen the occassella last and realised she must be one of Darius's creatures. She landed another blow on Sabina's face to keep her from gaining an advantage. Her knuckles bloomed raspberry-red with bruises as Sabina's beautiful face crunched from the force.

Sabina made a snorkelling noise through her battered nostrils, hacking on blood. "You—" A thin sound whistled out from her that sounded almost like a sob. Until Lyra realised she'd been laughing. "You should do that again—"

Any guilt that might have been formulating within her gave way to disgust as she attempted to tackle her. But Sabina was prepared for it this time, and it wasn't long before Lyra was flipped onto her back, head smashed against the granite floor until it left a crack.

Her mind swam from nausea as the impact blurred her gaze. All she saw was Sabina's fist coming down before she caught it, bending her wrist until it snapped to an unnatural angle and Sabina screamed. Then she launched her into the wall, sending priceless paintings toppling.

Lyra leapt to her feet in a bid for the door but not before a hex twisted her ankle and sent her tripping to the floor. Sabina was upon her again moments after, taking her good leg and snapping it in three different angles.

By the time Sabina was done, Lyra's throat was ragged from screams she hadn't realised she'd been letting out. She scrabbled her blood-smeared fingers into a slat on the floor as Sabina dragged her off to her bedroom.

XXVIII

Pacing up and down the room, Laila started to ruminate on the reliable avenues she had to use to reach salvation. She did not have the meticulous attention to detail Darius had crafted his plans with, only the intuitive sense of finding small gaps in hard places she could squeeze herself out of. What this meant was that she was now faced with the lone tool of her wits against the enigmatic combination of locks that was Darius's mind. And she wasn't sure how she'd emerge the victor. Not unless she had help.

A series of creaks on the staircase announced the aforementioned 'help' she hoped to secure. Serafina had been gracious enough to give her space and privacy to talk with Lyra, but Laila could tell the sorceress had reservations about the suppression of her heart's emotions, and she would need to put forward a compelling case to assuage her doubts.

"Have you given much thought to what you will do now your friend has left?" Serafina asked as she twitched at the curtains.

Laila first thought it was to busy her hands until it grew clear that Serafina was keeping vigilant for any ambush from her disgruntled son. "She wants me to return home with her. Understandable given the circumstances. However, I told her that is not practical. Not with the island under his control. He'll never let me leave."

"Well, despite our efforts, we never did succeed with the amended heartless ritual, so he's not quite unkillable yet." A jest on Serafina's end, but her smile withered upon its stone-faced reception.

"I don't want him dead."

"No, of course. I can imagine even in your condition a sense of fondness may linger."

"You misunderstand. I don't want him dead out of mercy. I want him alive because death is too quick. Too easy."

Serafina's half-amusement declined as something more cautious rose in its place.

"I want him to be *erased*. I want him helpless but to watch as I strip away every bit of authority until he has no more to wield. I want him to never again think to speak my name unless it's to curse it to oblivion."

Serafina sighed. "You are hurting. The spell might have suppressed your pain but it doesn't mean it can't still motivate your thoughts."

"If you think my judgement is clouded, you are wrong. I don't think I've ever thought with more sparkling clarity. As long as Darius is in power, nothing can be done against him. I say we remove him like Lanius before him."

"And how do you propose we do that?" Serafina scoffed. "Without killing him?"

Laila paused, as if meaning to consider it. There was no hesitation out of sentiment in her analytic gaze, simply pure hard logic. "There is a way that I can make Darius disappear. When that happens, you will have the support of Soleterea behind you to secure the Citadel from his prefects. And without him leading the chimeras…"

"It'll leave the Citadel leaderless and defenceless," Serafina deduced. "It can't be that simple. What would you even do with him?"

Laila would have to be careful with her words here. "Does it matter?"

"Of course it does. I presume you mean to hand him over to the mercy of the solarites, which could have any manner of consequences. Many of them positive for *you* but disastrous for the rest of us. I need to know whatever punishment you deliver to him will not be weaponised against occassi at large."

Laila canted her head and sought for any ulterior intent concealed behind her words. Her perception had dulled with her heart encased in stone, but she could still read the signals even if she couldn't intuit them with the same fluidity. "I know he's your son. So this must be difficult."

Serafina had to snort at the irony.

"I understand what it means to love him in spite of all the ill he does. And I know that's why you never raised your hand to him until now. Which is why I want to ask, is it really the fate of occassi you're concerned with, or his?"

Serafina tched in response, but her waver made it evident the question had staggered her.

"If it truly is the former then I give my word. No harm shall come to pass to anyone but Darius." A lie, but a necessary one. "If you can live with that then we can proceed."

"All right, I think I've heard enough of this." Katerina came prowling into the room with a grunt. "Serafina. Why are you even entertaining her inane babblings? We've gotten what we wanted."

Serafina shook her head. "No. We're going to need to resolve this new matter in some fashion. What can we do with her now?" She pointed Laila's way. "We can't return her to the Citadel like this."

"You acted on impulse, clearly," Katerina said.

"I was trying to prevent a bad situation from growing even worse." Serafina ruffled her hair in frustration. "No thanks to your efforts."

"Honestly, Serafina, you cannot possibly think she has a chance to take on Darius and prevail?"

"And why not?" Laila interjected. "I happen to think my idea is quite solid. And you can choose a successor. Someone who is likely to be more sympathetic to the Vidua Nocte than Darius shall ever be. You should want this."

"You are going to get us killed," Katerina sneered, "and I should emphasise the 'us.' Not you. I doubt a single golden curl on your little head will get ruffled if he uncovers this."

"Can't you see that is the point?" Laila's tone oozed with condescension. "He isn't going to harm me as long as he believes reconciliation is possible. That makes me the perfect person to get up close to him."

"I'd be wary of how close. Considering your... predicament." Serafina gave her a quick glance-over.

"Oh, don't worry about that." Laila waved a hand away. "If I know anything about Darius... it's that he loves a challenge. I don't intend to warm to him too quickly. He'll likely suspect something is amiss otherwise."

"How so?" Serafina asked.

"I'd not be as... affectionate to him as I once was."

"Ah, you'd become the frigid wife neglectful to his needs." Serafina's lips twitched in amusement before she shrugged. "Well, that's a simple enough fix. It's a physical function like any other. You may lack any emotional investment, but you can still perform."

"I can't do that with him. He'd notice."

"Then you need to put on a better show."

Laila gave her a humourless stare and shook her head. "You don't understand. Sex was never something we did out of obligation or simply to fulfil an urge. It was how we connected. It was intimacy. It was... Even when we weren't together, I felt passion with him I've yet to find with another. At times I question whether I could." She paused to keep at bay any impulse to reminisce. "In any case... it was unlikely to go unremarked."

"Hm, can concur," Katerina piped up from the corner. She draped herself lazily on an available chair. "For all his faults, Darius was always an exceptional lover. Sex with him never lacked meaning even in the absence of attachment. He had a way of making one feel valued during the act—like he'd made the language of your body a rigorous subject of study and was taking the time to express his knowledge of it. I can only imagine how much more elevated the experience would be when he's in love with you."

Something drained from Laila's face as the blood sorceress spoke with that wistful tone in her voice. There was a flicker of something embedded in her she couldn't quite put to name—annoyance would be the answer she'd cling to. Jealousy would be the one closer to the mark. Even emotionless, she didn't quite care to hear someone else discuss being with Darius before her. "Returning to the subject... with my mother here we have an opportunity. If we all collaborate together to subdue him then we should be able to deal with it before he can think to prepare for a counterattack."

"Smart." Serafina tapped her lips idly. "Rather than an outright offensive we trick him into letting down his guard."

"Then once we have him in hand we—"

A loud roar reverberated through the Widowlands, rattling the windows and sending loose objects clattering to the floor. The sorceresses let out a collective shout in alarm as their legs wobbled beneath them and crumpled.

"What in *oblivion* is that?" Katerina clapped her hands over her ears and felt blood spurting out.

"Chimera," Serafina grunted. She palmed her way to a window ledge to bring herself upwards while her legs shook. "Ugh... that shout..."

The least affected appeared to be Laila, whose legs barely twitched and quickly regained their full strength.

"He's here." She could sense him. His presence was an itch niggling along the nape of her neck. Perhaps that sensation might have heightened to fear without the shield she erected around her chest, but she faced the prospect of meeting him again undaunted.

She burst out of the door to meet the slimy perversion of a toad crossed with a crocodile leaping through the trees. "Don't get anywhere near it!"

Several blood sorceresses had already gathered to stand their guard, daggers at the ready to carve their runes.

"Don't!" Laila ran in front of them with her hands up.

The chimera snarled and frothed thick, stringy mucus from its fat lips. Black warts inflated and flattened with each of its snuffled breaths.

"It won't hurt me," she said, cautious and somewhat uncertain beneath her stoic demeanour. "It's here to fetch me." She sidled closer to demonstrate and reached out a hand to nudge the chimera's snoot.

The chimera belched a dank, putrid gas in response but remained docile at her gesture.

"See?" Laila said. "He wouldn't send something that he couldn't be sure would bring me back alive." She looked over her shoulder at Serafina. "I'm going home with it."

"If that's what you wish," she said.

Laila gave her a final nod before mounting the chimera's slippery back. She had to catch her foothold on the hardened scales to keep from sliding back down, but she soon managed it. Once she'd secured her place, the creature made full use of its powerful toad legs to escort them both home.

She wasn't sure how to face Darius with this new head on her shoulders. Now that love's rosy lens was stripped from her vision, how would she regard him with this unclouded sight? What would she see?

The answer came as soon as she drew into the courtyard and saw him standing there. Any emotion she might have braced herself for met a silencing blow against the stone wall encasing her heart. There was no fear. No longing. No need to cry or tremble. Nothing. If he'd once truly had such an effect on her it seemed difficult to fathom now, as she stared ahead at him as if she wasn't really seeing him.

"Welcome home," he said, reaching out a hand to help her down from the chimera.

Laila blinked before looping her leg to the opposite side of him and sliding down to the ground. Then she brushed past him into the Citadel without a word.

Of course, he followed her immediately up the stairs to the Regina Wing.

"Your room is exactly as you left it." Darius opened the door to allow her entry. It was true. Everything had been undisturbed from their initial argument. He had demanded the servants not touch it and dedicated it as an empty sepulchre to mourn his grief. Several times now he had found himself inside simply roaming just to run his fingers along the bristles of her hairbrush or rest his head atop her pillow.

Not that Laila cared to check, of course. Her eyes glazed in boredom the moment she stepped foot inside. She was merely grateful that Darius was being courteous enough to allow her sanctuary.

"I was thinking we could... we might..." He huffed, realising he was bumbling like a buffoon. "Dinner will be prepared soon. I hope to see you there."

"I think I'll take dinner in my quarters this evening." Laila pranced over to her bed and threw herself atop it. "I believe that's the least I could ask for seeing as you set your monster upon me."

"That chimera would never have harmed you—" He ceased himself from working into a temper. If there was any way to have Laila return to trusting him, then he would need to keep his claws sheathed. "Of course." His jaw flexed with irritation, but he was only biding his time. A little patience could go a long way, this he knew. And Laila had always been worth the wait.

He tried for something civil, a bid to take a leave of absence, but the words did not form. "How long do you intend to punish me with your silence, Laila?"

She turned her head from him to break the alignment of their eyes. "I have no desire to speak with you about this."

He rushed forward to clasp the side of her face to bring her back to him. "What must I do?"

Laila's breaths stuttered as she gathered her composure. He'd only slightly startled her before that too faded into apathy. She closed her eyes and sighed. The stroke of his thumb along her chin might feel deceptively tender, but she now knew the full extent of what his hands were capable of outside of her.

"I just want you to come back to me." He touched their foreheads together and let out a weary sound. "Please."

One had to commend him for how remarkably wretched he could render himself for her. It made something thud against the stone wall casing—some deep, contemptible crevice in her heart she had long needed stifled.

"I know you still feel something," he whispered, breath hot on her lips as he moved closer to brush them along hers. "Why else would you return if not?"

She moved instinctively towards him out of habit, if nothing else. The anticipatory tingle of their mouths sweeping together was too tantalising for her body to deny, even if there was no emotion behind it. However, she calculated what could follow if she let herself grow careless, and so she held fast. Giving him nothing but her cold, impassive stare.

"The only thing I feel right now... is tired." Her words made him start, and she took advantage of that weakness to push him off of her.

A faint ripple of hurt crossed his features. "Am I to assume I'm being dismissed?"

"If you wish to make amends with me, Darius, then the worst possible way you can accomplish it is by attempting to force the issue. Leave."

"Fine." Darius's shoulders coiled tightly as he marched to the door and closed it behind him.

Alone, Darius returned in defeat to his quarters, where Sabina was already awaiting him. A migraine pulsated from the altercation she'd suffered hours before, and she put a palm to her temple, concluding she needed a stiff drink. Something potent enough to silence her agony.

She helped herself to the strongest Mort whisky on offer and swirled the glass, downing it instantly. The burn on her throat cushioned the harsh twinges of pain from her injuries, a welcome reprieve—she never expected the sprite to have given her so much trouble.

When Darius came upon her he paused, a line of concern creasing his brow. "You look as if you've taken quite the beating." He approached her with caution to lift her chin and examine her closely. Her face and knuckles were dappled with fresh bruises and a cut sliced through her lip.

"You should see the sprite," Sabina quipped.

"I should hope you've left her alive." A serrated edge came to his voice at this, and it was clear it wasn't a question, but a demand.

Sabina shrugged, sucking in a breath as she rolled her throbbing shoulder. "She's fine. We got into it a little. I tried to approach her friendly, and she wasn't having it. Just took a bit more subduing than I anticipated she would."

He snorted. "Sounds like her."

"Who is she? Why is she so important?"

"She is called Lyra de Lis. Laila's friend and closest confidant. And I doubt she'd care much to learn my prime prefect had slain her."

Sabina made a sharp noise in response. "Yes, you'd be rather fucked in that case. Not to worry, she remains alive but uncooperative. I do have to wonder what you were hoping to discover."

"I was *hoping* I would find out more to do with Laila's state of mind. What she's thinking." Darius carded a hand through his hair. "This is bothersome. If we release her now there's no telling what she might say to get between Laila and me. She's never held me in high esteem." He paused. "What the fuck happened, Sabina?"

She flinched. She knew it was serious given the unlikely occurrence that Darius had resorted to obscenity, and her chest sank a little at having disappointed him. "We... I—I tried to cosy up to her at first."

"Cosy up to her *how*?"

Sabina's eyes were everywhere but on him.

"I see." Of course, his protégée would attempt to take a leaf out of his own playbook. "All right. You tried to seduce her. It failed. And then what happened?"

"She turned violent. I didn't know how to react. All I knew was that I needed to stop her from fleeing, so I subdued her. Threw her in the dungeons."

"And she's still there now?"

"Yes."

Darius paced about the room, hands on his hips. "This isn't ideal, but it's not unsalvageable. I'll... have to smooth things over with Laila. Keep her from noticing." He rubbed at his temples, swearing beneath his breath. "I've only just gotten her back... If she finds out about this she may never forgive me."

XXIX

THAT MORNING WHEN LAILA AWOKE SHE WAS greeted with a silk ivory gown floating in the draught on the doors of her wardrobe. The cycle had begun. Darius would present her with gifts the way a housecat might deposit the corpses of its kills, pupils broadened in the hopes that she would pet him in thanks.

This gesture might have had more effect if she still held the capacity to care for being pampered. As it stood, her taste for fine things had congested and she regarded the admittedly objectively beautiful garment with little more than a brow raise.

She scrunched her lips to one side as she moved close to run her fingers along the gossamer fabric. It was light as a morning dew's wisp against her skin. He knew her taste well; she could never fault him for that. The rich floral motifs of the gown were beautifully ornamented by glass beading weaving through multicoloured threads. A sheer spider's web of an overdress spiralled over it, embroidered in gold and silver.

Attached to the hanger of the dress was a note inviting her to tea in the rosarium he had gifted her. A chance to "talk" was his lacklustre pitch, signed with his usual steady hand. She would find no traces of his agitation here.

Her first impulse was to put the missive to the flame of her candle and watch it burn until it singed her fingers. However, that was a touch too wasteful for such a prime opportunity. So she decided she would attend and be the right balance of inviting and distant, muddling his mind on how to proceed next.

While Laila had little hope to outwit Darius, she could stumble him emotionally, and prodding that tiny patch of weakness might be enough to get him to make one of his rare missteps.

With the matter decided, she called on Yula to help her get ready and made a note to inform Lyra of her plans to meet her. After that, she had to count on her former guard to be able to come to her rescue.

Yes, that was the plan. Laila couldn't allow herself to think of what might come after, such as whether she and Lyra would even be able to escape this country unscathed. But as misfortune would have it, Amira was already prepared to tell her the worst when she called her mirror.

"Lyra is missing."

A chill seeped through her to the bone. "What?"

"She didn't return to the castle last night. I've been calling her for hours and have heard no word. Laila—"

She snapped her compact mirror shut.

Darius spread a blanket across the floor of the rosarium and littered it with rose petals he'd plucked from stray bushes. After that, he flipped the lid of the wicker basket and set out plates of food and voluptuous wine glasses that resembled roses, then placed a bottle of lightly chilled rosé alongside them.

He pulled the cork off the bottle and filled her wine glass to the brim, sitting down on the blanket to wait for her with his ankles crossed. Not long after, Laila entered, and a smile came to his lips when he saw her wearing the dress he'd picked out.

"I was starting to worry you'd stood me up." He scratched behind his ear, offering up a weak laugh for how ludicrous the scenario now seemed to him.

Laila did not join in his mirth, instead saying, "I needed time to look my best."

Before she might've had pages and pages worth of anecdotes to bore him with where he'd still happily lend an ear, riveted by the mere sound of her voice. Now she could barely muster a sentence.

"You look beautiful."

"The dress does most of the work; it would be rather difficult to look unattractive in it."

"You are being far too modest."

"Yes, well." Laila cleared her throat. "What is it that we're having?"

She looked over the steaming strawberry pie with its lattice pastry topping. Beside it were glasses of rosé, cold sandwiches stuffed with salmon and sour cream, and a bowl of handmade flower-pressed pasta. Her stomach burbled, not immune to the allure of a fine treat.

"I thought that might catch your attention." A smugness infused his smile so potent that, if one were to bottle it, it would leave you drunk within half a sip.

It almost made Laila frown, but her petulance merely made an undetected temporary entrance before switching off again. "I could never say no to a good strawberry pie."

"Then let me cut you a slice."

She got down on the blanket to allow him to do just that.

Darius served the lavish helping with a smile. There was something soothing in it for her, to simply allow him to play-act his role of doting husband and not look too strongly at what was lurking beneath. She could see why he'd upheld the act for so long. What chance had he for any form of inner peace other than to pretend at it? The only one who'd deign to love him unmasked would have been someone on his par. Or worse.

"I wanted to say I'm... glad you've decided to come down from your room. You've been away for so long, and I've missed you terribly. I even have one of your favourite topics lined up for discussion."

"Oh?" She picked up a fork to slice a bit of crust from the pie.

"I know how much you enjoy a party. And I was thinking with the first anniversary of our marriage approaching you might have ideas on how to celebrate."

Laila prodded at her pie with her tiny fork, watching it bleed juice.

"Now," Darius continued, "I do have ideas of my own, but I thought it best to hear your first and then we could compile our ideas." He smiled, head tilted in interest. Said smile faded when Laila made little reaction. "Is something the matter? You seem... out of sorts."

"I'm fine." Laila nudged the pastry around her plate.

He inched forward slowly, carefully, like she was a bird he sought not to startle. "Are you?" he challenged with a brow arched. "What's going on with you, Laila? Tell me."

He knows me too well, she thought. Then she gathered her skirts to step away from him. She needed to find a way to mask this rift he was feeling between them. The abnegation of her emotions could not yet be discovered. Laila traced the contents of their conversation with calculating precision and isolated an angle she could use.

He got up from the picnic blanket to join her, framing her face in his hands. "Tell me how I can fix it. I'll do anything."

"Anything?" She covered his hand with hers, as she was likely to do.

"Yes, of course. Laila, you mean everything to me. Ensuring your happiness is paramount."

Oh, but he is so very good at this. She couldn't help but admire him for it. Such a declaration would've softened her at the knees under regular circumstances, but without the filter of sentiment impeding her judgement all she could muster was a chilly respect. She could understand easily why she loved him, why she wanted to believe him, why even now she felt something push against the stone wall compressing her heart until she looked away.

"I miss my home, Darius." She slowly observed his response and found he had taken the bait, head bowed in contrition. "I was trying not to tell you because I thought it would go away, but... it hasn't. I thought I could come to love Mortos with the same fierceness, but with each passing day, I feel suffocated under the weight of the expectation that I will fail to be the regina that it needs. That *you* need."

Darius's face creased with sympathy. "That isn't true."

"Mortos needs someone with an iron core. Someone crude and durable. Someone who can withstand the heavy blows of violence that need to be dealt to keep it under control." She made her eyes well with tears until one slid artfully down her cheek. The physiological responses were simple enough to mimic even if she remained utterly indifferent. "I can't do it."

"Please don't say that." He shook his head at her. "It's my fault. I've been overwhelming you. Asking you to deal with too much too soon."

He paused for a sigh. "What if... you and I had some time away from all this? Not for long. Just... a few weeks. A month at most."

"In Soleterea?"

"Yes." He managed a crooked smile before his face fell once more. "You and I can have a break from all of this chaos, and you can show me all your favourite childhood haunts. The ones we didn't get to see before."

"That does sound nice." Her next movements, from here on, were ones she knew would have to be precise. "Oh, I'll have to tell Lyra the good news!"

"Lyra?" Darius glanced up in surprise. "You two are speaking?"

It had been the first time she had caught him lying to her so plain-faced, and yet the disguise was seamless. No flushed cheeks, no racing pulse, no unsteady eye movements. He didn't need enchantments as she did to render her so bloodless; such things came natural to him.

"Yes, she came to Mortos with my mother and we made amends." She speared through him with her gaze. Waiting. Waiting for a confession. Waiting for a display of remorse.

"When was this?"

"At the circus." She affected a quiver in her voice. "I hadn't told you because... of everything that happened." When he still made no motion of revealing himself, she continued. "Perhaps it might be nice if we can all leave together. Give the two of you the chance to mend the bridge, too."

"I don't think that's going to happen."

"Why not?"

"You must understand... it was never my intention for anyone to get harmed." He pinched the bridge of his nose. "I sent Sabina after Lyra. You'd been gone for days, and all I wanted was to know what you were thinking. However, Lyra did not take well to being questioned, and she grew violent. Sabina took matters into her own hands to subdue her and threw her into the dungeons."

"And she's still there now?" Laila feigned affront. "Why didn't you say so in the first place?"

"I wasn't sure how to explain myself."

"Well, then. Now that you have, you'd best let her out." She turned out her heel to start on a path to the subterranean floors, pausing when she noticed she wasn't being followed. "Darius?"

"I think considering the nature of the crime, it's best to keep her in custody. You didn't see the injuries she laid on Sabina…"

"I cannot believe what I am hearing. You sent one of your lackeys to menace her! How did you expect her to react?"

"Sabina meant no harm and has attested to not landing the first strike. As Sabina is my prime prefect, I cannot allow this matter to stand unpunished."

"So you're going to keep her locked up like a common crook. For how long?"

Darius picked up a glass of wine and took a long drink.

"For how long?"

"Until we return from Soleterea."

"Sounds a lot like you're holding her hostage."

"That is not my intent. But I need some assurance from you, Laila, that you're not about to disappear."

This was far beyond anything she might have anticipated, and she knew any response she gave would pale in comparison to the histrionics expected of her. Thus, she didn't bother to act. "I can't even look at you right now." As she turned to leave him his hand clamped around her wrist. "Let go of me!"

"Not until I hear you say the words." His presence overwhelmed her with a gravitational force that kept her pinned beneath his gaze—he needn't use his hand to keep her still. "Now, I've been patient, weathering your rejections and suffering through your absence for long enough. I need this to be where it ends. Return to my side. My loyal consort. My most beloved regina."

Her heart should be throbbing with fear at this moment, and yet her numbness soothed it. All the better for her to see how his own desperation stripped him trembling, naked, of his dignified pelt. She'd pity him if he didn't disgust her.

"Say the words, Laila. Say them and I will grant your every whim."

"And if I refuse?"

Her question crackled the ice in his stare, giving way to the watery uncertainty behind his gamble. Both realised in tandem he hadn't counted on her responding with anything but the affirmative. The threat had been a bit of fang displayed on his end, but he was still not prepared to follow through with the bite. Yet.

"I see." She left with him that ambivalence, slipping her arm away from his slackened grip.

XXX

Sabina took a seat at her father's desk and emptied it of his papers. She had left the office untouched since his imprisonment and subsequent torture, almost as if in wait of his return, but as days stretched into weeks and then months she had grown so accustomed to his absence that when the declaration came he was dead she could accept it as quietly as a bad turn in the weather.

Now she unfolded the contents of his tenure in official documents stamped with his seal. Outside, raucous hailstones rattled against the cobbled stone and windows. The sound soothed her, gave her an ambience to settle down in as she tried to extract his ghost from the writings he'd left behind.

She had let the spectre of his disappointment loom over her shoulder too long. Long enough that the first time she allowed herself to seek solace in the arms of her desired sex it had been an encounter mired in the language of transaction, of dominance, such as he had taught her. Her thumb traced the faded pattern of bruises along her knuckles as the only remaining proof that such passion had transpired between her and the sprite. A collision of bodies and a tussle of limbs that she recalled with such sensory sharpness but grew hazier the moment she tried to untangle the conflicting emotional states of carnal want and anguished rage that sent her from a kiss to a fist.

Part of her still agonised over what had led Lyra to strike the first blow. The spritemaid was clearly not as repressed as she but whatever disgust she held for occassi had been sedated enough that night to follow one back into her dwelling. What had changed? Was her inexperience as a lover so evident that she lacked the skill to numb reservations through lust as well as Darius could?

Sabina doubted she would receive answers if she were to visit Lyra's cell, leaving her instead to the cyclical torment of unsatisfied speculation. Another climax withheld. Her father would think that served her right. He could never understand why she couldn't set her 'debauched predilections' to one side as a secret indulgence to engage in after marital congress for the good of the kingdom. But she knew from an early age that the thought of lying placid was unthinkable, unstomachable, enough so that she would rather chance dying alone on a mountain in the First Rite than submit.

Delanus had been happy to let her do so. What he hadn't anticipated, what no one had, was that she would still have it within her to make her way back.

Once she'd removed the last of his affairs from every nook and cranny of the desk, she smoothed them out to observe. Here lay the last vestiges of his legacy on Mortos in which he had fought to preserve the decaying institutions of tradition that had governed her life to misery.

Sabina crumbled the papers and turned them to mulch with a curse. She was about to dust them away into the rainfall when the door swung upon and Laila came barrelling in.

"I demand you release Lyra de Lis at once." Her hands slammed on the desk and scattered the ashes of Delanus's work in clouds of dust.

"Afraid I can't do that, Your Majesty." Sabina suppressed a twinge of annoyance at being robbed of the chance to sweep her father out of her life on her own terms. "Rex's orders."

"Be honest with me, Sabina. You know full well you have Darius's ear enough to turn his head on this matter."

"And I happen to agree with his judgement. So there is nothing for us to discuss."

It occurred to Laila that had she not been so hasty to lock her emotions away she might have navigated this interaction with more finesse. Perhaps intuited more regarding the animosity behind Sabina's actions. Alas, she must make do. "I know Lyra, and she never would've assaulted you unless she felt she was under threat. Considering the nature of the attack, I see no reason why she cannot be pardoned."

"Regardless of her motive, I demand satisfaction for the injuries suffered. Her detainment won't be permanent, Your Majesty. But this sentence shall hold." Although for her it had become a matter of wounded pride more a search for justice. It embarrassed Sabina to think Lyra might tell others of her botched attempt at seduction.

"Well, I'd like to know what your father would make of all this. Domitia's execution and all the actions thereafter." Laila took a methodical turn as she folded her hands behind her back. "Perhaps I'll ask him personally."

Sabina couldn't withhold her flinch. "My father"—a coldness seeped into her voice—"had never wanted to accept you at the rex's side.

If he were present to see all of this now, it would... it would break his heart."

She knows. It was all Laila needed to hear to understand the extent of her loyalty for Darius. If this wouldn't flip her, then nothing would.

"Maybe he was accurate in his assumptions," she muttered underneath her breath and met her with a cool stare. "Rightly or wrongly, your father never hesitated to challenge Darius when he needed to be challenged. You ought to consider doing so yourself, Sabina, if you ever truly want to usurp his shadow." With that, she took off from the room and scampered down the steps of the tower to the main castle.

When she entered the hallway Darius was already standing there, staring at her, as if he had the prescience to anticipate her movements. She realised he likely had. This was, after all, his castle, his creatures, his kingdom. She was a mouse scurrying about a maze of his creation.

There was none of the soft, pliant fondness for her in his eyes now. He had scraped it off like rust and all that remained in its place was a cold light—nothing that ignited from his own soul, but rather a refraction of the impenetrable steel that forged him.

Was this his true face? The one he feared to let me see? She held his gaze, chin firm, unwilling to be intimidated. Then she turned and made her way to her quarters, locking her door behind her. She knew that would grant her no reprieve from his presence. He'd clothed her as an equal whilst reducing her to nothing more than a pet trying to wrest control from its omnipotent master.

Sabina proved to be a futile avenue, which left her with one person to whom she could turn. To do so she would have to keep up the ruse that their love was salvageable, and that meant one thing: She would have to leave Lyra in his clutches. No matter how much she loathed to consider it. Losing Darius would be devastating but survivable, but losing him and Lyra both would be a crippling blow she might never rebound from. However, she couldn't risk squandering her opportunity by worrying how the outcome would affect her in the future.

Thus it took little to convince her. She must be willing to get Darius to Soleterea. No matter how dire the collateral damage.

Darius approached the door his regina had sealed herself behind to escape him and put his palm against it, stroking it down slowly. "I know you're angry with me right now, Laila." He slumped the rest of his weight against the door. It'd be easy enough for him to shatter it with little resistance, but it wouldn't give him the vindication that he needed if she were to come to him. "When you're ready to discuss it, I'll be waiting. I can wait however long it takes for this to pass. Even if it takes twenty years. Or more."

She was giving nothing away, conspicuously so. But he could sense there was something wrong about her in the thing she didn't say. The little silences when she thought no one was looking, but he always was. He wondered what had happened to the vibrantly expressive star maiden that he'd married, and who was responsible for dulling all her colour. Had he done this to her? Had Katerina been right all along when she'd predicted her ruin at his hands?

He couldn't bear to face the despicable truth of it. No matter how it stared him down, demanding acknowledgement. All he wanted was for her to look at him again the way that she used to.

Then it came to him. A callous thought worming its way up from the dirtbed of his mind. If he could reach inside her skull to scrub away her memories of his monstrous acts, then he could be polished anew in her eyes. Her black velvet prince returned. Someone who might present a little dark, a little dangerous, but ultimately soft at his core.

It tempted him far too much for something so unforgivably vile, but that was how desperate he'd become to be welcomed into her arms again. It came so clearly to him now he wondered why he hadn't considered it before. The memory box. He could use the memory box to wipe and store all of this away so they could finally start anew. Of course, it wouldn't be simple. Tampering with the mind never was. She would question the gaps, the missing pieces of information. He would have to implant a believable enough narrative that cast his actions in a more excusable manner. Dim the lights, so to speak. Make things hazy.

Far too late did he realise what he was about to convince himself of. *What a despicable creature I am*, he thought, *to even consider drugging my wife and vivisecting her mind as if she were no better than one of my specimens.*

He shook his head at himself, knowing he couldn't cross that bridge as anything but a last resort. There were other paths he could find over the rift in the meantime. Such as the spritemaid he kept locked away in the dungeons below.

Since being informed of Lyra's imprisonment, Darius had been warring with his desire to approach her and mine her for the information he could not obtain from his wife. The reasons against it were clear. He knew better than to expect that Lyra would ever be forthcoming with him and that it would be more likely to persuade her to gargle poison before considering it. And yet, with the possibilities of such punishments or worse on the table, it would be interesting to test the limits of her stubbornness. To see how much of her fortitude was posture from privilege.

It was with this goal in mind that Darius journeyed downwards into the dungeon, hands clasped behind his back as he prowled through the aisle of cells before reaching the one that had been newly occupied.

Lyra still looked worse for wear. The purple bruises mottling her white skin tinged green at the edges, and the majesty of her silk armour had been left in tatters. Certainly, she had seen far better days. Huddled in the corner of the cot, hugging her knees, she seemed a mere wisp of the firecracker he once knew her as. Yet when her eyes met him, something flared to life in her. A potent hatred. That was the source he would need to stamp out.

"Hello, Lyra," he said in a soft, genial tone. No need to come barrelling in with the stick when he could employ the carrot first. "I must confess you had been the last person I had expected to make a visit. Though the circumstances have been... less than ideal. Do forgive the amenities."

"Rot," she seethed at him.

"Charming as always."

"I'm afraid that's your area of expertise. I've thought you capable of many lows, but I didn't think you'd resort to whoring out your prefects to obtain me."

"Sabina is no whore. She took her own initiative where you were concerned. God only knows why."

"Bollocks. If you could make Laila abandon her senses, then I expect far worse of the people living under the length of your shadow."

"Ah, yes... that brings us to the most relevant subject of discussion. What did you and Laila talk about?"

"She's your wife. Why don't you ask her?"

"I'd suggest you not try my patience, Lyra."

"You can threaten me all you like, but we all know it's empty words. If you kill me Laila will never stop loathing you. You might be bankrupt of any moral fibre, but I know enough that is the last thing you'd want."

"You're right. I can't kill you and I won't." His tone softened to a whisper so slight only the dead might hear. "But I can make living far more unpleasant for you."

"Touch me and see what will happen, you demonic piece of shit."

Rage flared in his eyes before dulling to a simmer. "I'll leave you alone with your temper, Lyra. It's only understandable. But when I return next, I'd strongly consider you mind the tone you take."

He turned from her and made his way up the stairs, where the last of his fury quieted.

XXXI

IN HER BEDROOM, LAILA TRADED HER DRESS FOR A SOFT LAVENDER lace negligee that rattled with butterfly beads and sequins along her thighs. A garment of enticement.

Darius was unlikely to fall for her camouflage, but it would torment him, and that was all she needed. So she took out a sheer peignoir to layer over her undergarments and sought him out in his quarters after tightening the sash.

When she found him in the antechamber he'd been helping himself to a drink, entirely unaware of the assault she'd been plotting against him. How amusing to hold the knowledge that she had switched their roles and shoved him into the seat of the ignoramus, as he had done to her countless times. Now she understood how one could become such a drunkard from an accomplished act of deceit.

It was clear he heard her enter when an uneasiness settled on his shoulders. "I hope you being here means you've had a drastic change in temperament—" Darius swivelled around in his desk chair, words failing when he caught a full glimpse of her.

Laila could see he was trying too hard not to look at her. "I know I've been... distant."

Darius watched her with a stuttered breath as she approached the desk and walked her fingers to approach his. Close, but not quite touching.

"I wanted to say I'd like for us to try again. Mend the rift, at long last." She put her hand on his, smoothing her fingers along his backhand.

"Would you, now?" His disbelief was evident, but his furrowed brow betrayed his lack of conviction. It was almost too easy. This paltry gesture shouldn't have affected him. And yet, here he was. Throat thickened with a yearning to believe it was real.

"I don't want us to fight, Darius." She lowered onto his lap so comfortably it was as if she'd never stopped doing it.

His body tensed as he glanced away from her.

"I spoke with Sabina." Gently, she took his face and guided it back to hers. "I see why you feel the need to keep Lyra in custody. I can't... say it sits well with me, but having seen her injuries—and as you both feel so strongly about it—I am willing to concede to your judgement."

"Sure you're not just saying that to get around me?"

"Perhaps I am..." She smiled at him with the same teasing mischief of their old sparring matches. "But isn't this more pleasant than a row?" Her lips hovered above his before she brought them together.

Darius was eager for the affection, so he closed his eyes and let himself lean into it. However, he noticed immediately that there was none of the typical heat within it. No passion. She was convincing enough, but there was a sense she was going through the motions. He broke the kiss to stare at her, betrayal flickering in his gaze.

"You're not connecting with me."

Laila gazed at him in feigned bewilderment. "What?"

"You're not connecting with me," he repeated as he drew back, the desire for passion now dissolved.

"Darius?" She made a mirthful sound as she reached for him. To bring him back to her. "What are you talking about? I'm right here with you."

"You're with me by proximity," he corrected, making himself cold to her hand on his face, impervious to her attempts to lure him. "Yet when I'm touching you, when I'm kissing you, I feel you'd rather be elsewhere. I know what it feels like when you're in the moment with me, Laila, and this isn't that."

"You're being ridiculous."

"If I wanted a whore to lie with me out of obligation I'd have paid for one. What I wanted was for my *wife* to return. Did you really think I'd be pacified with a few passionless kisses whilst you stare at me dead-eyed?"

Whatever expression she'd been forcing on her face smoothed down to stone. She'd underestimated his skill at reading her. Her disguise was unravelling faster than she might have anticipated, and she needed to find a way to keep it stitched for longer than this.

"You say I'm not connecting with you? It's true. But the fault is not mine alone. In truth... you haven't been connecting with me either."

"How could you say that? I have bared my heart and my soul to you."

"In pieces, perhaps. But not fully. And don't say you have because I know you're lying. For as long as I've known you and loved you, I have always known there were doors in your past that I couldn't enter. I was willing to accept that because there were parts of me I was equally unwilling to share. But you know everything about me, Darius. Every little thing. Can I honestly say the same of you?"

He hadn't liked that. She'd known it the instant she said it. Spite had a way of leaving a residual imprint even when she thought she'd scrubbed the last of it clean.

"What's brought this on?" he asked. "Why the sudden interrogation?"

"Because I need us to be partners going forward, Darius. Equal partners. That means you can no longer keep me in the dark. If you want me to open myself back up to you, then you need to open yourself up to me. Completely."

"I can't do that."

"Why? Are you so afraid of what I might see?" She placed her palm against his chest. "Do you think I might leave if I knew?"

He swallowed thickly, and she could tell she'd reached his soft spot.

"You once told me there is nothing I could do that you wouldn't forgive. Well, you should know there is no part of you I couldn't love. We're bound in this now, Darius. Don't push me away."

He wondered what had provoked it. This newfound curiosity. Perhaps it was that he knew she still bore the stain of Dominus's murder on her manicured fingers and needed the comfort of seeing his sins. Mutually assured devotion. Or destruction. For better or worse.

His instincts screamed this was a poor choice on his part, but his wounded heart outweighed it. Perhaps if he showed her, made a pledge of faith and trust, this might be what finally mended them.

Even if she did nothing but shout and scream at him, he could at least be assured that there was something to provoke at all.

In that moment, he grew thankful for a reprieve when a guard burst through the doors with grave news plain on his face.

"Your Majesty, I..." He trailed off when his eyes took in the arrangement of the regina on his lap and her state of dress.

"Out with it," Darius barked impatiently.

"There is something wrong..." the guard murmured, scratching nervously at his ear. "Something at Darkwater Towers."

Something akin to a claw seemed to graze down Darius's spine. "Get my carriage ready. We leave at once." He pushed Laila off of him without so much as a cough of acknowledgement.

"Where are you going?" she called after him. "We're not finished talking!"

He continued onwards to the staircase in silence.

A busy night had commenced in Darkwater Towers.

Artificers gathered at the forges to pour black sludge from the dying carcass of a recently decommissioned chimera and mix it with steel. The intent was to craft an alloy with the same chaotic, indestructible properties as a chimera itself. Through this they could craft weapons, armour, and even automaton soldiers that would withstand a chimera's life cycle.

After Emica Hariken's firstborn expired, he had discovered that a chimera could only sustain itself for a lustrum, after which the corpses would disintegrate back into chaotic sludge. It took much testing and observation for Darius to utilise this to his benefit, and this latest creation might, indeed, be his fondest child yet.

The sludge blazed a bright yellow from the heat of the flames as the metal took shape into an iridescent carapace of several limbs—two legs, two arms, a torso and finally a metal helmet. This figure, when fused together, had the impenetrability of iron blended with the malleability of leather.

Whilst the clank of metal reverberated through the overheated basement, Darius entered the Towers from the ground above. He observed the diligence of the workers as they toiled inside the foundry, secured behind six inches of reinforced glass, before he ascended to the top of the tower to the most secure room.

Emica remained as before, still ensnared in her writhing black net of chaos. Her already ragged figure was wearing from the toll of forging chimeras. Scholars had fretted over whether she would be able to hold out for many more decades, but such cautions were not enough to pause the hubris of their rex.

However, something had changed. Some nights ago they had been unable to summon chimeras from her body. It was as if she had vacated from her role. An unprecedented development, which had drawn Darius's attention immediately to examine her and see if he could root out the cause.

No matter how much he rifled through pages of medical scans, nothing seemed changed in her. Her vitals were reading as they should. Her pulse was steady. The oxygen and fluids keeping her body sustained were being changed at regular intervals.

That was when he turned to her neurological activity. And it was there he found it: a conspicuous drop in the waves of her nervous system to a point that she seemed hollowed out. A casket. But not enough to declare her death.

"What is going on with you, Emica?" Dread crept up his spine the further he progressed into the report. This could be troublesome, ruinous even, if he didn't figure out how to put a stop to it. Yet the scientist in him had reached a blockade to further expedition. He could not pass through until he found a lead.

"Perhaps she's simply exhausted," Faustus offered. "You've been keeping her at work for over twenty years now; it was bound to take a toll eventually."

"On her body, of course, but the mind I imagined to be more resilient."

"We must remember, she produces the chimeras from her body but that is not whence they originate. This is not the standard childbearing of a female, this is something—"

"Spiritual," Darius finished. Therein lay his answer. Whatever was wrong with Emica would be found in the realm of the soul, but he lacked such equipment to pursue this inquiry on his own.

Thankfully, he knew of just the country down south that would be able to give him exactly what he needed.

"What ought we to do next, Your Majesty?"

"Leave us for now," Darius said absently over his shoulder. He waited until the footfalls of the scholar carried away into nothingness before approaching his greatest creation, the closest approximation he had to bringing *life* in this world. "Come back..." A stone pit of pain lodged in his throat as he mourned her absence. "Come back..." He started, fruitlessly, to shake her in the hopes she would give him more than rattling bones in her sagging sack of skin. "*Emica.*"

He couldn't stomach the weight of another abandonment. To have yet another presence turn her shoulder to him. However, it was of no use. His shovel had finally hit hard rock on the bottomless plunder of her soul.

"Oh, Emica..." He closed his eyes to ignore the spider-like scuttle of Calante's laughter along his mind.

You see how easily I give... I can also take it away...

Quiet, Darius snarled in his mind.

I gave her to you as an offering, Calante revealed. *A little sampler, shall we say? An appetiser for the full banquet of power I can offer should you pledge your allegiance to me. All I ask in return is for you to permit me to wear this lovely flesh suit you have. Come, where's the harm?*

If I give in to you, Darius thought back, *you will not only lay claim to my body but also my soul. My mind.*

That was the original aim, but I am not opposed to negotiating shared ownership. There is no reason we cannot both hold captaincy over one vessel and take turns steering the helm, so to speak.

Darius squeezed his eyes shut. *I do not trust you.*

Think of what I am offering you, Darius. Far superior to the throne of one frozen rock. Together we could rule the entirety of this planet. And beyond.

I won't hear of this. What you're advising, it's…

It's the only way to preserve your skin. And the rest of your kind. You have set the needs of your own aside to please the aetherborn long enough. It is time you reclaimed your power. And your birthright. Believe me, the solarites will not hesitate when the time comes to take what's theirs. You are in an optimal position to beat them to the punch. So do it.

Darius hissed in pain as he touched his temple. A ring seemed to enclose around his mind, fastening him in its grip. *Stop,* he ordered.

You can't resist it any longer, Darius. I'm going to have you. You will bring about my reign…

A sensation akin to claws scratched along the surface of his brain. Darius's teeth gritted as he struggled against Calante's pincer clasp on his mind, enforcing his own will. *Stop!*

He wrestled for control as the talons sunk further in, carving Calante's initials onto his cerebrum to rebrand it for ownership. Snarling in resistance, he rooted deep within himself for something stronger than this. Stronger than the ancestral order in his blood to submit to destiny. Stronger than the compulsion to bend the knee towards godhood.

At first, he could think of nothing. Then he thought of Laila—and the pain stuttered to a stop. He thought of Laila, and the piercing of his skull receded.

I've loved you whether you deserve it or not... I always will. The memory of Laila's words liberated him from the binds of Calante's control. So palpable was her voice, her touch, her face, her *love* that it became a shield around him Calante could not hope to puncture.

Darius gasped for breath as pinpricks of sweat dribbled down to his nose. He realised Calante's godly gambit—the blueprint he had been tirelessly mapping towards escape for centuries—had such an easily exploitable weak point. One he knew precisely how to master.

XXXII

NCE THE CARRIAGE OF THE REX DREW AWAY from the courtyard, Sabina descended into the dungeons to take up the place of interrogator that Darius had left unoccupied. She could no longer deny herself the urge to visit the sprite again, to see the marks of their collision before they faded into the milk of her skin.

Even though she approached on as light a foot as she could muster Sabina could tell the huntress sensed her by the way her head snapped up. Her eyes, so much like fire opals, brimmed with unbridled fury. And that gave Sabina a thrill. The challenge. To think there was a carnal awareness that linked them, driven by pure instinct. For so long she'd been the hunter, unparalleled in battle, and Calante had finally delivered upon her a worthy opponent.

"Great." Lyra snorted. "Just when I thought I'd been rid of the master. The lapdog's arrived."

"You have the most defiant tongue for someone recently bested in battle."

"Forgive me, I wasn't up to snuff that night. Had a few drinks in me, some moongrass. The fact that I was willing to go home with you says enough of how impaired my faculties were. Rest assured, I am fully sober now."

"You make a tempting offer, huntress. Though I'm afraid my orders are to keep you in remand."

"You do everything that Papa Darius says?"

"Of course. Mortos instils in its young respect for those who rank above them. Do you not follow the orders of your leadership?"

"For the most part, yes. That said, when I think I might be furthering the plans of an evil mastermind, I, uh... might have a few criticisms."

"You truly believe your solarites are so immune to corruption?"

Lyra chuckled for a long time. "No... we're not doing that. We're not doing the 'You and I aren't so different' farce. Not after everything that's happened."

"You might not want to believe it, but it's true. What Darius Rex has done with the chimeras? That is fuelled by fear. I saw the way you razed Gravissia to ash during the coup. Do you think we'd be foolish enough as to leave ourselves unguarded?"

"If you want someone to soothe your guilty conscience then find another bleeding heart to proselytise to. Laila's the soft touch you want. I'm all steel."

Sabina snorted in disdain, pacing away from the cell.

As Lyra watched her retreat, she realised she was wasting a prime opportunity to mine her for more information. For weakness. She might not have the same gifts of charm and subterfuge as Laila, but her blunt force approach could have its own merits. "Why did you seduce me that night?"

Sabina halted, shoulders hunched.

"You could've arrested me the moment you saw me. Doubtful anyone would stop you, but you had to put on a show. Why? To what end?"

A ripple of tension went through Sabina as she returned to the cell. "That wasn't... the objective of my mission. I did that for me. I was curious about you. The valiant monster slayer from across the sea. When I imagined having your hands on me... that wasn't quite how I expected the night to turn, but I can't stop thinking of it all the same."

"I beat you until you were bloody, and that endeared you to me more?"

"That night we tussled... was the most exhilarated I have ever felt in my entire life. It made me realise how long I'd been neglecting the longings of my body. The desire to touch, to bruise, to feel the collision of my body against another drenched in sweat. You've unlocked something in me... and I want more of it."

"All right." Lyra cracked her neck. "Let me out of this cell and we can go all the rounds you want."

"I can't do that."

"Then why are you here?"

"Because you're the only one with whom I can unburden this torment. I cannot... I... I thought I could extract it from myself, fashion myself into little more than a machine to carry out Darius's justice. But..."

Lyra struggled with an uncomfortable sensation she soon realised was pity. "There is nothing wrong with you, Sabina. There is nothing you need to extract. And if this is what your country has led you to believe... why cling to it? Why defend it?"

"It is not the country I seek to defend but Darius. He is the only one willing to embrace me as I am and not attempt to bend me into the shape of a wife. How can I not pledge my loyalty to him?"

"What kind of life is it if you're only halfway living it? Denying yourself intimacy and masking it with pain? There is so much more to life than being a slave, Sabina. I'd suggest you learn that before Darius orders you into an early grave."

The occassella bristled at her words before turning away once more.

Darius started up the Citadel staircase to reach his wife when a sudden wave of pain nearly knocked him senseless. He clutched his head as a migraine split down the centre of his skull.

"Laila..." He stretched his hand forward in reach of her. His vision distorted into a fishbowl view, oscillating as if he were swimming underwater and pushing against a continual torrent of pressure shoving him backwards. "Ugh..." His ears congested before popping with a shrill ring, overwhelming him with a bout of vertigo.

Calante's claws grew more entrenched in his brain by the hour, and he wasn't certain how much longer he could retain hold of his faculties. If he didn't make peace with Laila soon, then he might lose the fight for his body and soul entirely.

He just needed to make it to the room ahead. If he made it that far, then he could drag himself into the nearest bed and hopefully sleep the rest of this away. Preferably in near proximity to his wife, where he could take shelter in her love. Whatever remained of it.

Thus it was with impenetrable willpower that he dragged himself up the bannister towards his antechamber where he had left her last, only to appear before her indignant stare.

"Where in oblivion did you run off to?" Laila put her hands to her hips. "We weren't finished talking." He brushed by her absent-mindedly until she took him by the shoulder. "Darius!"

That was when he inevitably collapsed. His final moments of awareness were the peer of his wife's expression—too blank to show concern for his wellbeing.

Laila inhaled deeply at the sight of her unconscious husband, grateful for his insensate state. She was spared, for now, the performance of concern. Cursed as she was, her pulse no longer rose to her throat, nor did nerves rattle the cage of her composure. She had been hollowed of such hindrances. And so, when she dragged him over to the divan, it was with a serenity bordering on reverence. She shifted his weight onto the cushions and rested his head on her lap, waiting for him to awaken.

When he next threw open his eyes, it was with Laila smoothing her hand over his brow in careful strokes. He looked almost childlike, gazing upon her with such naked relief. For all he presented himself to the world as unconquerable, he still needed her at his side to keep weaving the myth. It would unravel without her whispering threads in his ear to assure him of all he was and all he could be. And for as long as that was true, she had something to bargain with.

"Thank goodness, you're awake." She infused her voice with a sigh of relief.

"What... what happened?" Darius glanced around him, struggling to contain his wariness.

"You fainted." Laila cupped his face in her hands. "I didn't even know that could happen to you."

"I've been... under a lot of strain." He wracked the back of his neck. "How long was I asleep?"

"A few minutes." Her brow creased in concern too belated to feel genuine. "What's going on with you?"

"Honestly... I could ask you the same question. One moment it seems you can't stand to be around me and the next you have me cradled to your breast. I can't seem to figure out where I stand with you."

"I think you already know what the answer to that is."

Darius pushed himself up onto his elbows. "Do I?"

Laila went silent for a moment, then she withdrew from her seat to cross to the other side of the room. Further away from him.

"I think it's about time for you to finally be truthful with me," Darius said.

"About what?" Laila approached the table to pick up a bottle of orange brandy and popped off the topper.

"About why you really came back." Darius splayed his hand over the top of the divan for balance. "It had nothing to do with wanting to make amends, did it?"

Laila chortled as she poured herself a glass of liquor.

"Answer me, Laila."

She picked up the tumbler and knocked back the drink before pouring herself another.

"Laila, I swear on all of Calante's might that if you do not talk to me I will smash that glass."

She paused then, turning to face him with an expression of faint challenge poised on her lips. "You're really frightened, aren't you? You can tell that you're losing your grip on me... and it terrifies you."

He was afraid. That much was clear. He understood that whatever rift had formed between them was not one he could bridge with empty promises. To pave the way to reconciliation, he would have to lay down tangible bricks towards rebuilding her trust.

"What has *happened* to you?" Darius shook his head slowly. "You haven't been the same ever since you came back to the Widowlands. Just what sort of poison did my mother manage to spill into your ear in that short amount of time to make you... like this?"

"You really want to start blaming your mother?" Laila swirled the brandy in her glass. "Can't you take any responsibility for your part in this?"

"How long do you intend to keep on punishing me?" There was something colder in his eyes now. Even the softness of his voice had taken a sharper edge. "Try to see reason on this, Laila. I need to be strong enough to face down anyone who might attempt to hurt me. Or you. And after Domitia, I see I was correct on that gesture. She nearly killed one of us. And there'll be more after her. I spent twenty years trying to subdue Mortos on your behalf so you could have an easy ascension. It was all for *you*, Laila. With Mortos under my thrall, we could take Soleterea. We could take it all. Easily."

The more he spoke, the more one could understand the demented logic that had driven his actions.

Laila spoke carefully. "You say you were doing all of this to protect me. Us. I was wrong... for allowing you to do that for me. I understand now that I shouldn't have been willing to let you do something for my sake if I wasn't prepared to do it myself. No matter how bloody or awful. So, thank you... for your lesson."

A look of betrayal sparked in Darius's eyes, and then he chuckled. "Finally, she reveals her true face."

She knew now there were no more cards left for her to play. He'd outmanoeuvred her emotional appeal. He had sidestepped her attempt at seduction. Even her indifference had not forced him to relent. Darius was still clinging to the myth of their love—and worse yet, he was still *winning*.

She could no longer keep up the ruse that there was anything between them capable of being rescued. He'd seen too much and read her too clearly. And as long as he had hope, she knew he would never stop trying to "fix" her, own her, or rewrite their narrative into one of reconciliation. There was nothing left to her now but the truth. To hold up the mirror and see if he might cringe from his reflection—or finally be forced to reckon with it.

"I know everything, Darius. I know about the experiments. I know about what you did to Dr Hariken. I know about your foolish quest to become heartless like your father. I know all of it." Laila's eyes hardened. "You were deceiving me from the very start. Was there ever a moment between us that wasn't tainted with your lies?"

"Every moment." Darius groaned as he brought himself back to his feet. "Every moment I kissed you, held you, loved you. None of that was false. For either of us."

"You let me fall in love with you not knowing what you were. You knew that had I been aware of the full truth I would never have let you touch me."

"I don't believe that for a second." Darius shook his head, taking several steps closer to her. "You saw me for what I was and you loved me anyway. You may not have known everything but you certainly knew enough. And yet, you loved me. You still do."

"I don't." Laila's lip curled back in a sneer. "You revolt me."

"You said there was no part of me you couldn't love. Something like that doesn't just evaporate, no matter how much you may want it to. I understand you're hurting now, you're angry. And I don't blame you one bit. But we can overcome this, Laila. You loved me then and you can love me now. I'm not giving you up without a fight."

"You truly don't understand what's happened, do you? Because you're right. Something like that doesn't just evaporate. Not at once. But I've had a while to erase the hold you have on my heart, Darius. And when I look at you now... I feel nothing."

"Don't say that." His voice cracked as he cradled her face in his hands. Tears glistened in his eyes as he spoke. "Laila, don't say that to me. Look at me. Please." He seized her by the chin when she turned away from him, boring deep into her eyes for a mere fragment of what he'd lost from her. But there was nothing. It was as though she'd been scrubbed raw. And that was when he realised. "What did she do to you?"

"Who?" Laila asked, her voice bored.

"My mother. Don't play me for a fool, Laila. I know she's behind this. She's done something to you. I can see it in your eyes."

Laila tilted her head to one side. Had she the ability, she might have even felt vague amusement it had taken him so long. "Serafina did nothing to me that I didn't request."

"So you asked her to erase your emotions? To leave you as a husk?"

"Yes."

"Why?"

"Because I needed it."

Rage rippled through him, followed by the impulse to dismember his mother and leave her strewn about the courtyard. "Well, we're going to fix this."

"You will not," Laila said with just as much insouciance, but there was steel behind it.

"What in oblivion are you talking about? You think I'm just going to leave you like this? Out of the question. We'll get my mother to reverse what she did and then—"

"What do you suppose will happen when I get my emotions back, Darius? Do you believe I will be grateful to you? That you and I will weep into each other's arms and make love and all will be well?" Her lips twitched with the faintest impression of mirth. "So foolish. I had to give up my emotions because with them I felt crippled. Give them back and I'll only revert to how I was. Unable to handle the weight of how much you ruined my life. How you ruined me. Even if you could get me to love you again, why would you do something so cruel?"

"Oh, Laila." Darius's voice broke completely as tears streamed down his cheeks. "I'm so sorry. I never wanted any of this for you. God, what have I done? What have I done to you?" He collapsed to his knees and buried his face in her stomach. "Please forgive me. Please."

Laila closed her eyes and exhaled, feeling the burgeoning of something sprout within her chest. She fought against it. Fought with her entire might. She knew that within her battled two warring desires. The one she had to hold Darius to her, stroke his face and hair, open her heart to forgiveness. And the one that sought to claw out his vocal cords piece by piece so she might never again feel herself soften before his words.

The two could not co-exist inside her without destroying her from within, and so she let herself breathe a moment. Then she shoved him aside. "If you're quite finished... we have much more pressing matters to discuss."

He fell backwards, startled, before pushing himself up on his elbows. "Such as?"

"Such as..." Laila mocked his timbre. "How we can come to an agreement going forward. Because I can see this going one of two ways. The first: you confess to your sins, abdicate your throne, and give yourself up to justice in Soleterea. If you do that... I may find it within my heart to forgive you someday."

That tiny shred of false hope made his breath hitch. But he knew it was just that. False. A way of luring him into submission to her aims. "And if I refuse?"

"Then you and I are going to have a very, very difficult separation."

"Marriage is a lifelong covenant, Laila." Darius slowly rose to his feet and dusted the flint from his kaftan. "The only way either one of us is escaping this is when we draw our last breaths."

"You won't kill me."

"No..." he said softly. A frigid rage glittered behind his eyes, like the roar of an ocean crystallised. "I have something else in mind for you."

A twitch of alarm rippled through her, a dormant survival instinct, but it was enough to make her turn herself invisible.

"We've played this game before, Laila... you know you can't hide from me." He honed his senses and anticipated her phasing through the door and down the staircase. She would go to the courtyard, most likely. To the grounds to try for a hippogriff.

The hunt had begun.

A slow smile came to his lips, but it was not his own.

XXXIII

LAILA RACED DOWN THE HALLWAY AT SUCH A SPEED she snuffed the candles in her wake. It would do little to repel his night vision, but she would take any advantage she could muster. She couldn't afford to let him capture her. Not now. A fork of lightning illuminated the darkened corridor as a relentless downpour of rain rolled its drumbeat against the window.

Good, she thought. *The less better he will be able to hear me.*

It was foolish to think so. Futile. To consider she could ever outstalk the predator. The one who'd had his entire body honed for the hunt and the eventual capture. She tried for one of the ornaments strewn across the countertops all the same, seeking the one that opened a path to a hidden passage.

Heavy footfalls echoed behind her before she could remember the sconce on the wall as an arm swept for her invisible form. She stepped around it, manoeuvring his weight against him in an attempt to trip him up.

Darius landed on the countertop with a grunt, exploding one of the priceless antique vases.

She struck him again for good measure before she ran, knowing she wouldn't get far, knowing he was gaining on her with every step. When he caught her again, it stripped the enchantment from her body, and he dashed her against the wall with such force it left her winded.

Laila cried out in pain before curling her fist to punch him. He caught it in ease and twisted her wrist painfully before slamming her against the bannister rail, tipping the weight of her body over the long drop beyond the staircase.

"I wonder, did it make you feel good? Killing Dominus." Darius tilted his head to one side in contemplation. A ring of volcanic red encroached on the rim of his iris, searing with the fury of a godhead. "I heard there was nothing left but ashes once you were done with him."

Laila struggled against the frantic flutter of her heartbeat at being so near peril. If she broke that seal she feared she wouldn't be able to keep the rest at bay. "It felt like cleansing a stain."

"I bet it was gratifying to rid the world of him. I bet it felt like justice." His fingers dug into her sides. "Would it feel as good killing me, do you think?"

Laila risked a furtive glance to the fall only his grip braced her from and almost longed for him to release it. "Stop touching me."

"Answer the question."

"Death is too merciful for a fiend like you."

"Perhaps." He breathed a mocking laugh. "Or perhaps your true dilemma lies in not wanting me dead at all."

"Don't misunderstand." Her body flickered with a current. Rage threaded its way towards the surface. "My sparing your life has little to do with sentiment."

"Quite right, I'd imagine. It'd be far more convenient for you were I dead. Erased from existence. Then you wouldn't have to carry on this charade of cowering away from your feelings for me—"

Her head darted forward to strike his nose but he was far quicker. He had her arm painfully twisted behind her back as he pressed her face first into the wall.

"Get off me." She squirmed in futility against his expert hold.

"You would no longer have to fear confronting the truth of this..." His free hand hiked up her gown to slide along her thigh, the waistband of her undergarments, caressing her through the fabric.

His touch inflamed her with an unbearable heat. Laila muffled herself as he stroked her clit in that careful manner he knew she liked until a tightness coiled in the pit of her stomach. She wanted to protest, to bite her lip against the moan that threatened to roll up her throat as he circled his thumb, her toes already curling at the precision of his movements. He followed it with the slow glide of his finger along the fabric of her undergarments, so deftly that she couldn't help but give an involuntary buck of her hips.

"That these hands..." His voice was so silken that it crawled up her spine and seeped between her thighs, his fingers a rhythmic motion through the thin layer her drawers provided. He didn't even have to touch her, just the sensuous timbre of his voice in her ear was enough. "The ones that once brought you such pleasure and solace are the very same ones I used to commit those awful acts you so loathe."

That was enough to ignite her rage. She smashed the back of her head into his nose, stunning him, then pivoted round to knee him in the abdomen. With him winded she tackled him to the ground and tore open his shirt, infusing her palms with a divine glow and sinking them into his chest enough to leave an imprint. Wisps of steam coiled up to frame her face as he fried beneath her touch.

"Yes," Darius hissed in satisfaction, his blue eyes crazed with glee. "Scorch me. Mark me. Pummel me into the ground if you must. I'm yours to do with as you wish."

Her seething faltered at the sight of him, as she realised she'd let him get the better of her. She warred between withdrawing back into herself or burning him that much fiercer, wanting him to disintegrate into nothingness—to cauterise the blight of him from her mind and heart.

"Well, what's it going to be, Laila?" He remained placid and pliant beneath her in challenge, fully embracing his undecided fate. "Kill me like a coward or face your fears?"

Tears sprang into her eyes at his words. She swallowed them away. It would be so easy to walk from him right now and leave him on the floor in indifference. Her rage would be a small price to pay to maintain her emotional barricade. Yet he'd worn away at her too much already, slipping his way in through the fault lines.

Her palms extinguished with a sputter as she slid her hands away and let them fall limply at her sides. "I can't, I—"

Darius grabbed a fistful of her hair and brought her mouth down on his. Laila seized from the shock of it. The softness of his mouth paired with the intensity of his kiss caused her heart to race with a carnality that smashed through the first wall of stone. She tore away from him, gasping for air and distance, which he granted for mere moments before he took her by the chin to put his lips back on hers. At first she thought to struggle, putting her hands on his shoulders to shove him away. But the harder he kissed her the more she relented. Then she whined softly, responding to his passion in spite of herself as he wrestled her to the ground.

The sound of ripping fabric suffused the air as he tugged her gown off. Her undergarments followed. Her stomach lurched as he loomed above her, clenching with anticipatory excitement, thighs growing slick as he pushed her legs apart to position himself between them and pinned her down beneath his weight.

It was obscene to her how wet she was getting for him at this moment. He wasn't usually this aggressive. Not with her. Yet she preferred that to tenderness: In its absence she could retain her wall of indifference—or so she thought. There was nothing remotely apathetic about the way she was throbbing with need as he bit down on her breast, fangs exposed, before forcing his hand between her thighs.

Laila's gasp caught in her throat, the suddenness of his fingers entering her going through her like a shockwave. Her body shuddered in both revulsion and relief as his fingers crooked, forcing her open, igniting a war between her disgust and her desire. She'd been starving herself of him for so long that her body couldn't help but respond to the satiation of this gnawing hunger at her core.

He continued taunting her to release with his fingers as he lavished her breast with open-mouthed kisses, fangs sliding over her nipple. Laila whimpered, back arching despite herself as he mastered her body with a brutal, determined prowess and brought her closer to the brink.

The torrent of her orgasm made her come to grips. She shoved him off her and reversed their positions so she was the one mounting and peering down at him in fury. Her breaths were panting and hard, breasts heaving. She slapped him across the face so firmly its echo rebounded, delighting in the ability to vindicate her anger.

Her glee only increased from the dazed astonishment he regarded her with. Let him be the hapless, bewildered lamb for once. She roped her hands around his elegant neck and squeezed until he gasped for her. She liked the sight of it. Him choking for his next breaths with his throat straining. Before she knew it she was smothering his mouth with hers to claim his air. For a moment she hadn't understood what she was doing until their lips were sealed. Then she was kissing him with frustrated fervour, one hand pressing on his throat as the other raked through his hair and tugged.

She pulled back to discover his features had grown feral, veins snaking beneath his eyes, his pupils dilated until they were almost an abyssal-dark pit encircled by a slim iris of brilliant blue. When he reached for her she batted him away with a wasp-sting swat, and then yanked off his clothes.

He was stiff with excitement when she stripped him, but her rough treatment had made him compliant. It revolted her somewhat, to stoop to his level, but she let instinct take over as she took his shaft in hand and guided him so he could enter her, though only partially.

A low growl tore from the back of Darius's throat, making her stomach flutter. She kept his wrists trammelled above his head as she rolled her hips in short, shallow thrusts.

Darius grunted as though his throat were hoarse with unslaked thirst. He wanted to let himself close his eyes and enjoy the feeling of her, but she was still keeping him at a distance, still reserving an intimate part of her that he was yearning to reach. Each time he raised himself up to push inside her she withdrew from him with a smirk. Then she shoved him back down, smacking him in warning.

"Laila—"

"No," she snarled. She was getting wetter as her folds shifted from the motion of his head inside her. The more his muscles tensed in agitation beneath her the more self-satisfied she became, and she bore down on him inch by inch and allowed herself to envelop him.

Laila kept herself still as she clenched and gripped him with her muscles, squeezing him until she felt certain he might spend before she stopped. She so badly wanted to ride him, drive her hips into him until he was sore and bruised, yet she kept the impulse at bay, determined to keep him at the edge until he was near insane from it.

Darius groaned in agony from her grip around his long-neglected cock. The noise came low and desperate from the back of his throat, his forehead creasing from the rippling motion that travelled down to his base. He submitted to the cruel torment until he couldn't take it any longer and seized control.

He broke free of her hold and pinned her to the floor. Laila was dazed for mere moments before she readied to strike him, but he was faster and grabbed her wrist. Then he gripped her thigh hard enough to leave a ring of bruises as he tugged her legs around his waist and entered her with one forceful thrust.

Laila cried out, hand splayed on his chest as though she meant to push him away, but he kept her anchored to the floor by his hips as he pulled out leisurely, slowly, before thrusting in a manner that hit one deeply hidden spot. The sensation went through her in a powerful surge, making her entire body go slack from how good he felt.

Darius kissed her fiercely as he moved inside her at a fevered rhythm, hips digging into hers with relentless vigour. This was what he wanted, what he'd needed. "You don't know how long I've been craving this." His voice strained, a rich molten sound. "Craving you. You've driven me mad."

Laila couldn't think, couldn't breathe, couldn't feel anything other than him. Her eyes rolled back from the intensity as she urged him on with her hips. She wasn't sure whether her body could withstand it, a passion of this magnitude. But he didn't stop writhing, savage in his want for her. She didn't notice her back scraping away against the floor or the fractures forming from the impact of their bodies.

Her breath hiccuped as she tossed the curls that clung in a sweaty disarray to her face. Her barrier was cracking. Pleasure thrummed through her body with each frantic hammer of her heart and caused more to rupture to the surface. Comfort. Disgust. Love. Hate. Yearning. Contempt. She palmed his face in her hands, and she wanted to crush it as much as she wanted to kiss it.

She found she couldn't face him at all—she didn't want him to see what effect he was having. How he had her once more completely conquered and at his mercy. She bit down on her lip to halt the moans and sighs that threatened to escape.

"Don't." A bestial command, breath ragged from exertion. He grabbed her by the chin and wrenched it towards him before pressing his damp forehead against hers. "I want to hear you."

That alone was enough to make a sound slip out of her. It was the first time there had been this tacit acknowledgement between them. That a hidden, shameful part of her had always wanted and craved the monster. The taboo thrill of it. To be taken until her legs were trembling.

He paused inside her, leaning down to kiss her once more, their breaths quivering. He could see a glimmer of something had returned to her eyes, and he wanted to grab hold of it. He savoured her whine as he withdrew from her to slide inside her again.

"Darius," she sighed as her toes curled even tighter. His hot, ragged breaths only serve to increase her arousal and she came, gasping heavily, white heat spreading up her spine.

He pushed forward a few times to reach one particularly sensitive spot, and her body raced towards another release. Then she was coming again, her muscles spasming with a devastating sharpness. It did nothing to relieve her, only renewing the strength of this bottomless appetite she couldn't find a way to remove. Her need for him was embedded in her blood, in her marrow. You would have to scoop her out clean to extract it.

Darius kept a firm grip on the underside of her thigh to hold her in place and buried his lips into the crook of her neck. He wanted to whisper how much he adored her, how much he'd missed her, how glorious it felt to have her returned to him again. To watch her face contort with something other than blankness and know he was the cause.

Yet each time he opened his mouth his words came out strangled. So he kissed her neck, infusing the words unsaid into every expression of his body until he was edging towards climax. He sank his fangs into her shoulder before he came inside her, crumpling into a heap of satiation.

Laila knew in the surface cognition of her mind that she would have to face up to her mistake. But it wasn't until the last throes of her lust-addled haze had cleared, when he took his face in his hand with affection, that the first pangs of it hit her. Guilt. Loathing. Shame. Her barrier was fragmenting at the seams, crumbling faster than she could repair it.

She shoved him away.

"Laila—" Darius reached for her as she scurried away from him, scrambling for her tattered clothes. He ignored the painful stab in his chest, then shook his head with a chuckle. "Of course. Now you run away. After all, what would people say of their pure and perfect queen if they knew how eager you were for my cock inside you again?"

It would've been useless to deny it when she still wore his bruises at her thighs and the pleasurable ache of him still drummed between her legs. But she kept her eyes on the task of mending her clothes via enchantment.

"You're not going to get a rise out of me, Darius. I may not be able to control how my body responds to you, but it doesn't mean I desire you beyond empty pleasure. It meant nothing beyond that." She slipped on her gown and spared him a dismissive glance over her shoulder. "You are nothing to me."

He was on his feet in moments, speeding towards her. Those were the few words from her he couldn't stomach hearing. "Is that why you sealed away your emotions?" He cuffed her arms in his grip and shook her. "Because I mean nothing?"

Her face remained an impassable stone. "You can poke and prod at me all you like, Darius. I am never coming back to you. You destroyed any concept of that with your treachery."

"You speak to me of treachery when you conspire to steal my crown and country out from under me? I would have had anyone else hung by their entrails for less—"

Laila shoved him, her temper set ablaze by his words. "Then why am I alive?"

"The same reason I am. The same reason why the moments before we made love you couldn't push yourself to snuff the light from my eyes. To finally be free of me. It's because we do not wish to be, Laila. No matter how much you may snarl at me, we both know the truth of this."

Sorrow welled in her eyes and clogged her throat. "I hate you for what you've done. What you've done to me. I cannot bear to have you near me and yet I cannot silence the piece of me that reaches for you in spite of it." She wiped the tear that fell and stiffened herself with a breath. "But I'm getting good at mastering it, Darius. Of unfastening your claws from me bit by bit. And one day soon I shall have you removed entirely."

"You will not. I won't allow it." Darius grasped her chin in his hand, tenderly enough to be a loving touch but with a tightness that betrayed his dominance. "You are mine, Laila. You have been the moment you agreed to this." He traced his fingers along the marriage mark on her wrist. "Now, I've been patient enough to weather the storm of your vengeance. This is where it ends. I'll destroy us both before I let you free of me."

She took his wrist and firmly removed it, her smile vacant and yet serene with her emotional shield having rebounded into place. "We'll see about that."

Kill her, Calante's roar rattled against Darius's temple. *Free yourself from the shackles of mental servitude to this pernicious wench.*

No, Darius hissed back, feeling his hands flex against his will in the impulse to murder.

Deliver her soul to me, and the rewards will be immense.

I cannot... His brow crumpled as he fought for dwindling control over his limbs. *I cannot kill Laila.*

It's the only way... the only way to liberate yourself...

No! He took a step back from her.

Seeing her chance to escape, Laila bolted, and like a hound with the scent of game on his nostrils Darius pursued her until she was back in his grip. She squealed and squirmed, smashing his nose with the fat of her palm until he launched her away with a pained snarl.

Laila threw out her arms to balance herself, catching nothing but air, a scream lodging in her throat as she tumbled down the entire flight of stairs and cracked her head against the marble floor.

"No!" Darius flew after her and leapt the last of the way, handling her dented head with precious care as he assessed her pulse and breathing. Once he'd ascertained that she still lived, he looped his arms around her body and cradled her to his chest.

XXXIV

AURÉLIE ROSE OBSERVED ALL FROM HER PERCH IN THE Astral Realm, face drawn in disappointment. On one side she saw Emica Hariken's soul puppeteering the body of Sadik Yilan, thinner, ghost-eyed, but undeniably present. She spent her days scrawling spirals of chaotic glyphs across the walls in a language only Isuka could read. On the other side, she saw her fallen granddaughter being led away in the clutches of her monstrous beau. Though the Elders had long demanded that she not interfere in the dealings of her descendants, she knew the time had arrived for her to step out of passivity and lend a helping hand.

She outstretched her palm, summoning flakes of iridescent fire to shower upon Laila's shattered soul until it layered like a virgin snowfall. Each particle, once alighted, emitted the faintest bell-like chime and tremored with celestial energy. They began to float, forging a magnetic field around her that lifted her to the plane of the Astral Realm.

"Awaken, starlet," Aurélie commanded.

Laila's eyes slowly fluttered open as she pushed herself up from her bed of soft pink grass. "Where... where am I?"

"You're somewhere safe. Somewhere no one born of chaos can reach."

Somewhere their magic would wane was the part unspoken.

Before Laila could reckon with what that meant, her face crumpled as she shed the days of stagnant tears trapped inside the tomb where she kept her heart concealed. She wept for the disintegration of her deceitfully happy marriage, for the fear of her friend's safety, for the impossible choice laid out on how to salvage this.

"That's right. Let it all flow free." Aurélie rested her hand on her granddaughter's back as it wracked with sobs. "It's been a long time coming."

"I can't." Laila's voice strained through the torrent of her tears and the ache of her stomach. "I can't. It's too much. I can't."

Aurélie rubbed Laila's back in circular motions as she continued to wheeze. Then, once Laila's throat had run sore after the course of her weeping, Aurélie reached out a hand. "Come."

Laila rubbed the rims of her puffy eyes as she took the palm extended and allowed her grandmother to help her to her feet. "How long do we have?"

"As long as you need." Aurélie traced the last tear streaks on Laila's cheeks with a feather-light touch. "Before you're ready to awaken."

Laila nodded. Time didn't flow the same way in the Astral Realm. She could stay a decade or more, and it would be as if a minute had passed for whatever had become of her unconscious form. "I can't go back down there."

"You must, starlet. There is still business you have yet to finish."
Aurélie turned Laila's palm to reveal the glimmer of the phoenix feather.

"Why did you give me this?"

"Because I trusted Lyra to choose correctly. And you are the only one whom I trust to receive such a blessed gift and such a terrible burden. I've watched over you enough to know you will wield its power best in the aim of stopping this catastrophe. Of ending Calante before he can seize hold of your husband for good."

"Is that what's happening to him?" Laila reflected on his changeable moods, realising it made sense. "For how long?"

"Not long enough to exonerate him of all his ills." Aurélie palmed Laila's cheek. "As much as it might pain you to reckon with that."

Laila's eyes glistened with a moistening of tears as her last dwindling hope of redeeming him was snuffed. "So you want me to kill him? Kill Darius?"

"What would you like to do, starlet? Would you prefer your true calling to be at Darius's side for centuries, pulling him back from the brink when he threatens to fall to corruption? Or would you rather put a certain end to all of this strife so you can finally attain peace?"

"I want to stop Calante... but not at the cost of those who are innocent of his wrongdoing. There are those that rely upon chaos. Who would suffer greatly without it. I cannot remove it from them unjustly, not without due cause."

"Then what do you suggest?"

"A third option."

A debate unfurled behind Aurélie's pearlescent eyes in rapid undulations of colour. "You must make your case known to the Elders. It's up to them to make the final judgement. Plead your argument well, starlet."

She snapped her fingers. The moment she did, the landscape shifted to that of a cloud-carpeted void where the only surface present was a round table, silver as the moon.

Laila found herself seated at the head of a table surrounded by silhouettes of floating stars—five on each side. One for every dynasty of the solarites.

"You sit before the Divine Authority of the Celestial Court," the voices spoke in unison. "Tell us, Laila Rose, Descendant of the blood of Esterre. What summons you?"

She'd learned of the Celestial Court during her studies—as the highest authority in both the physical and spiritual realms they only made themselves known when it pertained to matters of cosmic importance. Otherwise, they remained withdrawn from worldly affairs and kept themselves hidden from those who hadn't the fortitude to behold them in all their ethereal glory.

For Laila to find herself sat before them now to hold an audience was something she would never have fathomed possible in her lifespan. Not until the time came for her to be called to membership herself.

She fidgeted in her seat and twisted her words around her tongue. "I seek to plead for the life of Darius Calantis."

"Request denied."

"Seeing as I am the one you want to deliver the killing blow, you are at least beholden to bargaining with me."

"Do not try our patience. Recall the vulnerable position where you find yourself in the Physical Realm. If you do not assist us, then we shall leave to your fate."

"And what will that accomplish?" Laila could feel her temper rising. "What is any of this accomplishing?"

"These creatures are irredeemable. They encompass all that is evil and wicked. Exterminating them would be the only reasonable course to rid the world of their uncleanliness—"

"Do you not think that you too hold the potential for evil and wickedness?"

"That is not—"

"Do you think that purging these creatures will extract all that is evil and wicked in ourselves?"

"You are obscuring the point."

But as she spoke, her conviction only solidified. "The point is that it is easy to externalise wickedness. It keeps us from looking within. But goodness isn't something you are, it's something you do, or choose to do, over and over again even when it's hard."

"Yet, you do not deny that they are evil, nor that they are monsters."

"That does not mean that there is nothing in them worthy of salvaging. I have seen great evil in them, yes, but also love, pain, joy, and despair. Who is to say it is simply their nature, that they are not capable of more?"

For had not she, too, been selfish? Or cruel? Or malignant in her own ways?

A star could only remain earthbound for so long before its shine began to fade. And even in her half-century of life, she had not escaped the world's slow corrosion. Blemished by grief, by pride, by a thousand quiet compromises—she, too, had darkened.

So why, then, should she wrestle with this conundrum? The occassi were a savage, blood-soaked race, gnawing at the bones of their own history, trapped in the wreckage of their ruin. A cycle they seemed fated to repeat.

Who could ever love such creatures?

She could. The answer came to her as swift and sure as the morning sunrise. *She could.* And if she could love them, she could spare them too.

"And how much monstrousness are you willing to tolerate in order to reach this supposed salvation? One's nature is not destiny—no, it can be fought against—but that requires willingness. Have they shown that they might be willing? Did Darius show it?"

Her expression hardened. "Darius is a complicated matter. He always has been. We haven't seen who he is when removed from his environment."

"And you believe now that he has the capacity to change?"

"I believe he should be granted the opportunity to try."

"Your compassion is admirable, princess, but it is short-sighted. We fear your judgement is being clouded by your emotions."

Laila couldn't help but chuckle at that. "On the contrary, I think having my emotions back has given me the clarity I've been sorely lacking. As far as I'm concerned, you are the ones clouded by your biases and thus cannot be trusted with a weapon of this magnitude." She held up the phoenix feather imprinted on her palm. "I shan't be complying with your wishes. If that means I have to face this alone, then so be it."

"If you deny our blessing the Phoenix herself will reject you."

"Will she?" Laila clenched her fist until her nails drew blood, and her palm was eclipsed by an orb of oscillating colour that spread to the rest of her body.

A manic laugh escaped her as she levitated above her disapproving ancestors, irradiated by pulsations of crackling electricity. The sensation was glorious. It was the most exquisite pleasure she'd ever felt or could ever hope to feel again. She drew that power in and allowed it to unite with her, enhance her, tear her soul asunder and remake it into something new.

Serafina sensed a subtle shift on the wind, enough to prickle down her spine as she realised what the cause must be. "Something's happened."

"What?" Katerina asked.

"It's Laila…" Serafina rested her fingers along her temple. "I can't sense my spell on her any longer."

"That could mean a number of things."

"And few of them are good." Serafina couldn't recall the last time one of her curses had failed her that hadn't been as a result of the recipient's death. And she doubted Laila would've broken the curse of her own volition. Thinking of Laila broken and bloodied at the claws of her volatile son was enough to make her pivot from her fellow sorceress and bolt towards the door.

However, the moment she opened it, she was met with commotion as an unexpected visitor to the Widowlands entered the fray. Her sorceresses had scattered with fingers raised in gnarled defence to summon a hex or baleful chant against the source of their distress—none other than Impératrice Amira sitting astride her bejewelled armoured unicorn, flanked by her silk-sheathed sprite guard.

"What is the meaning of this?" Serafina's eyes narrowed as she stepped forward, chest protruding in territorial pride. She refused to cow in the face of such a brazen display of intimidation.

"Forgive the intrusion," Amira responded sweetly as though she'd committed no greater faux pas than to arrive at an unfashionable hour. "I believe you may have something that belongs to me."

"And what is that?" Serafina rested her hands on her broad hips.

Amira hmphed as her head cocked to one side, unperturbed. "My daughter."

"She's not here."

"Then where, pray tell, is she? Because the last I was able to trace the whereabouts of my guard, Lyra de Lis, it was to this"—Amira's nose gave a delicate crinkle—"quaint little village of yours."

"I'm afraid your visit has come a little too late, impératrice. For my son Darius has already come to claim his wife."

"That's unfortunate news." All mirth faded from Amira's features. Then, as if signalled from the minute twitch of her jaw, her sprites reached for their rifles.

In return, the sorceresses cleared their throats to summon a retaliative curse.

Serafina sensed the carnage poised to erupt should she not tread carefully to defuse Amira's mood. Hers was not unlike the tempestuous male egos Serafina had been forced to subdue in the past—raw, unapologetic, and infinitely destructive. "Believe me, I no sooner wanted her to go than you did, but she made her choice and I'm sure you know well that your daughter is unlikely to be dissuaded once she sets her mind to something. But my coven and I are not against you."

Amira sniffed. "Considering you are the one who birthed the source of my ills, you can see why I have some trouble taking you at your word."

"Then let me assure you that my son is no ally of mine and likely wants me deader than anyone else in this forsaken country. It's proof of my most egregious sins as a mother." Serafina's lips drew into a wry smile. "And as a mother I speak to you with sympathy, not malice, when I say I wish no harm for your daughter has come to pass... but if you want to see her alive you are going to want me as an ally. Not an enemy."

Amira swallowed the acerbic words of blame on the tip of her tongue, seeing instead the opportunity for a much bolstered offensive against their shared foe. "You would take up arms against your own blood?"

Serafina canted her head to one side as a shrug. "Wouldn't be the first time."

Amira cast her one more searing glance. "This battle might take many of us. Be prepared for that."

"We're ready."

Thus they marched onwards to the Citadel, unified, casting enchantments so that the beasts of the forest would know not to get in the way of their path.

XXXV

A TRAIL OF SHIMMERING GOLD FIRE FANNED OUT behind Laila's careening spirit like a peacock's tail, spangled with eyes of sapphire and emerald. Once she had dived back into her unconscious body she jolted awake, the song of the Phoenix lilting through her veins in the midst of transformation.

"Shhh." A gentle caress glided down the side of her face. "It's all right. You're safe."

She tugged at the binds on her wrists and ankles until the bed she'd been strapped to rattled. "No..." Her heart hammered as she realised what had happened. "Let me out! Let me out—"

"Easy." Darius cradled her to him, and it reminded her how easily his arms could swallow her. How many times had she nestled in the hollow of his embrace feeling safe as a bird inside a bole of oak? Stupid. She was so stupid. "Everything is going to be fine. I'm not going to hurt you."

The soft syrup of his tone was how she knew her doom was sealed. For him to approach her sweetly meant he had something in the wings to delude him that a positive outcome was still possible. She directed a look of pure blankness at him, playing neutral. "If you're not going to hurt me... why am I all tied up?"

"To prevent you from hurting yourself."

"Is that what you told Emica Hariken?" She realised her body now lay where their miserable fates had been met. "Delanus?"

"Those were regretful actions, but we can't change the past." Darius picked up a sterilised medical utensil and lifted it up to the light.

"Darius..." Laila infused her voice with as much tenderness as she could muster. "It's not too late for you. Let me go and we can find a way to resolve this."

"It's far past negotiations for us now."

"It's not," Laila reasoned. "It's never been too late. Please... I know you don't want to do this."

He held her head down, stroking a palm through her hair. "It's the easiest way to deal with this. I cannot let you go. All that leaves me with is to—" A groan escaped him as he clutched at his temple. The very suggestion seemed to be unspeakable, rending his mind in two as conflicting wills battled for conquest inside his crowded mind. "I can't. Please. Don't make me."

Laila didn't understand. "The one that has the power to stop this is you!"

"All I wanted was to return to a time before all of this! When you were happy! When we were happy!" A hitch caught in his throat as the scalpel fell from his hands in a clatter. "Why couldn't you have just..."

He collapsed against the wall as a sob burbled to the surface. "Why can't you just forgive me?"

"Forgiving you won't make what you did go away, Darius. You have to know that. If I stay with you now, every smile I give you, every embrace, every kiss... it's all going to be a lie."

His lip trembled as tears leaked down his cheeks.

"You'll have to live with yourself every day knowing I can no longer love you. Not like before."

"Stop saying that."

"I have to. I have to let you know. No matter how much you may want things to be different. You'll never be able to remove the truth."

"Stop it..."

"I can't love you like this."

"Stop it!" Darius overturned a table and sent the contents scattering to the floor. He exhaled raggedly, gathering his composure with a swipe of his dishevelled hair.

"Darius..." Gold-flecked tears welled in Laila's eyes. "I know this isn't you. This is Calante, and he wants you to give in to him. Fight him."

"What's the point?" He gave a derisive cackle. "If not for you, then what am I even fighting him for?"

"If your goodness hinged upon my love, then it was never real goodness. It was merely a careful deception built in exchange for reward. My love will not make you good, Darius. No one's will. You have to decide for yourself whether or not you seek to embrace true retribution, one that comes without hope of gratitude, and when you are ready to make that step perhaps you will finally attain peace with yourself. Decide who it is you want to be."

"Sweet words, princess. You always had them in abundance." Darius's irises slid from crystalline blue to volcanic red. "But it seems you have already deemed me your monster. Why disappoint you?"

Pure chaos splintered his skin from the corners of his bloodshot left eye until chips of his skin disintegrated to reveal a charred black carapace of scales.

"Darius, stop this." As her anger blazed, the Phoenix embraced her into the fold and sought to merge their essences as one, amplifying the potential to wield aether to such an extent it was unfathomable.

"There, now." The ruby red eye on the side of his broken face twinkled. "I thought that would provoke the reaction from you I was seeking."

"Darius... please..."

"It's too late for pleading, Laila. You've made it perfectly clear what you feel."

Laila watched her opportunity to pacify him crumble to powder along with his once beautiful face, returning her to the only alternative. If he would not be talked down by reason, she would have to subdue him by force.

A shower of gold fire ignited her bindings and engulfed them into cinders, allowing her limbs to move free.

"What...?" Darius stepped backwards as all the whites in her eyes bled gold.

"I had hoped to avoid this outcome." Laila floated above the operating table, summoning orbs of immaculate flame. "But it appears you have forced my hand." She shot the fireballs from her palms in his direction.

Darius's eyes widened as he sped out of the laboratory before they could make impact, and they scorched holes through the wall behind him.

Laila exhaled a smoke puff in disappointment before she flew after him in pursuit.

Over the horizon, the cavalry of Amira's sprite guard and the Vidua Nocte were rapidly gaining ground towards the Citadel. The impératrice headed the charge as she ignored the aching groans of her still-ailing body craving its next treatment.

The path to her daughter was so close it was practically within her grasp. Too close to be dissuaded by the feebleness of her vessel. She dug her heels into the sides of her unicorn to move faster up the impossible steepness of the terrain that seemed to be degrading further with every hoofbeat.

Yet the further she trod the more the ground seemed to rumble into a maleficent activity at her presence that disturbed small pockets of sediment and sent rocks tumbling into her path. Amira tugged the stirrups of her mount to steer him away from an incoming collision at breakneck speed whilst the startled cries of her guards succumbing to a sickening crackle of bone signalled they were less fortunate.

She did not look back to see who had perished in the downpour as she erected a shield around her to rebound the rest of the debris. Too focused was she on the pursuit of her daughter. However, her tunnel vision worked to her detriment when a large hand exploded from below to seize her and her steed.

Amira cried out as she lost control of her enchantment, and the ravenous chimera met her with a saliva-slickened gleam before chomping its teeth deep within her skin, shredding clumps of flesh and muscle to hold her fast in its grip as she struggled against it.

On instinct, she unleashed a burst of electricity that dispersed her assailant into ashes, but not before more hands sprouted from below as the hidden army of Darius's chimeras revealed themselves.

"Why, if it isn't Her Luminosity!" Darius swooped before her on his hippogriff and launched himself onto the back of his largest monstrosity. "You can't imagine how pleased I am to see you."

Amira realised at once that she didn't have a chance, not in her weakened state, but she still very much intended to give him everything she had. "Let's dispense with the badinage, shall we, Darius Rex?" She held out her palm and summoned several bolts of lightning from the sky. "Give me my daughter."

He grinned at her, a good portion of his face having gone charred as coal under Calante's growing influence. "With pleasure. Come with me and I'll be more than happy to escort you."

"Do you really believe me that witless?"

"No," he conceded. "But I do believe you to have no other choices." He put two fingers to his lips and whistled, and his chimeras charged her.

Even armed with her bolts, Amira knew she had little hope of prevailing. Still, she emitted a radiance so powerful it blinded her assailants before using her bolts as javelins to spear through their matter.

"You've no mother to regenerate from now, fiend." She turned to Darius. "Your troops are finite. I'd suggest you use them wisely."

Darius smirked. "I intend to." He summoned more legions of his netherborn underlings with a lift of his hand until they spiralled around him as oily globules, and then he launched them at her.

Amira knew she was outnumbered, knew he intended to keep overwhelming her until she tired enough to become easy prey for him. Having no option but to battle for victory, she continued to slay his beasts by the dozen until her body wore down from the activation of the blight poisoning her aether.

No, she thought woefully as she fell to her knees. *I am better than this. Stronger. Superior. Get up. Get up, you miserable, worthless lump of flesh!*

Darius hmphed in amusement, taking scornful relish in every slow-paced step he took towards her as she pathetically tried to pull herself upwards and stumbled over her own limbs—reduced to no more than a starlet newly of walking age. He seized a handful of her silken white hair and wrenched her head back.

"I won't... let you..."

"Truly, Amira." Darius shook his head with a tut. "At least express some dignity." He punched through her stomach, rooting around deep until he'd found grip on her star.

Before he could go further, Serafina entered the fore with a chant barked in his direction.

The spell rebounded off of him with little damage, and he issued a chuckle for the effort. "You caught me off guard only once, Mother dearest. I've been bathing in tree sap since then." He responded with a counter-curse that mangled the bones in both her wrists, twisting and snapping them at conflicting angles.

Serafina snarled in pain as her ankles jerked next under the force of his curse and sent her to her knees.

"Step away from her!" Laila commanded, descending from the sky with orbs of fire in hand.

Darius responded by bringing up Amira's body to use as a shield. "Well, well. It's shaping up to be quite the family reunion, isn't it?"

"Let my mother go, Darius."

"Why?" He embedded his claws further into Amira's stomach. "One tug and I'll have given you everything you've ever wanted. Isn't that why you're doing all of this? For the glory? For the crown?"

A white-gold glow eclipsed Laila's eyes. "You know that's not why I'm doing this."

"Please," he sneered. "I knew deep down from the moment you left with me that whatever affection you felt was on borrowed time. You'd always do this. You'd always choose to secure your own power over me... and look at you now. It seems you've been rewarded handsomely if this new fire in you is anything to go by."

"You have the Phoenix..." Amira whispered in muted awe upon seeing her daughter attain her own greatest ambition.

"You misunderstand the situation, Darius." As Laila spoke, every fjord of her veins illuminated gold. "I have not been given this power because I intend to misuse it but because the Phoenix knew that I would burn myself to ashes if it meant I could scorch Calante out of you."

"Yourself, perhaps," Darius retorted, "but you would burn your own mother?"

"Do it," Amira commanded. "Incinerate me if that's what needs doing."

"Maman..." Laila couldn't help but waver. "I can still save you."

"Laila, look at me." Amira stared deep into her daughter's eyes with a weary acceptance. "Accept what you must do. Accept what you must be: my better. My successor."

"Maman, no—"

Amira clutched Darius's hand and tore it out of her, removing her star along with it. "Stand strong." She gave her daughter one final look, the look that Laila had long been seeking—that of pure maternal pride, before her body dispersed into golden atoms.

"No!" Laila unleashed a cry of sheer horror, tears misting her vision as she tried in vain to capture the fragments of her mother before she deserted her entirely. "Please. Don't go..."

Seeing his wife in such anguish jolted some capacity for compassion in Darius, if only temporarily. It wasn't to last, but Amira's noble sacrifice was precisely the distraction Serafina needed to regather her bearings.

She tapped into the source of her agony and used it to erupt spikes from the ground, impaling Darius, then drew blood from the stones of the Citadel wards to launch at him in the form of daggers.

Darius shielded himself behind the shadow of his cloak and used it to render himself intangible. Then he called for another chimera and sent it barrelling towards Serafina to rip her in two.

Serafina closed her eyes, her fate accepted: The non-existent breath of the chimera as it engulfed her would at least be a brisk end.

Then a slash of a sword through the air, so quick it was audible, and sliced off the lower jaw from the chimera before it could even fathom the idea of a bite.

Laila knew there was only one soldier who could be that swift with a blade.

The quicksilver knight known as Lyra appeared as the source of the ambush, retrieving her pistol and shooting a sunbeam through the chest of the beast, then watching as it squealed and dissipated into floating atoms.

Serafina communed with the demonic heart lurking beneath the core of the Citadel and erupted several geysers of blue-green flame to burn through the shapeless masses before they could settle into forms.

The geysers descended as droplets into the grass, clustering together into fully grown monsters. Too many of them. They were surrounded. They couldn't dare hope to dispense with the chimeras alone.

A whistle sounded in the distance as Sabina swooped low on her hippogriff and scooped Laila and Lyra both onto its back.

"Sabina!" Darius growled, realising he had lost his most staunch supporter to the other side. "You come back here this instant!"

He sent two flying chimeras in pursuit of them until Laila called down a strike of lightning from the raging clouds and scattered them into embers.

"You have to get me near him," Laila said, stifling her tears to ready herself. She would end this now. She would end this tonight.

Sabina nodded, steering her hippogriff to once more swoop low over Darius. A large hand lengthened from a chimera to snatch them, thwarted narrowly by a sudden swerve upwards by Sabina's careful flightwork.

Then Laila leapt off of its back to land on Darius with a blade-shaped flame poised at his heart.

"Don't kill him," Lyra cautioned. "We need him alive."

Despite her friend's wishes, Laila knew couldn't risk leaving him breathing after what he'd recounted in his plans to her. One sharp stab was all it would take to sever Calante's foothold in this realm for good.

She took the handle of the blade in both hands, sinking it into his chest where his pulse thrummed loudest.

What was most unnerving of it all was how he did not fight her. He arched towards her penetration with a perverse excitement as his lips parted with a whisper. "Do it." A soft chuckle rumbled in his throat. "End me."

It was a ploy. He didn't think she had it in her. She sank the blade in a few more inches, goaded on by his arrogance.

"Laila!" Serafina summoned another ring of unholy fire to dispense with the incoming chimeras before charging forward.

As she slid the blade home, a golden light crackled from her palm and travelled along his veins until it reached inside his heart.

Darius's neck arched with a cry of sublime pain before he burst into flames. A spectrum of colour rippled over every inch of his skin until he was engulfed, and protruding from the planes of his shoulder blades were the wings of a phoenix.

The conflagration spread throughout both their bodies and consumed the fields surrounding them. Laila watched him burn beneath her until the rot of Calante's influence disintegrated from his features and restored the face she'd once skidded her fingertips along so softly. The lips she'd lavished with kisses. The aquiline nose she'd playfully nudged with her own.

To see that face liquefy to wax was enough to make her halt the fire, craning her neck back in a birdlike shriek that exhausted the remaining reserves of her power.

When the flames extinguished, his body had been charred beyond recognition, mummified within a sarcophagus of ash. Then it cracked and splintered around him in disintegrating pieces until all that was left was a body inside. His original form remained but stripped of any of the characteristics that once defined him as a demon. What remained were the striations of phoenix fire pulsing through his veins. He was not quite occasso and not quite solarite, but some collision between the two.

EPILOGUE

O NCE NEWS HAD SPREAD THAT THE THREAT OF Calante had been successfully vanquished, the scientists of the Mountain gathered to witness Darius be paraded through all floors to the deepest crevice of the laboratories. Before the scornful malice of those who had worked tirelessly, for decades, to undermine the advances of his sadistic experiments.

If only one thing could be said in his favour it was that he did not once lose composure in the face of his enemies. Not even when they spat at him, hurled insults towards him, or whispered intent of tenfold retribution on his person for the harm he had caused.

Darius allowed this to pass through him like the scorch of liquor before the eventual numbing—his mind was far too weighed by Laila's treachery and this chimerical abomination of a body that had resulted from it. He felt his heart had been cleaved in two, pried away by hand, and patched up with foreign muscle. The heavenly blood that thrummed in his veins seemed like a slow poison.

He couldn't bear it. The wrongness. The vague dread of feeling incomplete. Knowing something within him had irrevocably changed and not being able to locate the source. The worst of it was how it severed his bond to chaos magic and rendered him impotent to wield it. He could no longer be tormented by Calante's raucous laughter but neither could he foster connection to anything else.

Before this, his mind had been a hive of unsavoury spells, rituals, and reckless experimentations, whirring between his ears at such speed it was nearly impossible to keep up. Now, all of it had gone quiet. The engine had run dry. He mourned that silence more than the loss of any title or treasure.

Once sealed inside a thick glass cell, it didn't take long for the thought of death to seduce him. His first attempt came when he managed to pilfer an ætherald-powered baton from one of the orderlies. He pressed it to his chest and short-circuited his heart until it stuttered and gave out. As he collapsed to the floor, a sigh escaped his lips. At last, the Nether would take him.

But fate had other plans.

He woke to the sensation of being burned alive—his screams ragged and desperate as golden fire surged through him, lashing his nerves, forcing his heart back into a brutal rhythm. When the flames finally died out, he clawed his way from the charred sarcophagus, reborn once again.

Had he not been the subject, he might've found the phenomenon fascinating. But any wonder was drowned by the sickening realisation:

Even death had been stolen from him.

The screens flickered through endless reels of surveillance as Darius attempted progressively more daring attempts at self-mutilation, testing the limits for how much pain he could cause himself before it triggered his body to regenerate.

Under strict orders from Dr Mielette, Laila did not attempt to intervene at any point. Even though her heart yearned to reach out and stop this spiral of destruction, she knew that this was her penance. To watch the one she had once loved more than any other in the world be in immeasurable pain and know he would reject her comfort should she offer it.

After a while she closed her eyes to it, unable to watch any longer, and turned towards Lucrèce methodically bobbing a tea bag inside her cup.

"Remarkable, isn't it?" She let her beverage steep to her desired strength before moving the tea bag to her saucer. "I received the bloodwork not too long ago. Whatever you've done to him with the Phoenix flame appears to have eradicated all traces of chaos from his body. It seems we have finally found the solution to unravel all of this mess."

Laila watched her wordlessly, keeping her suspicion withheld. "At the very least, we can save the mortals who'd been unfortunately afflicted."

"Indeed!" Lucrèce added sugar to her tea with a vigorous stir. "Though I can only imagine how this might be utilised beyond that. If such a thing can already be used to—"

"No."

Lucrèce's stirring halted as a frown of confusion deepened her brow. "I beg your pardon?"

"We're not weaponising this against the occassi. I gave Serafina Blackwood my word that no harm would come to pass when I removed Darius from power."

"Your Radiance—"

"It's not happening, Lucrèce. Put those illusions out of your mind." A white-gold glow flooded Laila's eyes in warning. She might have emptied most of the Phoenix fire into Darius's veins, but a small spark remained. "Whatever becomes of Darius—however he is used or treated—all of that falls down to me. When I leave here I will be taking him with me."

"I must advise against this," Lucrèce blustered.

"You can advise all you'd like, but you have no authority here. Until the completion of my mother's reign I am the acting impératrice, and all operations of your facility shall be approved by me."

As Lucrèce's frown progressed to a glower, Laila knew she'd be continuing the rivalry that had divided their dynasties for centuries. That would be a battle for another day, however, as for now there was a far more pressing conflict she would need to resolve, which led her out of the control room and into the cells where her husband resided.

Darius had huddled in a corner as he healed from his injuries, his hands tugging his hair as he exhaled a soft whimper. A pool of black blood speckled gold with ichor glistened around him like a night sky.

He elected not to look upon her as he spoke his first words since his arrival. "You should've killed me."

It hurt to hear it even if she'd been watching him destroy himself from the outside from the moment he'd been imprisoned.

"It would've been a mercy to let me die. Instead you've trapped me here in this purgatory for all eternity."

"I know," Laila admitted. "I just couldn't. I couldn't bear the thought."

"Even now I wonder..." He picked at an open scab on his arm, having used his fingernails alone to pierce himself. "I ask myself... why? Then it came to me."

"It's because I loved you." Her breath hitched with the weight of her confession. "Then and now and even still..."

"No," he sneered at her with fangless teeth. Even his ears had lost their sharpness and were filed down to a blunted point. "This wasn't about love. This wasn't due to some paltry emotion. You saw an opportunity in me and you chose to exploit it. To get ahead. You took a page straight out of my book, and now you are the wielder of the most powerful weapon in the world."

"That's not true."

"At least have the decency not to insult my intelligence, Laila." He finally looked up at her, and she discovered his eyes had lost their intensity with their now-rounded pupil. "Part of me ought to be proud or even impressed. I never imagined you'd have such a thing in you, and yet... here we sit."

"You have to understand I couldn't sit and do nothing. I had to stop you."

"Ending my life would've accomplished the very same feat as this. What you've done now is so much worse. You've completely unmade me. Erased everything I had to call mine. Now every time I look at you... all I can see is what you've cost me."

"Please don't say that."

"Why? Why does it even matter now? You've made your choice, and it wasn't me."

"You want to know why I did all of this? It's because I gave up everything for you and you made a fool of me!" Her voice raised with this tear-filled outburst. "And so I was angry. And I was hurt. And I wanted so badly to make you feel what you'd done, but then... then I watched you die." A meek sound escaped her. "And the pain of that loss was worse than anything I could fathom. Worse than anything you could've done to me. So I saved you, I brought you back, and I thought... I thought you might..." She didn't know what silly impulse made her think he was still worth being vulnerable for, but habits this ingrained were hard to stop. "Forgive me."

"I used to believe that I could forgive you anything. That loving you was worth misery. Worth weakness. Worth every single moment of indignity and suffering I endured for refusing to let you go. And now I find myself here asking... was it? Was it truly worth it in the end? And the answer I came to in the end was so clear." He paused to glare at her with a seething hatred she never would've thought him capable of. "It wasn't."

"I don't believe you." Laila glanced away from him, not wanting him to see the tears he brought to her eyes. "You're only trying to hurt me."

"Perhaps." The spite he exuded at hurting her made her chest tighten. "However, the fact that I still can speaks to how truly pathetic you are. Doesn't it? You found out I duped you and lied to you all this time and still you hold affection for me. How damaged must you be? It's any wonder it was so easy for me to do it."

"You're right." She swallowed thickly. "I do still hold affection for you. But what's more is I have hope for you. And perhaps that's even more foolish. I like to hope that one day... when you're past all of this hurt, you'll see the potential you have been given to change the course of your life to something better than it was. But I see now, when that day comes, you're going to have to take that step without me."

On a higher level in the Mountain, Dr Isuka entered the patient room where Sadik Yilan's body was seated. Through his eyes Emica Hariken smiled at her lifelong friend. "We did it, Akira."

Dr Isuka nodded, tears of vindication already sliding down her cheeks. "We did." She took Sadik's hand and brought it to her face. "We did it, Emica. You and me. We saved the world."

Sadik's own eyes sparkled in happiness. "I think... it's time I returned this vessel to its rightful owner."

"Where will you go?"

"You don't have to worry. Now Darius has been nullified of all magic, he no longer has any hold over my spirit. I can finally be free... be at peace."

Dr Isuka's throat hardened as she understood the meaning behind the words. She was going to pass to another realm now. One far beyond her reach. "I'm going to miss you, my friend. So much."

"Me too." Emica stroked along the outline of Isuka's face, tracing it to memory. "But I'll be waiting for you in the next realm, and you'd best have completed a whole host of new research discoveries to tell me about. Do you promise?"

Dr Isuka could barely speak through her tears. "I—"

"Please, Akira."

"I promise."

Emica smiled a final time before the spark in her faded from Sadik Yilan. Dr Isuka caught his slackened hand before his body collapsed, and she guided him carefully back onto the bed in a resting position.

After that, she waited for him to return to consciousness, using the interval to dry up her teariness before he rose up with a tired rub at his eyelids. "What the... what?"

"Welcome back to the land of the living, Sadik Yilan."

"How in the..." Sadik slapped his own face, tapping down his body to ensure he was still intact. "Oh, thank Naya. I'm back."

"You're back," Dr Isuka confirmed. "And I have good news. We defeated him."

"We beat Calante?" He looked elated. "And Elina?"

"Elina is... going to be fine."

Sadik burst into uproarious laughter to the point of tears. "We won?"

"That we did indeed, Mr Yilan. This time, the mortal world won."

Laila sat on the Solar Throne as Parlement poured in from all corners to discuss how to weather the disastrous sequence of events that had left both Soleterea and Mortos temporarily leaderless.

"Your Radiance, is it to be our understanding that you will stand as impératrice after your mother's untimely passing—"

"Your Radiance, as the former rex's consort, who do you think is best suited to take up the throne in his stead—"

"Your Radiance, is it true that Darius Calantis is still among the living and has yet to be sentenced to banishment—"

To her own shock, she realised she wanted her mother at that moment. If for no other reason than to channel her infallible composure while being bombarded by those who sought her as the answer to all their ills.

Laila raised a hand to halt their inquisition. "I understand you all have questions. Allow me to put your concerns at ease to the best of my ability whilst the Magisterium and I work in collaboration with the Rex's Council to ensure a smooth transition into new governance."

Once more the members erupted in desperation for knowledge

that Laila denied them as she descended from the throne and left the audience room. Her mother would be proud, she hoped, of the seamless way she navigated telling them nothing and just enough at once whilst she gathered herself together behind the scenes.

When she next wandered out onto the grounds, she realised it had been so long since she'd seen Soleterea that its impression had started to fade from her mind. The sights, sounds, and smells that had once been so familiar to her had been overridden by the spindly silhouette of spruce trees.

She found her way to the rose garden and passed underneath the pavilion, coming to a halt inside its perfumed air. Her fingertips skirted along the petals of a gold rose as she recalled the memory of when she'd sent Darius away the first time and agreed to marry him the second. And now, here she stood, for the third and final time, knowing he wouldn't be waiting on her word at all.

Laila sank to the floor, cuddled her knees to her chest, and began to weep. She buried her face so deeply into her lap she didn't hear Lyra approach until the sprite put a tender hand on her shoulder.

"Need some company?"

Laila raised her head with a sniffle, managing a wan smile. "I'm fine."

"You're not." Lyra sat down next to her. "And you don't have to pretend for me, either. I'm not one of them."

Laila didn't realise how badly she needed those words until she dropped her head to Lyra's shoulder and let the tears flow. "They're going to make me stand as impératrice until the next election."

Lyra hummed in response.

"It's all I ever wanted..." She patted the tears on her cheek. "So why do I feel so miserable?"

"You lost your mother," Lyra reminded her, "and you lost your lover."

"And they were both terrible people who did terrible things." Laila raised up her head to look at her friend. "Is that the misfortune that my love brings, or is that simply what *this* does to you?"

By *this* she could only mean the crown, the throne, the limitless power in deciding the fate of thousands with one pen stroke.

"Maybe." Lyra shrugged. "It can. If you're not strong enough. If you don't have people you trust enough to pull you back from the edge."

Laila nodded in agreement. "There's so much work to be done now."

"I'll be at your side through all of it. You're not alone, Laila." Lyra pressed a kiss to the crown of her head. "Not while I'm still with you."

"Promise me if I ever lose myself... that you'll be the one to bring me back?"

"Forever," Lyra vowed. "Always."

THANK YOU FOR READING!
WHAT'S NEXT?

A great big thank you for reaching the end of my novel!

Please do remember to leave a review on your website of choice if you'd like to support me further. Every little bit helps, even just a rating or sentence.

Feel free to drop me a line at contact@aninkwellofnectar.com if you'd like to chat with me—I love hearing from readers!

Go to www.aninkwellofnectar.com for exclusive content, snippets, and release updates for all future novels.

I can also be found on Instagram, Facebook, Tiktok and Tumblr under **@aninkwellofnectar.**

ACKNOWLEDGEMENTS

I can't believe we've made it to the end of this journey!

I have so many people I'd like to thank. First of all, thank you so much to Eeva Nikunen for accepting the offer to work on this project with me all the way back in 2022 when I was commuting towards a job I hated (that I have since left). The Essence of the Equinox wouldn't be nearly the success it is without your talent behind it, and I sincerely mean that.

Thank you so much to Molly Rookwood for sticking by me throughout the years, not just as an editor but as a cheerleader. You've truly gone above and beyond for both me and this story, and I couldn't have asked for someone better to work alongside. It is with a heavy heart that I part ways with you and Eeva professionally, but I can only hope social media allows us to remain tangentially connected in each other's orbits.

Thank you to my ko-fi members: Lau, Tyler, Nix, Han, Valmont, and DC for your continued financial contributions to me as a writer. That little extra each month really makes all the difference.

d a final thank you to my dedicated readers who've seen this narrative the whole way through. This was the series of my heart, and it's been a balm to the soul in some of the most emotionally difficult periods of my life. I hope Laila's journey speaks to you. I hope it lingers. I hope it comforts and disturbs in equal measure. But more than anything else, I hope you return to this page someday—perhaps in the near future or longer—having experienced the rollercoaster all over again.

ABOUT THE AUTHOR

Camilla Andrew is the award-winning author of THE ESSENCE OF THE EQUINOX trilogy. She lives in a leafy English town that sounds remarkably like a fairytale setting with talking animals in suits, and spends her days working diligently on her books and her non-fiction essays dissecting intersections of race, gender, and power. Her works also feature in Cloaked Press and midnight & indigo. For more book updates, newsletter sign-ups, and extra goodies, join her at aninkwellofnectar. com.

www.aninkwellofnectar.com